THE
PLAGUE
STONES

THE
PLAGUE
STONES

JAMES
BROGDEN

Titan BOOKS

The Plague Stones
Print edition ISBN: 9781785659959
E-book edition ISBN: 9781785659966

Published by Titan Books
A division of Titan Publishing Group Ltd
144 Southwark Street, London SE1 0UP

First edition: May 2019
1 2 3 4 5 6 7 8 9 10

A CIP catalogue record for this title is available from the British Library.

Printed and bound in Great Britain by CPI Group (UK) Ltd

FOR GRENFELL

1

GUARDIAN

THE OLD WOMAN WAS NEAR DEATH, AND THE TRUSTEES had gathered about her bed to pay their respects. Although she was not a member of the Executive Committee, she had been custodian of Stone Cottage for nearly sixty years, and having coped with its unique requirements for so long demanded recognition. No private hospice could have provided better care than she had received during her last months here, in the place she had guarded so well; no expense had been spared. It was the least they could do, given what she had kept at bay for so long.

The reverend's prayers were a sonorous murmur set to the slow ticking of the clock on the mantel '—*I will say of the Lord he is my refuge and my fortress my God in whom I trust surely he will save you from the fowler's snare and from the deadly pestilence he will cover you with his feathers and under his wings thou shalt find refuge—*' even though none there really believed that it would do any good.

The Trustees shuffled and sniffed. The director of environmental services, who had trained as a doctor in her youth, checked the old woman's pulse. The machines had all been removed; she was beyond machines now.

The chief executive cleared his throat. 'Is she...?'

Environmental Services shook her head. 'Not yet.'

'—*take up the shield of faith with which thou mayst extinguish the flaming arrows of the evil one*—'

Unbelievably, the director of financial services actually yawned, and nudged the director of housing and community. 'How are we progressing with the replacement?' she whispered.

Housing and Community made a so-so motion. 'Slowly. She had very few living relatives, which is surprising given her age. We vetted the immediate circle but none met the profile to a high enough degree so we've been widening out to a lower co-efficient of relationship than we'd normally like, but what can one do? These are the times we live in.'

'Has,' murmured the chief executive.

Housing and Community blinked. 'I beg your pardon?'

'You said she *had* few relatives. She's not dead yet.'

Housing and Community reddened, and was silent.

Environmental Services looked up from her ministrations to the old woman, plainly unimpressed. 'You've had six months to find a replacement,' she said. 'With no new custodian ready to step into her shoes we're vulnerable. This is exactly the kind of slip-up which costs lives.'

'There's no need to be overly dramatic,' replied the chief

executive. 'We've already been through this. The boundary will hold. It always has.'

'But you know what happens when things become disrupted. When they *change*. There hasn't been a new custodian in living memory! We've only got the reverend's reassurances and to be brutally honest with you—'

The old woman gasped suddenly – a dry croak issuing from a wizened throat – and her ancient claw of a hand clutched at the coverlet. The Trustees stiffened. After the gasp, a whisper, little more than the sound of dry leaves blowing across old tombstones:

'She is here.'

Someone made a small whimpering sound.

'Control yourself,' said the chief executive. He went to the drapes at the other end of the room and drew them aside. The others joined him, drawn by curiosity despite their better judgement – even the reverend, who knew better than most what was out there.

'*—as for the head of those that compass me about, let the mischief of their own lips cover them let burning coals fall upon them let them be cast into the fire into deep pits that they rise not up again—*'

The window overlooked the cottage's rear garden. It was tidy and well kept, since the Trust had taken over maintenance of the property as its custodian had aged beyond the ability to take care of such things herself. Neatly groomed shrubbery and trim flowerbeds bordered a lawn as evenly green as a snooker table, in the centre of which sat the stone from which the cottage got its name. It was three feet high and roughly the shape of a canine tooth, its grey surface mottled with lichen, and so old that the markings that covered it had eroded away to faint grooves and hollows.

Standing on the far side of it, glaring up at the house with burning, centuries-old hatred, was the dead girl.

The reverend's prayers died in her throat.

'My God!' said Financial Services. 'Is that Her?'

The chief executive shot her a withering look. 'No, it's the fucking tooth fairy.'

She wore a simple woollen shift, much torn and stained, revealing emaciated limbs which were maggot-pale and blotched with the livid black-purple bruises of plague. Her bare toes and fingers were black with gangrene, and buboes bulged at Her throat. One had burst, and from the crater of ruined flesh beneath Her jaw its rot streaked Her front. The only things about Her which seemed to have any life were Her eyes, black and glittering as She stared up at the window.

Environmental Services turned to the reverend. 'You said we'd be safe,' she pleaded.

'I said that we simply don't know how the death of the stone's custodian will affect things, but that as long as the stone remains blessed the boundary should hold, and She shouldn't be able to enter.'

'Reverend?' suggested the chief executive. 'If you'd be so kind as to remind Her of that?'

The reverend ahemmed and approached the window. 'You have no power over this place,' she said, her voice wavering just a little. 'As it is said in the Book of Proverbs, do not move an ancient boundary stone set by your forefathers; do not move the ancient boundary or go into the fields of the fatherless. The blessing of the Lord Almighty is on this hallowed sentinel, which you may not profane. I command you to stay where you are bound!'

The dead girl grinned, displaying a mouth full of teeth that were yellow as poison, black as death, and the same moment a scream came from the old woman in the bed behind them. The Trustees turned.

A rat was sitting on her throat, eating her face.

It had bitten into her cheek, and bright blood spattered the pillow and coverlet. Her frail fingers were in its fur, pulling and fluttering ineffectually as she screamed with a sound like cloth being torn. Several of the Trustees cried out in response. One fled the room, clutching her mouth. Housing and Community gave an inarticulate bellow of indignation and rushed at the creature with a raised fist, and it fled – but not immediately. It paused, glaring at him with the same glittering black hatred as the dead girl, a look which said No, I *will not* as clearly as a shout, and then it leapt from the bed and was gone.

The old woman, former custodian of Stone Cottage, was dead with her head thrown back, eyes staring at the ceiling glassy with terror, teeth visible through the hole in her cheek. When the chief executive looked out of the window again, the dead girl was gone. Only the living remained, shocked and weeping.

2

GREEN SKULL

HE SLAPPED ANOTHER CLIP INTO HIS MESH GUN AND popped up from cover to spray the Xenoan position with covering fire while the strike team surged forward, over and past him into the battle zone. Return fire from the aliens was fierce, tearing chunks off the carcass of the sky medusa that he was sheltering behind in roaring detonations of purple warp energy. Micro-fluctuations in local gravity pulled his own shots out of true but he compensated; not that it really mattered, since all that he had to do was keep the Xenos' heads down until the strike team could take out their nest. A piece of shrapnel glanced off his left upper arm but the HUD indicated that the armour rating there was still in the green, so he ignored it and kept firing. His headset was a babble of voices yelling commands, whooping with battle lust, or cursing as they got fragged. Then a DNA grenade from one of the strike team exploded in a howling double-helix cloud of bio-flux and the squad commander (a kid from Japan called Masahito who must have been playing at breakfast, given the time difference) was screaming at them to go! Go! *Go!*

There was a man standing in the kitchen doorway.

Toby hadn't seen him arrive or heard the back door open, and with a sudden liquid feeling of terror realised that his mum had told him to make sure the doors were locked, even though she and Dad would only be at the cinema for a couple of hours, because he knew what this neighbourhood was like, didn't he? As she was saying it he'd already been switching on his Xbox and said yeah sure of course he wouldn't forget, and he'd totally meant to, just as soon as this mission was completed – well, this or the one after it, anyway. And now there was a stranger in his home.

The stranger was in jeans, trainers and a black full-face hoodie zipped right up to hide his identity behind the leering mask of a green skull. He had a long crowbar in his right hand, dangling almost casually.

On the TV screen, Toby's avatar had stopped midway across the battlefield and was being peppered with alien fire. His HUD revealed armour ratings sliding from green through amber and into the red while in his headset the tinny voice of someone thousands of miles away was yelling at him in fury: 'What are you doing? What the fuck are you *doing*?'

I think I'm being burgled, that's what, he thought. His breath had stopped, caught up somewhere in the middle of his ribcage while his heart beat in a hollow vacuum of terror. *Police. Call 999. That's what you're supposed to do, isn't it?* He was sitting on the settee with his feet up on the coffee table, and his phone only an inch away from his heels, but it might as well have been on an alien world. His avatar was down now, the screen colours muted to indicate that he was out of the fight.

Green Skull stepped from the kitchen into the living room, looking around with all the ease and confidence of someone in a shop. 'All right, kid?' he asked. His voice was low, muffled by the hoodie. 'Mum and Dad not in?'

'Who...?' Toby's voice stuck dry in his throat. 'What do you...?'

The man moved so fast that Toby barely saw it, certainly too fast for him to get a hand up in defence as the crowbar arced towards him; it hit his upper arm and a jolt of pins and needles numbed him to the fingertips. He cowered on the settee, curled into a foetal ball and too stunned for the moment to even cry out.

'Ask another fucking question and I'll smash your fucking head in, all right? I'm going to ask you again: are your mum and dad in?'

'No.'

Green Skull nodded and backed off a bit. 'Good. I already knew that, anyway. Watched them go. But it's good that you're honest with me. You might just get out of this okay.' He turned and saw the TV screen, and gave a little laugh. 'Hey, I love this game. This is a sick game. Have you made it to the medusa armada yet?'

'Um, uh, no...' Toby's arm was waking up in agony. He thought it might be broken, and he could feel a wet, prickling heat at the corners of his eyes. He blinked it away savagely. He would not cry. He might scream and beg and bleed but he absolutely would not cry.

'Fucking sick *as*, man. You'll love it.' Green Skull pointed the end of his crowbar at the frozen avatar on the screen. 'You think you're a badass motherfucker like this guy?'

'Um, I don't know…' He felt his airway clench in the first warning spasms of an asthma attack, and realised with horror that his inhaler was lying on the floor of his bedroom.

'Hmm.' The crowbar swung to point at Toby's phone where it lay next to the discarded game controller. 'That your phone?'

Toby hauled in a wheezing breath. 'Um, yes…'

The crowbar whistled down, shattering the phone and gouging into the table underneath. It was only a cheap flat-pack thing with about as much structural integrity as a wet cardboard box, and the crowbar went straight through it. Toby cried out and shrank back as Green Skull continued to smash at the wreckage until it was an unrecognisable pile of chipboard and birch veneer and his phone was completely destroyed.

The man stepped back, panting a little. 'If you think maybe you're a badass and you make this go hard I will fuck you up in ways you can't imagine. You do exactly as I say, and you'll see Mummy and Daddy again. You get me?'

Toby nodded, chest heaving. His airway felt like it had narrowed down to the width of a pinhole, and his lungs were burning. 'Please…' he gasped. 'Please… I need… inhaler…'

Green Skull peered closer at him. 'Oh, fucking hell,' he

said. 'You're not having a fucking asthma attack, are you?'

Toby nodded, wheezing.

'Fuck!' the man spat. He turned away and smashed at the wall in frustration, gouging ragged tears in the thin plaster. 'Why does nobody ever tell me this shit?' He spun back to Toby and held the end of the crowbar an inch from his face. 'You better not be fucking with me.'

Toby shook his head, blinking back tears of panic which he couldn't prevent any longer. This was his worst nightmare. Having a stranger break into his home and threaten him was shocking, as mad as aliens landing, but the fear of suffering an asthma attack without his inhaler went bone deep and right back to his earliest memories of visits to the hospital, of his mum's frantic worry, of his dad's thinly burning anger at having to raise his son in a place like this.

The crowbar dropped away. 'Where is it, then?' asked Green Skull. 'Your inhaler?'

'... Bedroom...'

Green Skull waved the crowbar at the door. 'Go on then. But I'm right behind you, badass.'

Toby scrambled up from the sofa and lurched for the hallway. A pathetically optimistic part of him hoped that the neighbours might have heard the table being smashed up; the walls were so thin that he could usually hear them watching soap operas and arguing, which seemed to be their two main hobbies. But he knew that even if they were in, and even if they had heard anything, and even if they thought something bad was happening in Toby's home, they wouldn't so much as knock on the door to ask if everything was okay, never mind call the police. He wasn't even sure what their names were.

In his bedroom he scrabbled around one-handed on the floor amidst the clutter of clothes and schoolbooks, until he found his inhaler, jammed the nozzle into his mouth and fired off a puff of salbutamol, and immediately felt the clenching in his chest begin to loosen up.

'Better?' Green Skull was standing in the bedroom doorway.

Toby nodded.

Green Skull grunted and cocked his head, considering the mess and the football posters on the walls. 'Huh,' he said. 'Villa fan. Good job. If you were Blues I'd've had to kill you.' He laughed like this was the most hilarious thing he'd ever heard. 'How old are you, kid?' he asked.

'What…?'

'Oi!' That earned him another tap with the crowbar, not as hard as the first one, but Toby jerked as if electrocuted. 'I warned you about that, didn't I? How fucking old are you?'

'Thir-thirteen.'

'You had pussy yet?'

Toby stopped himself just in time from asking another question. 'I don't understand.'

'Pussy! Sex! You know? You got a girlfriend? Shit, are you gay? Not that I give a fuck one way or the other, you understand.' Toby turned crimson with embarrassment. Why was this guy trying to start a conversation? It was excruciating.

Toby took a deep breath. 'You can take whatever you want,' he muttered, 'but I'm not talking to you about that kind of thing.' He clenched his eyes shut, hunched his shoulders and waited to be fucked up in ways he couldn't imagine.

'Whatever. So, whyn't you show me where they keep passports, birth certificates, important shit like that.'

'Okay.' Clutching his arm, Toby got up and led Green Skull to his parents' bedroom at the end of the short hallway. He didn't actually know where his mum kept important documents like that, but it seemed like a good bet. Theirs was a cramped, claustrophobic ground-floor flat and there wasn't much to it beyond two bedrooms, the bathroom, kitchen, living room and a closet in the hall overflowing with coats, brooms and boxes of random junk.

He saw his parents' bed, with his mum's old silver crucifix – the one she never wore but sometimes took and looked at when she thought nobody was watching – hanging over the bedpost by her pillow, and felt a stab of guilt about how easily he was letting this guy get away with it. Even helping him.

'Look,' he said. 'You can take my Xbox, my games, all of it – just leave their stuff alone, please?'

Green Skull turned slowly to look at him, and for a moment Toby let himself think that it would be okay. He'd wrestle the crowbar out of the guy's hands, and maybe he'd get away or maybe he wouldn't, and the guy would do something like clap a heavy hand on his shoulder and laugh and say *Shit, kid, seems like you do have some badass in you after all* and the grizzled old career criminal would take him on as an idealistic apprentice and they'd run off and have adventures through which they'd come to acquire a grudging respect for each other, just like in one of those films.

What actually happened was that the burglar who had trashed his parents' living room because Toby had been too stupid and lazy to lock the back door grunted, 'Cheeky little cunt,' and backhanded him so hard his head bounced off the doorframe. He was too stunned to even beg as he slid to the floor and Green Skull kicked him twice in the stomach. He hoped he might pass out, but that didn't happen either. Later, at the hospital, the doctors told him that he was a very lucky young man: his arm wasn't broken, no ribs had been cracked and he'd suffered no internal injuries, and the worst that he could expect was some spectacular bruising. Right at this very moment, however, he felt far from lucky. He just lay there until the guy was finished, curled around a burning knot of agony in his guts which felt like it was eating him from the inside out; then, as the intruder went on to ransack the flat, he remained there pretending to be unconscious, lying in a puddle of his own tears and snot. Finally, when there was only the sound of his own sobbing to bruise the silence, he got to his knees and crawled in search of a phone.

3

BAIT STATION

TOBY FEENAN GLANCED UP FROM HIS PHONE LONG enough to look through the car window at the house that his dad had pulled up in front of, more because the car had stopped than out of any real interest in their destination. The glance became a stare and he sat up straighter.

'Wait, what?' he said, and pointed. 'We're going to live *there*?'

'Yep,' said his mum. She closed the folder of real estate documents that she'd been reading through and unclipped her seatbelt.

'So, are we rich now?'

His father turned and gave him a goofy, beatific smile. 'Only in our love for each other, my dearest darling son.'

'Sorry I asked,' he muttered.

'In other words,' added his dad, 'no.'

The estate agent's car had pulled up ahead of them – a

black Lexus, Toby noted with approval – and the agent got out to meet them. She was a little taller and a little older than his mum, wearing glasses and a smart suit, with an iPad tucked under one arm. Her name was Natalie Markes, and she was the director of property and development for the Haleswell Village Trust Estates department, but estate agent was the closest Toby had got to understanding what it was she actually did. She'd been around to their home several times – their *old* home, he supposed he'd better get used to calling it – in the months during which incomprehensible legal wrangles had prevented them from moving into the new place, but now that it was all sorted out she had insisted on personally escorting them to their new home. 'Short of a red carpet for our newest Trustee, I'm afraid I'll have to do,' she'd said. Toby didn't understand how his mother – Trish Feenan, about as ordinary a mum as any you could imagine – had come to be a Trustee of a posh village neighbourhood in the suburbs that she'd never lived in just because an old lady she'd barely known had died, but if it meant she got to drive a Lexus too instead of their current shitty old Peugeot that was fine by him.

Toby got out of the car and tugged with a finger at the collar which had been chafing his neck throughout the journey. He couldn't believe they'd made him wear an actual tie on a non-school day. Apparently after this they were going on to meet the rest of the Trust at an actual garden party at an actual vicarage, for which he needed to appear smart – or at least, in his father's words, 'as little like a Hunger Games reject as possible'. Repeat: garden party.

Vicarage. Like in those TV detective shows like *Midsomer Murders* or whatever.

It seemed impossible that they could still be in the city. The road was lined with broadly spreading trees, and the houses all sat back behind high hedges, but behind even those he could still hear the muted background roar which reminded him that he only had to go half a dozen roads in any direction and he'd be back surrounded by dodgy takeaways, snarling traffic and high-rises just like the home they'd left – what? He checked the time on his phone. Twenty minutes ago. Impossible.

He looked at the house for a moment, imagining how it might be described in an estate agent's listings. Then he took a photo, found a filter which made it fuzzy around the edges and a bit muted like an old postcard.

```
PICO507181 shows a high hedge of beech, its leaves
like sheets of beaten copper, and a gap with a
wrought-iron gate between stone posts. In one
of them is the rectangular slot of a letter box.
A glossy green veinwork of ivy twists through a
name which has been worked into the metal: Stone
Cottage.
```

He added a caption: *stoner cottage lol,* and picced it to his friends.

Ms Markes produced a set of keys and unlocked the gate. 'We couldn't be sure who Mrs Drummond might have given spare keys to, so we took the liberty of changing all the locks – though we couldn't change this one, obviously. The Estates office does have a copy of the new ones, but only in case of emergencies.' Toby caught an anxious glance pass between his parents.

Ms Markes pushed open the gate and then stood aside for Toby's family, holding out the bunch of keys, but his mother hesitated, standing with her hand to her mouth and her eyes shining as if she was either about to burst into laughter or tears, or both.

'Everything all right?' asked his dad.

'I just…' she started. 'It's hard to believe that it's finally ours, that's all. I keep expecting someone to come out of that door and say sorry, it's all been a big mistake, clear off. Things like this don't happen to people like us.'

'People like us is people like them, now,' said his dad. 'Listen, if you don't want those keys I'll take them, but then me and Tobes get first dibs on a games room, isn't that right, fella?'

Toby stared at him. 'We get a *games room*?'

'Oh no!' His mum plucked the keys from Ms Markes' hand and strode through the gate. Toby followed, taking photos all the way.

PIC0507182 shows a gravel path circling a trim
lawn and beyond it a detached two-storey suburban
house. It has a large bay window on one side of the
arched front porch, and a roof which is a lopsided
ziggurat of steep gables and dormer windows
set at odd angles to each other. Despite being
perfectly straight and neat, with cleanly painted

window frames and tidy guttering, it nevertheless
gives the impression of having been caught in the
act of turning around, like a man peering over his
shoulder at something following behind.

'Well it certainly looks a lot tidier than the last time,'
observed his dad.

'We haven't been able to do much to the garden, I'm
afraid,' said Ms Markes. 'There was so much that needed
doing on the house. I won't bore you with the details – it's
all in the surveyor's report – but basically it was the first
time since the seventies that anyone's been able to get in and
give it a really good going-over.'

'I remember we came here once,' said Mum. 'When I was
little; I think I must have been five. One of those big family
get-togethers, probably somebody's birthday. There never
were any again – not that there was a feud or anything like
that, it was just that you know how sometimes two sides
of a family will drift apart? Well, that. I remember it being
very dark and smelly in the house. Full of big old pieces of
furniture and things that you weren't allowed to touch.'

His mum unlocked the front door – a hefty latch with a
chain and a row of four thick deadbolts, Toby noted with
approval. Ms Markes saw him looking.

'We've replaced both the front and back entrances with
state-of-the-art security doors,' she said, 'with oak cladding
over a steel core and steel frame, though you'd never know
it to look. The windows are made of laminated safety glass,
like in cars or shop windows, so that if they break there are

no jagged pieces to hurt you, and anybody trying to break in is going to have a very hard time of it.'

His dad gave a low whistle. 'Expecting a siege, are you?'

'It's standard on all Trustees' homes. The Trust takes the security of its members very seriously.'

'I'm getting that impression.'

There was no darkness in the house, and no heavy items of furniture – not much by way of furniture at all. The interior had been stripped right back to allow light to flood every room and hallway; it shone from the freshly repainted walls and glowed golden from newly varnished floorboards, gleaming from worktops and modern appliances in the kitchen and glittering from mica-flecked granite in the bathrooms. The windows were spotlessly clear and, he checked, also fitted with solid locks. Their flat, being rented, was only as well maintained as the landlord needed to avoid breaking the law. It was permanently damp, which meant that his mother was fighting a continual war against an insidious variety of black mould that seeped out of the ceilings and from the bathroom grouting like shadows taken root, and so everything smelled simultaneously of bleach and dank plaster. From as early as Toby could remember, he'd been fighting off one respiratory problem or another. Here it was dry and smelled faintly of pine- and lemon-scented cleaning products. In the old place, mismatched and draughty floorboards were covered with cheap, hard-wearing carpet which had actually given him serious road rash once when he'd fallen down the stairs; here he reckoned that if he took his shoes off he could glide down the long hallway on his socks like a curling stone.

It was almost intimidatingly clean, and Toby followed the adults on tiptoe, afraid to touch anything for fear of leaving smeary fingerprints while his mum uttered variations of 'Oh my God!' as they went into each new room.

'We're going to need a bigger sofa,' said his dad, as they stood gazing in wonder at the expanse of the sitting room with its wide fireplace and the sunlight streaming in through the panes of the tall bay window. 'Honestly, this is just embarrassing now.'

'All of Mrs Drummond's belongings were put into storage while we were completing the renovations,' said Ms Markes. 'You can have your pick and what's left will be auctioned.'

His dad was peering at the old-fashioned light switches by the door. 'Hold up, are these original Bakelite?' Toby sighed. He didn't know whether being an electrician had turned his dad into a heath-and-safety freak or if he had always been that way, but once introduced to a new environment it was only ever a matter of time before Peter Feenan started judging how likely it was to be a Potential Death Trap.

Ms Markes shrugged. 'I imagine so.'

'Can you show me where the fuse box is?' There was no way he was going to take assurances about the quality of Haleswell Village Trust's own electricians on faith.

'Of course. It's down this way.'

Toby followed them as far as the hallway. 'Hey, Dad?'

Peter turned. 'What is it, mate?'

'I'm going to go have a bit of an explore outside, okay?'

There was a moment's hesitation in which he knew his dad was thinking about telling him *No, stay where we can see you*, but then he said, 'Okay. Just don't go too far.'

Too far. As if he were six and they were at the beach and afraid he'd drown or get abducted. Since the break-in his parents' baseline level of worry about their dodgy neighbourhood had escalated into something approaching full-blown paranoia; instead of walking to school he'd been driven and collected by Dad in his electrician's van, and his social life had all but died. All he wanted to do was check out what the rest of the property boundary was like – did the garden have any hiding places, was the fence or wall climbable, whether there was a back gate, and if it was secure. Surely that was just sensible in a new place: to know its vulnerabilities.

PIC0507183 shows a narrow passage down the side
of the house turned into an obstacle course by
piles of junk and debris: stacks of old fence
boards, terracotta plant pots, empty cement
bags, bits of trellis, a rusted bicycle frame
with no wheels, piles of glass panes from a long-
dismantled greenhouse, and more besides.

The wall of the house was on his left, and above it the steep roof slope, and above that still the cliff face of the house's upper storey, blank on this side except for drainpipes and the narrow window of what was presumably a bathroom. He could have taken the wider, clearer path on the other side of the house, past the windows of what he was already thinking of as the study, but he wasn't interested in that.

An intruder would never use something so open. These shadowed and narrow places were where the world kept its secrets and hid its true face.

```
PICO507184 shows, tucked in against the wall, a low
box about the same size and shape as an overhead
projector. It is made of black plastic with wide
holes in either end and the logo of a pest control
company stamped on it, along with the words
'Warning! Contains rodenticide! Do not touch!'
```

Rat poison.

Last year's school scandal had been a boy in the sixth form who had ended up in hospital after taking a batch of fake steroids laced with rat poison. Apparently they were all at it, juicing up either to get onto a team or into a girl's pants by turning themselves into one of the swaggering tools from *Love Island*. He'd looked it up, because it was one of those sick, nasty little nuggets of knowledge that were currency amongst his mates (the ones who emphatically *didn't* try out for teams or watch *Love Island*). Apparently it was like a maxed-out blood thinner which caused internal bleeding and slow death over a matter of weeks. Lethal stuff, basically. Do Not Mess.

He knelt beside the bait station and fiddled with the lid, managing to pop it open. Inside was a circular reservoir containing a handful of bluey-green pellets, with more scattered in the body of the casing. Disturbed by something that'd had a curious, maybe fatal, nibble.

'Winner winner, chicken dinner,' he murmured.

He clipped the lid back on and continued exploring, but found no furry little corpses, so it seemed that the resident rat population had gotten away with it for now.

The back garden had the same manicured look as the front, with a tall green hedge running along the rear and a raised area with a summerhouse. The only place where it was not tidy was in the centre of the lawn, where a large stone protruded from the ground. He pulled up short at the sight of it. It was only about a metre high, very roughly conical in shape and made of something which was probably granite though he couldn't be sure, and there were strange bumps and hollows all over it which might have been the traces of weathered carvings, so it was obviously very old. There was nothing especially striking about it in itself, but somehow its very existence here, in this place which was otherwise so ordered and sane, felt wrong. It jutted like an erupted molar or an open fracture, splitting the skin of the world. It shouldn't have been here. It should have been out on a desolate moorland, part of a circle with its brothers guarding the grave of someone long dead, not surrounded by flowerbeds and herbaceous borders.

PIC0507185 shows a close-up of the grain of the stone; coarse, pocked and cratered, a desert landscape photographed from high orbit, patches of lichen spreading in an archipelago. The soft furrow of a carved line long eroded invites a finger to trace its length. No, more than invites – insists. Demands.

This close, Toby fancied he could feel the chill radiating from the granite as he reached out to touch—

'I see you've found it, then,' said Ms Markes from behind him.

He leapt back and whirled, as if caught in the act of committing a crime.

She was in the back doorway, smiling. He hadn't heard it open, his attention in thrall to the stone.

'What?'

'The parish stone,' she said, and stepped out to join him. He wondered where his parents were. 'It's why this is called Stone Cottage, after all. Although it's been here for a lot longer than the cottage – probably longer than every other building in the village, for that matter.'

'Uh, really?' He was still flustered from having been crept up on, but she seemed to take it as an expression of interest.

'Yes, it's at least fourteenth century. Some people think it might even have been an Anglo-Saxon moot stone, which would put it at over a thousand years old. Archaeologists excavated around it in the eighties and found coins and the remains of a dagger; isn't that cool?' When he didn't reply she shrugged. 'Well I think it's cool.' He was beginning to get the distinct impression that she was trying to persuade him to like it, appealing to what she thought a fourteen-year-old boy would find interesting, as if she were selling the property, as if it didn't already belong to his mum.

'Is that why there's the thing in the contract about not messing around with it?' he surprised himself by asking.

'The leasehold? Yes, there's a covenant to prevent anyone

removing or damaging the parish stone. It was here long before any of us, and if we look after it properly it will be here long afterwards too. That's why your mum is an honorary Trustee; it comes with the house, and the house comes with the stone.' She gave him a sidelong look. 'I didn't know you were interested in property law.'

'Me neither.'

'I heard about the break-in, of course,' she said, still looking at the stone, her voice low and neutral as if talking about nothing more unusual than the weather – but his heart was suddenly thumping in his ears all the same. 'And I know that you were alone when it happened. I want you to know that this place is safe. It's looked after. It's… protected.'

Now she looked at him, but he couldn't meet her eyes. It was excruciatingly embarrassing. He'd barely said anything about the attack to his parents or the police, much less the school counsellor, and now this stranger was presuming to talk to him about it as if she was his closest confidante?

'Especially from the rats, I guess,' he said, not really meaning anything by it beyond finding something to fill the awkward silence, but when she spoke again there was a sharpness to her tone that didn't sit with the reassurance she'd just been trying to project.

'What do you mean?'

'Nothing,' he replied. Touched a nerve there, it seemed. 'Just you've got some heavy-duty rat killer lying around. This place isn't infested, is it?'

'Oh no, nothing like that,' she replied, trying to sound like she was breezing it off. 'It's just routine. Whenever we clear out a property we like to make sure it doesn't disturb or attract any unwelcome visitors, that's all. There's an old saying that you're never more than six feet away from a rat, but that's nonsense. Right then,' she added, 'I better go and see how your parents are getting on.'

She left, and he watched her go, wondering why, of all things, this was the one she should be lying about.

He chose a room behind one of the oddly angled dormer windows overlooking the back garden. At some point in the cottage's long past someone had converted the loft space into two rooms, which had probably been intended as a hideaway for a middle-aged husband to play with his train set or his porn collection. It definitely wasn't designed to be a bedroom: the ceiling sloped steeply in all kinds of directions so that the walls were only a few feet high and there weren't many places where a fourteen-year-old boy could stand up straight, and his mum wasn't at all sure that it would be suitable for his 'needs' (whatever she thought those were), but Toby was adamant that he loved it, so that was that. He liked its closed-in nature. It reminded him of something he'd read about Indian palaces being built with deliberately narrow passageways so that intruders would have to fight one man at a time to get at the maharajah. So while Ms Markes and his parents went through the last of the paperwork, he sat in the high, narrow window at the top of the house and looked down at the parish stone sitting insolently in the middle of the lawn as if daring him to do something about it. 'Protected' it might be, but from up here he would at least have a decent warning if that turned out to be a lie too.

4

WELCOME

THINGS LIKE THIS DON'T HAPPEN TO PEOPLE LIKE US.
  People like us is people like them, now.

Peter's words kept coming back to Trish all through the afternoon that they spent meeting the other members of the Haleswell Village Trust. It started with drinks in the garden of the rectory of St Sebastian's.

People like Richard Nash, Chief Executive of Haleswell Village Trust, whom she made a beeline for first thing, even though under other circumstances she would have found him to be more than a little full of himself. He was well fed rather than fat, with his belly emphasised by a check shirt tucked into mustard-coloured chinos – country golf club smart-casual, though he had a beer in his hand while most of the others held wine glasses. He wore glasses and the perpetual half-smile of a man who appeared to be laughing at some private joke. The sort of man her bosses at the warehouse aspired to have drinks with.

'Peter!' he beamed, shaking her husband's hand first before turning to her. 'And Patricia! And of course this handsome young gentleman, Tobias.' Right there, she thought, there was the pecking order. She saw Toby rolling his eyes and smiled to herself. 'Fabulous that you could all make it. How are you finding everything?' he asked, his attention defaulting back to Peter.

'Wonderful, thank you,' she said before he could reply. 'I just wanted to say thanks to you and your committee for everything you've done for my family. You've been more than generous.'

'It's a genuine pleasure, Patricia...'

'Trish, please.'

'Of course. Trish. What can I get you all to drink?' And he led them to a side table loaded with bottles, alongside plates of finger food: miniature sandwiches, pastry savouries that looked like origami, and not a cocktail sausage in sight. 'Red or white?'

She surveyed the options. 'I think I'll have one of those expensive-looking lagers, thank you, Mr Nash.'

He laughed like this was the best joke he'd heard all day. 'Richard,' he insisted. 'The only people who call me Mr Nash are the people I can fire.' The bottles were the kind with a wire contraption at the top which flipped a little ceramic lid on and off again. She and Peter took one each. Nash turned to Toby. 'And what about you, young sir? What do teenagers drink these days? When I was your age it was a can of Top Deck on the way home from school, though I suppose that doesn't even exist now. Top Deck, that is, not school. I'm fairly certain that's still around.'

'He'll have a lemonade,' said Trish.

'Absolutely. Plenty of time for the hard stuff, eh?'

While Nash was sorting this out Toby leaned in close to his dad, and though she couldn't hear the whole of the murmured exchange, definitely caught the word 'nob-end'.

People like Anik Singh, the Trust's director of human resources, who listened with absolute seriousness as Trish embarrassed herself by telling him about her ambitions to train as a mental health counsellor now that she didn't have to work all hours of the day at her crappy, ironically named 'zero-hours' contract.

'What is it that you do?' he asked. He was quite short and slim, with a dark-eyed intensity that somehow made evasive small talk impossible.

What is it that you do? The kind of question which she imagined in these sorts of conversations would usually be followed by something like. *Oh you know, international finance, hedge fund acquisition, the usual.*

'You know those shopping catalogues where you buy handy kitchen gadgets and dodgy jewellery?' she replied. 'Well they all get supplied by these great big robot warehouses out in the middle of nowhere. I'm one of the "distribution technicians", which basically means if something gets jammed I hit it with a stick until it's unjammed.'

He nodded as if she'd just told him she was a brain surgeon

by day but dabbled a little in rocket science on the side.

'And you?' she asked

'All the clichés, I'm afraid,' he said with an apologetic smile. 'Second generation off the boat, with a pair of pushy parents who I disappointed tragically by becoming a chartered accountant instead of a doctor.' He picked a vol-au-vent off a nearby tray and munched it unenthusiastically. 'Do you like these things?' he asked.

She shrugged, not wanting to offend. 'I imagine they're an acquired taste.'

Singh leaned in conspiratorially. 'Do you want to know something? My father owns a cash-and-carry business on the Stratford Road. One year when I was twelve we had some bad flooding and he tried to save what he could in the big chest freezer in our garage. We ate chicken Kiev for a month and I put on half a stone.' He grinned. 'It was fantastic.'

People like the reverend Joyce Dobson, a tall, angular, middle-aged woman with large hands that seemed to do most of the talking for her. They enfolded both of Trish's in a warm grip of greeting, flew open in laughter, tapped fingers in thought and clasped solemnly when sympathetic. Trish listened politely while Joyce told her about the voluntary and charity work that the Trust organised to help the more deprived housing estates under their management, and when she finished with 'I do hope you'll consider popping in to lend a hand now and then', actually found herself thinking that she might.

'Would you like a quick tour of the church, while we're here?' Rev. Dobson asked. 'Escape this madness for ten minutes?'

Trish glanced over at where Peter and Nash were chatting, with Toby at his father's elbow, sipping his drink and looking bored and restless. She'd ordered him to leave his phone in the car, and he was obviously suffering from withdrawal, but a bit of enforced *social* without the *media* would do him good. Visiting a church was the last thing she wanted to do, but it would have been rude to refuse. 'I'd love to,' she said.

A door in the rectory garden's brick wall let them straight into the churchyard, and onto a short path leading between gravestones to St Sebastian's church. It was a simple building, and smaller than Trish had been expecting, with a square, four-pointed tower at one end and a half-timbered porch with heavy doors set halfway down its length.

'We're not exactly Westminster Abbey,' said Rev. Dobson, as if reading her thoughts. 'But then congregations are usually so small anyway. I'm not sure what I'd do if my flock actually started turning up.'

'I bet Christmas is fun.'

'Bless the Lord for folding picnic chairs, that's all I can say.'

Reverend Dobson unlocked the doors with a huge cast-iron key that looked like it would have been better suited to a medieval dungeon, and stepped into the entry porch. Even from here, Trish could smell it: the heavy redolence of furniture polish, old carpet, and candle wax which was instantly familiar even though she'd never set foot in this place before. It was like smelling the cologne of an old, abusive lover, one you thought you'd said good riddance to and never expected to have to deal with again. Her pulse quickened, and she told herself not to be so bloody stupid.

What's He going to do, strike me down with holy retribution?

Inside there were a few dozen pews and shelves stacked with hymnals, their dark wood set against oak panelling and grey-gold sandstone. On the pulpit a huge Bible lay open at a wide bookmark richly embroidered and embellished with shining pilgrim badges. The altar was modest, even for an Anglican church. She hadn't set foot in a church of any description for twelve years, but even so she was surprised to find that the urge to approach the altar and genuflect was immediate and strong. *I'm sorry, please take me back,* she wanted to say, at the same time as *No, never again, you bastard.*

In one corner, crayon pictures made in Sunday school were stuck directly to the stone wall next to inscribed plaques commemorating notable parishioners and a table with an honesty box and a wicker tray full of small bottles the same size as hand sanitiser. A hand-lettered sign read:

WATER FROM ST SEBASTIAN'S WELL,
SUGGESTED DONATION £2.

She picked up one of the bottles for a closer look. Its label read:

A SIGN OF LIFE AND GOD'S HEALING GRACE FROM
HALESWELL, THE SITE OF ST SEBASTIAN'S WELL, A
PLACE OF CHRISTIAN PRAYER AND PILGRIMAGE FOR

900 YEARS. PRAY WITH THIS WATER; PASS THIS WATER
ON TO SOMEONE AS A SIGN OF YOUR PRAYER FOR
THEM; ASK FOR GRACE TO LET GO OF PAST HURTS OR
SORROWS WHILE POURING THIS WATER INTO
THE EARTH; WASH YOUR HANDS OR FACE IN THIS
WATER, PRAYING FOR GOD'S BLESSING FOR
YOURSELF AND OTHERS.

And then in red capitals:

NOT SUITABLE FOR DRINKING

Trish laughed.

'What's that?' asked Rev. Dobson. 'Oh, I see you've found our little holy moonshine operation. I hope you won't think it too cynical of us. Prayer alone won't replace stolen lead roofing, unfortunately.'

'No, I just thought it was funny how the grace of God isn't fit for human consumption.'

'Ah, well there's the power of the Lord, and then there's health and safety legislation. Come on, I'll show you our holy well.'

Rev. Dobson led her up to the chancel, then turned back to her. 'Oh,' she said. 'I didn't realise that you were a Catholic.'

Trish looked at her sharply. 'What? I'm not. I mean, I was. How did you know?'

'You just crossed yourself.'

'Did I? Shit. Oops, sorry.'

'No need. Do you mind if I ask…?'

'A little bit, yes.'

'Then the apology is mine.' Rev. Dobson continued to the altar, with Trish blushing furiously behind. Dammit, was it really that easy? She stared at the image of Christ carved into the glossy wood of the reredos behind the altar. *Oh no you don't.* Meanwhile Rev. Dobson had lifted the altar cloth, laying her hand on the stone beneath.

'Despite what it looks like, this altar isn't a solid block of stone. It's actually been hollowed out into a trough with a wooden board laid across the top. During the time of the Black Death this stone was placed on the parish boundary and used as a way for the villagers to trade with their neighbours without actual physical contact, to try to prevent the plague spreading. One of the things that Haleswell had to offer was healing water from a spring blessed by Saint Sebastian.'

At the opposite end of the nave from the altar, under the stained-glass windows in the western wall, there was a shallow stone basin built into the floor, full of water. At first Trish thought it was a particularly odd design for a baptismal font, but then she noticed that the water was actually bubbling up into the basin from underneath the floor and flowing away along a channel through a grated culvert in the wall.

'It was originally in the grounds of the church,' said Rev. Dobson, 'but at some point in the seventeenth century the church was rebuilt and expanded to incorporate it as part of the structure. As you can see, it's quite small. Parts of the church actually date back to the twelfth century and it's likely that there were people settled here since the Anglo-

Saxons. Even then this spring probably wasn't big enough to supply the village entirely on its own, but that wasn't why it was so important.'

'I imagine that fresh, clean water coming out of the ground must have seemed like a gift from God,' said Trish.

'It wasn't much of a jump for the church to attribute its miraculous powers to Saint Sebastian, who is supposed to defend against plague. People still come here to pray for healing, and so we bottle a little of it for them to take away with them.' She shrugged. 'It's harmless, and it helps towards our running costs.'

'Just as long as they don't drink it, that is,' Trish pointed out.

Rev. Dobson laughed.

'And do you really believe that it works?'

'Are you asking me if I believe in miracles?'

'You're a priest. It must go with the territory.'

The vicar smiled wryly, and the look she gave Trish was cool and measuring. 'Well, put it this way – if someone had told you six months ago that you would be living mortgage-free in a large detached cottage in one of the most affluent neighbourhoods in the city, what would you have called it? Luck? Just that? Or maybe a little more?'

'Fair point,' Trish conceded. She was beginning to feel that this was a bit more than just a friendly tour – something more like an interview.

'Aha, but you didn't answer the question,' Dobson said.

'Aha, but I have no intention of answering the question.'

Rev. Dobson's hands folded themselves together, the tips

of her forefingers tapping each other as if in conversation. 'Patricia Feenan,' she said, 'if it doesn't sound too pompous, and I'm sure it does, you have firm inner defences. I like that in a person. And I like you, which is just as well, since we basically have the same job.'

'Um…'

'No, not that one. I mean that you and I are both non-executive Trustees. We retain voting rights even though we have no portfolio as part of the Trust's day-to-day business.'

'All the privilege but none of the responsibility.' Trish nodded. 'Makes a nice change.'

Rev. Dobson frowned slightly. 'It's not quite like that. You are a Trustee because you have the guardianship of the parish marker at Stone Cottage. I, similarly, have the guardianship of this spring. Both are important to the history and heritage of Haleswell village – by which I mean the core of the village, the original parish, not the extended series of estates and properties which the Trust has built up over the years. I'm hoping that as a… er…'

'Lapsed? Recovering?'

'Yes. That you will appreciate that Rogation Sunday is a very important fixture in our calendar.'

'I'm afraid you're going to have to remind me about that one. It's been a while.'

'The Sunday before Ascension Thursday? May twenty-sixth. This year it's part of the main bank holiday so obviously we want to make it as much of an occasion as we can—'

'Joyce, if I can stop you there? I think I know what you're

trying to say, and it's okay. Honestly, it's all fine. Natalie was very good in talking us through all of the small print in the title deeds before we signed the contract. We know that there are various conditions that come with owning the cottage, and we're more than happy to observe them. Of course we'll open our garden for the Beating of the Bounds, you don't have to worry about that.'

Reverend Dobson's face relaxed, and her hands stopped fluttering around each other like nervous birds. 'That's lovely to hear. It's been a very long time since Stone Cottage has had new owners – certainly not within living memory of any of the current Trustees – and as you can imagine some of us are a bit nervous about the, ah, continuity.'

'Well you have nothing to be nervous about on my account. We know exactly what we're letting ourselves in for.'

Trish was surprised by how bitter Reverend Dobson's laughter sounded as she led Trish out of the church and back towards the rectory, saying, 'I very much doubt that, my dear.'

Back in the reverend's garden, Richard Nash got their attention in the time-honoured fashion of tapping his bottle with a fork.

'And now,' he announced, 'it's time that we properly welcome our newest Trustee and her wonderful family into our community. If you'll all…' He gestured towards the French doors of the rectory study, which stood open. 'Don't worry,' he added to the Feenans as the group headed in.

'We're not all going to throw our car keys into a big bowl and dress up in pointed hoods and shag each other, if that's what you're worried about.' It didn't seem to bother him that her son was listening, and trading smirks with his dad.

Reverend Dobson's study was exactly as Trish had imagined – lined with books from floor to ceiling and furnished with a heavy desk and several wing-backed armchairs. The only thing which surprised her was that above the fireplace, where she might have expected an image of the crucifixion, there was instead a reproduction of an oil painting showing shroud-wrapped corpses lying in the streets of a medieval town while townsfolk rolled their eyes in terror and priests prayed over the bodies. In the sky an angel and a demon did battle underneath the figure of a man pierced with arrows like a pincushion, who was kneeling on a cloud and pleading with the Lord. It was entitled *Saint Sebastian Interceding for the Plague-Stricken*. She nudged Peter and nodded at it.

'Bit grim,' he whispered.

'Catholics for you,' she whispered back.

Reverend Dobson led her to the desk, upon which lay open the kind of large leather-bound tome kept with a precision which might have done a Victorian accountant proud. It was a register of names, each written in a different hand, the dates next to them going back several decades. The most recent ones were the names of all the people currently in the room with her: *Richard Nash, Joyce Dobson, Donna Russell, Sean Trevorrow, Natalie Markes, Anik Singh, Alan Pankowicz, Esme Barlow* and, a few places above them, separated by names she didn't recognise going back to the fifties, her great-aunt, Stephanie Drummond.

'This is the ledger of the Trustees of Haleswell Parish,' said Rev. Dobson. 'A record of all those who have given service to the village over the years – and now you're one of them, the new custodian of Stone Cottage. If you still want to sign up, that is, after having met all of us.'

A ripple of laughter went around the room, but it was polite and subdued, unlike the easy banter from before in the garden. The kind of laughter a congregation might give.

'Oh! Ah…' Trish tried not to show how flustered she was, suddenly having everybody looking at her so expectantly. 'I don't think I've got, um…'

'Here.' The reverend picked up a silver fountain pen from the desk and gave it to her.

'Ah. Thanks. Do I have to… should I say something? I feel like I should have prepared a speech.'

'Oh Lord, no!' Dobson laughed. 'This isn't a formal thing at all.'

But it felt formal. Over the last six weeks she'd signed insurance documents, title deeds, and all manner of official paperwork, but seeing those names set out by the hands of their owners in ink which had dried long before she was born, this felt like the most formal one of all. The barrel of the pen felt cold and heavy with some unspoken irrevocability, a weight of implications to which she was committing not just herself, but her husband and son. She was half tempted to try and laugh it off, though if someone had asked her what she was afraid of, she couldn't have said.

Everybody was looking at her, Peter and Toby included.

The pen scratched her name on the next blank line down.

People like us is people like them, now.

Then there was applause and laughter and more drinks.

While Trish was having her glass topped up, Natalie Markes came over. 'If you need any help on moving day, just let me know,' she offered. 'I assume it'll be soon?'

'Oh we have one or two things that need sorting out. We had to give the letting agency a month's notice so there's still plenty of time.'

A small frown creased Markes' brow, and was gone. 'The sooner you can do that the better, I would suggest,' she said, sipping her own wine. 'Yes. Definitely sooner.'

5

REPORTING IN

AFTER THE CATERERS HAD REMOVED THE LAST OF THE dinner debris the Trustees met in the reverend's drawing room. As darkness had fallen the weather had closed in, and the sound of rain could be heard being flung at the windows like handfuls of gravel.

'So,' said the chief executive, 'what do we make of them?' He swirled the contents of his whisky tumbler thoughtfully.

'It's a bit too soon to tell,' said the director of human resources.

'I know. First impressions is all I'm after.'

'Well, according to the reports…'

'Oh for God's sake, we've all read the bloody reports!' he snapped. 'You've spoken to them; what do you *think* of them? Will they stay on when the inevitable ordure hits the ventilation system? Are they keepers? Are they our kind of people?'

In the awkward silence, Human Resources shot a glance for help at the director of property and development, who sighed. When the chief executive had been drinking there was no telling which way his mood would fall, but they'd always had a good working relationship so her voice was the least likely to get shouted down. 'Depends on how long it takes Her to make contact,' she said. 'The boy has already started poking around in the garden, and he's young; his mind is more plastic. She's likely to appear to him first, but I think it's unlikely he'll actually say anything to his parents for a while. According to his ed psych report – I know, I know, just hear me out – the thing he's most afraid of is people thinking that he's going crazy after the break-in.'

The chief executive hmmed. 'Let's get him bedded into the grammar school as soon as possible. Get him invited to a few parties; build his new social group. He's already had to leave one group of friends, so he'll be resistant to abandoning another.' He laughed shortly. 'Hopefully he'll get a shag from some girl who fancies a bit of rough.'

The director of financial services made a face.

'I recommend no counselling,' said the reverend. 'If he feels like his past is following him around and the teachers are talking about him behind his back that will just make him more resistant.'

'Fine then. The father?'

'Uncomplicated provider type,' said Human Resources, having regained his equilibrium. 'Feeling a little bit emasculated due to the fact that his wife is the leaseholder and not him, but give him a good job on the Clegg Farm development, promotion prospects, lots of macho bonding to scaffold his need to protect his family and he'll be fine – especially when he finds out about Her. That's assuming he even does find out. For him it'll be a simple risk/benefit analysis: do the advantages for my loved ones of living in this place outweigh the threat She poses? Ultimately all he'll need is a solution, and we can provide that.'

Financial Services frowned. 'Really? You think it's going to be that simple when it's the lives of his wife and child on the line?'

'When it gets to that point—'

'*If* it comes to that point,' interrupted the chief executive.

'*If* it comes to that point,' Human Resources corrected himself, 'we can revise the strategy and lean more on the safety-in-numbers angle.'

The chief executive looked around the table at his grim-faced colleagues. 'Now look,' he said. 'The thing with the rat unsettled us, to be sure, but it's not as if it hasn't happened before and She is still weak, remember. Despite what you all seem to think, She is not some kind of all-powerful Demogorgon. Yes, from time to time She finds a way to cause the occasional regrettable incident, but She has Her limitations, and if we all do our jobs properly there's no reason to believe that anything like it will happen again.'

Environmental Services gulped a large swallow of red wine and shook her head, muttering, '*Regrettable incident.*' Her eyes were shiny with tears. Financial Services laid a comforting hand over hers and squeezed.

The chief executive forged ahead into the awkward silence. 'So, tick "uncomplicated macho bonding". What about the mother?'

'Ah,' said the reverend. 'Now she's interesting. Lapsed Catholic.'

'My favourite kind.'

There was general laughter around the table.

'But she wants to belong,' Human Resources added. 'Her involvement in various charitable and voluntary organisations in her old home indicates a need to build connections and put down roots. Do you think you can find something like that for her, Reverend?'

'Oh, just a bit,' she replied sardonically. 'I've already mentioned it to her, and she seemed receptive to the idea. What caused her crisis of faith? Do we know?'

'We know that she suffered several miscarriages trying for more children after the boy, after which she became much less active.'

'That's a shame.'

'I know. Poor woman.'

The chief executive waved this away impatiently. 'Well yes, obviously, but the one thing guaranteed to build strong ties to a place is having a baby. Let's subtly push free fertility treatment as part of the Trustee health care package. And once the father is settled, well – after all, a happy hubby is a horny hubby.'

'You old romantic,' said Financial Services, not even trying to hide her sarcasm.

'She has already expressed an interest in acquiring the

cottage's original furniture, which is a positive sign,' put in Property and Development.

'Well let's get that sorted as soon as possible, then.'

'That, ah, might not be so easy.'

'Why on earth not?'

'It's all still in storage, waiting to be vetted.'

The chief executive glared at her. 'Good God, Natalie, why? You've had months!'

Property and Development shrugged, unperturbed. 'A simple question of priorities, Richard. The physical state of the building needed a lot more work than we'd expected. Stephanie had really let the place go quite badly. It was riddled with damp, rot, and God knows what else. We've been so busy working on it that we haven't finished a full inventory of the contents – she'd hoarded all kinds of rubbish, and there are literally hundreds of books on things like the plague, the paranormal, ghosts…'

This was accompanied by a mime show of wincing and uncomfortable shuffling around the table.

'…not to mention letters, diaries, scrapbooks and things like that. There's no telling what she might have written down; we can't possibly let the family have access to anything which might spook them. Not at this crucial stage.'

Financial Services drained her glass of red and laughed shortly. 'Spook them? Is that meant to be funny? Haven't you heard of the Internet? Besides, as soon as the Feenans move in and She realises that there's a new custodian of Stone Cottage, She's going to do everything She can to drive them out. A pile of old *Fortean Times* is going to look pretty bloody tame once rats start trying to eat their faces, don't you think?'

A babble of gossip rose over this until the chief executive tapped his pen against his glass to silence them. 'Let's all just try to remember that this is the first time in living memory any of us have had to do this. We have the wisdom of our predecessors to guide us but obviously they didn't have to reckon with the capabilities of digital technology, so we need to be realistic about what we can achieve. Our goal is not to prevent the Feenans from finding out the truth – that's in Her hands, not ours. Our goal is to manage expectations so that when they *do* find out they come to us rather than run screaming for the hills.'

An action plan was agreed. The Executive Committee of the Haleswell Village Trust broke up as its members each found his or her own way home through the worsening weather.

'What do you think, then?' asked Trish, putting a mug of tea on the kitchen table in front of Peter. Except that the kitchen in their old flat was so tiny that there wasn't room for an actual table – it was the kind that clipped flat against the wall along with a pair of collapsible wooden stools. *Bless the Lord for folding picnic chairs,* Reverend Dobson had said, but Trish was fine if she never saw another piece of bargain flat-pack furniture again. All the same, she almost felt sad to be leaving it. It was chipped and scratched and stained, but those scars were the result of innumerable meals prepared for her family, evidence of where her infant son had learned to cut and stick and colour, and even the arena for one spectacularly ill-advised attempt at off-piste sex which had resulted in Peter wrenching his knee and limping for a fortnight. It seemed absurd to be fixating on so stupid and small a thing as a cheap kitchen table, but she supposed that the small things were what helped you cope with the big things.

'What do I think about what?' he asked.

'Them! The other Trustees. Do you like them? Do you think they liked us?' Up until today Natalie Markes had been their only contact with the Haleswell Trust.

'I don't suppose it really matters whether I like them or not, does it?'

She sat down opposite him and sipped her tea. 'Well try not to sound so completely over the moon about it, why don't you.'

'That's not what I mean. I just mean that we're going regardless, aren't we? Doesn't matter if they hate our guts or invite us to their wife-swapping parties.'

'Ew.' She grimaced. 'You think they really have those?'

'Bloody hope so.'

She kicked him under the table. 'Git. Although, did you notice that none of them had partners with them?'

'Probably because it was a works do.'

'"Works do". Listen to you. Common as muck, you are.'

'Ah, you like a bit of rough, lady of the manor.' He lunged across the table and slobbered theatrically into her neck while she squealed and swatted him away.

The space was made even more cramped by the fact that most of the cupboards' contents were already packed in cardboard cartons stacked on the floor and counters. They weren't due to move for another two weeks, but now that the decision had been finalised and they'd given notice to the letting agent Trish had wanted to get started as soon as possible, even though it would mean living out of boxes until the start of April. As far as the Trust was concerned they could move in tomorrow, but she and Peter had agreed that Toby's schooling should be disrupted as little as possible, that he would see out the end of the spring term and that they'd move at the start of the Easter holidays. The good news was that he was still only in Year Nine and so the move wouldn't jeopardise his GCSEs, and he'd have the whole of the summer term to familiarise himself with his new school, wherever that was. There was a decent comprehensive in Haleswell but also a grammar school that had been rated as outstanding and which Natalie had even hinted might be persuaded to have a place for the son of the newest Trustee. Trish supposed that was how it worked now. *People like us is people like them.* It made her a bit uncomfortable but not half so much as looking at the scratches and gouges around the back door where the intruder had got in to terrorise her boy. She didn't care where he went to school – and she agreed with Peter, she didn't care whether she fitted in with the Haleswell people or not – so long as Toby was safe. The police had never caught the man who had beaten her son, and the thought that he was still out there somewhere terrified her.

'What do you make of all that high-security stuff?' she asked. 'You know, the burglar-proof windows and doors?'

He shrugged. 'Good thing? Especially given... you know...'

'I know. I just wonder if it's going to make us feel all claustrophobic and paranoid. She said it was standard on all their homes. You don't think that makes them sound a bit... oh I don't know. Closed in?'

Peter dunked a custard cream and munched it, thinking. 'I imagine if they've all got big houses like that they're going to be worried about getting burgled. I kind of think it'd be nice to be closed in for a bit. Cosy. Safer for Toby.'

She mulled that over for a bit, then raised her mug of tea to his. 'To fresh starts,' she said. 'For all of us.'

'Fresh starts,' he echoed the toast, clinked his mug to hers and they drank.

'Hey,' she said. 'You know what I'm going to do in that lovely big kitchen?'

'Other than letting me have my wicked way with you over that big table?'

'In your dreams. No – I, drum roll please, am going to learn how to bake bread.'

He looked at her for a moment and then burst out laughing.

She frowned. 'Not sure I find that encouraging.'

'Oh, honey, I'm sorry, it's just that, you remember the Christmas pudding, don't you?'

'Look, it was a simple mistake, okay? Three minutes, thirty minutes, whatever!' She grabbed a biscuit and munched in embarrassment. 'Besides, it was only in for ten, and half of it was still edible.'

He was still laughing.

'How hard can bread be, anyway? It's like the oldest thing people have ever cooked or something. I've always wanted to learn how. Yes, there shall be bread and scones and cakes and things – but only if you behave yourself.'

He reached for her again, and she swatted him away again, but not very wholeheartedly. 'I said behave!'

Later he didn't behave himself at all, and in the most delightful ways.

6

TOBY

'SONOFA*BITCH*!'

Toby liked hearing his dad swear. It was shocking, given how fiercely both his parents had policed his language since forever, but also made him feel more grown-up and oddly trusted, as if his dad felt like Toby wasn't a baby anymore, almost a bit more of an equal.

Between them they were attempting to move a writing bureau up the stairs of Stone Cottage into Toby's room; it wasn't particularly heavy, but quite awkward to manoeuvre, and it was making his dad swear a *lot*.

'Tobes, mate, try to get that bit over... no, over...'

'Dad, it's not going to...'

'See if you can... yes, little further...'

It slipped, one corner bashing a dent into the wall.

'Jesus *fucking* Christ!'

Toby grinned.

The day after they'd moved in, Ms Markes had called around to give them the keys to the lock-up where all the old furniture that had been moved out of the cottage was being stored, telling them that they could have their pick of what was there, and that whatever they left would be auctioned by the Trust. His parents had hired a van and they'd driven out to a large, bland industrial unit near the motorway. Toby had been fully prepared for another boring afternoon of going through old people's stuff, but it had been like opening an Aladdin's cave of antique dark wood and gleaming brass. There were wardrobes packed like dominoes beside bookcases and glass-fronted cabinets stacked on chests of drawers next to tables with scrolled legs and piled with rolls of musty-smelling rugs, ornate mirrors reflecting candelabras and bedsteads and vases and a massive metal gong and a coal scuttle full of peacock feathers and crates full of picture frames. His mum and dad had filled the van easily, chattering excitedly about where each thing would go, and it was nice to see them so happy. When Toby's eyes had lit on a writing bureau which he thought might actually be quite cool to do his homework on, that had gone in too.

It seemed more *real*, that was the thing. It had three drawers with rattling handles below a slanted face which folded down into a writing desk complete with an actual leather blotter, and inside were loads of little compartments for filing correspondence and small drawers for keeping stationery. It wouldn't have anywhere near enough room for all his drawing materials, obviously, but he could definitely use it to house his textbooks and write essays. It looked like it had been made by actual people using actual tools, rather than extruded from chipboard and laminate, sold through a warehouse and then put together with a screwdriver and lots of swearing. Though he couldn't have put the feeling into words, there was a weight to it which was more than just the amount of wood, but had to do with the lives of the people who had sat at it over the years and written birthday cards and job applications and letters of love or desperation. Like everything else, it smelled of dust and furniture polish.

It was a bit weird taking it back to the house from which it had been removed – he wasn't sure where it belonged but it probably wasn't his attic room – but he hoped that if objects had spirits then it would forgive him.

It was certainly putting up a fight so far.

'Bastard thing!'

Finally they shuffled it over the last step and into his bedroom, and his dad leaned against it, wiping the sweat from his forehead. 'All yours now,' he grunted. 'I better see what I can do about that dent before your mother finds out.'

'Thanks. I'll take the fucker from here.'

'Oi! Watch your language!'

His dad stared at him. Toby stared back and raised his eyebrows. *Really?* His dad turned and clumped downstairs, shaking his head and muttering, but Toby could hear the smile in his voice all the same.

Below its set of main drawers the bureau stood on four short legs, which made it impossible to slide along the carpeted floor of his bedroom to the wall where Toby wanted it, so he had to tip it up on one leg and pivot it a hundred and eighty degrees in the right direction, then repeat. Fiddly, but doable, as long as he didn't overbalance the thing and bring it down on top of himself. It was while he was in the process of doing this that he heard a creak from the back of the unit and saw something small and pale seesaw to the floor.

Toby lowered the bureau and bent to examine what had fallen out.

It was a single sheet of paper, yellow with age, about the same size as the page of a school exercise book and torn along one edge as if that was exactly what it had been ripped from. He guessed it had slipped between the writing surface and the back of the unit and been presumed lost. There was writing on one side – elegant, cursive handwriting which it took him a little time to decipher.

But when he did, what he read made no sense at all.

Toby meant to ask his mum about it over dinner, but it slipped his mind when mealtime conversation turned into an argument about school.

It had started with his asking a simple question: 'So what's this Rogation Sunday thing all about, then? Is it like a church thing?' His parents had the kitchen calendar out on the table and had been wrangling out their various commitments for the next month. The twenty-sixth of May had been marked out with a star.

'Sort of,' said his mum. 'But don't worry,' she added,

seeing his expression, 'you won't have to go. None of us has to go. In a funny way, it's coming to us.'

'Oh-kay,' he replied, still wary. 'Not weird much.'

'Rogation days are the days leading up to Ascension Thursday, which is the day Christ supposedly got taken straight up to heaven.'

'This was after he did his reverse zombie act?'

'His what?'

'Reverse zombie. Comes back from the dead and lets other people eat him.'

His dad laughed at that.

'If you want to put it that way, yes.' Mum seemed less amused.

Toby shrugged. 'Holy escalator. Why not.'

'Anyway, Rogation days are supposed to be all about fasting and prayer in preparation for this but there are a lot of other very old traditions which go along with it. Haleswell, like a lot of places, has a big fair on the Sunday. Carnival rides, balloons, candy floss, that sort of thing. Plus they have a tradition called the Beating of the Bounds.'

Toby looked up from his lasagne. 'People get beaten?' This was suddenly interesting again, and not in a good way. He blinked away a sudden flash of Green Skull's fist curving in towards him.

'No. It means they go around the old parish boundary to each of the stones that mark it. I suppose there are some prayers, but mostly it seems to be more of a parade around the neighbourhood with stops for drinking and eating cake. One of the stones is in the bar of the White Hart Inn down the road, so I don't imagine that it's entirely serious.'

'And,' his dad put in, 'since we have one of the parish stones, we get to open our back garden up to dozens of strangers and feed them cake.'

'It's going to be fine,' said his mum. 'Great-aunt Stephanie did it every year and there's no reason why we shouldn't carry it on. We actually have to, anyway. It's one of the conditions of the leasehold. It'll be fun; you can invite your friends and turn it into a garden party.'

'You mean like that sick spree at the vicar's with those really interesting old people?' He danced his knife and fork in the air. 'Bring it.'

His dad nudged his mum. 'I don't know where he gets this sarcasm from.'

She scratched the bridge of her nose with her middle finger. Toby knew that she was really flipping him off. Both his parents knew that he knew, and he knew that they knew that he knew. His heart swelled with love for them so he buried it by attacking his lasagne again.

'Anyway,' continued his dad. 'You should be grateful to those old people. I'm meeting with Mr Nash tomorrow about doing some work for him on one of the Trust's projects.'

'Jobs for the boys,' commented his mum. 'Oh, which reminds me…' She went to the fridge, to which an official-looking letter had been stuck with a magnet. While they'd been out at the storage place, the post had arrived, bringing with it an invitation for Toby to visit nearby Pittfield Grammar School, quite informally, and have a chat with the deputy master about whether he thought he might like to apply for a place in the coming summer term.

Toby's lasagne dried to ashes in his mouth. He swallowed and with difficulty managed to choke out, 'What? What grammar school? I didn't know anything about this! I thought I was going to the comp!'

'It's an excellent school,' said his mother. 'It's close by, and I hear it's got a great art department. We should at least go and look.'

'But you're supposed to sit the eleven-plus exam to get into a grammar, and I haven't done that! All the kids there are going to be really clever. I'm not going to be able to keep up with them. They'll know I'm thick the moment I open my mouth!' He looked to his dad, but Peter Feenan was chewing his food with that silent intensity which Toby knew meant that he'd decided to stay out of it.

'Of course you're clever enough,' said his mum, reaching to pat his arm. He pulled away. 'The letter says that they've seen your grades from your old school and that you seem to be a very promising young man.'

'How have they seen my grades? Who said they could do that? That's like, data protection or something, isn't it?'

'I think you might be overreacting a bit—'

'So, what? They're going to fudge it and let me in anyway? How's that going to look? I'm going to be the thick estate kid who only got in because his parents pulled some strings. They'll eat me alive!'

'You don't think you're jumping to conclusions just a bit?'

Toby made an effort to control his breathing and speak in

calm, measured tones; his voice had broken a year ago but it still had a tendency to squeak when he was stressed, and the last thing he wanted was to sound like a child. 'Mum,' he said, 'you don't understand what it's like. That kind of thing – that sort of unfairness, jumping the queue that everybody else has had to stand in – it's social death. They'll *crucify* me. Please, it's bad enough that I'm having to leave all my friends anyway, please let me just go to a normal school with normal kids.' He had no qualms about resorting to emotional blackmail. You fought with what weapons you had.

His mum sat back in her chair with a little sigh of surprised resignation, as if she genuinely could not understand why he was turning down such an amazing opportunity. 'Well then I suppose of course, if you really don't want to go, you shouldn't have to.'

'He's a clever boy,' said his dad. 'He'll be clever wherever. That wasn't meant to rhyme, by the way.'

It defused the tension to some extent, and the conversation quickly turned to other, more neutral matters.

A couple of hours after dinner, while Toby was at the big desk in his room drawing a stone circle but making it cooler by turning it into an interdimensional arena in which alien gladiators fought, his dad came to see him. One of the disadvantages of this being a converted loft space was the fact that it had no door – steps led straight up from the upstairs hallway, so by the time his dad had knocked on the wall and coughed he was effectively already in the room. He didn't say anything straight away, of course. He hovered. He glanced at the posters – Aston Villa, something with superheroes, something with zombies. He trailed around the furniture – new bed, new bookcases, new wardrobe, TV and games console – like an old-fashioned butler looking for dust. He even looked over Toby's shoulder at his picture and made approving noises even though it was obvious that he didn't get it.

'Room okay?' he asked.

'It's okay,' Toby replied.

His dad went to the window and looked out over the back garden. 'Bit far away from everything, right up here.'

'I like it.' He didn't mean that to sound as defensive as it came out; he knew his dad was only making small talk to build up to something. 'Also I won't disturb you with my loud rock-and-or-roll music,' he added, trying to make a joke of it.

Eventually his dad cleared his throat and said, 'Try not to be too hard on your mother, yeah?'

'Dad—'

'I know, I know. It's just that the last few years have been hard on us all, and now this has fallen in our laps,' he made an encompassing gesture which meant not just the room, but the house and the neighbourhood surrounding it. 'And I think she's just keen to make up for lost time, you know?'

Toby nodded. 'I get it. It was just a bit of a surprise, that's all.'

'Felt like people talking about you behind your back?'

Toby's heart swelled with sudden love and gratitude,

mingled with surprise that his dad understood – at least some of it. He hid it by turning back to his sketch and adding some more shading that it didn't need. 'A bit. But yeah. I know she means well.'

Dad nodded. 'Okay then.' As he passed, he laid a hand on Toby's shoulder. 'For what it's worth, I think you made the right decision.' He patted it, and moved on. 'Oh, hey,' he added. He'd stopped by the old bureau which was in one of the only really tall spaces by the stairs. 'This looks good here. Nice job.'

It was only after he'd left that Toby remembered the piece of paper that had fallen out of it.

7

THE DEAD GIRL

TOBY READ ITS SINGLE LINE AGAIN.
Heb13/2 Is58/7 Ez16/49–50

Lying in bed with just the screen of his phone filling the room with its cold blue glow, he googled it on the off-chance. The Internet threw up three biblical references:

—Do not neglect to show hospitality to strangers, for by this some have entertained angels without knowing it.

—Share your food with the hungry and provide the poor wanderer with shelter—when you see the naked, clothe them, and do not turn away from your own flesh and blood.

—The crime of Sodom was pride, gluttony, arrogance, complacency; such were the sins of Sodom and her daughters. They never helped the poor and needy; they were proud and engaged in filthy practices in front of me; that is why I have swept them away as you have seen.

Then he googled the story of Sodom, which he read with deepening unease. As much as the details were disturbing in themselves – of a father offering his virgin daughters to a violent mob in order to protect his house guests from being gang-raped, and the entire city being razed to the ground in punishment – more disturbing to him was the sense he got of the person who had written the note. He'd never given much thought to Stone Cottage's previous owner, other than as a distant relative of his mum. Never imagined her as a solitary, elderly woman living in a house of empty rooms, approaching her death. His imagination fashioned the shape of her sitting at her bureau, which now stood in the shadowed recess of his room, the curve of her spine against a straight-backed chair, paging through the crackling onionskin pages of an ancient Bible with liver-spotted hands as she read stories of betrayal, angelic curses, and genocide into the dusty silence. So easy to imagine her stop, straighten as she became aware of his presence, and turn to look at him with eyes which—

Toby jerked awake with a cry. For a moment he couldn't remember where he was. There was no familiar street light here or sound of traffic on the busy road outside. It was altogether too dark, too quiet. His phone had just fallen to the floor, uplighting the room and pulling the shadows high towards the odd-angled ceiling in skewed perspectives. He checked the time: 1:43.

Stone Cottage. New home. Not the flat.

Obviously there was nobody sitting at his bureau. Just another intruder nightmare brought about by staying up too late on his phone. Nothing to see here, folks, move along. All the same, he got up and went to the window just to be sure, listening to the strange new creaks of the floor under his feet, wondering how long before they became familiar, before this place would feel like home. *This place is safe. It's protected*, she'd said, but she'd lied.

Because there was someone in the back garden.

Toby's breath stopped.

He tried to tell himself that this was just another hallucination like the one of the old woman created by his doze, and for a moment he almost believed it.

A girl, he was fairly certain of that, from the slightness of her figure, the shift-type dress that she wore, and her long hair. Beyond that he couldn't tell much because of the darkness that left her face in shadow, but her pale arms looked somehow blotchy. She was standing in the middle of the lawn, right by the parish stone.

No green skull, no crowbar. She didn't look like she was about to smash her way through the kitchen window and beat him up. She wasn't doing anything, as a matter of fact, just standing there. It occurred to him that she might be a junkie, either looking for something to steal or simply too high to notice where she was, although he couldn't imagine how she'd got in because the back gate was firmly locked; she'd have had to climb the fence and she didn't look strong enough for that. In fact, given that it was still only April and had been raining all day, he wouldn't have been surprised to find that she'd caught her death of cold. She didn't look dangerous. For a moment he wondered whether he should get his parents to call an ambulance or something – maybe that shift thing was a hospital gown. Maybe he should let her in for some warmth and shelter.

'Some have entertained angels without knowing it,' he murmured.

The girl's head snapped up, staring straight at his window. Her face was still in shadow but now there was the glitter of eyes deep in sunken sockets.

Staring straight at him.

He yelped and fell back. It was impossible that she could have seen him – almost as impossible as her being there in the first place.

Warily, he approached the window again, expecting to find the garden empty.

She was still there, still staring. However, the ground around her was busy now with small, dark shapes, tumbling about her bare feet as if playing. Rats. The sound of their chittering reached him clearly.

She raised her arm, and beckoned to him.

Come down.

'No,' he whispered. 'No, this can't be real.' Toby crept back to bed, wincing at the creaking of the floorboards, convinced that either that sound or his own shouting would have awoken one of his parents, and that they'd come to ask him what all the fuss was about and why was he wandering around in the middle of the night? There was no way he was going to tell them that he'd seen someone in the back garden. He knew exactly how it would look: more nightmares of the burglary; obviously their son was more traumatised than they'd thought; time to take him to see the men in white coats. That was never going to happen. Besides, there was a passive-IR security light looking over the garden; if there really was anyone there, the light would have come on. It had to have been the after-effects of whatever he'd been dreaming. He reached for his phone, put his headphones on and then slipped himself deeply under the covers, trying to hide in the darkness and his music.

But still he heard the chittering, like delicate fingers tapping lightly on his window.

8

HESTER
APRIL 1349

WHEN FOURTEEN-YEAR-OLD HESTER ATTLOWE WAS sure that the rest of her family were asleep she crept out of bed, pulled on her woollen dress and a pair of soft leather slippers, and went to see the stranger sleeping in her father's barn.

Getting out of the sleeping loft was easy enough; as the only daughter in the family she had the space behind the ladder to herself, nestled like a bird in the comfortable angle formed by the floor and the underside of the steeply sloping thatched roof. Her brother Henry occupied the space in front of the ladder, so there was nobody to disturb as she rolled off her straw-filled mattress and tiptoed towards the hatch. His side of the loft space was thick with the warm and yeasty fug of ale farts.

She caught her breath and froze as the floorboards creaked, but all that happened was that Henry grunted and flopped over onto his other side, snorting like a wallowing sow. She shouldn't have worried – he was so drunk that nothing was likely to waken him short of the End of Days. As were her mother and father, asleep and snoring in the room below. There was neither candle nor window, but she knew every inch of her home and proceeded by touch to the top of the ladder without stumbling or knocking anything over.

The ladder creaked too, and she paused midway down in the pitch-darkness, a few feet above her parents' heads, listening for any change in their breathing which might indicate that she'd disturbed them. There was none. Theirs was the large wood-framed bed with the panels that her father had paid to have carved with vines and flowers – the finest in the village. Dick Attlowe was neither as rich as Gideon the miller nor as important as Father Cuthbert, and their village was really little more than a hamlet which struggled in the shadow of larger and wealthier neighbours, but he was generous with gifts and that generosity had won him as fine a reputation as any lord's, at least to Hester's mind. People would give the shirts off their backs for love of her father, though sometimes it was for fear of his reeve's staff too. If he caught her sneaking around at night like this she was sure to get a beating.

Hester eased herself the rest of the way down the ladder and slipped through her parents' curtain-door into the main room. There was a little light here, a ruddy glow from the embers in the central hearth for which she was grateful. She would never have been able to make it across the room in darkness, since the floor was covered in the sleeping, snoring, drunken lumps of her neighbours.

Like all the houses in Clegeham her home was cruck-built, the 'crucks' being tall A-frames made from entire tree trunks sawn lengthways and propped together, rising to the apex of the roof in one sweep and then braced and reinforced with timbers, walled with wattle and daub, roofed with thatch. The simplest huts had two crucks and the bay between; room for living and working below, sleeping above. Larger cottages had three crucks, and so two bays, like that of Nicholas the smith, whose forge took up one half of his home. The Attlowes' home had four crucks, which gave them three bays; the only other structures in Clegeham larger than that were the stone-built mill and church. On one end of the house were the bedrooms from which she had just come. The other end was a barn where Dick Attlowe's plough and two prized oxen were kept at night. In the middle was the main household workspace where Hester did the mending while her mother Cristina cooked the family's food and brewed their ale – and on festive occasions it was also the closest thing Clegeham had to an alehouse.

This year St George's Day had been celebrated with particular fervour. Rumours of the pestilence had been gathering for almost a year like smoke; at first, nothing more than a wisp or two of outbreaks in Weymouth and Bristol – places on the coast that might as well have been on the other side of the ocean, for certainly nobody from Clegeham would ever have travelled so far. Then the pall of it grew throughout Michaelmas as travellers brought tales from London of whole streets full of corpses, their flesh blackened with rot and bulging with tumours that wept pus and blood. At Easter came news of deaths in Worcester to the south and Birmingham to the north – not exactly on their doorstep but close enough for the smoke of fear to thicken about them, saturating their clothes and seeping into the walls of their homes. They breathed it in and exhaled it into the faces of their neighbours, so they prayed for protection. Father Cuthbert shepherded their souls in the ways of righteousness, and however disturbing was the news from places where people's ways were strange, the villagers of Clegeham slept soundly in the knowledge that their steadfast faith would be rewarded, and that the Lord would keep them from harm.

St George's Day was therefore a chance to forget, momentarily – or at least mask the fear with celebration. Spring was a lean time anyway, with food stores running low before harvest, and the last harvest had been particularly wet which only made it worse, but those who could be spared from the fields cut flowering branches of may and blackthorn to decorate the village houses and church. Gideon the miller began baking cakes of white flour rather than the black rye bread which was all the villagers could normally afford. Wives and mothers brewed up in their homes ale enough to fill every jug and tun in the village. Ordinarily they would have travelled on the Monday to celebrate with their neighbours in the larger village of Haleswell, where there was a tavern and dancing on their green, but this year the people of Clegeham stayed close to home. The decision was unspoken, hidden in the smoke of fear.

Hester started to pick her way across the room, and spotted the sleeping form of Robert, the miller's son. When she'd been sent to the mill by her mother for a bag of malt she'd tried very hard not to stare at him, but he hadn't made it easy, shovelling great loads of grain into the hopper with a broad-bladed wooden shovel, the sinews standing out in his forearms and his hair all floppy in his eyes. He'd seen her staring, and grinned.

'Will you dance with me, after, Hester Attlowe?' he asked.

She hmphed at him in a bid to regain her composure. 'I know very well what kind of dance you have in mind, Robert Hicking,' she retorted, and turned away. Robert the miller's son had a pretty leg, that was true enough, but he did not have her heart.

Clegeham had no tavern, and not much of a green, at that – more of an empty space formed by the triangle of the mill, chapel, blacksmith, and haphazard scattering of houses between. At its centre, as if anchoring the buildings, stood a large stone which was whitewashed and decked with garlands of blossom. Father Cuthbert – the young priest who spent more time in his own fields than at the pulpit – blessed it with water from the spring in Haleswell, and they danced around it. In the light of a great bonfire and to the music of wooden flutes and drums they wove in and out of each other in twirling, skipping steps, passing hand-to-hand, ducking under each other's arms and spinning behind each other's waists. Hester felt as if the springing turf itself was lifting and propelling her along, her friends and neighbours spinning by in grasp and pull, release and skip, their grins as wide as hers. Dorrie, the girl with the harelip who made beautiful beads; and Timothy, who knew the trick of charming blackbirds; and Janot, who was so strong he once carried a lame calf five miles; and Agnes, whose hair looked like spun gold; and Hugh, the blacksmith's cousin – and a dozen more, and their fathers, mothers, brothers and sisters. She knew all their names and their lives as they knew hers, and the weaving of their steps was the weaving of her life with theirs and theirs with hers. And yes, she twirled with Robert the miller's son and let him steal some kisses, and even stole a few for herself. She was fourteen – old enough to be thinking of marriage in a handful of years, allowing that her father should find a man he considered suitable, but while she was yet young enough to be dismissed as a child she saw no harm in dancing with whomever she pleased, be it miller's son or squire. The Black Death might fall on them tomorrow, but she thanked the Lord for today.

Daylight faded and the lingering dusk seemed to coil out of the ground like mist to wreathe about their legs while the sky held the last of the fireglow for a luminous moment, until it too was gone. A thin rain set in from the south and the villagers went – shadows staggering on dance-exhausted legs, arms about each other's shoulders, laughing and gasping – to the Attlowes' cottage for ale and simnel cake. Those who could not fit inside gathered as a group by the doorway to bask in the beer-rich warmth of crowded bodies that spilled out while Hester and a few of the older daughters of other families went about with earthen ewers and jugs so that no cup was drained empty.

She was tossing a bowl of slops into the night when she saw the shape of a man in the dripping shadows and shrieked, dropping the bowl.

'Forgive me,' he said, and stepped forward, meagre light from the doorway catching his features. Features she did not know. A stranger. 'I meant not to startle you. I have travelled long today and am bone-weary. Is this the village of the Holy Well?'

Hester shook her head. 'You are short of that by a mile yet.' His accent was as strange as the fashion of his hat, and he wore a cloak fastened close against the rain with a gleaming brooch. Travellers often passed through Clegeham, but as Hester's surprise at being startled melted away she found that he was by far the most interesting she had seen in a long while.

The man's shoulders slumped and he wiped a hand over his dripping face. 'Then I have been beguiled. They swore it were no more than a day's journey. May I shelter in your alehouse for the night?'

Hester murmured something about going to fetch her father, took up the bowl and ducked back inside, where she found him and young Father Cuthbert laughing together with John Naissh, the bailiff from Haleswell. She did not like Bailiff Naissh. He had lost his wife in childbirth a year gone and Hester could see the way he looked at her – it was an appraising look, the way a farmer might look at a cow and wonder how many calves could be sired on her. The fact that her father answered to him only made it worse.

'Papa,' she said. 'And, Father,' she added, ducking her head before the priest. 'There is a stranger y-comen, outside, seeking our hospitality.'

'What manner of man?' asked her father.

'A traveller,' she shrugged. 'One who is wet and weary, that is all I know.'

'Just one?'

'For aught that I could tell, but if he had companions they will all be drowned rats alike and we shall see them off with a broom straight enough.'

He laughed and kissed her brow. 'I will see this King of Rats.' But as he put down his mug Hester's mother arrested him with a slim hand on his wrist.

'Husband,' she said. Her face was troubled. 'These are ill times to be welcoming strangers. Is this wise?'

'It is our Christian duty,' he replied. 'I'll not leave a man out in the dark on a night such as this. What do you say, Father?'

Dick Attlowe could not pronounce the title 'father' without even the ghost of a smile, since Cuthbert himself was no more than nineteen years old. He was dark-eyed and dark-haired, and swallowed his ale heartily. Hester moved quickly to refill his cup before any of the other girls could, hoping that she might catch his eye, but he thanked her with a chaste politeness that tore at her heart. 'As Paul wrote in his Epistle to the Hebrews,' he declaimed, 'be not forgetful to entertain strangers, for thereby some have entertained angels unawares.'

'Then shall we be doubly blessed,' chuckled Bailiff Naissh, looking straight at Hester. 'For we are already in the presence of one heavenly creature.' He tipped her a lazy wink, and grinned.

Dick Attlowe kissed his wife's fingers and folded them back into her palm. 'I will see the stranger, and if he is a godly man he will be welcome under my roof.'

'And if he brings the pestilence?' Hester's mother pleaded. 'You will risk our lives and our children's lives for a stranger?'

'What pestilence shall we fear, obeying the Lord's gospel? How shall I refuse charity to a stranger at my door when tomorrow I may be the stranger at his? If it be His will that the pestilence comes here then we will suffer it and enter into His grace with clean souls.'

Cristina Attlowe pulled her hand away. 'Well, if and until that shall come to be, your guest shall have here the barn and you will attend on him yourself. My child will not. Hester, come.' Together, mother and daughter gathered up the ale bowl and cups and left the men to their drinking. The revels were not yet done, for those that remained were the hardiest of drinkers (or else the most reluctant to return to their own wives), and so Hester was unable to see the stranger welcomed.

'But, Mother,' she teased, pausing halfway up the ladder to the sleeping loft. 'What if it really is an angel that sleeps under our roof?'

Her mother hmphed, unappreciative of her attempt at humour. 'He'll be angel enough if he simply pays for his board, though with your father welcoming him I would not be surprised if he left with even more gifts. Probably one of our oxen.' She looked up at Hester, who was surprised by the glittering depths of dark anxiety in her mother's eyes.

'You're not to greet him, or talk to him, or linger in his company, do you hear?'

'But, Mother…'

'No! I know you, my girl. You are too curious for your own good. When he's on the road away from here with his back to us you can look to see if he has any wings then.'

Hester stomped up the ladder to the sleeping loft. 'No,' she whispered. 'I will not.'

In the safety and secrecy of her bed, she reached into the straw stuffing and felt for her one true treasure: a pewter pilgrim badge given her by Cuthbert on his return from Canterbury. It was small, the size of a baby's palm, and exquisitely detailed in the shape of a sailing ship, but even in the dark she could tell its shape with her fingertips, and feel the shine of it when she brought it up to her lips. She could never look at it in daylight, however – she could not risk other people seeing it. She cared nothing for her own reputation, but whether she liked it or not Cuthbert was now their village priest, and she loved him too much to risk the shame to him.

The stranger had worn something like it pinning his cloak, and Hester was seized with a burning curiosity to see whether it was of the same fashion. Her mother would find ways of keeping her busy and out of the way come morning, and besides, she was only going to have a quick look and then come straight back to bed.

She pretended to sleep while first her brother Henry retired, then her father, listening to the murmured argument of her parents. Her mother was from Hereford, close enough to Wales, it was said, to have some of that folk's wildness in her, because although she'd acquiesced to her husband's will readily enough in front of the other men, in the privacy of their bedroom it was another matter.

'I am the *reeve*,' Hester heard her father protest. 'It is my duty to set an example for the others.'

'You are *one* of Naissh's *many* reeves,' her mother pointed out. 'It is true, you were elected by your neighbours because you are an honest man and fair to all. That is one of the reasons why I love you. But if they want moral instruction then they should look to Cuthbert. Let him worry about their souls, and you worry about their work.'

After her parents' voices had become snores, Hester listened to the sounds of the household diminishing as those guests too drunk to make their way home slept in the straw of the family room, laughing and chatting and finally settling into silence.

She stood before them now in the shifting red ember light, and for a sickening moment she was certain that the people lying before her weren't just asleep, but actually dead – victims of the pestilence – and that if she were to step over them she would see blackened fingertips clawed in their final death agonies as if reaching out to grasp her ankle as she passed, to pull her down amongst them where she would stare into their glassy eyes and smell the pus weeping from the swollen buboes in their armpits and throats, corrupting their voices as they mocked her with rot-clotted laughter…

Hester whimpered, and nearly ran for the ladder back to her safe nest in the roof.

No. She would see the 'angel'.

Steeling herself, she stepped around the supine bodies, who she saw now were breathing quite peacefully and very much alive. Thankfully none of them was John Naissh; he had left soon after the arrival of the stranger, wending his drunken way back along the mile of road to Haleswell. The thought of him being here, asleep on her floor, to awaken unexpectedly and see her, and what he might think... She shuddered. In the embers of the fire she kindled a stub of candle, and by its wavering light crossed to the other side of the room and the door to the barn. She held her breath as she lifted up the heavy wooden latch, and winced at the creaking as she eased the door open just wide enough to slip through, convinced that someone in the room behind her would wake up and demand to know what she was doing, but nobody did.

The air in the barn was heavy with the smell of dung and the warmth of the two oxen who slept with their heads curled in towards their flanks; disturbed by her entrance, they woke and surged to stand upright, puffing and snorting in confusion. She stroked them down their long noses, hushing and calming them, then turned to look for where the stranger was sleeping. Perhaps her father had changed his mind, listened to his wife and turned the man back out into the rain after all.

But Dick Attlowe would never change his mind once it was set on a course of action. The only thing stronger than his Christian piety was his stubbornness – a trait which he shared with his daughter.

The man was asleep on a pile of sacking by the barn's main door. In the candlelight he looked very ordinary: dressed in homespun wool, with brown hair and a beard, and a large nose which looked red with cold. If he was an angel, Hester wasn't sure how she would know, or what to expect. Father Cuthbert's sermons were sometimes about saints being visited by angels but frustratingly short of detail about what they actually looked like. She assumed there would be light and the singing of heavenly choirs, or at least a sense of being in the presence of the Holy Spirit, whatever that felt like.

The stranger shifted in his sleep, moaned, and coughed. They were wet, hacking coughs, and they left blood on his lips.

Then Hester remembered that there were other angels – the kind that killed every firstborn son of Egypt, and appeared at the time of Revelation to unleash calamity upon humankind in the form of war, and famine, and plague.

'I'm sorry,' she moaned, backing away. 'I didn't mean to. Please, I'm sorry.' She wasn't sure exactly who she was apologising to, or for what. Her mother? For disobeying her orders? The Lord, for her stubborn curiosity and doubt? Had she somehow brought this down on the poor man herself, like Eve, by giving in to temptation? She blew out the candle and blundered out of the barn, past the shifting, restless shapes of the oxen, latching the door closed behind her with a clatter and not caring if it woke anyone up, for what now could it possibly matter? She fled back to her bed, pressing herself as closely as she could to the underside of the roof thatch, wishing that she could disappear into it like the birds that nested there. She knew she should say something, but he was in the barn, wasn't he? He couldn't have had that much contact with her family and neighbours. He'd be gone by morning. And lurking underneath all of that rationalisation was the plain fact that she was simply scared, for she was, after all, just a child.

9

JOBS FOR THE BOYS

PETER SHRUGGED ON THE HI-VIS VEST, STRAPPED ON the hard hat that Nash gave him, and followed through the gated entrance of the construction site.

'Safety first, eh?' said Nash, and chuckled as if at some private joke. 'How long is it now? Two weeks?'

'Nearly three.'

'Superb.'

They made their way along an access road between the half-constructed skeletons of residential houses; it was muddy and potholed, but if Nash was bothered by the mud spattering his shiny shoes and the cuffs of his suit trousers, he didn't show it. The Clegg Farm development had been fields on the city's periphery six months ago, but now it was almost the size of a small village itself, with new residents already having moved into properties at the town end while at furthest edge the plots were still little more than foundation trenches and piles of scaffolding. Where Peter and Nash were currently walking the only thing finished was the maze of roads and cul-de-sacs with the empty plots between them.

'So how long have you been an electrician?'

'Pretty much forever. Since school.' The only thing he'd ever really been good at as a kid was taking things apart and putting them back together, but high school had turned out to be not the total shit-show everybody was expecting and he'd just about scraped decent enough grades to get onto a college training course. 'Mostly domestic. Fuse boxes, house extensions, that sort of thing.'

'And it pays the bills?'

Peter shrugged, uncomfortable with talking about his family's finances. 'We get by. I'm self-employed – means I can take the jobs I want. My diary's generally pretty full.'

'Of course with all the Poles and Romanians buggering off back home that means more work for the home-grown talent.'

'If you say so.' On the occasions when he'd worked on bigger projects he'd always found the European lads to be hard-working and polite, and had never begrudged them a day's work. It was more than could be said for some of the new 'home-grown' lads he'd seen coming through. Nash had offered to take him to meet the guy in charge of the sparkies working for the site's electrical contractor, an invitation too good to pass up. It wouldn't be an interview, he was told, just an introduction. As much as he disliked the kind of favouritism which invited his son to jump the queue into a prestigious school, he was pragmatic enough to appreciate that you didn't get offered work if you didn't put yourself forward. 'This is some serious development,' he said, to change the subject.

Nash nodded with the indulgent pride of a lord showing one of his guests around the family estate. 'It's all part of the Trust. Not quite the tea-and-crumpets, cricket-on-the-village-green type of thing you were expecting? Oh, we have all that, of course. St Sebastian's, the White Hart. There is even a village green and a pond with actual ducks. Not to mention Stone Cottage,' he added, with a little elbow nudge. 'But you know that because you're part of it now. It looks great on the website and attracts a few tourists – as well as a nice little bit of funding from various heritage charities. It's what I like to call the village's heart. Its inner core. That core has remained the same for a good couple of centuries, even as we've been swallowed up by the city sprawl; it's only in the last few decades since the war that things have really... expanded, shall we say.

'These days the Trust directly covers about one and a half square miles – that's a thousand acres, give or take, with a population of twenty thousand. The vast majority of those people are just normal householders for whom living in the Trust is no different from anywhere else in the city, except that they pay an annual charge in return for slightly better services. Did you get hit by that bin strike the other year?'

'Did we?' Peter snorted. 'We had a ground-floor flat, right by the bins. I had to borrow a snow shovel to get to the road. Christ, the smell of it.'

'Mm-hmm.' Again, the indulgent nod. 'Never touched

us here. Good links with trusted private contractors. And I don't mean that to sound like bragging,' Nash added hurriedly. 'Just that I'm not ashamed to say that we look after our own, and we do it bloody well. Approximately fifteen per cent of our residents are classified as "in need" and the Trust is subsidised by the city council as a registered social landlord providing housing to some of the most deprived families in the city. We're building two hundred homes here, and a third of those will be "affordable" for first-time buyers. That's a lot of fuse boxes and extensions, if you take my meaning.'

'For a trusted private contractor.'

'Indeed. Come on, I'll introduce you to Dino. Top man.'

As they were approaching the ziggurat of stacked Portakabins which was the site's offices, Peter's phone rang, and he answered it to the tones of Trish's furious indignation.

'Wait, whoa, slow down,' he said. 'Tell me that again in full sentences.' Turning to Nash, and aware of the man's curiosity, he said, 'Excuse me a moment,' and turned away to walk a little back down the road, although there was a fair chance Nash would be able to hear her shouting through the receiver anyway. Peter had rarely heard her so enraged.

'I said the letting agency has refused to return our security deposit! Absolute bastards!'

'Why? What did they say?'

'Oh I don't know, some bullshit about breaching the terms of the original contents report and not leaving the flat in a "sufficiently neat and tidy condition", the way they always do. How dare they? I scrubbed that place from top to

bottom the day before we left! Absolute fucking bastards!'
He could hear tears in her voice now. 'That's nearly a
thousand pounds, Peter! We can't afford to lose that kind of
money. What are we going to do?'

He was tempted to say something about how now,
without a mortgage to pay, they probably could afford to
let it go, but he didn't think that would help the situation.
Scraping that deposit together when they'd been living in
her parents' spare room had been the first real test of their
combined strength as a couple, and its worth was more than
just monetary – it was pride in their self-sufficiency. He felt
her anger stoking his. Someone in an office was trying to
screw them over, and it didn't matter whether it was for one
pound or a thousand.

'It's going to be okay,' he said. 'There has to be some kind
of appeal we can make. Just as soon as I'm done here I'll
come home and we'll make an appointment with Consumer
Advice, or something.'

Gradually she calmed, though not by much, and when he
hung up he found Nash had moved to a discreet distance
but couldn't hide the fact that he'd heard Peter's side of the
conversation. 'Problem?' he asked.

'It's nothing.'

'It didn't sound like nothing to me. In fact, it sounded very
much like an angry and upset wife. I should know.' He gave
a rueful chuckle. When Peter summarised for him what had
happened, he nodded as if this was the sort of unfortunate
thing one could only expect from letting agencies. 'Let me
see what I can do,' he offered.

'No, really, it's fine. I can take care of this.'

'Oh for God's sake, Peter, I'm not threatening to cut off your dick,' said Nash, exasperated. 'I'm offering to help. I know people in housing. This is exactly my area of expertise. Now you can either accept that as freely and honestly given or you can go home and explain to Patricia why you turned it down and spend the next six months fighting it through arbitration and the small claims court.' He took a step closer. 'You might not be, but she is a Trustee, and we look after our own.'

Peter relented. 'Okay, thanks. I suppose I'm not used to having other people fight my corner.'

Nash clapped him on the shoulder as they continued walking towards the Portakabins. 'There's fighting, and then there's dirty fighting,' he said.

Two days later, Nash was sitting across the desk from a Mr Cyril Doherty, manager of Doherty Property Lettings, a man who looked like someone had taken a meerkat, shaved it, and put it in a suit. He even had the twitchy head movements, which had increased as he'd become more incensed as Nash had laid out his case for why the Feenans should be given their deposit back immediately.

'You're out of your mind!' Doherty sputtered. 'You can't just come swanning in here, demanding this, that and the other!'

Nash looked at his watch. He was enjoying himself immensely. Sometimes it was a relief to get out of the citadel and mix it up with the mob, safe in the knowledge that any collateral damage wouldn't wash up against his own walls. 'Well I did try calling several times,' he said, 'but you seemed to be out of the office quite a bit so I just thought I'd pop down on the off-chance that you were in.' He smiled and spread his hands. 'And voila, here you are. It must be my lucky day.'

'Get the fuck out of my office now, or I'll call the police!'

Nash sighed and stood, straightening the cuffs of his coat. 'Very well, Mr Doherty, I understand that you're a busy man, so I won't impose on your time any further. Just as a friendly courtesy, though, just between fellow property managers, to show that there are no hard feelings so to speak, I would suggest that you make sure all your properties are fully compliant with environmental health standards. Angela Parry-Jones – sorry, did I tell you that I was on good terms with the council's chief environmental health officer? Lovely woman is Ange – very, very thorough, and some of those fines can be quite steep. Not quite as steep as the cost of having to repair the damage should anything, ah, *happen* to them, of course, but a lot more than the Feenans' pissy grand we're talking about here.'

'You're *threatening* me—?'

'No,' he sighed. 'I'm not threatening you. I'm having a perfectly reasonable conversation with a fellow professional about the importance of making sure that one's properties are fully compliant with health and safety legislation, and incidentally asking him to reconsider an unhelpful decision regarding some new friends of mine. As they say, it never hurts to ask.' He checked his watch again. Somewhere in the main office outside, a phone was ringing, and just as Mr Cyril Doherty of the oh-so-amusingly-rhymed Doherty Property Lettings was seething to his feet, scarlet with rage, his office door opened and a young man with an apocalyptic acne condition popped his head around.

'Er, Mr Doherty—?'

'Not now, Barry, can't you see I'm in a fucking meeting?!'

Barry flinched. 'Er, yes, sir, but it's the police on the phone.'

Mr Doherty stopped, his mouth open, head jerking like an electrocuted chicken.

'The…'

'Yes, sir. Apparently there's been a fire at one of the properties. A ground-floor flat on Amphlett Way. They say that fortunately it was empty at the time but it looks like it's been completely gutted. Shall I put them on hold?'

'No, I'll… Put them through.'

'Yes, sir.' Barry's head retreated and a moment later a red light began to blink on Mr Doherty's desk phone.

'That sounds nasty,' tutted Nash. 'Still, I suppose it could be worse. According to my information, your company currently manages twenty-seven rental properties in the Brownhills area, for a combined insurance cost of, ooh, half a million pounds, I'd say.' He spread his hands as if the answer had been simple and out in the open all along. 'All I'm asking for is a single thousand.' He nodded at the phone. 'You'd better answer that.'

It was the efficiency of it that he liked most, Nash decided as he walked back to his car. Killing two birds with one stone. For the Feenans, the deposit was more than just money – it was a demonstration and a reassurance that the Trust would protect them. But if they did decide to do a runner when the inevitable happened, their old flat was now a nice, big, smoking reminder that there was nowhere safer that they could run to. No home other than Haleswell. No going back.

10

WITCH MARKS

TRISH FOUND THE FIRST ONE WHEN SHE WAS EXAMINING the wide fireplace in the living room. At some point in the past it had been covered over with plasterboard and a gas fire put in – a truly ugly one with fake coals and a red light which was meant to give the impression of it being a real fire, despite the fact that the space for an actual fire was sealed up behind. As soon as they'd seen it, she and Peter had looked at each other and experienced one of those moments of marital telepathy in which each knew exactly what the other was thinking: roaring open fire, bottle of wine, sheepskin rug. They might even be able to get something that she could use to bake bread over the open fire, if that were possible. She knew that she was getting a bit ahead of herself on that score – her early experiments had left the kitchen looking like an explosion in a flour mill. It would take some work to rip out all the junk and restore the hearth to its former glory, but it was the kind of project that both of them loved – she as project manager, him as grunt monkey.

All that remained visible at the moment, however, was a massive oak beam set lengthways in the wall above the fake fire, which had both supported the original opening and acted as a six-inch-deep mantelpiece. It looked like a medieval ship's timber, dark with both age and the centuries of fires that had been lit beneath it. She was exploring it – curious as to how far back it went into the wall, how much it must weigh, and whether it was still structurally sound – when her fingertips detected carving in the middle of the underside. She bent down to look.

Six perfect circles, overlapping to form a crude flower shape. The kind of thing you drew in primary school with a pencil and compass, but etched deep into the oak. It couldn't have been decorative because it was hidden on the underside, and it was too deliberate to be idle doodling.

She took a photo and texted it to Natalie. *Just found this. Any idea?*

She was surprised when Natalie called her back, almost immediately.

'Where did you find it?' asked the director of property and development.

'Underneath the mantelpiece in the living room. Why? Do you know what it is? It's not vandalism, is it?'

'Not as such, no.' There was something in the other woman's voice – some sense that she was dancing around an uncomfortable truth that she didn't want to admit – that made Trish uneasy.

'If you know what it is, just tell me. You don't have to worry about us backing out of the move – we're in now. This is my home.'

'Well,' Natalie drew a deep breath. 'It's a witch mark.'

'A what mark?'

'No, a witch mark.'

'Ha ha. You mean as in broomsticks, pointy hats, black cats, dancing naked in the moonlight?'

'I mean as in just that. Loads of old houses have them. Back in the day when people actually believed that witches existed, they drew protective marks above doorways, windows, fireplaces, in roofs and cellars – anywhere they thought a witch might be able to sneak in.'

'So there might be others?'

'There may well be. Listen, if you find any others, don't be tempted to remove them, will you? They're part of the historical fabric of the building.'

'Why on earth would I? This is all kinds of exciting – it's like having a direct link back to the people who used to live here. I can't wait to show Toby. He loves this kind of thing.'

'Yes. Well. If you say so. Sorry, but I'm right in the middle of a thing…'

'Sorry, no, my fault. You get on. Thanks!'

Trish hung up, tapped her phone thoughtfully against her chin for a moment, and then went to see if she could find any more witch marks.

* * *

She found them *everywhere*.

They were above the back door, carved into the floorboards in the cupboard under the stairs, in the wooden frames of every single one of the original sash windows, and there were four carved into the rafters of Toby's loft-space bedroom alone. They weren't all the same kind of flower design as on the mantelpiece, and it took her a bit of googling to realise what she was looking at: some were zigzags, while others were kites, crosses and patterns of stars. They could easily have been dismissed as random scrapes and scratches, which was probably why she hadn't noticed them before.

There was a sense of desperation in the way they had been carved in every room multiple times. If these were meant to be protection against witches, then someone who had once lived in this house had been seriously and genuinely terrified.

'Has anybody seen my Leatherman?' asked Peter, peering about.

A chorus of nopes came from the blokes working in the building around him.

He sighed. It wasn't necessarily the best for a lot of the jobs that he had to do, but it was a good little general-purpose multitool and even something of a good-luck charm. It had been a gift from Trish when he'd passed his apprenticeship, and those things weren't cheap; it had taken her months to save up for it. Normally it sat in a little pouch on his belt but when he'd reached for it to crimp a couple of wires together he'd found the pouch empty. It was like discovering that his wedding ring was missing off his finger.

Then there came a snigger. 'Actually I think I saw a pigeon taking off with something shiny in its beak just now.' The sniggerer was a new apprentice – a thin lad called Lance Purslow whose facial piercings, they joked, had more metal than one of these buildings – and suddenly Peter knew what was going on.

This was a wind-up.

Pranks and wind-ups were as much a part of site culture as boots and hammers. Most were as unimaginative as dropping stuff on blokes' heads or spraying them with fire extinguishers, but occasionally they displayed streaks of truly creative sadism, like getting apprentices to hoover up puddles, or collect steam samples, or one he'd seen where a lad was asked to help out with a 'seismic test' by repeatedly whacking a spray-painted dot on the ground with a heavy sledgehammer while his supervisor pointed a voltmeter at it and pretended to take readings and everybody else just fell about as the lad got more and more exhausted. In construction site pecking order the only thing lower than an apprentice was fresh meat like Peter, and Lance was obviously enjoying the novelty of being able to roll some shit downhill for a change. This had probably been his idea in the first place, a way of becoming one of the lads. As a practical joke, nicking and hiding someone's stuff wasn't particularly original or funny, but that wasn't the point. It wasn't even about whether or not you had a sense of humour. It was about whether you took offence and showed that you thought you were better than the other blokes, or whether you shrugged your shoulders and sucked it up like everyone else had done when it had been their turn. Everyone was a victim, so everyone was equal.

He went over to where Lance was working with two other chippies – Arun Aliman and Craig 'Bully' Turnbull – to fit insulation batts into the spaces between wall studs. 'So did you happen to notice where this irritating little shit took it?'

Bully chuckled at the dig but Lance was either too thick or enjoying himself too much to notice. 'Dunno,' he grinned. 'I think maybe over to Lot 9.'

'Lot 9, you say?'

Lance shrugged. 'That's what I saw.'

Peter nodded. 'Cheers, mate.' He slapped Lance on the shoulder in gratitude, good and hard.

As he left the half-built house, Bully said, 'Hey, Peter.'

There was something in his tone that made Peter turn back. Bully was a thickset Scot who had a good thirty years on all of them. He'd worked on rigs in the North Sea, pipelines in the Gulf and construction all over the UK, and could give and take a joke with the best of them, but when he was quiet and serious and turned those granite-coloured eyes on one of the lads, they listened. 'What is it?'

'You be careful, okay? That part of the site's more dangerous than it looks.' It seemed like Bully wanted to say something else, but he just nodded and repeated, 'Just be careful.'

Puzzled at the older man's intensity, Peter just muttered, 'Okay.'

The Clegg Farm development was being built on farmland next to an existing estate from thirty years ago with roads all named after mountains or hills – Snowdon Avenue, Nevis Close, Kinder Scout Road – and whose residents had for decades used the neighbouring fields for dog-walking, jogging, and collecting blackberries. The path that they had worn along the field's edge had become a de facto right of way which the Trust had been forced to temporarily block during construction, as it simply wasn't safe for members of the public to be walking so close to a load of heavy machinery, the intention being to open it again as an alley between the old estate and the new when it was finished. A temporary fence had been built across the access point next to a row of garages on Bredon Road, and the entire ten-acre site was enclosed with modular wire-mesh security panels six feet high, like crowd-control barriers, clamped together and seated in concrete blocks. This stopped all but the most determined of trespassers, who tended to be either angry middle-aged suburban warriors who Knew Their Rights and refused to have their Right to Roam curtailed under any circumstances, never mind whether or not they got a pile of bricks dropped on their heads, or local kids looking for somewhere to fuck or get high, or both.

Which was why, on his way through the development, Peter wasn't particularly surprised to see a young girl. This was a quiet part of the site where the units were virtually finished: roofs on, tiled, windows in, electrics done, ready for new owners and looking like the shrink-wrapping had just come off.

'Oi!' Peter yelled at the girl. 'This is a building site! Clear off!'

If she heard him she gave no sign, but she wasn't moving in either direction, through the site or out of it. She was just standing there, bare feet on the muddy path churned by heavy workmen's boots and wheelbarrow tyres. Now that he looked closer, he saw how dirty and ragged she was – obviously neglected and probably malnourished, and his blunt anger took on an edge of concern. If there was a mother or father in this child's life, they needed a rocket put up them by social services.

'Look, it's not safe! You can't come through here! You'll get hurt!'

That must have done the trick because she turned and walked away – except instead of turning back to the fence she wandered off between two of the units and disappeared around a corner.

'Fucksake,' muttered Peter, and jogged after her, trying not to imagine her falling off a scaffolding tower or disappearing into an open drainage culvert or any one of a dozen ways that a kid could hurt themselves in a place like this. But when he rounded the corner she'd disappeared. He walked quickly past these units to the next open space where he had a good view of the immediate vicinity, but there was still no sign of her. Obviously she was scared and hiding from him. *But did you notice the way she moved?* a sceptical little voice whispered. *Kids who are scared tend to run. She was more like strolling, wouldn't you say? Like she felt at home here?* Didn't matter – he was going to have to tell site security either way. But their office was right at the other end of the site and Lot 9 was just around the corner, so what he'd do was pop in, find his Leatherman that Lance had so hilariously nicked, and then call it in.

He was in the oldest part of the development now, the finished units just waiting for decorators and landscaping. Beyond this was the perimeter fence and then the houses which families had already moved into. It seemed unreal to him that anybody could walk into a property showroom and buy a house off-plan maybe a year before it even existed, and then move in while watching the houses of their future neighbours being built. But then he supposed that it was just as unreal to have moved into a house like Stone Cottage that had probably been built when his grandfather's grandfather's grandfather was a baby.

Lot 9 stopped him with a frown. It was still only half built. Barely that; it was a shell of breeze blocks with a triangular ribwork of open roof trusses pointing to the sky and windows which were nothing more than rectangular holes opening onto darkness. Why hadn't it been finished? Was there something wrong with the plot – some kind of subsidence, perhaps? It wasn't unknown for new builds to run afoul of old mine workings that didn't show up on surveyors' maps. Maybe that was why Bully had told him to be careful. The problem with leaving something like this unattended for so long was that it inevitably attracted vandals; above the main doorway somebody had spray-painted a rosette of six interlocking circles that formed a crude flower shape where they overlapped at the centre. A step up from tits and dicks, he supposed.

Swearing to come up with some supremely evil retribution

for Lance, Peter moved cautiously inside.

The smell of damp concrete, mortar, and wood enveloped him. Without the first-floor supports having been put in, the grey breeze-block walls rose to their full two-storey height so that even though he could see the sky through the roof trusses he was still walking in shadow. Water dripped, forming wide puddles in which litter and building debris floated, and the sound of his sloshing reverberated in empty rooms further on. Sheets of plastic flapped in ragged strips from rafters and window openings. Chalk marks on the bare bricks showed where cables and pipes were supposed to have run, drawn by the men who had abandoned this place. He saw a half-empty packet of cigarettes in one corner, and that was when he felt the first fluttering of something which he refused to acknowledge as fear. Nobody left their cigarettes. Nobody.

Then, in the middle of the main hallway, sitting on the base of an upturned bucket, was his Leatherman. Heaving a sigh of relief, he stepped forward and reached for it. 'Lance, you fucking—'

The attack came from a dark doorway to his left, the shape pale and blurred, screaming at him through the smudged suggestions of mouth and eye sockets, and he fell backwards, yelling, thrashing at the clammy limbs that it wrapped about him which were more like wings and were cold and slick and... plastic.

Lance pulled the plastic sheet off from over his face and wailed, 'Whooooo!' then fell about laughing.

'Lance, you fuckhead!' he shouted. 'That's not fucking funny!'

'Yes it is!' cackled Lance. 'The look on your face, man! Absolutely fucking priceless!' He chucked the rest of the sheeting to the ground and took out his phone, beckoning Peter over. 'Selfie, man, yeah? No hard feelings?'

There was a moment when the urge to punch Lance's smirk through the back of his skull was almost overwhelming. But he and Trish had toasted a fresh start for all of them, himself included, so he swallowed it and forced himself to simmer down. Besides, he had to admit that the boy had got him good. Fast on his feet, too, to have got here before him. His heart was still hammering, but he let Lance take the selfie, and while the younger man was checking it out he scooped up a couple of inches of filthy water in the bucket and dumped it over his head.

'No hard feelings,' he agreed, and left with his Leatherman as Lance gasped and spluttered behind him.

'Hey, Peter,' grinned Arun, as he returned. 'What's the matter? You look like you've seen a ghost.'

'Nice one. Think of that one all on your own, did you?'

'What did it look like?'

'Like a twat wearing a shower curtain.'

They all laughed at that, including Lance, because he was now one of the lads. Peter went back to what he had been doing, up a ladder in the roof trusses putting in the main run of the first electrical fix on this house, looping thick grey cables through the open roof joists and stapling them to the beams in neat bundles. He took pride in doing a tidy job.

He liked to think that any domestic electrician who worked on these for whatever family ended up living here would be able to find everything – and then he realised that it might very well be himself. He found the idea that he might be here for as long as Bully, updating and maintaining the systems that he'd put in place right at the start, oddly reassuring.

'Hey, Bully,' he called down. 'What's going on with Lot 9, then? Why's it unfinished?'

'Haunted,' replied Bully, as terse and matter-of-fact as only a Scot could be.

'No, cut the bullshit. Really, what's up with it? It looks like it hasn't been touched for months.'

'That's because nobody'll work on it. Too many accidents. Lads working that plot have been electrocuted, put nails through themselves, lost fingers, even an eye. One old fella had a heart attack and nearly karked it.'

'Hasn't anybody looked into it?'

'Looked into what? A bunch of cack-handed chippies? They'll look into it when it's the last one of this phase that hasn't been finished; in the meantime there's too much else to be done and not enough lads to do it.' Bully's voice dropped, and he edged closer. 'I will tell you one thing, though; the kind of thing that doesn't have a box for it on an accident form and you don't tell your supervisor because he'll call the men in white coats to cart you off to the nuthouse if you do. In some cases, the man concerned has said that just before it happened he saw a wee girl hanging around – quite a few others won't say anything at all. They're too scared.'

Peter put down his cable stapler and looked down at Bully.

'A girl. Seriously.' She'd been barefoot, raggedly dressed and starved-looking. He felt his skin crawling with a sudden chill that couldn't be explained away by the weather.

Bully returned his gaze without any of the smirking or signs that this might be a wind-up. 'Aye, seriously. Nobody knows who She is, all they can say is that if you see Her, you'd best keep your wits about you because She's a vicious little bitch. Y'ask me it was a stupid idea Lance playing his joke there, but what can you do?' He shrugged as if to say that the motivations of ghostly girls and apprentices were equally unfathomable and turned back to his insulation job.

Peter manufactured a laugh which was meant to sound casual and unconcerned. 'Okay, mate, whatever you say.' He continued stapling his cables – but he checked the ladder to make sure it was properly secured all the same.

The rest of the day passed without any problem.

The accident – he refused to call it an attack or an ambush, despite how it felt afterwards – happened on the way home.

He was making his way past a house with only half its roof tiled; the other half had its red felt open to the air, crossed with the horizontal lines of yellow pine battens so that the whole thing looked uneasily like the raw flesh of skinned muscle. A few small stacks of brown roof tiles rested on the battens, and the whole building was surrounded by roof-high scaffolding. At the point where Peter passed it, on top of the scaffolding were two pallets of more roof tiles ready to be broken out for the rest of the job. They were packed vertically and bound with thick strips of blue plastic tape, although someone had removed the shrink-wrapping.

Later, nobody could provide a satisfactory explanation for how the tape had snapped. Someone said that the broken ends didn't look as though they'd been cut with a knife, so much as frayed, or chewed.

At first it sounded like a set of giant fingernails dragging down the world's biggest blackboard. He looked up – and he might have seen the dark shape of something like a rat scurrying away across the scaffolding, or in hindsight that might have been his imagination – as two hundred vertically stacked concrete roof tiles cascaded one after the other like a pack of cards pouring out of a magician's hands, except each card weighed nearly seven kilos and could easily have cracked his skull from that height. He flung himself to the side, into the road which at that point was little more than a muddy, puddle-filled track, as the first tile fell inches from his left hand. He scrambled backwards through the mud as the other tiles followed – ricocheting and rebounding, shattering in the debris and stinging him with shrapnel, deafening him with their clatter and din. By the time he'd shuffled to a safe distance he was drenched and filthy down his back from shoulders to ankles, sitting in the gutter, shivering with shock and adrenalin and staring at the debris in a daze. People came running to help him up, asking him if he was all right, and he said yes, he thought so, and by some miracle – with the exception of a few minor cuts – that turned out to be true.

By the time he got home his nerves had settled enough for him to spin a harmless tale for Trish about how he'd simply slipped and gone arse over tit in the mud, and she didn't question it because it was exactly the sort of thing he'd do. No way was he going to say anything to her about the strange girl; in the safety and sanity of his home there was no reason to believe that she'd had anything to do with the accident, or Bully's tall tales. A series of improbable coincidences, that's all it was. *But if it was just a coincidence*, said a small, sly voice in the back of his mind, *if She was just an ordinary estate kid, why didn't you mention it to site security?* Peter told that small voice to shut it, dumped his clothes in the washing machine, got changed and sat down to a normal dinner with his family. He asked Trish if anything interesting had happened to her today and she said no. Toby was quiet, but that wasn't anything to write home about for a moody fourteen-year-old.

The only way in which it was different was the large loaf of home-made bread which sat on a wooden board in the middle of the table along with a butter dish and a long serrated knife.

'What's this?' he asked.

'Packet of pork scratchings, what do you think?' she replied. 'Try some!'

He cut himself a slice, buttered it, and chewed, frowning as if in deep concentration.

'Well?' He hadn't seen her this nervous in a long time.

He chewed. 'It's…' he started, choosing his words carefully. 'Substantial.'

'Look,' she said, pointing the bread knife at him. 'That's ten thousand years of human civilisation you're munching on there, mate. Bit of respect.'

'As in healthy! Substantial as in good, healthy, home-made food!'

'It's possible that the dough needs to rise a bit more.'

'I think it's great!' said Toby. 'Have we got any chocolate spread?'

'Bloody heathens, the pair of you,' she muttered.

After Peter had finished the washing-up he kept turning to the selfie that Lance had messaged him later that afternoon. It showed the pair of them bleached fish-white by the phone's flash, Lance grinning, Peter managing a reluctant smile. It wasn't their faces which demanded his attention, like a broken fingernail snagging cloth – it was their shadows cast on the bare brick wall behind them. Hard to tell because of the angle, and it could have been nothing more than the peculiar lumps and bumps of the wall, but it definitely looked like there were three.

Then, in the morning, he deleted the picture, because of course he didn't believe in ghosts.

11

GOADING THE GHOST

THE GIRL CAME BACK THE NEXT NIGHT, AND THE NIGHT after that, and the night after *that*. She didn't do anything more than stand by the parish stone – the Beating Stone, as he thought of it now – stare up at Toby's window, and beckon to him whenever he appeared. Oddly, and despite his initial alarm, he wasn't frightened by this. She was freaky-looking to be sure, but She made no aggressive moves and the rats didn't reappear. Not that this made him any more inclined to tell his parents; part of him was terrified that he was going mental, and that this would be confirmed if it turned out that they couldn't see Her. Preferable to believe that She was real, however impossible. But *how* real? There was a limit to how much he could know by hiding in his room, and since She either wouldn't or couldn't do anything more, that really only left him with one option.

On the fourth night he went out to talk to Her.

It wouldn't have been the first time he'd sneaked out of his room, but it was the first when he'd had to deal with stairs. He found that if he hung on to the banister and put his weight only at the very edge of each step he could get down with the minimum of creaking. The back door alarm and the security light weren't a problem; once he'd made up his mind to do this he'd carefully watched his dad locking up so he could deactivate them.

When it was open he hovered by the back door, watching Her carefully for any sudden movements. If She was a junkie She might have a knife. The thick foliage surrounding the house muted both the street lights from the front and the sky's ambient city glow, leaving Her in rustling, restless shadow. It was late April, and despite Easter having come and gone, spring wasn't yet far enough advanced to put a balm on the night air. It was chilly as if with the ghost of winter, and his breath plumed.

Hers didn't.

'Who are you?' he whispered. 'What are you doing here?'

She remained unmoving. A thin breeze trickled past, though it didn't seem to touch Her. Was She even really there? Was he still asleep and dreaming Her? He moved closer, halfway to the Beating Stone. She stood on the other side of it, as if sheltering in the shrubbery, and though the details still eluded him he could see now that there was something wrong with Her face and neck. Some kind of damage to Her skin.

'Are you okay? You asked me to come down, so here I am. What do you want?'

Still no response. He was starting to get annoyed now.

There was an arrogance in this silent treatment which reminded him of the man in the green skull mask – it was the same sense of entitlement, but in this case demonstrated as an unspoken scorn, as if by capitulating to Her and coming down here he wasn't worth Her attention anymore.

'Okay,' he said. 'Fine. Blank me, whatever. Whoever you are, I'm not afraid of you.'

She stepped closer to the stone, into a shifting blur of light, and he saw Her properly for the first time: the sores, the patches of black necrotic flesh, the open wounds that nobody could suffer and live, let alone stand. She stank of the grave.

Toby fell back a step. 'Jesus…'

She smirked. It might as well have been a taunt: *You were saying?*

It was just a mask, he told himself. Just movie make-up, that was it. He'd seen enough zombie movies to know how real it could look, and he knew that people costumed up and chased each other around in the real world. This was some local nutjob trying to put a scare on the new neighbours, that was all. Probably someone pissed off that his mother had inherited Stone Cottage instead of them. All the same, that smell…

'Yeah, very clever,' he rallied, hoping that he sounded a lot more confident than he felt. 'Why don't you fuck off before I call the police? You can't do anything to us, you know.'

The smirk broadened as She tilted Her head and raised Her eyebrows at him. *Really?*

Later, as he lay in bed, he told himself that She must have

slipped away into the bushes too quickly for him to see, but at the time it did look an awful lot like She simply dissolved into the formless play of shadows.

In the broad light of day it was much easier to relegate such events to the realm of an overactive imagination, especially when his attention was consumed by the vastly more terrifying prospect of having to start a new school.

First, it was getting to grips with the physical layout of the place. His old school in Brownhills had been a simple series of red-brick blocks and corridors which hadn't changed much since the eighties, with all the aesthetic appeal and educational *joie de vivre* of a Victorian iron foundry. Haleswell Specialist Academy School, on the other hand, was part of a multi-academy trust which had been given a ridiculous amount of money by the government to 'renovate and reinvigorate' local education provision, and so had been redesigned by someone who had presumably been inspired by pictures on the Internet of cutting-edge work environments created for hip, maverick Californian tech companies and decided to replicate this for eleven- to eighteen-year-olds in the West Midlands.

It was all open plan, with sofas and weird coloured panels hanging from the ceiling and 'learning hubs' – small clusters of computers which the other kids didn't use because they had access to all the games and video streams they needed on their phones, as opposed to the school network which, he quickly discovered, was so tightly buttoned down that he couldn't even look up the subject of 'Sodom and Gomorrah' without getting a firewall alert warning him of SEXUALLY EXPLICIT AND/OR OFFENSIVE CONTENT. It had hydration stations and big LCD screens on the walls scrolling through pithy motivational quotes which didn't actually mean anything, like 'You Never Fail Until You Stop Trying' and 'Work Hard in Silence; Let Success Be Your Noise'.

What it didn't have was books. At the end of his first day he took home a list of all the stationery he was going to have to buy for himself, which at first his mum thought was a joke. 'All this?' she asked, incredulous. 'For just one term?'

'And this is the bog-standard comprehensive school,' his dad observed. 'God knows what he'd have ended up needing to buy at the grammar. His own bloody polo pony, probably.'

Toby's new registration tutor was a young history teacher called Mr Willis who looked a bit like one of the sports reporters on the local news. Mr Willis assigned Toby a 'buddy' in the form of Krish Mittal, who inhabited a strange no man's land in the school pecking order because despite being a lanky sports-phobe he already had enough facial hair that he needed to actually shave. Krish had a twin sister called Nandini and was quite at ease hanging out after school at the corner shop with her and her crowd of galdem, which was how Toby met Maya Gorić.

His interaction with any of the girls outside the classroom in those first few days had been limited to hurrying by, mortified, as they stood in groups looking at the fresh meat sidelong and laughing, but Maya introduced herself by walking straight up to him with a broad grin, saying,

'Pocketa-pocketa-*queep!*-pocketa-*queep!*' and prodding him in the ribs with a finger on each *queep!*

'Shut up,' he groaned. It had been only his second English lesson and the teacher, Mrs Chamberlain, had got them reading aloud from 'The Secret Life of Walter Mitty', in which the hero took passage aboard a steamer whose faltering engine made that noise, and whereas everybody else in class had read their bits in the standard expressionless monotone, Toby had decided to get a bit of a laugh by reading it the way it should have sounded. No laughter had been forthcoming – only an awkward, embarrassed silence.

'I liked it!' she said. 'I mean what's the point of using onomatopoeia if you're not going to *use* it, right?'

Looking at her properly, he found that she wasn't particularly pretty, hadn't hoisted her skirt up short or unbuttoned the top of her blouse like the other girls, was slightly taller than him and didn't have much by way of tits, but the open frankness with which she was grinning at him arrested his attention utterly. There was no mockery in what she'd said, only the simple desire to share in something funny, and maybe even something like respect. See also: *onomatopoeia*. She was clever and not afraid to show it, which was a rare thing in his – albeit limited – experience of girls.

'Right,' he replied. 'Hi. I'm Toby.'

'I know.' She was still grinning. 'I'm Maya.'

'Good name. As in ancient civilisation, pyramids and human sacrifice?'

Her grin, if anything, widened. 'That's the one. So watch

yourself, new blood, or I'll tear your heart out and hold it up beating before your dying eyes.'

Funny, he thought, *it feels like that's happening right now.*

After she'd gone, Krish elbowed him and waggled his eyebrows.

'What?' Dear God, now he was actually blushing.

Krish didn't reply, just elbowed him again and waggled his brows even more salaciously.

'Shut up.'

Whereas Toby's home was within walking distance, Maya's family lived in a flat on the Pestle Road estate, right on the edge of Haleswell. Most afternoons she had to pick up her ten-year-old brother Antony, whom she referred to simply as 'the Ant', from his junior school and walk home with him, but every so often they would both get picked up by her older brother Rajko, who was studying something mechanical at the sixth-form college half a mile away. Raj drove a white Vauxhall Corsa hatchback which could be heard long before it was seen thanks to the bass thumping out of a ridiculously over-powered stereo system. It was pimped out with a spoiler which was about as necessary as a shark's fin on a goldfish and alloy wheels worth probably more than the whole lot put together.

The first time Toby saw Maya's big brother, Rajko barely glanced at him, curtly ordering Maya into his boy-racermobile in a language which Toby later discovered was Serbian, before screaming off in a stench of burning clutch fluid.

The second time did not go even half so well.

Raj had texted to tell her that he was having to stay late

after lectures so she'd be on foot with the Ant. 'Do you want to come with me?' she asked Toby. 'I can help you with your science.' As if he was ever going to say no; it was the closest he figured he was ever going to get to an actual date, but on a very practical note the end-of-year exams were coming up at half-term and there were some topics which his old school hadn't covered. So he said yes. They picked up the Ant from his after-school club. Maya's usual route home took them along the High Street, where they bought bubble tea and kept the Ant distracted by letting him chase pigeons with a stick, and then through the Rec.

The Rec was short for Recreation Ground, something of a misnomer given that there was little to do by way of recreation except one small playground for little kids next to the Asda supermarket at the far end. The Rec was a shortcut between the village and the Stratford Road, used by teenagers getting to and from school and on weekends to sit in circles under trees smoking and just hanging out. It wasn't as nice as the village green for family picnics but some people walked their dogs and raced remote-control cars.

The journey wasn't long, but it took them out from where the leafy streets and closes of central Haleswell – what locals called simply 'the Village' – sloped downhill towards a neighbourhood of flats and blocky houses known as the Pestle Road estate. He saw the shabby Victorian townhouse that was subdivided into the flats where her home was, and squirmed with guilt when he realised exactly how grandiose his own new home was in comparison. If he went inside, he would have to return the invitation, and then she would see

Stone Cottage and think he was rubbing her nose in it and she'd never talk to him again. When she invited him in to meet her mother he balked. See also: *meeting her mother.*

'Listen, I'm really sorry, but I, uh—'

'You uh what exactly?'

'I've just remembered I have some jobs I need to do or my mum will go skitz at me.' It was a lame excuse, and he could see that she knew it.

'Suit yourself,' she said, and went in. He tried explaining as she was closing the entry hall door but she ignored him and he was left apologising to a panel of frosted reinforced glass.

Catch u 4 bubble tea before school 2moro? he texted her, but there was no reply.

Kicking himself for his own gutlessness and how he'd managed to offend her, he turned and headed for the bus stop, when the familiar *doompf-doompf-doompf* of a pair of 300-watt speakers came rolling up the road to meet him.

'Oh shit.'

Toby tried to ignore the white Corsa as it slowed alongside him, matching his pace, its tinny exhaust snarling like a wasp in a bottle. Maya's brother was only a short distance from his own front door, and Toby prayed that it was close enough that Raj would carry on home, park up, and leave him alone – or come back for him on foot, which would at least give Toby a chance to outrun him. The tinted driver's window scrolled down, replaced by Rajko's unsmiling face. His eyes were the colour of sump oil. His head was shaved down the sides, leaving a thatch of close-cropped curly hair, and he had a fag on. Gold chains were at his throat and wrist, and the sinews in his forearm shifted like cables. 'What are you doing here, *šupak*?'

Toby walked faster, not quite allowing himself to run.

'Hey! Don't you ignore me!' The car snarled and leapt forward, the passenger's side wheel coming up onto the pavement in front of him, blocking him, the door opening, Rajko surging out and around the front of the car, coming right up and into his face, so close that Toby had to back up against the wall. Rajko's cigarette hovered an inch before his eyes, the sting of its smoke mixed with the sweet reek of the bigger boy's aftershave making him cough.

'People tell me you been sniffing around my sister. Is that true, you posh piece of shit? Hey?'

'Sorry, I'm sorry, look, I—'

Rajko planted a palm on the side of his face and shoved it against the wall, grinding his cheek into the brick. He moved even closer, if that were possible, dragging on the cigarette so that its tip glowed red and Toby could feel its heat. 'Posh *kopile* like you got no reason being interested in my family, you understand?'

Toby nodded as best he could. He couldn't breathe; it felt like someone was taking a cheese grater to his cheekbone and jaw. All he could see was a green skull and a crowbar. *You think you're a badass?*

'You say yes, or I burn it into you in Morse fucking code.'

'Y-yes.'

'*Dobro*. Now piss off home where you belong.'

Rajko let him go, flicking the cigarette at him, and he ducked as it hit the wall in a shower of sparks. Then the gut-punishing bass resumed as Maya's brother got back in his car and drove off. The vacuum which seemed to have surrounded Toby popped and the world rushed back in, bringing daylight and the sounds of the world as he propped himself against the wall, trembling and breathing in great shuddering gasps, praying not to have an asthma attack and trying not to cry. There was blood on his face. People passed him without comment, let alone stopping to see if he needed help. Why would they? As far as anybody else was concerned he was just as bad as the rest of them.

When he had got himself more or less together he walked the rest of the way home, giving himself the time to calm down and think of a plausible story to tell his mum. But when he got there he found that he needn't have bothered, because his mother – who had been vocally anti-Church for as long as he could remember – was preoccupied with hanging a large and ornate crucifix in the hall by the front door.

12

THE FOOD BANK

'KNOCK KNOCK?'

Joyce Dobson appeared around the side of the house while Trish was pegging out the laundry. It was the first time Trish had seen her wearing anything other than a dog collar and suit; she was in jeans and a hoody with a printed slogan which read JESUS IS COMING – LOOK BUSY.

'Is this a bad time?'

'No,' Trish replied emphatically, dropping the sheet she'd been wrestling with back in the basket. 'This is most definitely a very good time. Cup of tea?'

'Hmm, not right now, thanks. I was actually off to help out at the food bank and wondered if you felt like lending a hand. You know, if you're at a bit of a loose end.'

Much to her own surprise Trish found herself glad to take up the offer. It wasn't as if she was bored in the house with Peter at work and Toby at school. There was plenty to keep her busy, what with having to wrangle the financial arrangements of their new life and the upkeep of a home three times the size of their old. Her previous job at the distribution centre, as she had pointed out frequently and loudly, had been badly paid for long hours working under a management which was petty and draconian to the point of paranoia – but at least it had felt like actual work. 'You know what? Yes. I think I would like that, actually.' She chucked the peg bag into the basket as well and took it all back into the utility room.

'Don't you need to finish that first?' asked the reverend.

'Finish what?' she said, all wide-eyed innocence.

They took Joyce's car back into the centre of Haleswell. At the heart of it was the green, a small but immaculately maintained park surrounded by narrow-fronted heritage-listed buildings occupied by smart little cafés, gift and jewellery shops, insurance agents, a branch of Lloyds Bank, a holistic therapies clinic and a cake-craft shop. St Sebastian's and the rectory formed one corner with the Manor House diagonally at the other; this was a half-timbered building three storeys high which dated back to the seventeenth century, and although it had genuinely once been the home of the de Lindesay family, it was now where the Trust had its main offices as well as housing the village hall, children's library, and Citizens Advice Bureau. At the back of the CAB Joyce showed her to a storeroom piled with cardboard boxes full of assorted tins, packets, bottles and jars.

'These are the donations that come in from all over,' the reverend said. 'Some of it comes from parishioners but an awful lot from corner shops and supermarkets. What we need to do is check the expiry dates to make sure it's all okay and then take it in the van to the big food bank on the Stratford Road.'

Trish rubbed her hands together. 'Let's get started then.'

As they worked, the reverend asked her, 'So I hope you and your family are settling in all right?'

'It's only been three weeks, but I think so, thanks.'

'One of life's most stressful events, isn't that what they say? Death, divorce and moving house?'

'Hmm?' Trish made a show of concentrating on the label of a packet of rice. 'Do they?' Happy as she was to help, she had a sinking feeling that the reverend thought she would benefit from baring her soul in a Deep and Meaningful Conversation. For years now her soul had been her own concern.

'Personally I think that's a load of tosh.'

Trish snorted a laugh. 'Did you just use the word *tosh*?'

'I was trying to protect your sensibilities. You would prefer bollocks?'

'I don't have any sensibilities. And you might want to rephrase that.'

The reverend mentally replayed what she'd just said, and burst out laughing. They carried on sorting and repacking.

The food bank itself operated out of an anonymous industrial unit near the busy dual carriageway, in a buffer zone of chain-link fencing, breeze blocks and roll-up doors between the estates of Pestle Road and the Willows. It was staffed by volunteers in green tabards who helped Trish and the reverend unload and told them where to put the boxes. It was what Trish imagined the food store of a nuclear bunker would look like: rows of industrial metal shelving neatly stacked with boxes and pallets of groceries – not just food, but household goods, children's clothes, sanitary products... anything with a decent shelf-life that a destitute person might need.

And there were so very many of them.

Trish was shocked to see them actually queuing outside. Parents, mostly mothers, trying to hush squalling children too young to be in school. Elderly folk standing in quiet dignity. Solitary men and women, some of them with the pinched cheeks of junkies or the raggedness of the homeless, but by no means all; many of them she would have passed in the street and never imagined that their circumstances had reduced them to this.

They arrived with vouchers provided by doctors, social workers, or other charities, and had them stamped and authenticated by volunteers who would then talk to them about their needs and help them put together a package of supplies to see them through their immediate crisis. She overheard the story of a father who had missed his benefits appointment because his baby was in hospital with bronchitis and whose welfare had been stopped for six weeks as a result; that of an accounts manager who had lost her job when the company had relocated to Portugal and hadn't been able to make her rent payments; that of a sixty-two-year-old Falklands War veteran who hadn't eaten for two days and had been forced to come, despite his pride, by his granddaughter. Her blood ran cold at the thought of how close she and Peter could have come to this: one redundancy, one workplace injury was all it took. She thought about going home to her nice new cottage with the laundry basket that she'd been fed up with this morning, and felt sick with guilt.

That was the point at which Trish first noticed the girl.

She couldn't have been much more than eleven, very thin, with lank hair and dressed in the simplest of plain cotton dresses, but what caught Trish's attention most of all was her bare feet, which were filthy – it was a minor miracle that they weren't already lacerated. God alone knew what kind of broken glass or bits of metal were underfoot. She was standing a little off to one side, looking at the queue as if unsure whether or not to join it. She didn't seem to be with anybody; either that or she had lost her parents.

Trish headed towards her, about to ask if she was missing her mummy or daddy, but the girl chose that moment to look around and saw her approaching. Her eyes widened in alarm and she walked hurriedly away, around the back of the queue.

'Excuse me!' Trish called out. 'Wait a minute! I'm not going to hurt you!'

She rounded the end of the queue and saw the girl disappearing down the narrow alleyway between this unit and the next, a Volkswagen repair specialist. Not running, but still walking briskly, as if with a purpose. If she'd scared the kid and caused her to be hurt she'd never forgive herself.

'It's okay! I just want to talk to you!'

The girl looked back again and picked up her pace, disappearing around a corner in the alleyway.

Trish ran after her. She got to the corner in time to see the girl disappearing around yet another one in the opposite direction.

'Wait!'

Trish pursued again, concern turning to frustration and annoyance as she started to suspect that the girl wasn't afraid of her at all, but was playing some kind of silly prank. Those backwards looks hadn't been glances of fear – more like checking to see if she was being followed. Well, if she wasn't in sight around this next corner then she could sod off.

Around the next one, Trish nearly ran into the back of her. She was right *there*, almost within arm's reach, bending down to duck through a hole in the chain-link fence, on the other side of which cars and lorries flashed past. She was going out onto the dual carriageway, where she was certain to get hit, and now it didn't matter whether she was scared or stupid.

This close, Trish noticed the girl's smell – it was rank and foul, like the stench of something long dead and rotted in stagnant water – but she didn't have time to process this fact properly because then the girl slipped through the gap into the stream of traffic, and Trish yelled, 'NO!' and ducked through after her, grabbing...

...and nearly lost her balance on the edge of a yawning pit.

She flailed behind herself, fingers finding and hooking in the chain-link fence, arresting her forward plunge.

It was a storm-drain culvert, about a metre across and several deep, into which the drainage under the dual carriageway flowed before being carried away by a much wider pipe. Safety barriers prevented access from the road only on three sides, with the fourth supposedly being the fence that she'd just ducked through. The fall probably wouldn't have killed her, but she'd definitely have broken something. She shook her head in disbelief. The little bitch had lured her here deliberately.

'Dear God!' she whispered, aghast. 'Why?'

Then movement on the far side of the carriageway caught her attention – it was the girl, standing there, staring back at her. Somehow she'd made it across four lanes of busy traffic, including the central reservation barrier, in a few seconds. There had been no horns or tyres screeching – somebody *must* have seen her and yet the traffic was moving as smoothly as if nothing had happened at all.

'That's not possible,' she whispered.

As if hearing her, the girl grinned.

And changed.

Her face was a cadaver's, dead eyes glittering with malice as sores blossomed across her skin and her fingers grew black, while larger swellings erupted at her throat, some bursting to disgorge streams of blood and pus which stained the crude woollen shift which she now wore. Trish screamed, and the dead girl nodded as if pleased by the sound, and then was gone.

* * *

Trish had no memory of making her way back to the food bank. She couldn't have been gone more than five minutes, but when she returned the reverend came running up, her face lined with concern.

'Good heavens, Trish! What have you been doing? You're white as a sheet!'

'I'm just...' Trish croaked, only realising then how badly she'd strained her vocal cords with her own screaming. She swallowed, feeling something click. 'Felt a bit unwell, that's all. Could I maybe have a glass of water, please?'

Water was fetched, as well as a chair, and when she felt steady enough the reverend drove her back to Haleswell. On the journey she was aware of Joyce's speculative sidelong looks directed at her, and the reverend's expressive hands were restless on the steering wheel.

'Don't think me rude,' said Trish, 'but you might want to keep your eyes on the road instead of me?'

The reverend didn't say anything at first, just kept looking at her. She seemed to be weighing up the pros and cons of some internal debate. It must have been resolved one way or another because finally she said, 'What did you see?' in a tone so utterly sober, so lacking in the usual chumminess of her public demeanour, that for a second Trish thought it was the voice of a different person.

'What do you mean, what did I see?'

'Experience, then. Listen, Patricia, I'm sure you see me as some sort of well-meaning but basically quite ineffectual Little England village vicar, but I know the difference between sickness and fear, and you, my dear, have had the willies put up you by something.'

Trish laughed despite herself. 'Willies.' She shook her head. 'I've had... I've had a bit of a funny turn, that's all.'

'Suit yourself.' The reverend faced straight ahead and said nothing for a while as she continued to drive, and Trish knew that somehow she'd disappointed her. Well, tough. She wasn't about to go spilling a story which was bound to sound insane just to satisfy the reverend's need to be sticking her holy nose into everybody's business. 'As long as it is just yourself, of course,' Dobson continued. 'And not your loved ones too.'

'What's *that* supposed to mean?'

Now it was the reverend's turn to laugh, but she sounded far from amused. 'It means that if you ever need to talk to me about anything – you, or Peter or Toby – there is literally nothing I am not prepared to listen to. Do you understand what I'm saying?'

Trish thought she did, and the idea was far from reassuring – if the reverend was suggesting, however obliquely, that she might be prepared to take such a story seriously, it meant that she was just as deranged. Because it couldn't be true. It absolutely could not.

Even though they didn't have enough stuff to be living out of cardboard boxes after the move, one of the upstairs spare bedrooms had been designated a box room for the various bits and pieces which couldn't be found an immediate home. It still took Trish a while to find what she was looking for; it was one of those things that had been scooped straight from the back of the wardrobe and into a packing crate without looking, as if she'd been subconsciously trying to ignore it even then. After all, she'd been successfully ignoring it for the past twelve years.

It was an ordinary Clarks shoe box, tied up with a piece of tartan ribbon from some long-forgotten Christmas. The contents shifted and slid as she lifted it with sweating hands. This was a different kind of fear to this afternoon's terror – less sharp, but bone deep.

Even though nobody else was at home, she shut the door and drew the curtains. Some things were to be kept from the casual gaze of the outside world, even if the world didn't care anymore.

Taking a deep breath, she unknotted the ribbon and lifted the lid.

Envelopes, mostly. A lot of them contained doctors' notes. One was full of printouts of ultrasound scans. A book of baby names. But alongside these were other relics, these ones of her faith that had died at the same time: her first rosary and the little book of psalms for children that she'd received at her First Communion when she was seven. The veil she'd worn at her Confirmation when she'd been Toby's age (and dear Lord hadn't she been so proud of herself!). A large crucifix – gilded Christ on a rosewood cross.

She lifted out this last item and closed the box quickly before the tears could escape.

'Well then,' she murmured, regarding Him. 'Let's see what you're good for, shall we?'

After some deliberation about where to hang it – not in the living room, where it would be in their faces all the time, and definitely not in their bedroom, since Peter had made it clear a long time ago that he wasn't sharing it with another man, even though he'd tried to make it sound like a joke – she settled on the main hallway just inside the front door.

She was in the process of hammering a picture hook into the plaster when Toby came home from school.

'What's that for?' he asked.

'Fine, thanks!' she replied brightly, ignoring the question. How would she answer it anyway? *Today I had what can only be described as a paranormal experience and nearly got hospitalised by a little girl who I'm pretty sure wasn't alive and it's making me second-guess everything I disbelieve in, but other than that just peachy, darling.* 'How was school?'

Toby mumbled something and started upstairs. She finished hanging the crucifix and turned to ask him again just as he was rounding the landing halfway up. He had his hand up to the side of his face, and she knew instantly that something was wrong.

'Stop right there, young man!' she ordered, and he froze like a dog jerked on a leash. She looked closer. 'Toby, what's happened to your face?!'

13

TITS ON A FISH

'HE SAID HE WAS HAVING A KICKABOUT WITH HIS friends on the way back from school, and he fell over,' said Trish. They were in the living room, the remains of a Chinese takeaway and several empty posh lager bottles on the coffee table between them. They should probably have been developing a taste for something more exotic like Thai food and starting to drink wine, but that was never going to happen. Neither of them had felt like cooking. Something was bothering Trish, and Peter knew that the thing with Toby was only part of it. Their son had taken himself up to his room the second dinner was over, as if wanting to give them a clear space to talk about him.

'And do you believe him?'

She snorted a laugh. 'Of course not.'

'What makes you think he's lying?'

'Because when I asked if he'd hurt himself anywhere else

he said no, and I know that when you fall you go over hands first, don't you? So I was looking at his hands when he was eating dinner and there wasn't a mark on them. Nor on his uniform, either – no scuffed knees, nothing.'

'Blimey,' he laughed. 'Sherlock Holmes or what? Good thing I've never tried to cheat on you.'

'I hope that's not supposed to be funny.'

Peter's smile vanished. 'Not really.' He'd just given her an open goal to tease him, and she'd refused it. If their usual banter wasn't working, whatever was on her mind must be serious.

'Plus,' she continued, 'it's not like he's never been in a fight before, is it?'

Peter sighed. 'No, it isn't.' He took a long swig from his bottle and grimaced. 'Shit – I really thought we'd put that behind us. I thought maybe this new place, new school...' He shook his head.

'What if he gets suspended again? I knew that comprehensive was a bad idea.'

Peter felt his temper surging in response to the I-told-you-so, but forced it back. If she wanted a rise from him she was going to have to work harder than that. 'Trish, he's only been there a week – he's finding where he fits into the pecking order. Give the poor little sod a chance, yeah?'

'So are you going to talk to him about it?'

'I'll try.' He shrugged. 'But I'll be honest with you, I can't see it being any more successful than before.'

'For God's sake, Peter! Can't you at least try to summon up some sense of urgency about this? Pecking order! He's not a zoo animal! You sound like you've given up already!'

'Well what can I do? If he won't talk to me, he won't talk to me! I can't force it out of him with red-hot irons and bamboo splinters under the bloody fingernails, can I? He's a teenage boy! He'll talk when he's ready.'

'It's been six months! When is he going to be ready? You're his father! You should be able to... I don't know—'

'Wait, now it's *my* fault?' he snapped.

And there it was. He just about managed to keep his voice below shouting so that their son wouldn't hear.

'That's not what I meant—'

'No, you never *mean* to blame me, do you? It just sort of happens. Is that why we've got the big man himself staring down at us again? Bringing out the captain of Team Guilt Trip for reinforcements?'

'What? No!' She blinked and frowned, trying to make sense of that. 'What's that got to do with anything? I told you, I put it up for good luck, that's all.' Her fingers were playing with the front of her t-shirt collar – back in the day it had been a crucifix around her neck that she'd fiddled with when she was nervous or lying, and he didn't think she was even aware she was doing it. He wanted to call her out on it but he knew from past experience that this would just escalate things to a point which frankly he didn't have the energy for.

'Okay. Fine. I'll talk to him. Happy?'

'Thank you,' she said, very quietly.

But he didn't go upstairs to Toby's room. He took his beer and went out through the kitchen, the utility room and finally the connecting door into the garage. It had enough space for two vehicles but at the moment there was just his van – an old blue transit with *Feenan Electrical* decalled in white down the sides – which for so many years had been his only truly private space. It didn't just carry his tools and gear, it had a gas camping stove, a little 12-volt fridge and a couple of folding chairs, and some days when a job wasn't taking quite as long as planned he'd take off for a couple of hours to somewhere green for a cup of tea and a bit of a think. He'd never had garage space before. Now that he did, he envisaged the blank brick walls racked with new kit, giving him space to convert the van into something with maybe a fold-out table or bunks that they could take on actual proper family holidays, like he should have been able to do when Toby was much younger. He felt the sucking vacuum of lost time and missed opportunities pulling at his gut, so to distract himself he got in the van's cab and picked up the thing lying on the passenger seat – the thing that had been bothering him all day and making him ratty with Trish.

It was a smoke detector, its sleek silver-white plastic case looking like a movie model of a UFO. Its packaging declared that the HomeSafe3000+ Combined Smoke and Carbon Monoxide Detector was a 'next-generation security device employing dual ionisation sensor technology and loud piezoelectric alarm to guard your family against the threat of fire and deadly CO fumes'. It was also, in Peter's professional opinion, a mass-produced piece of Taiwanese crap which was about as much use as tits on a fish. It just about scraped EN14604 and EN50291, but some of the other sparks he'd spoken to had told him horror stories of how unreliable it was. One said he'd rather trust his family's safety to a canary with a bad head cold.

And Dino Periccos, on-site supervisor of the electrics firm that Richard Nash had subcontracted to wire the houses of the Clegg Farm development, had four hundred of the bloody things that he wanted Peter to install.

One of the last things that Peter wanted to do was go over anyone's head to their boss – it was a dick move guaranteed to lose an independent sparks like himself a lot of goodwill and future work. But he tried to imagine waking up to find his own home full of smoke (or worse, not waking up at all) and it didn't leave him much choice but to take his concerns directly to Nash. After all, the Trust looked after its own, right?

Nash had refused to listen.

'I'm sorry, Peter,' he'd said, in apologetic tones that didn't convince him one bit. 'But it's a budgetary issue. The costing has been finalised and there just isn't any wiggle room. I'd love as much as the next man to fit these properties with top-of-the-range fixtures for everything but it just can't be done.'

'These aren't luxury items, Richard,' he protested. 'They're required by law.'

'But these ones aren't illegal, are they?'

'No, but—'

'Well then.'

Peter had paced Nash's office in frustration, trying to find some way to make the man see reason. 'But the cost difference is peanuts! You're talking an extra twenty quid per unit for one that will do a decent job. That's only eight thousand pounds on a development which must be costing a good couple of million.'

'Yes, and where do you think all of that's coming from? Not out of my back pocket, that's for sure. Investors, Peter. Look, I'm going to tell you this in confidence because you're a good man and I can trust you not to go spreading gossip, but the truth is that the budget of Clegg Farm is already in overspend, and the investors are breathing down my neck. I can't justify tacking on a few thousand here for super-duper smoke detectors and a few thousand there for, I don't know, dimmer switches or something. What if the plumbers all decide that they'd rather install swanky granite hand basins instead of the bog-standard ones? No pun intended.' He chuckled a little and Peter could quite easily have punched him in the face right then and there. 'The investors would have my guts for garters.'

'A granite hand basin,' Peter said with iron control, 'isn't going to kill someone if its alarm doesn't go off. What happens when there's a fire – because it will happen – and the detector fails and a family dies? How will your investors feel then?'

Nash's complacent smile faded. 'Listen, Peter, I don't know how you and I have managed to get off on the wrong foot with each other after everything I've done for you so far, but just listen to yourself for a moment. Do you seriously think that I would knowingly put families' lives at risk? Let's talk about families, then, shall we? You remember how I told you that a proportion of the new development is being set aside for affordable housing?'

'Yes? So?'

'What do you think makes them affordable? Yes, we have a legal obligation to provide a certain proportion of cheap housing, but if the developer's financial viability assessment shows that the profit for the landowner isn't high enough at the end of the day they can simply walk away and sell those houses for prices way above what ordinary folk like you and me can afford.'

Nash's office in the Manor House overlooked the emerald sward of the village green, with its church opposite and its surrounding parade of olde-worlde boutique shops, and its families strolling with pushchairs or parked in gleaming SUVs. Peter looked at it all and listened to Nash talk about himself as 'ordinary folk' and nearly laughed. 'I'm glad you're so passionate about it,' Nash continued, 'because it shows that you care, and I do too, I really do, but there simply is nothing I can do. Anyway, there's absolutely no point in making wild speculations about... incidents like that.'

He could have walked away then. He really should have, but something in Nash's arrogance made him want to see the man squirm, just once, just a bit. 'People are entitled to speculate whatever they like, given the right information,' he said carefully.

Nash took a long time before answering, measuring him up as if seeing him properly for the first time. 'As a tradesman you'll appreciate this analogy,' he said. 'Information, like any tool, can be dangerous to all concerned when used irresponsibly. Here's a piece which I think you might be neglecting: the Trust looks after its own, as you know, and while your wife is a Trustee, you aren't. We'll see that she's looked after regardless of whether or not you're able to support her. Don't be under any illusions about that.'

The threat was clear. Peter felt his temper rise at the sight of this smug arsehole acting like the lord of the manor chastising a wayward peasant. He did his best to hide it but it must have shown because Nash's smirk widened a fraction.

'Are you going to hit me, Peter?' he asked. His tone was mild, even slightly surprised, but something danced in his eyes that gave Peter the impression that Nash would like nothing so much as for him to reach over the desk and take a swing. 'I know you want to. I know you have a history of it. We were very thorough in our background checks on your family when assessing Patricia's eligibility to be custodian of Stone Cottage, so I know about your police record. The assault charges. Please be assured that whatever happens to you – wherever you end up – your wife and son will continue to be looked after by the Trust.'

Seething with impotent rage, Peter bit his tongue and stalked from Nash's office. Then he came home and discovered that his son was getting into fights at school, again, and his wife was hanging up crucifixes in the house, again, and it seemed to him that rather than this move to Haleswell being the opportunity for a new start, things were sliding irrevocably back into the past.

14

HESTER
MAY 1349

IN THE FOLLOWING WEEKS, AS THE PESTILENCE BURNED
its way through her village, Hester would blame herself even
more bitterly for running straight back to bed, telling herself
that maybe if she had woken the household immediately the
stranger would still have had the strength to walk and so
could have been driven out. But as it was, by the time the
family was waking he was so ill that he could not move, his
throat bulging grotesquely with blackening lumps the size
of plums. Nevertheless, he could not be left where he was
and the Attlowes could not simply abandon their home.

'We should take him to the Priory of St Thomas,'
suggested William Priour. 'They will look after him there.'
He was a freeman farmer, one of a number of villagers who
had gathered outside the Attlowes' house upon hearing the
news and now stood in a fearful knot at what they evidently
believed to be a safe distance. Hester saw other good men

amongst them, their normally affable faces lined with anxiety: John Hastynge, father of Agnes of the golden hair; Richard Colleson, the charcoal burner; Henry Clech, who had the best pear tree in the village.

'The priory is in Birmingham, and that is nearly eight miles,' pointed out her father. 'Will you carry him yourself?'

'A cart, then,' insisted Priour.

'And who will pull it? Who will let their cart be used for such a purpose? And if he should die on the way, how shall he receive his last rites? How shall he be buried?'

'Haleswell, then!' Priour's voice was becoming shrill with fear. 'Take him to St Sebastian's Well for healing! We can do nothing for him here! Think of our families!' There were mutters of agreement from the group at this.

'It would be quicker to send someone to bring here the water,' said Hester's father. 'Easier for him, too.'

'There is also this, which you are forgetting,' put in Father Cuthbert, in tones of calm reason which none could ignore. 'The Lord has sent this man to our village. A charge has been laid upon us and we must not fail this test of our faith. We must not be as the priest and the Levite who saw the wounded stranger and passed by on the other side, but rather we should be as the Good Samaritan who took care of him and healed his wounds. For how shall we expect charity in our own need, rendering none to others? The stranger will come with me to the Lord's house, and I will tend to him.'

That being the word of their priest, backed by the decision of their reeve, the men of Clegeham had no choice but to acquiesce, and returned to their homes, though there was much muttering between them as they went.

Father Cuthbert blessed Dick and his son Henry with holy water from the spring at Haleswell, and they wrapped their faces around with cloth stuffed with crushed blackthorn blossom and cloves to protect them from the dying man's pestilential vapours, and they carried him to the chapel where the priest could tend him and administer his last rites.

When her father beat her for disobeying her mother's orders, he did it with his reeve's stick rather than his hand, so that she knew he was only doing his duty and that there was no anger in it.

As elected reeve of the village, Dick Attlowe's duties involved ensuring that each serf and villein worked his allotted share of the manor's lands without shirking; he was accustomed to being obeyed and now turned that to his advantage, ordering work to continue as normal, and the villagers went about their daily business, albeit with a strained calm. They would not look at the church directly, casting only sidelong glances at it and giving it a wide berth – especially when the stranger started calling for water in the most piteous tones. As the morning wore on his pleas diminished into little more than gurgles, groans and occasional barking howls of agony, resembling more the sounds of an animal dying slowly in a trap.

There was some heated argument about the best way to treat him, for this was beyond the petty day-to-day injuries and illnesses with which they were familiar. Father Cuthbert avouched that prayer would sway the Lord's mercy in his favour. Dick Attlowe fancied himself a more worldly man who had travelled as far as Warwick and spoken with men learned in physick, and insisted that the pestilence was caused by an imbalance of humours, for which evidence he pointed to the man's raging fever.

'It is obvious that there is too much blood in him,' said her father. 'If he is to stand a chance of survival he must be bled. We should send for Hordern the barber.' A Haleswell man, Hordern was the closest any of the surrounding villages had to a physick. As well as trimming the beards of the great and good he set broken limbs, pulled teeth, and lanced boils. A boy was sent to run the mile to Haleswell and beg his help, and by mid-afternoon he had arrived: a stooped man with hooded eyes and a sour demeanour.

Hordern hesitated when he saw the sick man. 'I was not told that he has the pestilence. I will not touch this man.' He moved to leave, but Dick Attlowe arrested his attention with a silver penny which he held up, shining in the spring sunlight.

'Will you touch this instead?' he enquired. 'Father,' he said to Cuthbert. 'Will you bless this man to protect him in his work?'

Father Cuthbert shook his head in disapproval. 'I will take no part in this,' he replied. 'The Church expressly forbids any man of the cloth to participate in such a practice.'

'Then pray for us, Father, if that is all you can do.'

So they removed the plague-stricken traveller back to the Attlowes' barn, since Father Cuthbert would not have this in the church, and they bled him.

The barber of Haleswell bound a cord around his arm above the elbow so that the veins stood out on his forearm.

Then he took a slender but wickedly pointed knife and, with his long pale fingers, pushed the blade lengthways into the largest blood vessel as the patient screamed and writhed against the hands that held him down. The jet of crimson which arced out of the wound was caught in a small bowl by her father with trembling hands, and a little slopped over the side. Hordern let it flow until the man's struggles eased sufficiently for him to judge that some of the excess had been removed, then repeated the procedure on his other arm, so that his humours would be balanced in both sides of his body. Then, because the grotesque swellings in the man's throat indicated that the worst of the excess had built up there, he was bled from the throat also. His wounds were treated with a mixture of clay, meadowsweet and treacle, and by the time the barber had finished Dick Attlowe was paler than the patient. Hordern was paid, and hurried from Clegeham without looking back.

'Will he live, Father?' asked Hester, looking at the patient lying as if dead amidst piles of bloodstained sacking.

'That is in the hands of Father Cuthbert now,' Attlowe replied, and went back out into the daylight on slightly tottery legs.

15

HISTORY LESSON

THAT MORNING, THE DEAD GIRL WALKED WITH TOBY to school.

He had to admit She was dead – quite apart from the fact that Krish obviously couldn't see Her – in the broad light of day there was no way to pretend that it was just movie make-up. Even the most realistic prosthetic effects couldn't hide the fact that fake flesh had to be built up on the actor's own face, so that they always ended up looking slightly chunky and oversized. The slight figure of the girl walking calmly beside him was ravaged with marks of a terrible disease which had not just bloomed out of Her in sores and pustules, but eaten craters of infection and necrosis into Her flesh which could not be faked. He could see the deep tissues of Her muscles working as She walked, though he tried not to look at Her directly, partly because he was terrified of Her reaction but also because, well, staring was rude. The idea made him want to laugh, but he was afraid of how it would sound, and that he might not be able to stop. It was hard enough trying to keep up a conversation with Krish, who was walking on the other side of him and totally oblivious to the dead girl's existence.

'So I'm chasing this noob across the Plains of Pain, right?' Krish was chattering away. 'Because points multiplier decreases the longer they're out of the Shell, yeah?'

'Mm-hm.' Toby knew how the game was played but Krish liked to explain everything anyway to prove that he knew what he was doing because he actually wasn't all that good. Besides, Toby was slightly distracted. The girl's fingers were black to the knuckle.

'And he's like, "You can't do this! It's soul-farming! I'm reporting you!" And I'm like, "Bitch, how old are you, twelve? This is *Hellscape*! If you can't handle it, go back to some baby game like *Fortnite*!"'

'Yeah, absolutely.' Toby watched from the corner of his eye as She walked right over a crisp packet without disturbing it, which meant that She wasn't real and only in his head. Or actually dead and a ghost.

'So then he finally ghosts and I stack him with the rest of my Flock—'

'Hey listen,' he interrupted. 'Did you spend any of last night doing the history homework?' Listening to Krish rattle on about a game involving soul-harvesting demons was just too weird. The girl gave a quiet little snigger and then wasn't there anymore.

* * *

'I was sorry to hear what Rajko did,' said Maya on the way in to morning registration. She found Toby by the lockers as he was getting his books out for the morning. History, Chemistry, Maths. Nice, safe, ordinary lessons. He'd been keeping his head down on his way into the building because the last thing he needed to see right now was the dead girl standing in the corridor, so Maya caught him by surprise.

'Oh! Yeah, right. Um, it was just a thing. No biggie.'

'But he hurt you!'

'Look, I don't want to make a fuss.'

'He was massively out of order. My mother has invited you to tea to apologise. Please say yes? If you don't then she'll be offended and *I* will beat you up.'

'Put like that, how can I refuse?'

'Good decision.'

She went off to join her friends further down the corridor who were looking back at him and whispering amongst themselves. He grabbed his books and shuffled off to registration. One thing about ghosts: at least they didn't gossip.

'Sir,' said Toby, 'if a person died from sores all over their body and huge lumps in their throat and black fingers, what would that be?'

Without looking up from his marking, Mr Willis replied, 'A very unusual death for Joseph Stalin, which is what you're supposed to be revising right now.'

This burn elicited a chorus of good-natured jeers from most of the lads in the class, but Toby didn't mind. Willis was a legend and never meant anything maliciously.

'Would it be the Black Death, sir?' He knew the answer already because he'd just been googling it under the table, but he was angling after something more local that might not be on the Internet and he figured that a history teacher would be the person most likely to know.

Willis put down his pen and regarded him warily. The classroom psy-ops tactic of distracting the teacher by getting them to talk about their pet subject (which in Willis' case was medieval Europe) was standard and well known to both sides, but he obviously decided to indulge them for a moment. '*Yersinia pestis*,' he said. 'Came to Great Britain in the bellies of fleas on the backs of rats in the holds of traders' ships from Gascony. That's in France. In three years it killed somewhere between a third and a half of the population.'

'How does it kill you, sir?' asked Shereen Patel.

'It attacks the lymph nodes in your armpits, throat and groin...' Willis paused to wait for the boys' sniggering to subside '...and your body's overwhelming immune response causes septic shock and catastrophic loss of blood pressure, leading to internal bleeding, gangrene, hence the 'black' in the name, multiple organ failure, and – unless someone gets antibiotics into you – death.'

'So it's curable?'

'Today? Easily. In the fourteenth century, not so much. The people then had literally no idea what germs were, or even that something as basic as washing your hands could help prevent the spread of disease. They thought it was a punishment from God, so everything they did to try to stop it involved finding out what had upset God and making him happy again. The usual minorities were blamed, obviously – Jews, Romany gypsies – and some people called flagellants even took to beating themselves with whips to atone for whatever sins they might have committed. They had some mad ideas about cures, too, such as eating crushed emeralds or ten-year-old treacle.'

'What's treacle?' someone asked.

Willis took a deep breath and carried on. 'So yes, antibiotics, which means that you don't have to worry about catching it. What *you* need to understand is that the whole of society changed as a result of so many people dying. You know all those films about survivors in a post-apocalyptic society? Well, you're living in one, just a few hundred years after the fact. Because labour was so short, peasants could choose who they worked for and earn a lot more money. More women could find jobs and make themselves wealthy and influential, choose to marry later in life or even not at all. The lower classes became more confident and less inclined to simply do what they were told, which led to protests like the Peasant's Revolt of 1381 in which thousands of poor people tried to rise up against their feudal overlords. Just like?' He waited for someone to make the connection.

'Russia in 1905?' queried Sean Davis.

'Sweetie for that man,' said Willis, and tossed him a boiled sweet from the jar on his desk, which was probably against health and safety but nobody cared. 'And so we come full circle and you're back to revising Stalin. Damn, I'm good. Get back on with your work.'

After the lesson, Toby caught up with Willis in the corridor outside.

'Sir, about the Black Death.'

'Yes? Please don't tell me that you're running a fever.'

'No, sir. I was just wondering if you knew anything about it that was a bit more, well, local.'

'You mean Haleswell? Not myself personally, but I think I was given something a few months ago by the neighbourhood amateur historical society. Come with me and I'll see if I can dig it up.'

Toby followed him to the door of the staff room where he waited until Willis reappeared with a small photocopied leaflet. 'Here you go,' he said. 'Fill your boots.'

It was a very ordinary A5 flyer inviting anybody who was interested in learning about the history of the Village Trust to a monthly meeting of the Haleswell Historical Society, so far so boring, but it was the details of the venue and the society's chief secretary which made him catch his breath:

Stone Cottage.

Stephanie Drummond.

And hadn't he seen boxes of books stacked in the lock-up where all the old lady's belongings were being stored? She must have known all kinds of secrets about the village, including the dead girl. Grinning, he folded the leaflet and stuffed it into the pocket of his blazer, then went off to lunch.

The sin of Sodom, Toby read, *was not, as traditional conservative interpretations would have it, that of rampant homosexuality. Apart from anything else, consider the simple practicalities: if homosexuality was so prevalent that the entire population of the city was considered to be polluted by it, how could it sustain a population? Where did their children come from? It may be possible to argue that the men of Sodom kept wives for procreation and had homoerotic relationships for recreation, but that is a far cry from a mob threatening to gang-rape the angels that Lot was sheltering in his home. Lot's decision to offer his daughters to the mob is extremely problematic, obviously, but why would he have thought that the men would be interested if their motivation was homosexual gratification?*

A violent mob assault of this kind isn't about sexual pleasure, or even about control, but about humiliating the outsider, dominating the stranger. Regardless of whatever other sinful, lustful, or idolatrous practices the Sodomites had previously engaged in, it is this violation of their scriptural obligation to offer hospitality to strangers which is the root cause of the Lord's displeasure, and the cataclysm which followed – a cataclysm which destroyed not only the men in the mob, but every human being in the city, wives and children included. Hospitality is a sacrament, to be profaned at great cost.

Toby closed the book – *New Interpretations of the Old Testament* – and put it in his school bag with the others. Then he checked the time on his phone and swore; he'd been squirrelled away here amongst the dusty furniture and storage crates containing Stephanie Drummond's belongings for over two hours, and if he stayed any longer his mum and dad would be pissed. He'd told them that he was going out to the cinema with Krish and Sean, but even so he was cutting it close. They were still very wary of letting him out on his own, except that he'd managed to convince them that he wouldn't be on his own, would he? He'd be with his mates. Thankfully they were more keen on him settling in than worried about him getting hurt again. Or in trouble. He knew they thought he was getting into fights again.

He looked around at the dim, cavernous space cluttered with boxes and furniture shrouded in dust sheets. Anyone could be hiding in here with him. Anything. He closed the main compartment of his bag and reached into the outside pocket, his fingertips touching the reassuring cool hardness of the knife that had been sitting there since yesterday. It was the small one that his mum used for cutting up vegetables. In the long run he would have to replace it with something that his mum wouldn't miss, but it would do for the moment.

He didn't plan on getting into any more fights, but he didn't plan on having to take it like a pussy, either.

Stealing the key from the cupboard under the stairs had been almost as easy as taking the knife. So, surprisingly, had been finding the information he needed, since Mrs Drummond had bookmarked everything significant she'd found with slips of paper and her own marginal notes, just like the one which had fallen out of the bureau. Most were obscure academic annotations, but one had been a revelation:

She waits outside the stones, it read. *Endlessly patient, She circles them like a wolf circling a campfire. If it should burn low…*

It meant that the old woman had seen the dead girl too, which meant that She was real and he wasn't going mental.

He wasn't sure that this was a good thing.

There were dozens of books on biblical interpretations like this one, plus many more on the supernatural, ghosts, epidemiology, complexity theory, UFOs, medieval life and culture, the Black Death in general and the history of Haleswell Parish in particular.

In another book he read: *To the people of the fourteenth century, the cause of the Black Death was very simple: God was displeased, and so God had punished humanity just as He had with the Deluge or the destruction of Sodom and Gomorrah. We like to think that we are more rational in this day and age but the media cycle demands a causal, reductionist narrative in which any given disaster can be attributed to a limited number of simplistic 'faults', which in turn feeds into the subsequent investigatory process manipulated by politicians so that they are seen to be doing something. According to the* Daily Mail, *a 'young boy playing near a colony of infected bats' was to blame for the Ebola epidemic of 2014. Scapegoating is alive and well and blinds us to the uncomfortable truth that the world is vastly more complex than we can probably ever understand, with the result that some disasters terrify us by appearing to be spontaneous, inevitable, and ultimately inexplicable.*

None of it was exactly his ideal choice of reading matter – he didn't understand most of what he read, for a start – and it had taken him a while to decide on the few that he could carry back to hide in his room.

He pulled down the heavy roller door of the storage unit as quietly as he could, snapped the padlock shut, turned and nearly ran straight into Ms Markes.

'Hello, Toby,' she smiled.

Toby gawped.

'We have CCTV on all our properties,' she explained, and pointed to the camera that he hadn't even suspected was there. 'In case of burglars. I was just making sure.'

'I was just... er...'

'You know that if there's anything you want – anything at all – you only have to ask, don't you?'

'Yes, I, that is, I wasn't...'

'Give my regards to Trish, won't you?'

He mumbled something, clutched his school bag tightly and fled.

16

HESTER
MAY 1349

HESTER'S OLDEST BROTHER ALAN CAME TO HIS FATHER on the evening of the bloodletting, and she saw the first real, serious argument between them. Alan had married a girl called Margaret from neighbouring Ulverley; she had brought to the marriage three cows from her own father's dairy herd, and while Alan worked them she was busy producing her own domestic herd in the form of a son and a daughter, with a third on the way. Hester relished being an aunt and whenever she had time to spare, which was precious little, she enjoyed going to Meg's house and looking after her niece and nephew. In the fullness of time she looked forward to her own children playing with their older cousins, and seeing the Attlowe family growing ever closer-knit in love as the years passed.

There was not much love evident in the conversation between her brother and her father that evening, however.

'You cannot allow that man to spend another hour in our village!' Alan insisted. He was pacing back and forth before their fire, plainly nervous at having to confront his father. 'You put all of our lives at risk – those and the lives of our children!'

'Did William Priour send you thus to me?' demanded Dick Attlowe. 'Did he think that my son could sway me when he could not?' He squinted at Alan with disdain. 'How little you must think of me. Do you not at least respect the wisdom of Father Cuthbert?'

'Cuthbert is a man of God, and a good man besides, but he is not a father. For pity's sake, he is barely older than Henry!' Henry, who had been mending one of the leather ox traces quietly in a corner, turned crimson at his name being dragged into the argument. Hester herself carried on with her sewing, head down, hoping not to be noticed, while Cristina Attlowe glanced anxiously between her husband and her eldest son, reluctant to interfere on either side.

'Father Cuthbert understands that we have a responsibility to more than just our families in this matter. I had hoped you would understand that. I hoped to have raised you better.'

'It is not just me. Many of the tenants are worried. Simon Yonge has already left with his family, and three serfs have run away. More will leave if you do not act.'

'So there is talk behind my back, is there?'

'God's nails!' shouted Alan in exasperation. 'Is that all you can think of? What is *said* of you? Yes, there is talk behind your back! It would be to your face had you the wit to listen!'

Their mother tried to come between them then. 'Alan...'

'Wife, be still!' snapped her husband. He stood and folded his arms in front of his broad chest, glaring at his son, red-faced, his own temper on the edge of boiling over. 'It shames me to hear you speak thus, to blaspheme before your mother and sister. To demonstrate so weak a faith. To talk of fear. It shames me.'

Alan's voice was low and dangerous as he said, 'You were not too shamed to undervalue my rent for the manor this year gone and pocket the difference for yourself.'

Dick Attlowe's rage finally overspilled. 'Get out!' he roared, snatching up his reeve's staff and brandishing it in Alan's face. 'Get out of my home before I beat you out!'

Cristina flew to her son, putting her body as a shield before him, pushing towards the cottage door. 'Go!' she said. 'You've said enough. Just go now!'

Alan went, cursing into the night, while Dick went into the barn and took his rage out on some piles of straw, and Hester and Henry stared at each other with terrified eyes as their mother sobbed quietly in the open doorway.

The following day, Haleswell closed its border against them.

The boy that Cuthbert had sent to St Sebastian's early that morning with a leather bottle to bring back more of the well's holy water returned with empty hands and a bruise purpling his brow. Wide-eyed and babbling, he ran straight to Hester's father, who was reckoning the village's accounts at his table in the house's main chamber. Hester was sweeping on the other side of the central hearth, but not so busily that she couldn't eavesdrop on the conversation.

'They have blocked the road, sir!' cried the boy. He was a child of one of the villeins, and as such she did not know his name.

'Who have?' asked her father. 'Bandits?'

'No! The men of Haleswell! They stand in the road in great number, armed with pitchforks and sharpened poles! They demanded that I halt a good half furlong from them or be driven off, on account of the pestilence. They have placed a great stone in the middle of the road, hollowed out like a horse's trough, and they say that if we desire trade with them, goods and payment should be exchanged in the stone at a safe distance. I said that I had not come to trade but to seek the healing water from the well just as I had yesterday, at Father Cuthbert's behest, at which they replied there was no water, food or protection in Haleswell for anyone except those from Haleswell, and that I should go back.'

Dick Attlowe frowned in puzzlement. 'There must have been some misunderstanding. You have not conducted your errand properly. Go to them again, and do not fail lest you earn a whipping.'

'Not I!' said the boy. Her father aimed a cuffing blow at his head but he dodged it and ran, wailing.

'Very well,' her father grunted. 'I shall go myself.'

Hester had never seen her father so outraged. Even when as reeve he'd had to beat one of the serfs for stealing or shirking their duties, he'd done it apologetically, as if concerned that the miscreant should know that there was no rancour in the beating; nothing personal. This he seemed to take personally.

He took up the staff that Sir Roger's bailiff had given him as a symbol of his authority, collected a number of the men, including Henry, and set out that very moment. Her mother tried to stop him, but her efforts were no more use than they had ever been when her father had made up his mind.

It was only a mile to Haleswell, a short journey by foot, but the group did not return until later that afternoon. The reason was obvious the moment Hester saw them appear on the road beyond the mill: her father was limping severely, dragging his left leg and being supported with an arm across the shoulders of John Hastynge on one side and her brother Henry on the other. Henry carried the broken pieces of his reeve's staff in his other hand. Their father's upper tunic was caked in blood, with more of it matting his hair and caking his face, which was swollen with bruises.

Hester and her mother rushed to help carry him into the house. He had lost several teeth, had a four-inch gash in his scalp and his leg seemed to be broken in more than one place; it flopped hideously as they manoeuvred him onto his bed and his screams were like no sound she had ever heard her father make. In response to their tearful enquiries he was sullen, cursing them for every jolt, and even though she told herself it was just the pain speaking, the way he turned his face away from his wife and daughter made her think that something much deeper had been broken too – something in his soul.

'How could they dare?' he kept repeating. 'We are freemen. It is our right to seek the protection of our lord and the Church.' His voice shook with what Hester at first took to be fury, but quickly realised was a kind of bafflement. This development seemed to shock him more than the coming of the plague; disease was to be expected, a punishment of the Lord to be endured without question or complaint, but this wilful rebellion of man against his neighbour was somehow worse.

She prayed harder than she ever had in her life that night, and cried herself to sleep listening to his whimpers and groans in the bedchamber below her while her mother tried to comfort him in vain.

Without the healing water from Haleswell it took the stranger three more days to die, by which time Father Cuthbert was stricken with fever himself.

Finding that their priest was sickening, folk began to mutter that the Lord had abandoned Clegeham, and half the freemen quit the village altogether, packing what belongings they could into sacks which they carried, for few of them were wealthy enough to afford a cart. Several of the serfs slunk away in the night, though their fate was more uncertain, since abandoning their plots was a serious crime punishable by flogging. Clegeham was tiny, barely a hundred souls at the best of times, and their desertion was a hard blow. Most of the refugees took the Stratford Road south towards Warwick or east towards Ulverley but a few attempted to skirt Haleswell to the north and thereby come to the larger settlement of Birmingham. Whether or not they succeeded, Hester never heard.

While Cristina Attlowe tended her husband, the other women, Hester included, shared the honour of nursing the priest as he worsened, by which time two of the men who had passed the night on the Attlowes' floor had begun to sicken with the pestilence too. Their families caught it from them in turn, and the increased burden of caring for the sick was spread amongst fewer people capable of shouldering it. Where once she could walk past her neighbours' cottages and hear their chatter and laughter coming from behind the doors and windows, now the village echoed with agonised moans, screams of pain, and hoarse voices begging for release. Eventually Hester was left to care for Cuthbert in his last hours alone, which was some comfort as they could at last speak the truth to each other without fearing gossip-hungry ears.

'I am sorry,' he whispered, stroking the tears from her face. It was one of the few times he had touched her since he'd been away on his pilgrimage, and she relished even this little. Every movement he made seemed an agony. His flesh festered with boils and the lumps in his throat were distended, the skin stretched livid and shining over them.

'It is not you who should be sorry,' she said, trying to sound gruff and strong like one of her brothers, though her heart was a wailing thing. 'It is the bishop, for taking you away from me for what little time we might have had. It is the men of Haleswell, for denying you the water of Saint Sebastian's Well.' *It is my fault, for defying my mother's will.*

'You must accept this.'

But her rebellion had always been stronger than her guilt. 'No, I will not. I will do anything to stop this. *Anything.* I will bleed you. Maybe that will—'

He placed his feverish hands over hers. She saw that the last three fingers of his right hand had turned black, but she didn't flinch from his touch.

'No,' he croaked. 'You will let it be, for my soul's sake. Please.'

In the end she found that she could deny him nothing, not even his death.

As if the village priest's death were the final stone to fall from a leaking dam, Clegeham haemorrhaged altogether. The pestilence was terrifying enough, but the fear of dying without the Church's last rites produced a soul-deep horror which drove even those who were already gravely ill to find someone who could minister to them. Hester saw the corpse of an old woman at the edge of the village, her hands and knees bloodied from crawling, who had obviously decided that there was nothing more to be lost by dying on the road rather than in her home. Flies were feasting at the open sores on her scrawny legs, and rose in an angry, buzzing cloud when Hester disturbed them. She froze at the sight of the woman's body. No attempt had been made to even cover her, and Hester well understood why. When her own mother's mother had been dying, Father Euan (who had been the village priest before Father Cuthbert), had taken her confession and delivered her last rites and when she'd died Hester had watched the village women prepare the purified vessel of her dead body for burial with reverence and love, knowing that she was with the Lord. No such care had been taken with this nameless old woman, because her soul, unshriven, was screaming in the torments of eternal damnation. Her corpse lay as if something diseased had pushed itself out of the soil, ready to burst and spill forth the vileness of hell. That was what awaited them all now.

Alan lingered in Clegeham with Meg and the babies for as long as he dared, but in the end came to the cottage to try to persuade the rest of his family to leave with him. He was pushing a handcart loaded with their belongings, atop which sat their two-year-old son Edmund, bawling. Meg carried their infant daughter Judith on her hip, and her belly was round with their third on the way.

'Come with us,' he pleaded at the doorway. 'You cannot stay here.'

Their mother gestured inside, from whence the cries of her husband could be heard clearly. 'I cannot just leave him!' she said, indignant at the suggestion. Whether it was because of his leg or the pestilence, Dick Attlowe had spoken no word nor made any other noise than groans of pain for days now. 'What then of my marriage vows? Would you leave Meg? Would she leave you? What has made you so cold, Alan, to even talk this way? But your brother and sister should go,' she added, taking both Hester and Henry each by an arm and propelling them out of the cottage.

'Mother, no!' wailed Hester, turning back. 'Who will look after you?' With her mother tending her father, Hester had taken over the running of the household, not that there was much to take over. Food was running low, and Henry had taken to scavenging scraps from the deserted cottages; he'd already been in one fight with a group of hungry villein boys who'd had the same idea.

'You will go,' ordered her mother. 'I will not also watch you die damned.'

'Please, Hester,' echoed Meg, her brown eyes swimming with tears. 'Who will be aunt to my children if not you?' Baby Judith was sucking her fist and grizzling.

Hester felt her wilfulness swelling up behind her breastbone, the sinful heat of it which had caused so much damage already and which she knew she should swallow down and obey her mother. She knew she couldn't save her parents' souls, but equally she knew that she couldn't leave them to die, crawling and flyblown on their hands and knees like that old woman. It was too much after everything. Too much.

'No,' she said, setting her face against her mother. 'I will not. I will stay, even if you do not want me to. Alan will have to carry me like one of his children or else tie me up and drag me behind, but I will not leave.'

Henry – always the middle child, always the peacemaker – put himself between them. 'I will go,' he said.

'No.' Alan shook his head firmly. 'There must be a man in the house. You cannot leave your mother and sister unprotected.'

'Wait, hear me,' said Henry. 'I will come with you but only as far as the next town where, if the Lord wills it, I may find a priest or a friar, who I shall bring back here to save us.' He turned to Hester and his mother. 'I swear to you that I will return,' he said.

And so it was decided. The family which was all that Hester had ever known rent itself asunder and she waved goodbye to her brothers, her sister-in-law and her niece and nephew with tears blinding her last sight of them as they disappeared around a bend in the road that led out of Clegeham. She and her mother went back into the cottage where her father moaned in his delirium.

Hester wished she could have been surprised to find the first signs of death swelling in his neck. She wished she could have been more distraught, but all she had the energy for was a kind of numb, exhausted horror.

17

BREAD AND SALT

'WHAT HAPPENS IF YOUR BROTHER TURNS UP?' ASKED Toby.

'Don't worry,' Maya replied. 'It'll be fine. Mama has invited you; he won't cause a fuss.' The other good bit of news as far as Toby was concerned was that her dad was on a late shift at the post office, so he wouldn't have to run the gauntlet of any more violently overprotective male relatives.

Maya's home on the Pestle Road estate was one of three flats in a converted Victorian townhouse which had seen much better days. It was three storeys tall, with wonky roof slates and weeds peeping out of the guttering. The window frames were scabrous with peeling paint, and a brown veinwork of dead ivy still clutched at the crumbling brick. Half a dozen wheelie bins were crowded into a small front yard, like an honour guard leading up to the front door which boasted a stained-glass panel of tulips, though several pieces had been replaced by duct tape.

As they approached it she stopped and looked back at him. 'You're sure now?' she asked.

'Yes.'

'No second thoughts?'

'No.'

'Not going to suddenly change your mind again?'

'Definitely not.'

'Good. Because this is my mother who's invited you, and if you think Rajko is dangerous wait until you make *her* angry.'

'Maya, open the door!' whined Antony.

'Shut up, bug-face,' she replied, and let them in. Antony barrelled straight past them and inside, his footsteps thundering upstairs.

The first thing that hit Toby was the smell of damp. Ahead of him was the door to the ground-floor flat, and next to it a large plant pot with something green and glossy lurking in it. A faded carpet runner did little to soften the chill seeping up through the ancient floorboards. The old wooden balustrade shone darkly, and the stairs creaked as she led him up to the first floor. At some point in the distant past someone had tried to brighten the stairwell up with a coat of magnolia paint, but it couldn't hide the bulging of damp plaster and there was a long dark streak down the wall where countless shoulders had rubbed it over the years.

'Good job you don't live on the top floor,' he said.

'Bit of a pain for the old man who does,' she replied.

At the first landing the door to Flat 2 was already open, and framed in it was a woman about the same age as his mum; small with a broad, smiling face and waves of blonde-grey hair. She wore a violently multi-coloured jumper which stretched down to her knees and yoga pants below that. Gold dangled and flashed at her ears, neck, wrists, and fingers.

'*Dobrodošli!*' she beamed. 'Hello! Come in!'

'Hello, Mrs Gorić,' he said and held out his hand to shake hers but she ignored it and swept him into a jangling hug.

'*Mum,*' Maya growled. 'Don't embarrass him.'

'You'll have tea, yes?' said Mrs Gorić, ignoring her daughter. 'Before you study?'

'Of course. Thank you.'

He was led down a hallway with richly patterned carpet and walls covered in family photographs, and into a kitchen. It was cluttered and colourful with racks of pans and hanging cutlery; countertops busy with jars, bottles, canisters, and cartons; the cupboards a patchwork of postcards from all over the world. Mrs Gorić steered him to a breakfast counter where Antony was already installed, munching a biscuit, and said something to Maya in Serbian which must have been an order, judging by her sulky reply.

Mrs Gorić opened a tin and took out a round loaf of bread, richly patterned with plaits and rosettes, and a small ramekin filled with something white and crystalline which might have been sugar. 'Hleb i so,' she said. 'Bread and salt for the guest. The bread is pogača, to bring togetherness for our family, and the salt is to bring you prosperity and happiness in our home. Here…' She showed him how to tear off a chunk of the bread and sprinkle a pinch of salt over it before eating. It was light but not too dry, baked with nuts and dried fruit, and he enjoyed it more than he'd been expecting.

Maya went to the fridge, its door almost hidden behind a glittering mosaic of magnets, while her mum negotiated a complex routine of shifting some brightly coloured tins from around the kettle so that she could fill it at the sink. 'Mint or hibiscus?' she asked.

Maya groaned. 'She thinks she's being funny. Sorry about this.' She turned on her mother. 'Mum! Normal brown tea like we always drink!' It was interesting and kind of funny to hear her getting so wound up when she was normally so calm and collected at school.

'You know what?' said Toby. 'I think I like the sound of mint tea. I've never had that before. Is it a Serbian thing?'

Mrs Gorić turned a smile on her daughter which was part gloating, part conspiratorial. 'What a nice boy you've brought home!'

Maya groaned again. 'Kill me now.'

Mrs Gorić produced from the fridge a large pie dish, its contents obviously home-made, with a big wedge already missing and its filling a bright berry-red against the white ceramic.

'*Pita od višanja*,' said Mrs Gorić. 'Cherry pie. It's a family favourite. You need to feed your brain before studying.'

As she began to dish up two large slices Toby racked his brains for something to say; his one experience at the Trust's meet-and-greet had confirmed that he was terrible at social small talk, but he couldn't keep sitting there just grinning and nodding like an idiot. 'Maya's been great,' he said, for lack of anything better. 'Like, helping me catch up with the things I've missed. She's much better than me at maths.'

'You're new to Haleswell, I think? It seems an odd time to change schools. How are you settling in?'

He sketched out the details of how his family had come to move, obviously leaving out the more problematic details such as the break-in. The kettle boiled and Maya's mother made him a cup of mint tea, which was a lot more bitter than he'd been expecting so he sipped it politely and chased it with forkfuls of the pie, which was miles better than anything he'd had from a shop. He must have passed some kind of test because Mrs Gorić eventually shooed them out of the kitchen and into the living room where Antony was watching cartoons and a gas fire was blazing against the pervasive chill. They got their exercise books out on the large dining table and Maya helped him revise probability, which was the one thing that he just could not get his head around.

He'd lost track of time, but it couldn't have been much more than half an hour when he heard keys jingling in the front door and Rajko's voice yelling cheerfully in Serbian. Toby froze with his pen halfway to the paper. A few hours, she'd said. Maya's brother appeared in the doorway to the living room with a bag slung over one shoulder, saw him, and stopped dead. '*Šta će on ovde?*'

'He is a guest,' said Mrs Gorić, the warning clear in her tone. 'So you be nice. And talk English.'

Rajko hesitated a moment longer, then grinned. 'Okay, little landlord, good to have you here.' He dumped his bag on one of the armchairs and reached over the table to scuff Toby's hair. 'May I borrow him for a minute?'

Maya turned to her mother in protest. 'Mama!'

'What? I'll be nice! But if he's a guest then we've got some air to clear between us. Just a quick chat. Man business, you know?' He winked at Toby, who felt his bowels clench with anxiety. He thought about the knife in the outside pocket of his bag.

Rajko led him back out onto the landing where he produced a packet of cigarettes and offered Toby one.

'Um, no thanks, I don't.'

Rajko shrugged, lit up, put the pack away.

Toby waited for the threats, the fist in his shirt, the lighted cigarette end in his face. 'Anyway,' he added. 'Won't it set off the smoke alarm?'

Rajko barked a laugh. 'You think they actually fucking work?'

Toby supposed they didn't. Looking around, he couldn't even see one.

'Before,' said Rajko. 'You and me. You know that wasn't personal, right?'

Toby unclenched ever so slightly and looked at Maya's big brother more closely. He was looking out over the balustrade to the ground floor, blowing smoke thoughtfully. He didn't look like he was about to go psycho, but Toby wasn't about to dismiss the idea that this might be a trick. Still...

'Felt personal at the time,' he said.

Rajko gave him a look as if he'd suggested that the earth was flat, or that the moon was made of sparkly unicorn shit. 'You were being interested in my *sister*,' he said. 'I'd have done the same to anyone. She's too young.'

'Don't you think that's for her to decide?'

Rajko took another lungful and appeared to consider this carefully. 'No,' he decided. Still no threats, no fists, no burning. This was going well – or at least better than he'd feared.

'What's made the difference?' asked Toby. 'Why aren't you threatening to beat the shit out of me still?'

'Because you're a guest, of course. You're invited. Invitation changes things.'

'So what did you mean when you called me "landlord"?'

Rajko leaned over the rail and pointed to the ground floor. 'Down there lives Tamanna and Stuart. He does something in IT. She's a primary school teacher. His brother is living with them and she's getting fed up with it; we hear them arguing a lot.' He turned around and pointed up the stairwell. 'Second floor is the Ashoks. Mum, dad, grandmother, three kids. Very crowded. Last summer we had a big barbecue and the old lady made some fantastic vegetable koftas. See right up the top, in the attic conversion?' Toby found himself staring up the stairwell towards the topmost floor. 'Up there lives an eighty-two-year-old Jamaican man called Mr Griffith. He's a Windrush man – you know them?'

'Something about Caribbean immigrants after the war? The government deported a load of them illegally?'

Rajko nodded. Toby was surprised at how much Maya's brother knew about his neighbours, and a little embarrassed for himself. He'd never even known the names of the people living around them in his old place, let alone where they came from or what they ate.

'This is a very old building,' continued Rajko. 'Used to be

a home. Now it's flats, but all our heating still runs off the one boiler. You know that big freeze we had in February? Well Mrs Griffith died of pneumonia in it. They couldn't afford to run their gas fire and the central heating has been fucked for a year and a half. Now, guess who owns this building, and a dozen others like it, and gets kickbacks from the council to run it as cheaply as possible?'

Toby gestured helplessly.

'Haleswell Village Trust. The same organisation that your mother is the new Trustee of.'

'How did you know—?'

Rajko waved it away. 'The Internet, obviously. And so here you come, like the lord of the manor checking out the peasants, one of them being my little sister.' He said it quite conversationally but it got Toby's hackles up all the same.

'No, it's not like that—'

'I know, I know. I'm just fucking with you. So my father puts in a request to the Trust to come fix it and some maintenance guy comes and dicks around for like, ten minutes and then says it's fixed and fucks off, and it is fixed – for about a month. Then it dies again. So we complain and nothing happens, we complain and nothing happens, we complain and by now you see there's a pattern here, yeah? Eventually we pay for an engineer to come out and he takes a look at it and he just laughs, man. Fucking laughs. Says it should have been scrapped around the time JFK was shot. Tells us how much a new boiler will cost, but there's no way we can afford that, and why the fuck should we?' Suddenly he was angry again, spitting at Toby: 'It's your mother's people who are responsible, for fuck's sake! Eighteen months, and no central heating, and Mrs Griffith fucking dies because they can't afford to run their fire.'

Toby suspected that the reality of the situation was somewhat more complicated than that, but Raj didn't strike him as a person who had much patience with complications. The older boy finished his cigarette, stubbed it out on the banister and flicked the butt contemptuously down the stairwell, then turned to him. 'Now, you want to know about the fire escapes and smoke alarms?'

'No, I think I know what you're getting at.'

'Do you? Do you have any fucking clue what I'm getting at, little landlord?'

Toby watched him light another cigarette. 'Give us a go on that, then,' he said.

The corner of Rajko's mouth twitched upwards in a smirk, and he held up the cigarette. 'What, this? You want to be one of the big boys?' The idea seemed to amuse him. 'All right then. Try not to be sick all over yourself.'

He passed the cigarette over and Toby took a drag. It wasn't the first time he'd smoked, though he'd never made a habit of it, and he was able to hold it down without coughing and humiliating himself.

'You think I'm posh because I can use long words and live in a big house that I have nothing to do with,' he said. 'Fine. Whatever. I could have gone to the grammar but I didn't, not that I expect you to give a shit about that.' He took another drag. It was easier the second time. 'Before here I was living in a block of flats, and a while back we got broken into. I was the only one at home. Bloke knocked me around a bit. Yeah, I know, boo fucking hoo. They made me go to the school counsellor in case I was "traumatised" by the event, but the only thing traumatic was when the other kids found out why I was being taken out of lessons. Like the sessions couldn't have been arranged after school or on the weekend, I don't know. So there was this kid in the fifth form, George Cox, who kept following me around making spaz noises and shit jokes about bedwetting. Then one day I just had enough of it and put his head through a classroom window. George nearly lost an ear.' This was a slight exaggeration, but it had the intended effect of making Raj look at him with something other than contempt. Toby took a third and final drag on the cigarette and passed it back to Rajko, who was listening very closely. 'I'll talk to my mum. All you had to do was ask.'

In his head, Green Skull's mocking voice laughed *Oh you're such a badass motherfucker!* but he ignored it and went back indoors to work on his probability.

The walk home was only about half an hour, and he set off in plenty of time to get home for dinner. Mrs Gorić had wrapped the rest of the *pogača* in a tea towel that she said he could send back with Maya from school, and he munched it while walking. The shadows of late afternoon were lengthening, and a pall of dark rain cloud hung overhead except at the margins of the horizon, so that the light of the setting sun streamed in underneath and caused the shadows to fall at peculiar angles, as if the world had been turned sideways.

He tried to pretend that he couldn't see pale, bare feet pacing silently just behind his, and of course when he turned to look nobody was there.

18

HESTER
MAY 1349

HENRY DID NOT RETURN.

Over the following week, work in the fields faltered as those few villagers who remained spent most of their time digging graves and collecting as much spring blossom as they could, burning it in their homes to keep the plague out. It was too early in the year for any useful herbs to have matured, so when the blossom was stripped from the nearby trees they started collecting dung from the farm animals and burning that outside their doors.

Hester didn't recognise her own home as she made her customary trip down to the millstream for water. It was as if her father's surrender had given the disease licence to ravage the village unchecked. On the white stone on the village green someone had placed a bowl of honey and another of eggs in the hope that the Devil would be sated with it and leave them alone, but both had broken and spilled, and in the sun had festered into a foul-smelling mixture which was crawling with ants and flies. It was impossible to imagine dancing and laughing with her friends here less than a fortnight ago. Many houses were abandoned, with their doors wide open and dark like the eye sockets of skulls and random belongings strewn on the ground outside – either by animals or thieves or just in panic – while from those cottages that were still inhabited came the coughs, moans and pitiable begging of the sick. Veils of black smoke which stung the eyes and stank of burning shit hung in the air like something out of the Revelation, and through them her neighbours wandered like ghosts on whatever errands they thought might make a difference to their dying loved ones. Water from the holy spring at Haleswell might have helped, but Haleswell was still closed off from them, and the bitterness at this betrayal stung worse than the smoke. On the one occasion when a cloth merchant came down the road from the north in a cart, he told of how the villagers there were aggressively patrolling their parish boundary in armed groups, and then hurried on his way, crossing himself.

When Dick Attlowe died, Hester was given help in digging his grave by her neighbour Janot, who had once carried a calf five miles. There was nobody else, her mother now being sick and bedridden in turn. The day was damp, the ground thickly sodden, and though Hester was accustomed to physical labour she hadn't eaten properly for days and was weak. With the miller having fled, she was forced to bake with old rye flour which had become rancid and infested with weevils.

'You should stop,' said Janot. 'Let me finish this.' He was pallid and feverish himself, leaning on his shovel and panting.

'No,' she grunted, heaving at the soil. 'I will not.' Her father's stubbornness was in her still, even though he lay on the ground next to them, stitched into a sheet. The grave was far too shallow, but the prospect of leaving him unburied and at the mercy of whatever scavengers would call this place home after all the people had died was unthinkable.

She did pause for a moment, though. 'Why do you suppose I have not yet taken sick?' she wondered aloud. 'I saw the stranger first before any of us. It should have been me.'

'Maybe it is because you are the reeve's daughter,' replied Janot. 'The Lord will protect you if nobody else.'

But she was beginning to wonder about the Lord, too. It seemed much more likely that she was being kept alive as a punishment to see everyone she loved die one by one because she hadn't told her parents about the sick stranger as soon as she'd known. She looked at the line of fresh graves, nearly two dozen so far but with many more lying dead in their homes even so, and then at the church which now lay empty.

After they buried her father and Janot went to his own home to rest, she went into the church to see if God was still there.

It was tiny compared to that of Haleswell, with a few benches and a table for an altar, though its simple plaster was decorated with bright paintings of stories from the saints' lives. The candles had all been stolen so that what dim light there was came only from the one small louvred window above the altar, for Clegeham was too poor to afford coloured glass. Hester closed her eyes and listened carefully, trying to find that still, calm core of herself where she sometimes felt the sense of a comforting presence during Cuthbert's sermons. But she felt utterly hollow, empty of love or hope. This time the only thing she heard was the growling of her own belly.

And something skittering in the shadows.

Onto the altar leapt a rat. It was sleek and glossy, obviously well fed, and it watched her fearlessly with eyes which gathered the meagre light into two hard points. It might have looked like a rat but Hester knew who it really was, and she knelt before it in weary acceptance. 'He has truly abandoned us, then,' she said. 'This place is yours now.'

The rat tilted its head, listening.

'Please, take me. But spare the life of my mother, I beg you.' She clasped her hands and held them out in supplication. She was damned, she knew, but if it was the price of her mother's life and soul then it was no price at all. And if she failed, they would all burn anyway.

The rat leapt off the altar and reappeared, closer, sniffing at her. Considering.

'I pledge myself to your service if only you will spare my family.'

The rat darted in and sank its teeth into the soft flesh at the side of her right palm just underneath her littlest finger. Hester screamed and tried to pull back, but the creature held on for a moment, its yellow teeth locked in her flesh, its glittering eyes locked just as mercilessly on hers.

Then it let go and disappeared into the shadows.

Hester clutched her bleeding hand, gasping at the pain and staring after where the rat had gone.

'Thy will be done,' she whispered.

She bound her hand with moss and a scrap of linen, and when she returned home she found her mother seated in a chair by the hearth in the centre of the main room, filling a small clay jar with old needles and rusted nails. It also looked like she'd thrown her household broom onto the fire; the birch twigs of its brush end were crackling brightly.

'Mama?' she asked carefully, fearing that her mother had taken leave of her senses. 'What are you doing?'

'I am making a witch bottle,' her mother replied, dropping in another nail. Then she looked up at Hester. 'The *gwrach clefyd* is here.'

'The... goo-rack...?'

'She is from my mother's country to the west. She is a hag that brings winter and pestilence. The Church has failed us, but the older remedies will not. Sharp iron will repel Her.' Her mother took up a pitcher of the house ale and topped off the jar with it, then began to seal the lid with a wooden plug and some waxed thread. 'Ale from my hearth marks this as protection for my family. My only regret is that I feared your father's anger and did not do this sooner.'

'But why are you burning your besom?'

'The *gwrach clefyd* carries either a broom or a rake with which to strike us down – if a rake, you may be lucky that you will pass between its teeth and survive. If a broom, She will sweep all before Her, and none will live.' Her mother smiled grimly as she worked. 'I do not intend to give Her any more help than necessary.'

19

THE FOX AND THE RAT

IT WAS A FLICKER OF MOVEMENT – JUST A FLASH OF tawny fur in Trish's peripheral vision, too fast to be sure it was there at all – which caught her attention.

She was in the ground-floor study overlooking the side of the house, surrounded by box files and folders, her head full of the household finances. It was ridiculous that they should still be finding themselves in tight circumstances, but there it was. Peter's income, which as a freelancer had always been a bit erratic, was more reliable now that he'd taken on work for the Clegg Farm development, but that was offset by her quitting her job at the distribution warehouse and the higher rates of household insurance, council tax, and the blizzard of other unexpected costs. All of this would have been enough of a headache now that she was a homeowner rather than a tenant, but even more so since the home in question was a place like Stone Cottage. Put simply, Haleswell was a bloody expensive part of the city to live.

Then there had been the nightmare of sorting out utilities providers, transferring the TV licence, setting up the broadband...

Nothing more than a flash, left to right, of something furry and orange coming in from the front garden, scooting right under her window and towards the back.

She rose and peered out through the glass, seeing only the dark glossy leaves of the rhododendron bushes guarding the fence a couple of metres away on that side. Whatever it was, it was gone. A stray cat, most likely. Then a new idea hit her, of another cost which she hadn't considered because in the flat it hadn't been allowed, but which nobody in the family would begrudge: they could finally get a pet! They could visit the nearest animal shelter and find a rescue cat. Or a dog. Toby would love a dog. Having something to look after and be responsible for might help to stop him sliding into the pit he seemed to be digging for himself lately, the deepest part of which so far had been him coming home reeking of cigarettes, though Lord knew how deep it might go. It was a shame that he'd never been able to enjoy one of the simplest of childhood experiences, that of playing with his own puppy; it would at least have been some companionship in the absence of any younger brothers or sisters.

And just like that, a small voice spoke up in the back of her skull: *Well we all know whose fault that is, don't we?*

She hadn't heard that voice in a very, very long time. Or if she had, she'd learned to ignore its sly insinuations.

All through the years after Toby's birth it had taunted her, whispering with hope at the start of each new pregnancy and then sneering at the barrenness of its end, through the arguments with Peter, the series of humiliating doctors' examinations and tests to determine what was wrong with her – as if anything was wrong with her and not the bastard who had stolen her unborn babies. *He has gathered them to His bosom and you will be reunited with them in His kingdom*, that voice told her. *Be strong in your faith and your love for your husband and the Lord. Try again.* And she had, until she'd realised that the problem wasn't that her faith lacked strength, it was simply that nobody was listening anymore. *Try again* wasn't a reassurance but a goad, to see how much she could take before she broke. So she broke, and went on the pill, and for a while that was gasoline on the flame of the voice of guilt that screamed inside her, burning, but with each month that passed it became a bit less shrill, and every time she and Peter made love it was just about the two of them, nobody else, until eventually it was silent altogether. Or at least bearable.

'Fuck you,' she said to the voice, the silent house around it, and the indifferent heavens above. 'My little boy's getting a puppy, so fuck you.'

She found some ham in the fridge, cut it up with the kitchen scissors onto a small plate and carried it outside to the back garden to see if there was a stray animal she could befriend. When she saw it, she was simultaneously delighted and dismayed, because it was so unexpected and yet she knew that it could never be house-trained.

There was a fox in her garden. Not exactly what she had in mind as far as dogs went.

It was right at the very back, where the fence was screened by thick shrubbery and trees, looking back towards her though not directly at her – past her, at something in the direction from which it had come running.

There was something very wrong here. It should have run off at the first scent of her, but it didn't even seem aware that she existed. If it had been disturbed in its den and was being chased, what was chasing it, and why hadn't it continued straight through, over the fence and into next door? Why was it just standing there, rigid and panting hard, one paw poised as if paralysed in mid-stride? Now she saw that its eyes were wide, ears flat back against its head, serrated white teeth bared against its pink tongue. What could be scaring it so badly that it would ignore a human being?

Then she saw the dead girl standing in the bushes blocking the fox's escape, and she knew.

Trish wasn't aware of Her appearing; it was more like one of those hidden picture puzzles where an image which had been there all along suddenly became visible out of the jumble of supposedly chaotic background elements. There were no shadows to hide the girl's condition, nothing to provide the comforting illusion that She could be alive, however catastrophically ill. Trish took in the lank hair, the corpse-white flesh abloom with festering sores, some so deep that bone showed, the primitive shift dress and the bare feet, and she fell back a step towards the door, clutching the frame for support. The crucifix hanging by the front door seemed laughably inadequate protection now, or maybe she'd made it so with her doubt.

'I'm sorry…' she whispered. 'Please, make Her go away…'

From underneath the stained and ragged hem of the dead girl's dress, the rats came, tumbling over and between Her feet, and also from the passageways down both sides of the house where they had driven the fox – because She was certain now that the animal had been herded here, and there was only one reason why that could be.

'Oh God no…'

The fox attempted to make a dash for the back fence but the rats were on it in moments. The sound of the attack was like nothing Trish had ever heard: the fox's cries sounded distressingly like a child's high-pitched screaming over the chorus of the rats' high, looping squeals, which themselves had a texture like hundreds of nails being dragged repeatedly down blackboards. They swarmed all over the fox as it spun and snapped at them, grey bodies against the red, and then a glossier red still as they bit, tore, and fell away with shreds of flesh in their teeth.

'No…' Trish said louder, becoming angry now. This was monstrous. Mindless butchery. But the dead girl continued to watch Her sport, grinning.

The fox's head rose up, thrashing in an attempt to dislodge two rats which had their jaws fastened in its throat, and for a split second Trish thought that its rolling white eyes met her horrified gaze. Then it was brought to the ground by the sheer weight of its enemies, and they were attacking its belly, ripping it open to get at the soft internal organs, and suddenly there was a shriek from the fox that tore at her ears like claws and a lot more blood as coils of purple-grey viscera unspooled. Her own stomach lurched as she saw that there were rats burrowing inside the dying creature; she could see it bulging with the press of their invasion like some obscene parody of birth, and that was too much for her.

There was a rake leaning against the wall; she grabbed it, screamed, 'No! Get the fuck off!' and began to beat at the seething swarm. They were reluctant to give up their prize. One or two even made nipping darts at her ankles. But when several lay crushed and others had to drag themselves away, wounded, the spirit of the swarm seemed to be broken, and they melted away as quickly as they had appeared, leaving the fox dead on her lawn in a mess of itself.

Shoulders heaving with exertion and the impulse to throw up, Trish turned to brandish her weapon at the dead girl. 'What exactly the fuck is going on here?' she demanded. 'Who...' she swallowed thickly. 'What are you? What do you want from me?'

The girl said not a word, but simply pointed at the eviscerated animal and then at Trish herself, making the connection clear. Her grin had disappeared. This was not sport anymore. Then She too was gone, melted into the background of the world.

Trish fell to her knees in the grass beside the butchered animal. When she saw that one of its back legs was still twitching, she thought that things couldn't possibly get any worse.

Then her phone, tucked into her jeans' back pocket, buzzed.

'Oh Jesus, what now?' she groaned.

It was a text from Peter: *Tobys in A&E. On way now. School wont say why but T says he was bitten by something.*

She watched a rat, whose spine she'd obviously broken with the rake, dragging itself into the bushes with its forepaws, and knew what it was that had attacked her son.

From where Toby was sitting, near the middle of the school dinner hall, all he could hear at first were shrieks of alarm and the plastic scraping of chairs being hurriedly shoved back as kids leapt to their feet.

'Food fight?' said Krish.

He shrugged *dunno* and kept a wary eye forward in case the stupidity spread in their direction, but otherwise it wasn't worth moving for, yet. He took another bite of his budget chicken zinger burger.

Then excited cries of 'Rat! There's a rat!' reached him as kids came running past, though not all of them; a decent number had pulled back to a safe distance in a semi-circle around the serving hatch, their fascination overpowering their fear. Most of them had their phones out, videoing something that the press of their bodies prevented him from seeing properly.

Krish grinned at him. 'Come on! Let's have a look!'

'Ah, I'm not so sure that's a good idea.' All of a sudden the sound of the crowd's excited chatter sounded too much like rats chittering below his bedroom window.

They were tumbling about Her feet, almost as if playing.

'Whatever.' Krish ran to join the others. Curious despite himself, Toby followed at a wary distance.

A large black rat was sitting on the glass counter of the school kitchen servery, and the dinner hall was descending into bedlam.

The rat, for its part, seemed utterly unfazed by the crowd that it was attracting or the disturbance that it was creating. Behind it, Toby could see the kitchen staff absolutely shitting themselves. Someone was yelling into a phone. Others had picked up whatever makeshift weapons were to hand – spatulas, serving spoons. One had a massive knife. The prospect of seeing this routine lunchtime descend into a chaotic slapstick scene of panicked adults chasing a rodent around a large industrial kitchen was too good to resist, but the rodent in question didn't seem interested in playing. It didn't even seem particularly interested in the food in the steel serving tubs directly underneath. It was crouched on the glass, wary and alert, its black-bead eyes glittering, its pointed nose in the air, sniffing. Almost as if it were searching for something. Or someone.

Its head snapped around, just like hers had done, as if it had read his thoughts, and it saw him through the crowd.

'Oh shit—'

The rat made a chittering noise and leapt. It weaved its way between the feet of kids who leapt away, shrieking, and then it was clawing up his left leg, digging for purchase through his trousers and into the skin of his legs beneath. Its black eyes locked like needles on his, and he knew that it was coming to chew them out of his face.

Toby managed to get his left hand up in self-defence just in time for the rat's teeth to sink into the soft flesh below his pinkie finger. The pain was like nothing he had ever felt before, like having his hand clamped in a vice made of bone – and worse, because he knew that the creature's bite was poison and his imagination told him he could feel it pumping into his flesh which was already hot and swollen tight with infection. And the *weight* of the thing squirming, claws raking his forearm as it fought for a tighter grip, pink tail lashing like a soft, warm worm. It revolted him on every level. It shifted, gnawing, making a muffled high-pitched snarling, and blood began to flow more freely, his blood in its mouth, and he fell back screaming for someone to get it off him.

After their shock, people ran to his aid. Krish beat the rat with a plastic tray. Somebody else got the long metal handle of a serving spoon into the hinge of its jaws and tried to lever it off. Hands grabbed it and pulled, even though that made its teeth tear his flesh more. Eventually it was prised off him and it turned its bite on his rescuers so that they dropped it and it streaked from the dining hall.

Someone was bandaging his hand with a tea towel as he felt shock begin to wash away the world in waves of grey. Faces crowded around, ignoring the shrill voice of a teacher yelling at them to get out of the way, and right at the very back of them he thought he saw the dead girl, ignored by the crowd because of course She couldn't really be there, enjoying the spectacle with a mocking grin.

20

EMERGENCY

SIX HOURS.

That was how long the receptionist at Accident and Emergency told him it would take for them to treat his rat-bitten child. Six. Fucking. Hours. And they couldn't even guarantee that. He was told that the Minor Injuries Unit in Shirley was temporarily closed due to staffing shortages, and he could either wait until it reopened tomorrow or take a seat.

Peter had almost lost it then, but both Trish and Toby looked so wrung-out that he couldn't bring himself to inflict on them the stress of seeing him Make A Scene, so he swallowed his temper and took his seat.

He could easily see why it might take so long – even at mid-afternoon on a weekday the waiting area was rammed. Every one of the orange plastic chairs, bolted together in racks, was occupied, mostly by people who also had

203

'minor injuries' such as Toby's, but that included a lot of bloodstained dressings and limbs clutched while waiting to be told how badly broken they were. He saw lots of elderly people, some obviously distressed rather than injured, some who should have been treated in their homes by district nurses or care workers who hadn't appeared because there simply weren't enough of them. One middle-aged man was gasping with chest pains, waiting to be told whether or not he was having a heart attack. A young mother was trying to soothe a squalling, red-faced infant while her two toddlers rolled on the floor. He watched the police bring in a young woman covered in blood and hurling verbal abuse at everyone around her – possibly an addict, possibly with mental health problems, most likely both – looking to pass her off into care which didn't exist.

'First thing I do when we're out of here,' he muttered, 'is get Environmental Health on those fucking idiots. Rats in schools? It's like the fucking dark ages, this country, I tell you.'

Toby had told them what there was to tell, but Trish kept quizzing him anyway. 'Are you sure there was nothing else, when the rat bit you?'

'What do you mean, else?' asked Peter. 'Isn't that enough?'

'Anything,' she continued. 'Were there any… people there that you didn't recognise?'

Toby was gripping his hand; the bandage that the school first-aider had put on was already spotted with red. It could have been worse, he'd been told; the rat's teeth had made deep punctures but at least nothing had torn. Funny, but he didn't feel like he'd gotten off lucky. He looked up, wariness in his eyes, like when he knew they were trying to catch him out in a lie. 'People?' he asked. 'Like who?'

'I don't know,' she continued, but Peter could tell from her voice that she knew *exactly*. 'A strange boy, maybe? Or a girl?'

Toby inhaled sharply. 'A girl? What kind of girl?'

'What in God's name are you two on about?' Peter demanded.

'Patricia!' interrupted a new voice. Reverend Dobson was heading towards them briskly, along with Nash and another of the Trustees who he recognised from the meet-and-greet but couldn't immediately put a name to. She had dark, shoulder-length hair framing a wide face which gave the impression that she was smiling even though her face was set in the same expression of concern as the other two. 'What a terrible thing to have happened!' continued the reverend. 'Is Toby all right?'

'Um, sorry, but what are you doing here?' Peter asked, not meaning to sound rude; it was just so utterly unexpected.

'I called her,' said Trish.

'You called a priest? What the hell for? Did you think he needed the last rites or something?'

'Peter,' said Nash. 'Calm down. We're here to help.'

'And these two? What are they here for?'

The dark-haired woman stepped forward. 'Mr Feenan, as well as being the Trust's director of environmental services, I'm also a qualified doctor.' His memory supplied a name for her now: Esme Barlow. He'd only ever met her that one time. 'I was wondering if you'd like me to take a look at your son's hand? Somewhere a bit less busy than here? Somewhere closer to home. A bit safer.'

'What, you mean like a private clinic?'

Nash laughed softly. 'Do you really care?'

Peter looked around at the desperate faces in the waiting room and found that he didn't.

One of the many things that the Feenans hadn't got around to arranging yet was a new doctor, so they were taken to Covenant House General Practitioners' Surgery in Haleswell. It was just as busy as anywhere else – albeit on a much smaller scale and with more comfortable chairs, magazines, a coffee machine and a table of toys for small children to play with – but Esme Barlow had a few quiet words with the receptionist and they were all ushered through into an empty treatment room. His son sat up on the examination bed and in Peter's mind there was absolutely no difference between now and when his little boy was three and sitting in a room exactly like this one having his MMR jab and needing Daddy to hug him. He knew that it didn't matter how old Toby became – how independent or wise or experienced, maybe even with kids of his own – somewhere he would always be three and needing a hug.

'Now then, young man,' Barlow said to Toby. 'Let's have a look at where you've been chewed.'

As they watched Barlow gently examining Toby's wound, Nash turned to Peter. 'I suppose it's only natural, isn't it, dialling 999? Adrenalin's going, your brain goes on autopilot, you do what you've been taught. Like the joke about the nun in the launderette – old habits dye hard? Difficult to remember the priority contacts in a situation like that.'

'I have no idea what you're on about,' Peter replied. 'What priority contacts?' He hadn't actually called 999, but correcting Nash on this point seemed utterly irrelevant right at this very minute.

'What – you mean nobody arranged that with you?' Nash seemed genuinely surprised, and even upset. 'Oh shit, Peter, I am so sorry!' He took out his wallet while muttering darkly about someone getting their arse handed to them for this, dug for something that looked like an ordinary business card, and handed it over. 'Pop these names in your phone,' he said. 'Next time you need the emergency services, make sure you ask for one of these chaps by name.'

'What does it do?'

'Gets you the emergency services, obviously. Standard fire, police, ambulance – just without so much of the waiting around. Bumps you up the priority chain.'

'Queue-jumping, you mean?'

His disapproval obviously wasn't the reaction Nash had been hoping for. 'Listen, Peter, the NHS uses private ambulances all the time, more and more each year. Private contractors are getting billions of pounds' worth of health service contracts. There is a subscription-paid private police force already on the streets in London. Even the bloody military, for God's sake, pays other people to run its fire and rescue service. Everything is outsourced. You live in the twenty-first century, you must know this!'

'But surely,' said Trish, 'if there's someone dying of a heart attack they're not going to attend an animal bite first, are they?'

'Well obviously we're not talking about driving past people dying in the street. That would be much too obvious.' Nash shrugged. 'Everything is contracted for. It just depends on the terms of the contract.' Seeing their expressions, he ploughed on before either of them could protest. 'Oh I know, of course it's not fair, swanning past all those people out there waiting their turn like good citizens. Why should you get to jump the queue? Why should any of us? It's entitled. Privileged. And yet your son's sitting there bleeding, so do you care? You'd be a liar if you said that you did.'

Peter turned to him. 'Why are you even here?'

Nash nodded at Reverend Dobson. 'Because she asked me. Because your wife asked her. Because the Trust—'

'Looks after its own, yeah yeah yeah, I get it.'

Nash laughed. 'Oh, you do not remotely get it.'

Trish sat next to Toby and stroked his hair. 'Tell us about the girl,' she said.

So Toby did. And just when Peter thought that what he was hearing couldn't become any more unbelievable, Trish told her side of the story.

'Who is She, Joyce?' Trish asked the reverend, when she had finished. 'Why does She want to hurt us?'

21

HESTER
LATE MAY 1349

TWO DAYS LATER CRISTINA ATTLOWE DIED VOMITING
blood and raving with delirium. She resembled something
inhuman, with her misshapen flesh livid with purple-black
patches and weeping sores, and her fingers hooked into
gnarled black claws. Between moans of pain and coughing
fits that brought bright red blood up onto her lips she asked
repeatedly after her husband whom she believed was away on
village business. 'Is he not returned from Haleswell even yet?'

'No, Mam,' replied Hester.

'But how can he be away so long? He has not taken his
tally sticks so he cannot be at reckoning with the sheriff. Oh
where is he?'

Her mother's anxiety was directed at the pile of her
father's tally sticks which, like so much of the household,
lay in a jumbled mess on the floor. One of his main duties
had been to carry accounts of the produce from Sir Roger

de Lindesay's lands to the sheriff in Haleswell, for the purpose of which such sticks were commonly used since most folk, including her father, were unschooled in letters. A stick would be carved with notches to represent quantities of grain, or wool, or any commodity, then split lengthways with one half going to the recipient and the other to the producer, so that each had a copy and neither could cheat the other. She remembered the long hours her father would spend laboriously carving those notches, and the weeks – months, years – of scrupulous reckoning they represented, accounting for the work of Sir Roger's serfs, dealing with their thefts and idleness and receiving only surly resentment from them in exchange, and having to manage the manor's ever-increasing demands so that the poorest of Clegeham would still be able to eat.

And now, all those sticks lay in a discarded pile and her father lay in an unhallowed grave with his wife soon to join him while the great and the good of Haleswell closed themselves off from their neighbours' need, having taken what they could for as long as it didn't threaten them. Even the Devil had abandoned her, reneging on their deal, if there had ever been one. Her rat-bitten hand was swollen red and burning with infection.

Unbidden, a cold fury rose up in Hester Attlowe's soul, black and blinding. It overwhelmed and drowned her reason for an unguessable time, and when she came back to herself she found that her mother had died. No words had been said over her. There would be no peace for her in the Lord's embrace. Another crime to lay at the door of Haleswell.

'There shall be a reckoning,' she promised – not just to her mother's corpse, but the empty cottage and the dying village around her. 'Their debt shall be paid in full.'

She felt the first scratching itch at the back of her nose, and it was almost a relief.

Lacking the strength to move, let alone bury her mother, Hester simply drew the coverlet over her face and wept; all the while the fury brimmed so high within her that she was surprised her tears did not come out as black as pitch. Then she shook herself, for weeping had never accomplished anything, said a last goodbye and left her home.

The church was as dark as it had been before, but now there was an unmistakable stench of putrefaction about the place, as if something had crawled in to die. There were three rats sitting on the altar this time, which Hester thought seemed only appropriate; one each for the souls of her father, mother and brother.

This time she did not kneel.

'I am done with begging,' she told them, and their master who she knew was listening. 'I am done pleading for lives which cannot be saved. Take them. Take us all if that is your will. I no longer pledge myself to you out of love for my family, but out of vengeance for them. Take my service or not, for I am done.'

Without waiting to see the reaction to this, she strode out and went to make her reckoning.

Her family's cottage lay at the southern end of the village, to take advantage of the sun, and so the road north to Haleswell led past the homes of all her dead and dying neighbours. She saw Janot digging through a pile of refuse in search of something to eat, and in spite of everything that had happened she was still shocked at how gaunt his once-muscular frame had become. He was pale and sweating, red-rimmed about the eyes. He saw her and stopped, wincing as if caught in some shameful act.

'I was...' he started, gesturing at the heap. Then he coughed with a sound like stones being churned in a bucket, bent double with the hacking. 'I have it,' he gasped, when the spasm had passed. 'The pestilence. I will be dead soon, so it can hardly matter if I am starving or not. Still.' He coughed again. 'Where are you going?'

'Haleswell,' she replied. 'I mean to speak to the sheriff. I will remind him of his obligations. They must help us.'

'You will never see him. They have sealed themselves off from the world.'

She raised her chin. 'Then I will die at their door if that is all I can do, but at the very least they will see me. They will close their eyes to our plight no longer.'

He considered this for a moment. 'May I join you? I might just as well die there than here, and it would be nice to have the company of a friend for a while.'

Hester hesitated. It had not occurred to her that she might not have to do this alone. The black fury abated somewhat and she moved to embrace him. 'You can keep me safe on the road,' she smiled into his shoulder.

'I shall be glad if I can keep on my feet.'

Nor had it occurred to Hester that there would be others remaining in Clegeham who wished to accompany her, but as she and Janot walked past the untended fields and cottages, their surviving inhabitants appeared, curious. To those who asked, Hester told them just what she'd told Janot. Some were scornful, and turned back to tend their dying, but quite a few joined her on the road northward. Many had armed themselves with farm tools and muttered darkly about taking what was rightfully theirs. By the time she passed the mill at the northern end of Clegeham she had nearly thirty souls at her heels. Many were sick and had to be helped by their neighbours, so that it took them most of the morning to cover the single mile through woodland to Haleswell. Several didn't make it, but sat down by the roadside to rest and simply never got up again. After the stench and smoke of their home, the woods were full of birdsong and sunlight, and bluebells carpeted the ground in a violet haze, but for all that it was perilous now. Not just for the fear of simple violence, but because if their neighbours had closed their doors to them, breaking that oldest and most powerful of customs, then this was now an alien country and their journey a more dangerous pilgrimage than anything Father Cuthbert had attempted.

They heard the hounds first: a great baying which sounded like a hunt echoing through the trees.

Then around a turn in the road, they saw the clearing where a large stone like a horse's trough had been placed, and an anxious, shuffling group on the other side. The men of Haleswell were also armed with farm tools, though here and there metal glinted from blades set on longer poles. They were scarved with rags tied across their mouths and noses, either as protection against the pestilence or to hide their shame, and every so often one of them would lift his mask to drink from a leather bottle which was being passed around. Dogs strained at the leashes in their hands, and one or two were mastiffs which must have come from Sir Roger's own kennels. Hunting dogs. It was a disquieting combination: dogs and ale and a large mob of fearful men.

'Come no further!' one of them cried. 'You may not enter!'

'We are from Clegeham!' Hester called in reply. 'Of the manor of Sir Roger de Lindesay. We have come to see him, to beseech his help. Our village is dying. Please, do not deny us this!'

There was laughter amongst the mob, and one stepped forward. He was better dressed than the rest, in a blue tunic and a wide leather belt, and carried a heavy bailiff's staff. Though she could not see his face, hard eyes glinted at her above his mask.

'Who is this girl?' he sneered, and with a shock she recognised the voice of Bailiff Naissh. 'Are the men of Clegeham brought so low that they must have women and children to speak for them?'

Hester walked right up to the stone, and into its hollow she threw several of her father's tally sticks. 'My father was Richard Attlowe, reeve of our village, accountable to Sir Roger's sheriff,' she said. 'As are you, John Naissh. He managed the manor's lands and collected its rents, and never was fault found with his reckoning. My father, who you drank with not but a fourteen-night ago. You drank ale brewed by my mother at her own hearth and poured by my own hands! How can you do this, now? How can you? We have given all that is owed to our lord, uncomplaining, year in, year out. Our fealty and our faith are beyond question. And now we ask for his help.'

Naissh's voice was cold in reply. 'You bring death to our home. What shall we give you, then? The lives of our own wives and children?'

'I had hoped simply for some water, at least.' One of Naissh's mob tittered at that, though she had not meant it in jest, and the bailiff shot him a venomous look.

'You are insolent, girl,' he growled, turning back to her. 'Take your rabble and leave now.'

The black fury began to rise in her again; it had subsided during their walk along the road but not left her entirely. 'No, I will not,' she said to him, her voice low and cold like a stone at the bottom of a well. 'I have lost my brothers and watched both my mother and my father go to a godless death. Insolent is only one of many things I am. I ask only for water, from St Sebastian's Well. Surely you would not begrudge us that which was blessed for the good of all?'

Naissh approached the other side of the stone, so that she was well within reach of his bailiff's staff. He raised it, and for a moment she was sure that he was going to strike her, but instead he put the end of it to her chest and shoved so that she stumbled backwards. There were angry murmurs from her people.

'There is nothing for you here!' the bailiff shouted, to her and the rest. 'Not a single crumb of bread nor a single drop of water! Any man, woman or child who sets foot over the Haleswell parish boundary – whether they have the pestilence or not – will be met with swift and certain punishment!' From within his tunic he pulled a roll of parchment which he brandished aloft in one fist. 'It is so set out in this warrant, agreed by a jury of freemen in the court baron, ratified and sealed by Sir Roger de Lindesay, and enforced by these his bailiffs.'

'It seems to me that fear makes for poor law-making,' she replied, seething. 'So it is murder then? You will turn to brigandry?'

'Not brigandry. The defence of our homes and livelihoods is right and just, and we are acting in due accord with the laws of man and God.'

It might have ended there, but the blackness raged so violently within Hester that she let it flood her, filling her eyes and taking over her voice. 'Why then damn your warrant!' she screamed. 'And your jury! And the sheriff and all your pox-ridden mob of little bailiff bully boys, and that whoreson Sir Roger himself! Damn your God! The Devil take all of you!'

There was a gasp from one of the bailiff's men, who let slip the hold on his dog's leash. Its snarl was like a shout of glee as it bounded across the clearing and leapt on the nearest Clegeham man, a serf named Jacob. He fell back, screaming, the dog fastened to his arm, while the men on either side hacked at the animal with sickles and its owner gave a howl of outrage and dashed to its rescue, followed by his mates.

The uneasy peace of the clearing disintegrated into a

maelstrom of screaming and barking, with the already weak villagers of Clegeham falling under the scythe blades and cudgels of their neighbours. Over and above the noise Naissh's voice rang out: 'They are Satan's imps! Kill them all! For the sake of your families let none live!' Blood splashed the tree trunks and dripped from the leaves like rain. With neighbour attacking neighbour it was hard to make sense of the chaos, but Hester thought she saw behind it all, standing still and silent beneath the trees, a tall figure veiled in grey. It did nothing but watch, and it held a broom in its hands just like her mother's. Then Naissh's staff slammed into the side of her head and the world went away in a bright blur. She was dimly aware of falling, and when she hit the ground he struck her again, this time in the ribs, and something there caved in with a deep crunch like someone stepping on ice. She couldn't breathe, nor could she move as he stood above her and raised the end of his staff above her face and screamed, 'Die! Just die, will you?'

All she could do was glare up at him with her eyes full of glittering black hatred, and as the final blow came down said to him the only thing that had ever seemed to make any difference:

'No. I will not.'

And the rats came.

They poured out from the undergrowth by the score, the hundred, the thousand, in a seething tide of grey bodies that flooded across the clearing and around the legs of those who fought there. The dogs went berserk, abandoning their human prey in favour of a more ancient enemy, snapping and worrying and flinging furry corpses in all directions. The swarm ignored the villagers of Clegeham – what few were still standing – with their main mass concentrating on the body of Hester Attlowe, boiling over and burying her completely. When the combined efforts of dogs and men finally succeeded in driving them off, there was no sign of her whatsoever – not a scrap of hair or clothing, or so much as a drop of blood on the ground where she'd fallen.

Profoundly unnerved, the men of Haleswell carried the bodies into the woods far to one side of the road and buried them in a pit, then vowed amongst themselves to forget everything about it.

They continued to patrol the boundary of their parish as the course of the Black Death ebbed and flowed over the next two years, and even though there were some unpleasant confrontations nothing came close to the scale of that massacre. It was never spoken of – except in the silence of haunted glances passed between those who had been there.

When some places die they leave monuments of their passing by which they are remembered: green mounds in the grass, broken stumps of pillars, or pieces of wall. Others, like their inhabitants, disappear utterly, as if they had never existed. All word of Clegeham was erased from the manor's records, and the village itself died. Woodland crept back to reclaim the fields; birds stole the roof thatch for their nests; wind and rain did the rest. Travellers on the Stratford Road crossed themselves and hurried past the overgrown ruins which could be glimpsed between the trees. As the years passed and Haleswell prospered and expanded, farmers clearing the ground for new pastures to the south found the derelict remains and took the last of the useful timber for their barns, while the crumbling old mill and the church were demolished stone by stone for walling. The bones of Clegeham were subsumed into Haleswell, and vanished.

22

REVELATION

'SEVEN HUNDRED YEARS AGO THE PEOPLE OF Haleswell committed a terrible crime, and our village has been cursed ever since,' said the reverend. She stood by the large picture window in Stone Cottage's living room, looking out at the parish stone in the garden. It was late afternoon and the light was dimming. Nash and Esme Barlow flanked her, sitting in armchairs while the Feenans sat in a tight, protective knot on the sofa. Toby's hand was heavily bandaged; he'd been given three stitches, a tetanus booster and a week's prescription of amoxicillin to guard against infection.

'Historical records are sketchy so we don't know the exact circumstances,' Rev. Dobson continued, 'only that one of the victims was a girl named Hester Attlowe whose undying rage causes Her to haunt the outskirts of the ancient parish boundary. In a sense the *why* is academic – what She wants is very simple: vengeance on the leaders of Haleswell. Which is to say you, me, and every other member of the Trust.'

'But we haven't done anything!' protested Toby.

Nash gave a hollow laugh.

'She doesn't care,' said Joyce. 'It's not what we've done or not done that matters to Her, it's who we *are*. We represent everything She despises, so we must be punished.'

'That's not fair!'

'You say that like it means something,' Nash muttered.

'Shh,' said Trish, stroking Toby's hair. 'Let her finish.' She turned back to Dobson. 'You say the records are sketchy. So how do you know any of this?'

'Towards the end of the nineteenth century there was a surge of interest in occult phenomena – clairvoyance, mediumship, reincarnation – anything esoteric was tremendously fashionable. Secret societies and churches like the Hermetic Order of the Golden Dawn attracted respectable intellectuals like Yeats and less respectable ones like Aleister Crowley. Even Arthur Conan Doyle was fooled by two girls who had faked photographs of fairies at the bottom of their garden. Séances became very popular, and most were debunked as fakes, but since the Trustees knew that they were the targets of a malicious entity that was very real, it made sense to try to contact that spirit to find out what it wanted, maybe even to placate it or come to an accommodation. It was a terrible, tragic mistake.

'What happened was recorded by a clerk of the Trust, who was committed to an asylum shortly afterwards. The medium, a man by the name of Joseph Beely, was imprisoned and later hanged for the murders of the six Trustees who were in the room at the time. Since the séance had been conducted in secret they had only the clerk's testimony about who was there, because what Hester did to them – using Beely's body and only the furniture in the room – made it impossible to identify specific individuals.'

'But how did that work if She wasn't invited in through the barrier or anything?' asked Toby.

'But that's exactly what the séance *was*,' explained the reverend. 'An invitation.'

'Oh my God,' said Trish.

'Since then there has been no further attempt to make contact with Hester. It's simply too dangerous. She will exploit any gap in our defences, however small, and over the centuries She has become very good at finding them.'

'When you say defences…' said Toby.

'At the beginning it didn't take the village leaders very long to realise what was happening, so they stuck to the model they had learned during the Black Death and maintained a vigorous policing of the parish boundary – except instead of doing it with a mob of armed men, they accomplished it with prayer, establishing a perimeter of boundary stones and blessing them each year at the Feast of the Ascension so that the power of the Lord would keep Her out. And it worked. It's been working for centuries, evolving into the Beating of the Bounds on Rogation Sunday. There have been mercifully few instances in the past where She has been able to slip through the village's guard, but whenever it happens She doesn't stop until She has killed those whom She holds accountable. On May seventeenth, 1941, the day before Rogation Sunday, a major German air raid hit many areas of the city and fire caused a building to partially collapse, burying one of the parish stones and preventing it from being blessed. On the following Monday, every member of the Trust was found hacked to death – some in their homes, some in air raid shelters surrounded by other people who had seen and heard nothing.'

'But I don't understand,' said Toby. 'If She wiped out the whole Trust back then, who took over after them?'

'Deputies,' said Dobson. 'Temporary administrators appointed by the council, the War Office, the diocese...' she shrugged. 'Bureaucracy will always find a way to fill a vacuum. That wasn't the first time it happened, either. Of course by the time those poor people discovered what they'd let themselves in for it was too late. For most, the Beating of the Bounds is little more than a quaint folk tradition, an event on the tourist calendar, but for us it is quite literally a matter of life and death.'

'Right!' said Peter, getting to his feet and clapping his hands together decisively. 'I think we've heard just about enough of this bullshit, thank you very much. I'd like you three nutjobs to leave my house now.'

Nash glanced at Esme and looked at his watch. 'Two minutes fifty-seven seconds. You owe me a fiver.'

She grimaced.

'Peter—' Trish started.

'No! Have you been listening to this? It's absolute bullshit! Not even original bullshit, either! Get out, the lot of you, now!' He approached the reverend, hands clenched into fists, and Nash got up to meet him.

'Not going to happen,' he said. His voice was very quiet, very low.

'Get out of my fucking house before I call the police!' Peter shouted, and Trish could suddenly see how terrified he was. Something was happening to his family that he couldn't understand and was powerless to stop.

'But it's not your house,' replied Nash. 'It belongs to the Trust; has done for decades, will do long after you're gone. Specifically, it belongs to that Trustee there,' and he pointed at Trish. 'We'll go if she asks us. Not you.'

'Peter,' said Esme, 'please, you need to calm down. Your wife and son are owed an explanation for what's happened to them, even if you don't believe it.'

Trish moved over to him and laid a hand on his shoulder, and he jumped at her touch. His muscles were taut and trembling, as if he was being electrocuted. 'Peter, please. You're scaring Toby.'

'*I'm* scaring…?' He stared at her, incredulous. 'All right, then,' he announced. He turned on his heel and strode into the kitchen, through it and into the utility room, where Trish heard the jingling of the back door keys.

'What are you doing?' she called, running after him. By the time she caught up he had the back door open and was disappearing outside.

'I'm going to talk to this non-existent dead girl myself!' he shouted.

'No! Peter, don't!'

Toby came after her. 'Dad, no!'

But by then he was standing by the parish stone and yelling into the gathering gloom at the end of the garden. 'Come on, then! If you're even fucking there! Hester, is it? What kind of stupid name is that for a ghost? You don't scare me, dead girl, and you know why? Because you don't fucking exist.'

Trish had both hands on his shoulders and was trying to lead him back to the house. 'Please,' she begged, but by then it was too late, because the shadows were already moving.

The shadows unwreathed themselves from around Her like garments slipping to the ground, and She stepped right up to the stone, as close as She dared so that he could see Her properly. Peter fell back, letting Trish pull him away.

'Fuck me,' he breathed. It was the girl from the construction site.

Hester smiled and blew him a kiss. Then She turned to look behind Her, where the darkness was seething more busily than before, and made a beckoning gesture to it.

This time She had brought company.

Men and women, haggard and plague-ridden, dressed in shifts and shirts, woollen caps and leather shoes. The victims of the Clegeham massacre bore the marks of their deaths as proudly as the weapons with which they had tried to defend themselves: scythes, rakes, shears, billhooks, pitchforks and knives. They assembled behind Her in a wide line across the garden, held back by the prohibition of the parish stone, but the avidity in their faces and the light from the picture window spilling on their blades left Trish in no doubt that if that prohibition were to fail then they would kill without mercy. They didn't leer or threaten; they didn't need to. They'd been patient for centuries, and that sheer force of will carried its own weight.

'Costumes…' Peter said vaguely. He seemed to be mesmerised, or at least frozen with shock. 'Hallowe'en costumes. This is a… must be some kind of prank…'

'I tried that,' said Toby. 'It didn't work.'

Peter turned to see him standing in the back doorway and that broke his paralysis. 'Get back in the house!' he yelled, seizing Trish by the arm and dragging her inside after him. She was too surprised to resist; she'd never seen him so panicked before.

The three Trustees were still in the living room. In the glass of the big picture window behind Joyce Dobson the reflections of the living were superimposed on the figures of the dead, who hadn't disappeared and were still out there, as patient as the grave. Peter let go of Trish and marched across to Nash. She knew exactly what was in his head but it all happened too fast for her to do more than shout, 'Peter, no!' before her husband punched the chief executive of Haleswell Village Trust square in the face. Nash collapsed back into his chair, bellowing, hand to his nose which was already squirting red. Toby was yelling at his dad while Trish, Joyce and Esme all tried to drag Peter away, but he had his fists bunched in Nash's shirt and was screaming into his face.

'And you put us in the middle of this, you lying fucking bastard! You let us move in to this nice big house with your village green and your grammar school and your jobs-for-the-boys bullshit, and all the time you knew what was going to happen! You fucking knew! You've been playing us from the start, haven't you?'

He was shaking Nash like a doll, but the three women managed to drag him away to the other side of the room and get him up against the wall.

'Peter?' said Trish, trying to sound calm, even though right at this very moment all she wanted to do was slap him. 'Now you really are scaring our son. You need to deal with this. We all do.'

'You seem to be coping just fine.'

'No!' she hissed, and shook him with each sentence: 'I am fucking terrified! And I'm as pissed off with them as you are. But I am not going around punching people!'

'Have you got this?' Esme asked her, looking back at Nash, who was staggering into the kitchen with his hands cupping his face.

'I don't know,' Trish said, staring at Peter. 'Have I got this?'

His gaze met hers for a moment and then it slumped, along with the rest of his body. 'Yeah,' he muttered.

'Good.' Esme went off to check on Nash.

'As long as we remain inside the old parish boundary, we are safe,' Dobson continued. 'Hester cannot touch us, directly or indirectly. Even outside the boundary, She isn't able to cause physical harm by Herself but you saw how easily She was able to manipulate you into nearly breaking your neck, Trish. She also has some control over rats, probably because they were the original plague carriers, and as Toby can testify, She uses them very effectively.'

'That's why She never came further into the garden than the stone,' Toby realised.

'Yes. It's also why we encouraged you to take up a place at the grammar school – it's inside the parish boundary. All the children of Trustees go there. You will be tempted now to run – to get all your things together and escape with your family as far away as you can. This would be a mistake. Hester will find you, and find some way to kill you, Patricia. She's done it before; no Trustee who leaves the parish survives for very long. Mostly She drives them to madness and suicide, or else they meet with unfortunate "accidents".'

'I saw Her,' said Peter, his voice barely above a whisper. 'Before, I mean. Weeks ago. At the site. She tried to…' He swallowed. 'Tried to kill me.'

Trish was aghast. 'My God, Peter, why didn't you say something?'

'Like what? "Hi honey, I'm home! Just another day on the site, nearly got decapitated by a dead medieval peasant girl, you know how it is, what's for dinner?" Because it sounds insane even now when we know it's true – what would it have sounded like then?'

He sketched out the details of what had happened at Lot 9, by which time Esme returned from the kitchen, drying her hands on a tea towel. 'My predecessor died in a car accident,' she said. 'He was walking outside the bounds when a car mounted the kerb and pinned him to a wall, crushing his pelvis. The driver later stated that he had swerved to avoid a girl who had stepped out into the road, but no witnesses reported seeing a girl, and no girl appeared on the street CCTV.'

Peter snorted. 'How did the Trust trick you into taking this gig after that?'

Esme looked at him levelly, and her voice was bleak. 'Because he was my husband,' she replied, and went back to her chair.

'It's only the Trustees She's after,' said the reverend to Trish. 'But She'll go through anybody to get to you, especially your loved ones.'

'But if we leave and I give up the Trusteeship, let someone else take over the house, maybe…'

'You think it's that easy?' said Esme. 'You think you can just wash your hands of the whole thing, say "sorry, changed my mind" and walk away? Do you imagine, if that were possible, that any of us would still be here? You're a Trustee now, and that's for life – not because *we* say so, but because *Hester* does. She doesn't give a shit who you are, what you think, or what you want. She will kill you if She can.'

'And even if you could walk away,' added the reverend, 'who would you choose to replace you? How would you choose them?' Trish couldn't answer that. 'Not so easy to commend the poisoned chalice to somebody else's lips, is it? Now maybe you start to appreciate that we do this with nothing but the heaviest of hearts.'

'Oh, poor you,' replied Trish, feeling her bitterness etch the air between them. 'This must be so hard for you.' But now she understood why Great-Aunt Stephanie hadn't left Stone Cottage to any family members or loved ones in her will – who could you inflict this on except strangers?

Nash returned from the kitchen. He had a bag of frozen peas wrapped in a tea towel pressed to his face. 'I can't say I blame you,' he said to Peter, his voice nasal and thick. 'I might have done the same thing in your position. But you only get one free pop, mate; the rest you pay for.'

Peter's frustration had by now channelled itself into the much safer act of pacing about the room with his arms crossed tightly over his chest, hands shoved deep into his armpits. 'But do there have to be people living here? Why can't you just use CCTV or something like that?'

'It's been tried,' said Nash. 'Her rats just eat through the wires. And yes, now we have Wi-Fi, but even if you mount the cameras inside the house the rats still get in without anybody to keep an eye on the place. Plus She gets them digging under the stone, trying to upend it. There needs to be a human caretaker.'

'But it's more than just a practical point,' added Joyce. 'Houses are like people, and when they're empty they attract unwholesome attention. Hester is an empty spirit – She has no soul, nothing to keep Her going except rage. With a family living here, a close-knit family who love each other, it seems to strengthen the blessing on the stone and keep Her more subdued. Every time Stone Cottage has been empty, Her activities have increased. When we had gardeners looking after the place we would only ever let them work in pairs.'

'Hasn't anybody tried to, I don't know – exorcise Her or something?' asked Toby. 'I mean you're a priest, right?'

'But, Toby,' said the reverend, 'that's exactly what the Beating of the Bounds *is*. By blessing the parish boundary stones we banish Her from our village and keep ourselves safe for another year.'

'Yes,' said Peter, 'but She's still fucking *there*, isn't She?'

'I'll admit, it's a less than perfect solution, but it's what we have. Please try to remember, the people of Haleswell have had nearly seven hundred years to try all kinds of more, ah, *definitive* attempts to remove Hester and those who follow Her, but each attempt has ended in tragedy.'

'We did a huge amount of research before we were sure about you,' Joyce continued. 'All three of you. Stephanie had very few relatives to begin within and for one reason or another we were forced to reject those who were a lot more closely related to her. That's why the house was empty for so long and why the legal procedures dragged on.'

'Trustee positions are often hereditary,' added Nash. 'Some of us come from families that have lived in Haleswell for generations, and see the responsibility of protecting our home as a great privilege rather than a burden.'

The reverend glanced at him as she said, 'Some of us argued against the introduction of a child into the Trust's business, but at the end of the day we agreed that you are the best possible person to be the custodian of Stone Cottage. You were not just the nearest warm body – you were carefully selected for your strength of character. Have faith in that if nothing else.'

Trish shook her head. 'I'll never trust you. Ever.'

Dobson nodded acquiescence. 'That's fair,' she said. 'But never is a very long time, even for the dead folk outside. I sincerely hope that as the years pass you may find that you come to think of Haleswell as your home rather than a prison.'

'Don't hold your breath.' She gathered Toby to her on one side and Peter on the other. 'I suppose I should thank you for finally telling us the truth, at least.' She nodded at Barlow. 'And thank you for seeing to Toby's hand. We have a lot to process. But one thing I am in firm agreement with my husband about,' she said to the three of them. 'I'd very much like it if you all got the fuck out of my home.'

Quietly the three Trustees left. When they were gone the first thing Trish did was go to the big picture window and draw the curtains on the darkness and the things that waited in it.

'We should take off on our own, just the three of us,' said Peter, his words slightly slurred. Once the Trustees had gone and Toby had disappeared into the cave of his bedroom they'd broken out the bottle of spiced rum that Peter liked to save for Christmas and special occasions, and had gone through half of it. Trish was mixing hers with cola but he was slurping it neat. 'Put as much distance as we can between ourselves and this bloody madhouse. We can live in a caravan. Join the circus. Become the Flying Feenans.'

'Which puts us in no better position than we are already,' she pointed out. 'At least here we're surrounded by people who know what's going on and can help us. Who knows? Maybe we can even work out a way of stopping it.'

Peter hmphed and took another swig of rum, grimacing. He swirled it around in his glass thoughtfully, watching the toffee-amber liquor catch the light. They'd shut all the doors and turned off all the lights except for one small table lamp next to the sofa, where he was sitting and she was curled up next to him with a blanket up to her shoulders. The warmth and safety was an illusion, she knew, but hopefully getting drunk would help them both forget that for a while. 'We could stay with your mother again,' he said with a little snorted laugh. 'Remember how much fun that was last time?'

'And explain all of this how exactly?' she replied. 'We can't take this anywhere near anyone we love. What if something happens?'

'So who can we stay with that we really, really don't like?' She chortled. 'Your cousin Geoff.'

Peter tipped his glass to hers in salute. 'Hi, Geoff! Mind if we crash at yours for a bit? What? How many? Oh, just the three of us. Don't mind the mob of angry undead medieval peasants, they've brought their own sleeping bags.'

Her chortling became giggling, and her giggling infected him until they were crying with laughter and clutching each other. Toby came downstairs to see what all the noise was, and found them in a heap on the floor by the sofa, laughing like drains.

'You two are weird,' he scowled, and went back up.

23

VOLUNTEER

JOYCE WAS WISE ENOUGH TO LET THINGS CALM DOWN for a few days before she approached Trish again, and the reverend didn't insult her intelligence by trying to pretend that everything was back to normal. She simply showed up at the front door of Stone Cottage one morning with a wide, low cardboard box in both hands and an offer: 'If you like, I can show you all of the information we have on Hester,' she said. 'You're owed that, as a Trustee. I don't promise that it'll make you any safer, but it might help to know that we're not hiding anything from you. It will also help you to understand Her limitations, and how safe you and your family can be here.'

Trish still had the front door on its chain, and she regarded the reverend without replying. Her eyes glanced down at the box and back up. Joyce flipped open the lid. Inside were four cream buns covered in squiggles of what looked suspiciously like strawberry syrup. 'I also have cake.'

'That's low, even for you,' said Trish. She unhooked the chain, opened the door, and jerked her head towards the hall. 'In with your buns,' she ordered.

Joyce smiled and stepped inside.

Later, she invited Trish back to the vicarage to show her the Trust's archive. An ordinary-looking door in the hallway behind the stairs opened onto a flight of steps leading steeply down.

'Mind your head,' Joyce warned. 'This used to be the cellar and the ceiling is still quite low.'

At the bottom there was a second door, much older and more solid, with heavy iron hinges. Joyce took out a set of keys. 'We keep it locked not just for security,' she explained, 'but also because some of the documents in here are incredibly old and very fragile, so the room is climate-controlled. You're welcome any time you like, though.'

She unlocked the door and led Trish inside, flicking on a row of wall switches.

Low-wattage fluorescent strip lighting blinked into life along a ceiling which was made up of rows of intersecting arches so that what used to be the cellar wasn't so much a tunnel as an interconnected series of low, vaulted chambers. Where they met the walls they formed arched alcoves that Trish could well imagine being full of dusty wine racks in an earlier century, but now they held bookcases, filing cabinets, display cases and storage racks crammed with archive boxes. Just a cursory circuit of the nearest chamber showed Trish a collection of bound sermons of the vicars of St Sebastian's church, Haleswell, 1714–1756; index-card boxes full of carefully catalogued postcards of Haleswell in the Victorian era; large cartographic journals of proposed urban redevelopment projects on Pestle Road; and a locked glass case full of neatly labelled animal skulls. She saw racks with old flintlock muskets next to agricultural tools, rails of antique clothes in protective plastic wrappings, chamber pots, paintings, wax recording cylinders and microfiche films, brass lamps, stuffed animals (one was a fox, she noticed with a jump), and this was just one alcove – there were dozens more.

'My God,' she breathed. 'You've got the village's entire past down here.'

In the midmost chamber was a circular reading table with hooded desk lamps where Joyce had sat herself while she let Trish explore. 'Not quite, but a lot of it, yes. We even have some of the original fourteenth-century manorial records. There are some gaps in the continuity, due to events like the Reformation, the Civil War, the Great Plague. But it's not indiscriminate – everything you see here is in some way connected to Hester Attlowe. The witness accounts of people who have seen Her, the possessions of Her victims, even the remains of some of the rats She's used to do Her bidding. Anything which might one day give a clue about how to lay Her to rest.'

'You still think She can be stopped?'

'I can't believe that She is entirely evil. There has to be some way of reaching Her.'

Trish trailed a hand over a wardrobe rail of old dresses in their shrink-wrap, trying to imagine the number of lives this treasury accounted for, the weight of history which pressed down on the arched ceiling overhead.

'And yet despite what it looks like,' Joyce continued, 'Her attacks are actually quite few and far between.'

Trish uttered a short laugh. 'Well She's certainly upped Her game recently, I'll give Her that.'

'That's because this is a time of instability, as you establish yourself as the new custodian of Stone Cottage. She's not some continually prowling beast, watching and attacking at every opportunity. When things calm down She becomes quieter – often a decade or more might go by without a sighting or an incident. In some way Her... *moods*, shall we say, are tied to the prevailing spirit in the community, so in times of uncertainty like war or social unrest or a new Trustee taking up their position She becomes more active, testing the Beating for gaps and weaknesses. As you and your family settle in and become a part of the village, She'll subside again, and you'll all be able to live here almost as peacefully as if it were any other ordinary part of the city.'

'Almost.'

'She is completely unable to harm you in any way when you are inside the Beating and it is secure. Even outside She can only act by proxy and within the limitations of what is available to Her. And even then, She is only ever seen by Trustees or those closest to them. The ordinary residents of Haleswell have no idea of Her existence because She's simply not interested in them. If we were continually being inundated with hordes of flesh-eating rats attacking people at random do you think there would even be a village?'

'Yes, I suppose you'd think people would have noticed that. But what I still don't understand is why the Trust continues to exist at all. You mentioned those times when She got in and managed to kill everyone – why didn't the powers that be just leave it alone then? Why put new people in the same position of danger? If Hester isn't interested in just any old bugger then surely She would have just – I don't know – stopped? Disappeared? Been at rest, like you say?'

'Let me see how good your detective skills are.' Joyce led her to where a large mahogany honour board hung on a wall, its columns of gold letters listing the names of past vicars of St Sebastian's church. 'Notice anything unusual?'

It took Trish a few minutes of scanning up and down the list of names and dates before she thought she knew what Joyce was hinting at. 'Why was there no vicar between 1843 and 1851?' she asked.

'Because in 1834 the Poor Law Amendment Act was introduced, which allowed small rural parishes like Haleswell to amalgamate with their neighbours into a poor law union run by a board of guardians. This gave the old Haleswell Parish Council the perfect opportunity to do exactly what you suggested: abandon their posts and give Hester no target. The de Lindesay family had died out half a century before, so there was no complication there. But they couldn't simply resign en masse, of course, so they allowed their roles to fall vacant by natural attrition and old age over many years. Edward Bould was vicar at the time, and when he died in 1843, nine years after the law came into effect, the bishop simply didn't send a replacement. The last member of the old parish council lived on after him for another eight years, and when he died in 1851 Haleswell came completely under the control of the Solihull Poor Law Union's Board of Guardians. They were in charge now. They were responsible.'

'Oh no,' breathed Trish, realising.

Joyce nodded. 'And they didn't have any boundary of blessed parish stones to protect them. They were all killed within a few days of each other. Instead of removing Hester's prey, they had simply been replaced by some further up the food chain, so to speak. Hester does not care who is responsible, only that someone is. That was why the Trust was created and why it is maintained – to keep Her malice localised and focussed on those best placed to defend against Her.'

'So how did you get this gig? Did you inherit it like Nash or were you tricked into it too?'

Joyce sat back down at the central reading table and fiddled with the switch of the desk lamp in front of her. 'I was a twin, you know,' she said eventually, without looking up. 'Her name was Claire. We grew up in the Lake District, near Ambleside, and I wanted to be a vet when I grew up.' The reverend's voice was becoming thick with old grief; Trish didn't know where this was going, but couldn't offend her by interrupting. 'Claire was the eldest by four minutes, and being the first one into the world she was the first into everything – first to dive into a pool, first to lose a tooth, first in line for ice creams. The only thing where I came ahead of her was in science at school, but there was never any animosity or competition between us because that was just the way it was.

'So anyway, we were twelve and walking back from school one day along one of those narrow lanes they have up there – you know the kind with high banks on either side – and I heard a lamb bleating from somewhere up to my right. Well, it sounded like it was in distress and being the animal lover that I was I had to go up to see what was wrong, and I found that the silly little idiot had gone and got its head caught in a section of wire fence along the top. Claire was still down on the road, eager to get home, and she called up to me, "Get a move on, slowcoach!" Those were the last words I ever heard her say, alive or dead. As I got the lamb's head free and it ran off to be with its mother I heard the sound of the car's engine, and then the brakes screaming, and then the thud. A tourist, driving much too fast and completely unable to stop. And that was how my sister Claire died.'

Trish sat down opposite and laid her hand on Joyce's. 'I'm so sorry,' she whispered.

The corners of Joyce's mouth curled up slightly, and she blinked back tears. 'That wasn't the last I saw of her, though,' she continued. 'The first time she came to me was during my school exams. I'd been revising so hard the night before that I'd forgotten to set my alarm, and I would have slept right through it and probably been late except that I was woken by someone shaking me and saying, "Get a move on, slowcoach!" Well I woke up, and in that moment when your eyes are all gummy and blurry I swear I saw Claire standing beside my bed. Of course when I blinked she was gone, but it had definitely been her.

'She came to see me several more times over the years, always whenever I was under stress or slacking off and needed a boot up my backside, and for a long time I thought she was looking out for me. But then it started to change.

'I remember when I'd just learned to drive and I was still a bit unsure about pulling out into a junction, she was there on the back seat behind me, whispering, "Get a move on, slowcoach!" and I, trusting my big sister, moved out into the junction and nearly got flattened by a lorry. It all came to a head when I was at college, and there was a party where I'd had rather too much to drink and I found myself in the upstairs bathroom of a strange house looking at a pile of pills in my hand and a bottle of vodka by the sink, and Claire's reflection was behind me in the medicine cabinet mirror. "Get a move on, slowcoach!" she said, and I knew that she wasn't trying to help me at all, she was trying to make me catch up with her like she'd always done when we were children. She was waiting for me to join her.

'For a long time I thought I was going mad, and so did quite a lot of other people. I was medicated, hypnotised, analysed, and none of it did any good – Claire was still there – until I thought well, I literally have nothing to lose, and tried talking to a priest. Let me say right from the outset that what he did was not an exorcism. There is a ministry in the diocese called the Diocesan Deliverance Team that specialises in helping people who believe that they are suffering from spiritual assault. Their first port of call is to exhaust all possible rational explanations, so they do a lot of liaison with medical and psychiatric agencies before they even begin to consider that something truly supernatural is happening. I was offered counselling and prayer...' She shrugged. 'And it worked. Claire left me, and at the same time I found my faith and my vocation. I quit college, got myself ordained, and began looking around for a flock to serve. That was when my Deliverance counsellor mentioned to me that there was a parish called Haleswell that came with its own set of "unique challenges", as he put it, but which he thought my particular experience might make me well suited for.'

'So they know?' said Trish, not quite able to believe the implications of it. 'The Church knows about Hester?'

'Of course they do. How could they not?'

'And they maintain the Trust if, when, it... breaks down.'

Joyce nodded. 'We come to the Trust in a variety of ways,' she said. 'Some, like Nash, are born to it. Some, like you, are manipulated into it, I'm sorry to say. And some crazy idiots like me,' she added with a wry smile, 'actually volunteered for this gig.'

24

THE BEATING OF THE BOUNDS

'LET ME GET THIS STRAIGHT,' SAID KRISH. 'THEY'RE going to pick you up, hold you upside down, and smack your head against a rock.'

'When you put it like that you make it sound like something a normal person wouldn't want to do,' said Toby.

'I think we've pretty much established that you're not normal,' said Maya.

They threaded their way through the Rogation Sunday festival crowds, checking out the stalls and eating hot dogs, even though it was still barely mid-morning. Toby had thought the day itself would be little more than a bunch of old people wandering around town singing hymns like a party of roving geriatric Jehovah's Witnesses, but could not have been more wrong. It was more like a carnival. He hadn't appreciated what a big occasion it was and how many visitors it would attract, but when he considered that

Haleswell's Beating of the Bounds was a tradition almost unbroken for centuries, it made sense.

PIC260519-4-through-12: The green park at the centre of Haleswell village is crammed and bustling with fairground rides, sideshows, food stands and craft stalls – so many that they overspill out into the surrounding roads, which have been closed to traffic while marshals in hi-vis tabards with walkie-talkies direct visitors foolish enough to travel by car towards parking on nearby school playgrounds. There is candyfloss and popcorn, hook-a-duck and whack-a-mole. There is a beer-and-pie marquee, but also street-food vendors serving out of trailers that look like miniature Caribbean beach huts or Parisian bistros on wheels, selling everything from gourmet burgers to stone-baked vegan pizzas. Music thumps from speakers. Historical re-enactment clubs give demonstrations, like the Thegns of Mercia in full Anglo-Saxon chain mail who duel on the grass, the sun flashing on their blades. In the ornate green and gold bandstand by the pond, the Haleswell Village Brass Band plays show tunes for families sitting on picnic blankets, and small children run around with coloured paper pennants streaming behind them.

None of it was enough to help him ignore the presence of Hester Attlowe, unseen and unheard behind everything.

She hadn't shown Herself since appearing with Her small army that night, and he didn't know whether to be reassured by this or freaked out even more. If everything that the reverend had said was true, it didn't seem likely that Hester had been intimidated by their defiance, and in a way he might actually have preferred it if Her fellow pitchfork-wielding revenants had turned up below his window every night; he might have got used to that. As it was, Her prolonged absence made him nervous. It gave the impression that She was waiting, biding Her time, and as the Beating processed around one stone after another he found himself examining the crowds, dreading but hoping to see a feral and unflinching stare amongst the smiling and laughing faces. A turn of shoulder, a lift of hair, a flash of eye; any could be Her.

It was like when he took a picture and used a filter that maxed out the contrast or oversaturated the colour: it was a bit too bright and happy. The laughter was a bit screechy, a bit too in earnest, and when anybody shrieked he jumped as if cut. The smells of hot dogs, popcorn, doughnuts, cooking oil, axle grease and diesel fumes roiled thickly in his guts if he stood too long in one spot. The axis of the world teetered on the balance point of tipping over into sensory overload and it was only by making it stand still in the frame of his phone's camera that he was able to make sense of it.

The day itself had started with a church service at St Sebastian's, but Toby had been offered a trade: he wouldn't have to attend the service itself if he agreed to be bumped – a part of the Beating which involved a village youth being upended and having his head bumped against one of the parish stones. According to Rev. Dobson it was a holdover from a time when the young folk needed to be taught the boundaries of their home, but agreed that it seemed a bit too drastic for this to be true. Toby had shrugged and agreed; if it helped keep Hester away from his mum, he'd do it. His life couldn't get much weirder.

In the two weeks since the Day of the Rat, as he called it to himself, his mum started going to services again, even though it was Church of England rather than Catholic – not that he was all that clear about the difference, but at least St Sebastian's had the advantage that it was safely inside a zone where the vengeful dead couldn't get at you. It was amazing how quickly you could adapt to insane circumstances and treat them as normal life, he thought. All the same, neither he nor his dad had been converted into happy-clappers for Jesus because of what they'd seen. As far as Toby was concerned, accepting the existence of ghosts didn't necessarily open the gates for everything else. He knew from his biology teacher, Mrs Ascough, that a fish had been discovered that everybody had thought extinct for millions of years, but that didn't mean that there was a Loch Ness monster too, did it? Besides, he thought that his mum quite liked worshipping on her own.

She had tried to get him to help with the preparations for Rogation Sunday, but when he started calling it 'Rogue Nation Sunday' and whistling the *Mission: Impossible* theme tune every time the reverend came around to their house to sort out the arrangements, she told him the best thing he could do would be to just keep out of everybody's way, which suited him fine.

To his knowledge it was the first time she'd ever organised anything resembling a proper event with people and food and drinks, and she was going at this like it was an episode of *Bake-Off* crossed with the invasion of a small country. When they'd lived in the flat his parents' social life had revolved around the Golden Cross down the road – his birthday parties had been celebrated at the kind of family pub where the mums and dads could get a free drink with a burger for under a tenner and the kids could get wired up on sugar and spend the afternoon flinging themselves around a soft-play arena. For the Beating she'd plundered napkins, disposable plates and glasses from their nearest Waitrose supermarket (and get this, had actually *dressed up* to do it, declaring that she wasn't going to be sneered at by the Yummy Mummy brigade for doing her shopping in sweat pants and a hoodie), and actually gone and *baked* things, but behind the frenzy of activity he thought he detected the same kind of twitchiness in her. Hester had done this. Like a low-level electric current fizzing constantly through their nerves, Hester had made it impossible for any of them to simply enjoy what should be enjoyable, even when She wasn't there.

The service ended and the congregation emerged to set out on the Beating, each carrying a long, thin stick of hazel, and led by Rev. Dobson and Richard Nash, though the majesty of the chief executive's golden chain regalia was undermined a bit by the fading black eye that Toby's dad had given him. The remainder of the Trustees followed, including his parents, and he caught up with them, while Krish and Maya and their families joined the large crowd of revellers who followed the procession as it made its way out of the carnival and through the streets of Haleswell towards the first of the seven parish stones.

At the edge of the Rec was the parish marker known as the Sunrise Stone, protected from vandals by an enclosure of high, spiked railings and a heavy padlock. It and the stone at the cottage were the two oldest, believed to be the only ones to have survived from the time of the Black Death. Nash unlocked the cage and Rev. Dobson moved inside to bless it.

'We are at the most easterly point of our parish. Here, Lord, we pray for all those who live and work in this district. We especially remember all those who live in overcrowded homes, those living in hostels and on the streets. Those who commute daily into our neighbourhood for work and for those who cannot work. Let us pray for those who have recently been elected to positions of power over the life of this place, that they may use their power wisely and for the common good. Amen.' She drew a cross on the stone in water from the holy well of Saint Sebastian and stepped aside as the procession moved past, each tapping the stone with their hazel stick several times and repeating the amen.

This procession moved on through residential streets, down alleyways, across parks, and over busy roads to repeat the blessing, with variations on the prayers and offerings, at each of the other stones. If the *amen* that followed each blessing was said more earnestly by the Trustees and their families, only they noticed. If the fairground music struck a discordant note or the laughter of children faltered into tears, only they heard. There was something familiar about the whole process, even though Toby had never seen it before, and it was when he looked at his dad that he realised it was just like watching him lock up before bedtime, going around each window and door in turn, checking the locks and making sure that everything was safe for the night.

We're not locking the dead out, he thought. *We're shutting ourselves in.*

On the war memorial by the library, the Red Stone was set in the other side of the column from the honour roll, and a wreath of remembrance poppies was laid.

In the White Hart pub, the Ale Stone was part of the hearth of a large open fireplace, and instead of holy water the reverend used a thimbleful of beer while the bulk of the procession waited on the pavement outside.

The Horse Stone was in the wall above the doorway of an Oxfam charity shop which had once been a coaching inn, where a handful of straw was used to draw the cross.

In a wall next to a red postbox where a post office used to be, there were gaps around the Epistle Stone into which members of the procession stuffed folded-up banknotes (which were discreetly removed to add to the church collection later).

Cemented into the pavement of an otherwise ordinary suburban street was the Bumping Stone, which Toby regarded warily.

'Come on, you!' grinned Sean Trevorrow, the Trust's

director of housing and community, appearing beside him. On the other side was Alan Pankowicz, the bush-bearded landlord of the White Hart, who was another non-executive Trustee like his mum because of the stone he guarded in his pub. He was aware of other people standing close behind, and then his dad was in front of him, looking embarrassed.

'Ready to do this, Tobes?'

'No.' He wasn't at all sure this was a good idea anymore. That stone looked extremely hard. Shouldn't he be wearing some kind of harness? What if they dropped him on his head? He might get brain damage.

'Good. And a-one and a-two and a…'

On three they lifted him with strong arms, holding him by his arms, legs, shoulders and hips, and turning him upside down. Gently they lowered him so that his head just touched the stone – it wasn't even a bump – three times, to tumultuous cheering from the procession, and even though his mind was racing with *this is stupid this is so unbelievably stupid I look like an absolute tit God I hope Maya isn't watching*, by the time they set him upright his heart was thumping and he was grinning like a loon.

'That was actually pretty cool,' he said.

'Loser!' shouted Krish from the crowd.

Which left only Stone Cottage.

There obviously wasn't enough space in the garden to admit the hundreds of people in the procession, so numbers had been limited to the church congregation, including the Trustees, and a few specially selected friends. The Gorić family had been very surprised to find themselves on the guest list, but not half as surprised as Toby's mum when he had suggested it.

'What?' he'd said. 'I'm just returning the favour. She asked me to tea, I'm asking her to... whatever this is. I'm just being polite. It doesn't mean anything.' But the knowing look in his mum's eye suggested that it did mean something.

The Reverend Dobson blessed the garden stone: 'Dearest Lord, we ask Thee to bless this stone which has stood guard over the lives that have dwelt in this house for generations. Bless this family – Patricia, Peter, and Toby – and bless all the families of Haleswell that shelter in its protection. May they find support and joy and love in one another. Keep them and watch over them, and defend them from the evil that lies within and the evil that lies without.'

Toby's dad was leaning on the garden rake as if it was no big thing, but his knuckles were white where he gripped the handle and his eyes were scanning the shrubbery rather than watching the reverend.

If Hester was there, She remained in hiding.

The procession continued in its roughly circular route until it came full circle at the holy font in the church, where Rev. Dobson poured the remainder of the water back into the stone basin, and the ritual was complete. The members of the procession drifted apart to enjoy the festival while the Trustees and guests returned to Stone Cottage for drinks.

'See?' said Nash, clapping Peter on the shoulder. 'Nothing to worry about. You've got more to worry about with that lot coming in.' He nodded at the Gorićs – Maya, her mother, father, and two brothers, the older one scowling around as if looking to pick a fight. 'Lock up the family silver, eh?' he chuckled, and poured himself a beer.

25

GARDEN PARTY

'SO WHAT'S THE BIG FUSS OVER ALL THESE OLD stones?' asked Maya, prodding the garden stone with a toe. Toby wanted to tell her not to, but couldn't possibly begin to explain what he was afraid might happen if she somehow damaged it. Plus, the other half of his attention was taken up with keeping an eye on the side passage to the front of the house where the guests were, in case his mum or dad had noticed that he and Maya had sneaked away.

'It's like a village tradition. Bit stupid really,' he said, glancing around.

Nobody came into the back garden much these days. Although his parents had made it presentable for the Beating, the curtains on that side of the house were permanently closed and the washing line was bare. His mum hung the laundry on radiators around the house, making it smell damp and claustrophobic. No way were they going to entertain guests back here, and he knew he'd get a bollocking if he was found. Dad's temper in particular was frayed and unpredictable, and Mum's wasn't much better.

And he couldn't even tell Maya that they were sneaking away at all, because then she'd want to know why his own back yard was off-limits, but she'd asked to see the stone closer up, without all the other people crowding around, and he couldn't refuse because that too would have been weird.

'What are these markings?' she murmured, bending close and tracing them with her fingers. 'They look really old.'

Ancient sigils of protection carved by the villagers centuries ago to ward off a vengeful undead peasant girl, he thought. 'Dunno,' he muttered. 'Hey, I found something out the other day. Did you know that the name of your road, Pestle, actually comes from the words "pest hole"? Pest as in pestilence as in disease?'

'So what?'

'So I think that somewhere near your home is the site of an old plague pit – you know like a mass grave?'

'Well that's reassuring. Where did you find out this particularly delightful piece of information?'

'Oh, just, you know, online stuff,' he said airily. He was slowly amassing a small library of dead Mrs Drummond's books on her old bureau in his room, but telling Maya that would have invited more awkward questions. He felt like he was having to second-guess everything he said and did these days.

* * *

'Maya!' yelled her little brother Antony. The Ant was standing at the side passage, whacking the bushes with a stick. 'Maya, there's cake! Come on!' And he disappeared again.

'God, he's *such* a pain,' Maya muttered.

'Must be pretty noisy in your house, huh,' said Toby.

'Oh I don't really mind,' she replied, her mood brightening as quickly as it had darkened. 'It's kind of nice being surrounded by people.'

'Yeah, must be.'

As they returned in the direction of the party she said, 'I hope you don't mind me saying, but I think it's sad that you don't have any brothers or sisters to share this with.'

He didn't know how to respond to that. The issue of his only-child status was something that had never been discussed openly, at least not between him and his parents. He was dimly aware that it was tied in to his mother's feelings about religion, but it had always hovered, unspoken and accusatory, like the smell of cigarette smoke on clothes. Maya stating it so baldly left him utterly at a loss for how to respond. She left and he followed her, glancing back briefly over his shoulder, expecting to see Hester's mocking grin but seeing nothing except the stone. Her absence should have made him relieved, but instead it simply made him more worried about where She was and what She was up to.

Back at the party there were plenty of people to be surrounded by. The Trustees, each with their small number of invited friends and relatives, were chatting in groups on the lawn, his dad was deep in conversation with Mr Gorić about Serbia's fortunes in the UEFA Nations League, and Mrs Gorić was exclaiming over the beauty of Stone Cottage's flower beds. Rajko was leaning against one of the front gateposts as if eager to leave, glowering at his phone.

Also, as the Ant had said, there was cake.

His mum, determined to throw herself with both feet into the customs of village life, had looked up an old recipe for an Ascension cake and added a few touches of her own. It was basically a large ring-shaped fruit cake decorated with walnuts and glacé cherries that shone like green and red jewels. There was probably more rum in it than was strictly traditional, and she'd even bought a genuine old sixpence from the Thursday flea market to bake into it as a lucky charm. It was Donna Russell, Director of Financial Services, who found it, which prompted a round of good-natured jeers about her rigging the finances. Then Nash nudged her suggestively and said that if she played her cards right she could get lucky with him later. She looked obviously uncomfortable at this and Toby watched his mum take Donna aside later to ask her if she was okay.

'That man is a misogynistic dungheap,' Russell growled.

'I'm so sorry. Shall I get my man to beat him up for you?' She thumped a fist into her palm and scowled.

'Hah. Don't tempt me. If it comes to that I'll do it myself.'

But when the fight came, it was from an entirely predictable direction. Rajko left his post as gate sentinel and strolled over to Toby and Maya. 'Nice estate you've got here, little landlord.'

'Raj,' Maya warned. 'Don't call him that. We're guests. Be nice.'

Rajko looked wounded. 'I am being nice! We're having a nice conversation, aren't we? With tea and cakes on the lawn! This is about as nice as it gets! So,' he turned back to Toby. 'Have you asked your mum yet about looking into our boiler situation?'

'Yes,' he lied.

Raj laughed in his face. 'Bullshit you have.'

'Raj!' Maya protested, trying not to shout. She took him by the arm and tried to drag him away. 'Don't make me get Papa.'

'No, go and get Papa,' said Raj, his eyes still locked on Toby's. 'Maybe then we can have a conversation about something that actually matters instead of all this *nice* bullshit. Go on, get him!' He shoved against Maya's grip and sent her sprawling.

Without warning, the Green Skull filled Toby's vision, along with a ringing in his ears that became a roaring, and gradually he became aware that the roaring was his own voice, and he was punching something, kneeling half on the ground and half on somebody's chest, and he was punching Rajko in the face over and over again with his rat-bitten hand, screaming all the while, and Raj's lips were split open and bleeding and then adult voices were yelling at him and strong hands were pulling him away and a shocked silence descended over the garden.

'There we go,' said Nash with quiet satisfaction. 'There's the Feenan in him.'

'Shut up, Richard,' snapped the reverend, and went to see if she could help.

* * *

'He was your guest!' shouted Trish. 'It doesn't matter what he did!'

Peter had dragged their son upstairs to his room and then gone back to apologise to their guests, but by then Toby had gone limp, submitting to his mum washing his hands and putting sticking plasters over where his knuckles had split on Rajko's teeth. He was lying on his bed, arms tightly crossed, and furious, as if he had any right to be.

'Oh, right, so are we all supposed to suddenly start turning the other cheek now that you've got religion?' he retorted. 'You're such a hypocrite, Mum!'

'Why? Why am I a hypocrite?'

'Because you're just doing it to get in the good books with the Trustees, obviously. You're baking cakes and working at food banks and it's not you! It's bullshit!'

'It's not me?' She laughed. 'Toby, you're fourteen! You haven't got the faintest idea of what's *me*!'

'Well why don't you tell me, then?' he yelled. 'There's all this shit happening around me and I don't know what's going on and why the fuck won't someone just *tell* me?!'

He was crying by the end of it, the heels of his hands pressed deep into his eye sockets as if in an attempt to dam the flow of his tears.

'Oh, Toby, Toby, Toby,' she moaned, moving to sit beside him and stroking his head. He flinched away but she persisted, and eventually he sagged in towards her side, and she pulled him tight to her – her son, her baby.

'Toby,' she said, stroking his head, 'after you were born, things were difficult for me. You don't need to know the how and the why of it, just that I was so angry and upset that I pushed away something that had once been very important to me. Now, for lots of different reasons – some good, some bad – I've decided to let it come back into my life, and it's making me happy. That's all. It doesn't mean I love you or your father any the less, and it's not about everybody in the household suddenly having to get religion. You're not going to be made to go to church on Sunday and say grace at dinner times. But I might, and I hope that you'll respect that even if you don't share it. Do you think you can do that?'

He sniffed and nodded.

'And I promise I'll get better at making bread,' she added.

He gave a wet laugh, and they just sat that way for a while together.

Reverend Dobson addressed the Trustees after their guests had all left.

'There is one last service, just for the Trustees and their families. Hester will now test our defences, attempting to profane the blessing and undermine the Beating. Part of what makes it so powerful is the depth of tradition and the willing participation of all the people in the carnival and procession, all those thousands of souls in our community, but we must never forget that first and foremost we are Her targets and must fortify our souls accordingly.'

'I understand,' said Trish. 'We'll be there.'

'Hey, wait up,' replied Peter. 'Will we?'

'Yes,' she answered. 'Or are you not convinced that there's something supernatural trying to hurt our family?'

'Oh, I'm convinced. I'm just not so sure that throwing ourselves into the deep end of the happy-clappy pool is necessarily the answer to our problems.'

'I'm not sure what you think the alternative is,' put in Rev. Dobson. 'Surely once you accept that the powers of the Devil are real, you must accept that the power of the Holy Spirit is real too.'

Peter shook his head. 'See, it's that either/or thing where it falls down. I've seen something I can't explain – doesn't mean that I've seen the Devil, and it sure as hell doesn't mean that I'm about to start trusting you people any more than I absolutely have to.' To Trish, he said, 'You and Toby go to the service if you want. I have no problem with that. I'll look after things here. Take care of the tidying.'

'This is a bit more important than the washing-up,' the reverend objected.

'Come on now, Joyce,' said Alan Pankowicz. 'You've gained one more convert – why not quit while you're ahead?'

She rounded on him. 'Are you seriously accusing me of exploiting this situation just to get another notch on the altar?'

'No, of course not. Just that you don't have to hector the pair of them about it. They'll come to us in their own time.'

The reverend walked away, shaking her head. 'This is exactly the sort of gap She likes to exploit,' she warned.

'Maybe you all should have thought of that before you lied to get us here!' his father shot after her.

Pankowicz placed a hand on Peter's chest. 'Peter,' he said. 'You won this one. Stand down, mate.' Mild-mannered though he was, the landlord of the White Hart was also half a head taller and a physical presence not to be ignored. Peter stood down.

After the sideshows had gone and the streets been swept, the glasses washed and the bunting packed away, night fell on the last of the Rogation Sunday festivities, and the dead came out to beat their own bounds.

26

THE PARADE OF THE DEAD

BANISHED TO HIS ROOM IN DISGRACE, AND WITH HIS
phone confiscated, Toby fell back on going through Mrs
Drummond's notes. They were cryptic at best, tangential
reminders and references to a body of knowledge built up
over a long lifetime which he was having to acquire from
scratch by going back through her books, and even then he
had to find online explanations for most of what he read.
Slowly, like teasing the loosening strands out of an intricate
knot, isolated insights would fall out of the tangle:

Hester's family had lived in the medieval village of
Clegeham, which was mentioned in Domesday records but
was never in the manorial rolls after 1350. Nor did it appear
on any of her old maps.

Richard Attlowe had been reeve of the village – a sort of
combined head man and tax collector.

Hauntings could often be dispelled by finding the physical

remains of the unquiet spirit and giving them a proper burial.

The problem was that he didn't know how any of these loose ends fit together and he felt that he was simply amassing a collection of Quite Interesting facts without any idea of how to use them to inform a course of action. He sat up late into the night, long after both parents had gone to bed, with books spread out around him on the floor of his room, feeling like he was reading around and around in circles.

And then, just like that, he knew She was in the garden below his window.

If asked, he couldn't have said *how* he knew – maybe repeated exposure to Her presence was knocking loose or waking up some part of his brain that controlled senses people didn't normally use, like the way birds could migrate for thousands of miles using the earth's magnetic fields, or sharks could sense a molecule of blood in a million gallons of ocean. She was just suddenly *there*, and he felt it like he could feel the hairs rise on the back of his neck.

Leaving the books, he crept to his window and peered through the crack between the curtains.

She had brought Her people again. They crowded as closely as they could to the Beating Stone on the other side of the intangible boundary that it marked, but for once they didn't seem interested in the house. Neither did She. She didn't even glance at his window. Instead, She raised in Her fist a stick which was carved down one side with many notches, and struck the stone hard, three times. He distinctly heard each *clack!* and then the collective clatter as Her followers each hit the stone with the farming tools that they carried.

Then, still without paying the slightest attention to the house upon which She had been so fixated every other time, She led Her people out of the garden, through the shadows at the side.

Toby scrambled to get his jeans on. 'Don't be an idiot,' he told himself as he shrugged on a hoodie. 'She'll fuck you up if She gets the chance.' Socks, trainers. 'Going out on your own like this is literally the dumbest thing you can do.' He knew all this. And yet She hadn't been bothered with the house. Maybe She wasn't interested; maybe for once She was distracted or too busy conducting Her own beating ceremony. She would be doing a circuit of all the stones, and by the way She'd left it hadn't seemed that She was finished. He could follow Her, staying on the safe side of the boundary, and maybe learn something that he could use. If She saw him and disappeared then he'd have lost nothing.

'What you've lost is your mind, dumbass,' he whispered to himself as he crept downstairs. By the time he got outside they had all disappeared, but if he was right then he didn't need to see them to know where they were going.

He caught up with them by the Bumping Stone and watched from hiding in a side street, though they weren't paying the slightest attention to anything about the modern world around them. It was late, but not so late that there wasn't the occasional passing car or pedestrian. Maybe Hester's people simply weren't interested. Maybe they couldn't see because, locked in an eternity after death, the ritual they were enacting was so old and removed from the petty present that they were incapable of perceiving anything so transient as *now*. If they were really over six hundred years old, his fourteen-year life must seem as brief and meaningless as a mayfly.

The world of the now couldn't see *them*, that was certain. He watched a car pass, its headlights picking out the stone and everything surrounding it except the shadowy revenants who crowded close about. The light slid straight through them. Toby didn't know why he could see both. It was like seeing overlapping images, or being at the centre point of two intersecting sets in a Venn diagram.

Then they turned, apparently done with their business, and moved off into the suburban streets on the southern outskirts of Haleswell, away from the village and much further than he was expecting. He'd assumed that the original villagers of Haleswell would have disposed of their murdered neighbours where they fell on the parish boundary and that the unquiet spirits would return to that spot if anywhere, but they were way past that now and still going. Haleswell was right on the edge of the city; in a few streets there would be nothing but fields.

Then he saw the signs for the Clegg Farm estate where his dad worked, and they were walking past clean, new houses with tidy gardens and shining cars in the driveways to the barrier fence which marked the edge of the active construction site. Hester and Her people walked right through it and disappeared into the labyrinth of skeletal buildings.

A terrible, wonderful suspicion began to grow in Toby's mind.

He ran all the way back home, letting himself into

the house as quietly as his escalating excitement would allow, dragged onto the floor of his room all of Mrs Drummond's old maps and spread them out like a second carpet. She had originals going back to the First World War and reproductions going back further than that – the earliest was dated 1731, which still left a gap of almost four hundred years since Hester's time, but that wasn't an issue because towns didn't shrink, did they? If the thing he was looking for wasn't there in 1731 it wouldn't have been there in 1349 either. He'd been looking for the wrong thing: evidence of a mass grave somewhere close to the parish boundary. What he should have been looking for was quite literally further afield, and it had been staring him in the face so obviously that his own stupidity stunned him.

Clegg Farm. Clegeham.

He traced it through the maps, scrabbling across the floor on his hands and knees. It had been there in the sixties when the post-war building boom had created estates like the Willows, and before that in the 1860s when houses had been built along Pestle Road nearby, and woodland before that, and probably never built on since Haleswell and Clegeham had been two separate villages.

He checked and double-checked everything before running into his parents' bedroom and waking them by shouting, 'Mum! Dad! I got it wrong! She's not been going back to Her grave – She's been going *home*!'

* * *

'But that doesn't make sense,' said Natalie Markes. 'I saw the archaeologist's report. I signed off on it. It was an empty field; nothing there.'

'Wait,' interrupted Trish. 'You mean that you suspected it at least?'

'No. Yes. Sort of. It's complicated.'

'Then uncomplicate it for me.'

The day after Rogation Sunday was the spring bank holiday and they were driving to Peter's parents in Coventry, and Natalie's voice on the phone kept dropping in and out as the signal varied. Trish really should have called before they'd left, but in the whirlwind of the Beating festivities she'd completely forgotten about the traditional family visit and so the morning had been a mad rush, not helped by them having been up half the night trying to get a coherent story out of Toby. He was slumped in the back of the car, having made plain his incredulity and disgust that they could possibly be thinking about going to his grandparents' place given everything else that was happening, but Trish had been firm: ghostly curses or no ghostly curses, a bank holiday meant a visit to the relatives.

'Any new build needs planning permission, yes?' said Natalie.

'Obviously.'

'Well that gets handled at council level, and part of the application process means running it past the county archaeologist's office in case there's the danger of damaging anything heritage-worthy. Sometimes they look at the plans and decide that they want to have a look under there, which they obviously did in the case of Clegg Farm, probably for exactly the same reason that Toby spotted. So they ask for a pre-determination assessment – which is basically dig a trench, have a look, write a report.'

'Which they did.'

'Which *I* did!' said Markes. 'This is what I do! We picked an archaeological contractor from the council's list, hired a digger, cut trenches where they told us and the contractor wrote a report saying that there was nothing under there. That would have been a year and a half ago. Planning department gave us permission for the development and boom, here we are.'

'Is there any chance I could see that report? It's not confidential, is it?'

'No, but it is quite technical. I'm not sure how much use it's going to be.'

'What about the archaeologist – the one you hired? Can I speak to them?'

'Of course, if you want. I'll text you his contact details.'

'Thanks.'

A few minutes later Natalie's text came through with a PDF of the archaeologist's report and a link to his website: *Lewis Simms Archaeology, an independent archaeological consultant providing reliable and cost-effective services for planning officials and building contractors*, and, as she suspected with most small independent specialists, he was operating out of an office in his home, because the postal contact was a residential address: *3 Andrews Coppice, Clegg Farm Estate, Haleswell, B90 3SN*.

Trish didn't need to read any of the report further than

the first page, where Lewis Simms had listed himself as consultant with an entirely different address in Sparkbrook. It seemed that at some time in the eighteen months between being contracted to write the pre-determination report for Haleswell Village Trust and today, he'd moved into a nice new house close to the countryside, courtesy of, drum roll please, Haleswell Village Trust.

She texted Natalie back:

thx 4 this.

Then she hesitated, wondering how far she could trust the director of property and development, before deciding that it really didn't matter one way or the other and adding:

What if they had found something? Would that have affected development? Delays?

Certainly.

Delays costly?

Always. £££. ☹

Refusal of planning permission entirely???

Potentially yes but depends on how much there.

How about a whole medieval village?

There was no reply to that for long moments during which she watched the motorway traffic and the landscape unroll past the car.

Then Natalie's response came:

I'll get back to you on this.

Be careful. Maybe not mention this to Nash.

Natalie sent her a thumbs-up. Trish put her phone away and continued to stare out at the passing countryside.

Peter glanced at her. 'Everything okay?'

She shook herself as if waking up. 'Yes, why?'

'You've got that frown.'

'It's nothing. Just Trust issues.'

27

PRE-DETERMINATION

NATALIE MADE SURE THAT HER ID LANYARD WAS straight and put on her best Trustee smile before knocking on the door to 3 Andrews Coppice. It opened onto a tall and slender man somewhere in his forties, greying stylishly about the temples and dressed in exercise gear.

'Hello, Mr Simms?'

'Yes?'

'My name is Natalie Markes. I work for Haleswell Village Trust. I don't know if you remember, but you did some work for us last year? On this very site, as a matter of fact. I'm sorry to trouble you on the long weekend, but I was hoping you could help me with a quick question.'

He had a broad smile with lots of very even teeth. 'Of course I remember – please, come in! And call me Lewis.'

She was welcomed into a home which was open and bright, furnished with an eye towards stylish minimalism but without being spartan. Large abstract tapestries and framed fabric works were placed carefully about the walls, giving warmth without clutter. At the breakfast bar of the open-plan living room a younger man with skin the colour of toasted cinnamon had the back off a computer and was prodding it with a screwdriver.

'This is my partner, Cal,' said Simms.

'Pleased to meet you.' They shook hands.

'We were just talking about you actually,' said Simms. 'Or rather the village festival yesterday. Completely fantastic. There aren't that many places which have that sense of tradition anymore.'

'I'm glad you enjoyed it. Hopefully you'll both stay to enjoy it for many years to come.'

'Can I get you a tea? Coffee?'

'Thank you but no – this really is a flying visit.'

'No problem then. Shall we go into the office?'

'Actually I was rather hoping that we might talk about this in your back garden? It's such a nice day. Minor miracle for a bank holiday, it seems a shame to waste it.'

With a slight frown of puzzlement he agreed and led the way through the house to a garden dominated by a patio obviously intended for entertaining large groups, with a table, many chairs, a chimenea for the winter and a barbecue that looked like it could run a small restaurant.

'What a lovely space!' she said. 'I hope you had no trouble having it fitted?'

'Uh, no – is there any reason why we would have?'

'Oh I don't know,' she replied airily. 'You find all kinds

of odd things in the ground when you start digging, don't you, Lewis?'

Simms' frown deepened and he went very still. 'I'm not sure what you're getting at.'

She turned to face him squarely. 'Then I'll be clearer. Eighteen months ago you submitted a pre-determination report to me, which I accepted in good faith, in which you concluded that there was no evidence of previous human habitation on this site, but I've since found good reason to believe you were lying. Now before you say anything,' she continued, as she saw him start to puff up defensively, 'let me just point out that it would be the easiest thing in the world for me to find out exactly when you bought this house, under what kind of financial terms, and whether or not you received any kind of preferential treatment. It would also be very easy for me to commission a second assessment of the part of the site which is still undeveloped, and, assuming I find what I suspect to be there, to call into question your competence and integrity with the Institute of Archaeologists. Frankly, I'm not interested in getting you into trouble. You seem like a nice man. And anything you tell me now will remain strictly confidential, but I really would like to know: what did you hide? Are there the remains of a medieval village underneath this site?'

Throughout her speech he'd turned increasingly scarlet and now looked like he was on the verge of bursting into tears. 'Oh God, yes, all right!' he said, his voice thick. 'But there was no way I would ever have been able to afford a place like this otherwise! And your chief executive Mr Nash offered me such a good deal! And it made me sick, honestly it made me sick!'

'I believe you,' she said, and it was true. 'I checked your references back then and you struck me as a decent man and I don't think this is a thing you would have done lightly. You just wanted a proper home for you and Cal, and I understand how persuasive Mr Nash can be. But here's what I'm not so sure about: were you so sick that maybe you did a bit of quiet looking around on your own? You know, once the diggers had started excavating the foundations, maybe you went through the spoil heaps at the end of the day to see if there was anything you could rescue?'

Simms was staring at her with a combination of awe and embarrassment, as if she were a stage hypnotist who had just made him squawk like a chicken. 'Do you want to see?' he asked.

'I'd be honoured if you showed me.'

He led her back through the house and into his office. Aside from the computer, noticeboard and bookshelves, there were photographs of him on various digs all over the world looking young and sunburnt and happy, and a large set of wide shallow drawers of the kind usually found in museum storerooms. He unlocked the unit and pulled out one of the drawers, and she gasped at what he'd found.

There were potsherds, belt buckles, nails, coins, beads, spoons, knives, scraps of cloth, and even a leather shoe, all in plastic grip-seal bags – physical remains of the village of Clegeham which had disappeared so many years ago. She wondered if any of this had belonged to Hester, if She'd touched it as a living, breathing child. Then she recognised something from Trish's story of what Toby saw: a stick like an old-fashioned wooden ruler, but with notches cut all down one side.

'What's this?' she asked, pointing.

'It's a tally stick,' he replied. 'A way of keeping accounts without having to use written records.'

'May I please borrow it?'

'I'm not really in a position to say no, am I?'

'I promise to look after it and return it to you if I can.'

He hesitated at the last moment before handing it over. 'You will be careful with it, won't you? You won't... sell it, or anything like that?'

'Why on earth would I do that?'

'Mr Nash. He asked me to keep an eye out for anything which might be, you know. Valuable. Just as a favour, he said.'

'Dear God.' She shook her head in disgust. 'This just gets better.'

'I know, I know—' he started to apologise.

'Oh it's not you, Lewis. Don't worry, you're not the one who needs to apologise.'

'Well?'

Nash stared at the tally stick on the round pub table in front of him as if it were something about to rise up and bite him. 'This is utterly preposterous,' he snorted.

The Trustees were meeting in the function room upstairs at the White Hart, which was designed to resemble an eighteenth-century gentlemen's club, with hunting prints on the walls and heavily upholstered armchairs. Trish had insisted that both Peter and Toby attend, so Nash had refused to let them use their usual meeting room in Manor House as there couldn't be an official minuted agenda. Alan Pankowicz had offered drinks on the house (Toby was allowed nothing stronger than a lemonade shandy, despite his protests), and to any stranger entering the room it would have seemed like nothing more than an afternoon drink between friends.

'Which bit is preposterous?' replied Anik Singh, Director of Human Resources. 'The bit where this is evidence of Her home being right under your precious development? Or the bit where you get someone to bury a report that could damage it by bribing them with a whole bloody house?'

'We can't be sure that place has any significance for Her...'

'Other than all the injured chippies who have tried to work there, of course,' interrupted Peter, but Nash ploughed on as if he hadn't spoken.

'For all we know this could be a setup; She could have been leading Toby on. I mean how do we know he saw anything in the first place? Kid was probably high on spice or monkey dust or whatever it is they're snorting these days.'

'Oh you did not just go there...' Peter growled, getting to his feet.

'Oh yes I did,' grinned Nash, pushing back his chair. 'Care to come with me?'

Trish pushed Peter back down while Natalie kicked the leg of Nash's chair. 'We're not going to let you derail this into an argument,' said Natalie, and Nash shrugged as if to say *Well you can't blame a man for trying.* 'You owe us an explanation of why you kept this information from us.'

'Why I kept it from you? Why do you think? Because there are some people around this table afflicted with an excess of conscience, who would like nothing more than to run every hiccup and setback through a committee and allow Trust business to get bogged down in paperwork from external agencies. Because they don't have the first clue about what we have to deal with on a daily basis. This is life and death for us, or have you forgotten that?'

'None of us have forgotten that,' said Esme Barlow with quiet venom. She was onto her second large gin and showed no signs of stopping any time soon.

'Good! Then perhaps you more than anyone will appreciate that there's a time for procedure and discussion, and there's a time for swift and strong leadership. Sometimes things simply need to get done. Isn't that why you voted for me to be chief executive?'

Sean Trevorrow downed the rest of his pint. 'I swear to God, if you tell us that we "can't handle the truth" I will glass you.'

'You all know what sort of a knife edge the Trust's finances are on,' Nash continued. 'If anything had happened to delay the Clegg Farm deal and those investors had pulled out we'd have been in a hole so deep none of us would have seen the light of day again. Besides,' he added, 'it's not as if I didn't tell *anybody.*'

Donna Russell swallowed a large mouthful of wine and

ahemmed. Natalie stared at her. 'Wait – you knew?'

Russell gave curt nod. 'Yes. And he was right.'

'I don't fucking believe this,' muttered Trevorrow.

'The Trust's financial director was in full agreement with me all the way,' said Nash.

'But you called him a misogynistic dungheap,' Trish pointed out.

Nash tipped his drink towards Russell in salute. She ignored him.

'I did, and he is. But that doesn't stop him from being right. If there was a medieval village under there the excavation could have taken years, and most of our budget projections along with it. I can name you half a dozen development companies who have gone to the wall for precisely this reason.'

'I don't think you're getting it,' said Anik. 'This is not just any other excavation we're talking about. Those other companies didn't have to deal with Hester Attlowe, did they? This could have been an opportunity to find out more about Her – how She lived, maybe even where She died. Something we could have used against Her!'

Nash shrugged and yawned as if the matter were one of supreme indifference to him. 'Why? What would have been the point? Granted, we might have found out a bit more about how and where the dead bitch lived, but there was no guarantee that anything useful would have come out of it. Certainly not worth risking the Trust's future over. The Beating of the Bounds keeps us safe like it has done every year. Isn't that right, Reverend?'

Joyce Dobson, who had remained silent up until then,

sipping her port and lemon, nodded slowly. 'Although I disagree with almost everything about the chief executive's methods,' she said, 'I have to say yes, we are as safe as we have ever been.'

'Safe?' Trish shook her head. 'The level of complacency here is staggering. Has She never attacked you, then? Have you never had any near-fatal accidents yourself?'

'Of course I have,' said Nash. 'But only when I've been careless, and never inside the boundary stones, obviously.'

'I still don't understand why someone who knows there is a vengeful medieval ghost after him who may well be connected to these finds would want to sweep this under the carpet.'

'Don't you? Here, let me demonstrate.' He took two of the smaller empty glasses from the table and his own nearly full pint of bitter. 'This is the possibility that a full excavation of the site might have revealed something we could use against Her, assuming that it had anything to do with Her at all.' He poured a tiny amount of beer into one of the small glasses. 'Here's the possibility that a full excavation of the site would have bankrupted the Trust.' He dumped beer into the second glass so that it overflowed and slopped over the table.

'Hey!' Anik shoved his chair back as beer spilled into his lap.

'The mistake you are making,' continued Nash, 'is in thinking that I am a selfish and manipulative bastard whose primary motivating factor is personal survival and enrichment – and to be fair, I can understand why you'd think that. But my family is one of the oldest in the village; there have been Nashes in Haleswell as far back as records go, even before there was a Trust, and we have always kept it safe from Her. The village is more important than any one person living in it – you, me, anyone. Compared to the hundreds of years behind us and the hundreds to come, the tiny spans of our little lives are completely insignificant. If I die, someone will replace me as chief executive. It's the way of things.'

Peter laughed. 'Well that's terribly noble and altruistic of you.'

Nash looked at him squarely, and when he replied, 'No, it's the exact opposite,' there was no bombast in it or self-satisfaction or mockery. It was the clear and implacable expression of a judge delivering a sentence. 'The welfare of the village comes first. Everything and everyone is expendable to that end. Try living here for more than a couple of months, then you get to judge me.'

'But all of that is by the by,' the reverend added. 'All of the he-saids and she-saids don't matter. Now that we do know, we have to decide what to do about it.'

'What *can* we do about it?' asked Esme.

'Exorcise it,' said Toby.

It was the first time he'd spoken. He'd listened to the squabbling adults, afraid to draw attention to himself while they did what adults did, which was to apportion blame, but this was something he knew. He'd read all about it in old Mrs Drummond's books on ghosts and the paranormal. Everybody turned to look at him.

'Or at least,' he added, suddenly intimidated, 'not exorcise as such. That's for people who are possessed by demons. Houses are "cleansed", aren't they, Reverend?'

'That's right. You seem to have done your homework. Although in the Anglican church we refer to it as "deliverance".'

'Find this on Google, did you?' laughed Nash.

'Richard, for once in your life just shut the fuck up and let the boy speak!' snapped Russell, and to everyone's surprise he subsided without another word. 'Go on, Toby,' she added. 'Tell us what you know.'

'I'm not sure about any of it…'

'Then guess,' said Trevorrow. 'You've as much right to an opinion here as anyone.'

Toby swallowed. 'Okay. So. It's pretty clear that the building site is on top of the old village of Clegeham. Most of the things I've read say that an unquiet spirit will return to its grave or a place of significance to it in life, so I would put money on that haunted unfinished house being somewhere special. Maybe where She's buried.'

'I'm not sure,' frowned his dad. 'I don't think the Haleswell villagers would have carried the bodies of their victims all the way back to Clegeham to bury them. Probably wouldn't even touch them, if they were infected with the plague.'

Trevorrow nodded. 'More likely burn them or bury them in a mass grave close by.'

'It could be the site of the village church,' suggested Rev. Dobson.

'Or Her own home,' suggested his mum.

'Look!' Toby interrupted, getting exasperated. 'It doesn't

matter! It's important to Her, okay? It's a place of refuge for Her. If you cleanse it or deliver it or whatever, maybe it will weaken Her. Maybe get rid of Her altogether.'

'That's a barrel-load of maybes,' grumbled Nash. 'I'm inclined to think that, for better or worse, we have achieved a kind of equilibrium in the village which I'd be reluctant to disturb. The plague stones protect us from the worst She can do, and we know the limits of what we can safely get away with. I worry about what might happen if we stir things up. What do you think, Joyce?'

'I think,' said the reverend slowly, 'that if we are not tampering with the blessing of the stones themselves then we have nothing to lose by trying.'

'There's always something to lose.' Esme Barlow's voice was low, but its weight of grief carried it into all corners of the room. She stood and waved her empty glass at them. 'I'm going for another. Anybody?'

Nobody took her up on the offer, and they watched her head to the bar.

'But it's not quite as simple as that,' the reverend continued. 'A proper deliverance has to be authorised by the bishop, which would entail a full investigation and report, and that could take weeks. It's a multidisciplinary approach, so they would take into account a history of accidents in the building, maybe health and safety or ground surveys, I don't know. Plus the final ceremony wouldn't be conducted by me, but by a member of the Diocesan Deliverance Ministry also appointed by the bishop.'

Nash frowned. 'I'm not sure we need to escalate things to

that kind of extent. Not until we're sure.'

'I bet you're not,' said Natalie.

'The alternative,' added the reverend, 'is that I conduct a simple home blessing. That's well within my remit and it might tell us something if She reacts. Then I can go to the bishop with something a bit more definite than educated guesswork.'

Nash clapped his hands once, decisively. 'Good, then.'

'Wait,' said Natalie. 'I thought you said you were worried about disturbing the equilibrium?'

'Regardless of what any of you think of me, if it's a good idea I will listen to it and I will always defer to the experts. But, to avoid any more accusations that I'm riding roughshod over the democratic wishes of the Trust, shall we put it to a vote? All those in favour of blessing the construction site?'

Hands rose around the table. Markes, Trevorrow and Barlow abstained but only Nash was actively against it.

'Fair enough,' he conceded. 'That's carried, then. Joyce, how much time do you need to set it up?'

'It's likely that we'll meet with some resistance from Her, so those who wish to be involved should take some time to fortify their souls through prayer or meditation or what you choose. I'll arrange a private service, obviously. But not long. I would suggest this Sunday, as the Lord's day. We should use every advantage we have.'

'Excellent. Sunday it is.'

Toby watched as round the table the adults took out their phones and tablets to enter it as an appointment in their calendar apps. He took out his own and texted Maya:

Hey. Want to see a building get exorcised?

She hadn't contacted him since the punch-up or replied to any of his apologies, which meant that she was pissed at him. Not that he could blame her – Rajko was her brother, at the end of the day. He figured he'd try this one last time, and then wait to see what happened when they got back to school. When she texted him back he was so was surprised that he almost dropped his phone in the puddle of beer on the table.

That's ur idea of a date is it? Weirdo.

Toby grinned.

28

THE CLEANSING

TOBY LAY IN BED AND PRETENDED TO BE ASLEEP WHEN his mum opened the door to check on him. He heard her murmur, 'We'll be done and back before he's even awake,' to his dad, and the door closed again. They had absolutely refused to let him attend the cleansing. Even his dad didn't want to go, but had decided that he needed to be there to protect his wife, since she was equally adamant about supporting Rev. Dobson. The pair of them no doubt thought that because he was fourteen and it was a Sunday morning, he wouldn't be awake before midday – although he had to admit that on any other weekend that would probably be true. It was half past five in the morning, but he'd already been awake long enough to watch the dawn.

He listened to his parents shut the front door behind them and jumped out of bed, shrugging on yesterday's clothes as he texted still up for this?

up dressed and already waiting 4 u dozer

she replied.

He dressed quicker.

The streets were empty and the early morning was bright and clear but still had the pre-dawn freshness which carried a chill even for the beginning of June. The thinnest fingernail paring of May's old moon was hanging low in the sky.

Maya was waiting for him at the Rec, trying to look cool but obviously as buzzed as he was about it all. Her hair was back in a single ponytail, and she was wearing a pair of trainers which looked immaculately clean, her most stylish jeans with the knees out, and a plain yellow sweater over which she'd wrapped one of those big scarves that had lots of tassels over it. It looked suspiciously like she'd dressed for a date. He was suddenly aware of the fact that he hadn't even stopped to brush his teeth.

Jesus, man, just focus, would you?

'Your brother isn't going to come screaming after us, is he?' he asked, before he could engage his brain.

She stared at him, stony-faced. 'Is that meant to be funny, psycho-boy?'

'No,' he muttered, chastened. 'Sorry.'

Then she smiled and bounced on the balls of her feet. 'So where's this haunted house, then?'

* * *

'Visit, Lord, we pray, this place and drive far from it all the snares of the enemy. Let your holy angels dwell here to keep us in peace, and may your blessing be upon it evermore, through Jesus Christ our Lord.'

Peter stood a little to one side, watching Reverend Dobson leading his wife and the rest of the Trustees in a prayer in front of Lot 9. It didn't seem to matter that it was the brightest part of an early summer morning – the sun was behind the half-built house, casting a long, tongue-like shadow over the group, as if it had soaked up the night and now clasped it jealously to its grey concrete bones, reluctant to part with it. Its window spaces gaped at him, shreds of plastic stirring restlessly in a breeze that couldn't be felt in the sunlight, or possibly moved aside like curtains by dead hands curious to see who had come to visit.

'The Lord be with you,' said the reverend. She was holding a large wooden cross in one hand, and reading from a copy of the Book of Common Prayer with the other. Trish herself was carrying a small bottle of holy water from St Sebastian's Well to sprinkle in each of the rooms, and Nash was wielding the church's huge Victorian Bible in both hands like a shield.

'And with your spirit,' responded the others. Trish had her head bowed and her eyes closed, deep inside that place Peter had never been and couldn't understand. He'd never felt like he knew her less than at this very moment.

'In the name of the Father, the Son and the Holy Spirit,' Dobson said, and led them inside. The shadow of the front doorway swallowed them, and Peter hurried to catch up.

They should have been in the long hallway which ran into the depth of the house; the plan, as he understood it, was to bless each room of the house and then move on, but they weren't here, and he felt a little flutter of panic. Had he stood so long outside, lost in thought, that they'd already finished in this room and moved on, or had they decided to skip it? The interior seemed unchanged since Lance's prank: the same pools of stagnant water, the same floating debris, the same looping chalk scrawls on the walls. Even the bucket was still here. Almost as if he'd never left at all.

He shook his head to clear it. How long had he been standing here, staring at a stupid bucket? He could hear the voices of the others coming from another room, the echoes of their murmurs spreading out like ripples on the water that lapped about his shoes.

There were no doors, just suggestions of exits and entrances sketched in rust-streaked concrete, opening on darkness.

He followed the murmurs.

'O God,' Joyce declaimed, 'give your blessings to all who share this room, that they may be knit together in companionship...'

Trish looked up to the sky that she could see through the ribs of the roof trusses, but the early-morning sun was still too low for its direct light to penetrate the gloom. Whatever this room was supposed to be on the plans, it was small, and with the water around her feet and the bare block walls rising two storeys around her it was like being at the bottom of a well, or an oubliette – somewhere to be forgotten, left to starve and die and rot.

'...thank you for this place to live. We claim this room as a place of spiritual safety and protection from all attacks of the enemy...'

All of a sudden the people around her felt too close, hemming her in, taking up her oxygen. She looked at them to see if they seemed to be feeling anything similar – Anik, Pankowicz, Nash, and Donna – but their eyes were closed in prayer, their lips moving silently.

'By our authority as children of God, we command every evil spirit claiming ground in the structures and furnishings of this place to leave and never return...'

The smell of damp brickwork was thick and over-powering in Trish's throat, the promise of fresh air too high and unreachable.

'I can't—!' she gasped. 'I can't—!' and shoved her way through the people crowding her, fighting to find the door. There was an opening, but less light there than here and no suggestion of what might be on the other side. Voices behind her were calling out in concern but she couldn't hear them properly through the roaring in her ears. She curled her fingers around the edge of the doorway and pulled herself through.

And into a pair of outstretched arms.

Peter knew this doorway shouldn't be here. He'd been working on the site for almost six weeks and the floorplan variations of these units were as familiar to him as walking around his own home in the dark – and this doorway absolutely should not be here. Unless somehow he'd become turned around. Or the owners had ordered some customisations which would never see the light of day because nobody in their right mind would work on this unit.

This house is stillborn, he thought. *Dead before it ever lived.*

Still, this was the direction in which he'd heard the murmuring voices so this was the direction he had come.

'Trish?' he called. The concrete soaked up his voice – tasted and swallowed it without echo.

Whatever this chamber's intended function, it was large, most likely the living room. Sheets of shredded plastic hung down from the ceiling joists, making it hard to be sure, but it looked like there was a group of people standing in a little cluster at the far end.

'Reverend Dobson?'

Then Trish's voice, screaming, '*Peter!*'

Coming from behind him.

He spun around as she lunged out from another doorway opposite and fell into his arms, gasping and sobbing. Behind her hurried the reverend and the rest of the group, asking if she was okay, what was the matter, was she all right?

'I'm sorry,' she gasped. 'I just, I think I had. Anxiety attack. Just, oh God, can we please just *leave*?'

'Peter,' said Reverend Dobson, 'maybe you should take Trish outside for some fresh air.'

He nodded. 'Maybe we should all leave. This place is *wrong*.' Who had those other people been? Had they been real? Shadows cast by the plastic sheeting? Was he simply going crazy?

The reverend shook her head. 'We knew there would be resistance. This only proves how right we were to come here in the first place. We must be strong in our faith and our trust in each other.'

'Great. You do that. But I'm telling you, this was a mistake.'

Then Nash started in. 'Peter—'

'Where's Donna?' asked Pankowicz, looking around.

'Didn't she come out with the rest of you?' replied Trish.

Dobson turned back to the small room that they'd just left. 'Donna!' she called.

In response came the sound of a girl's voice, singing. It was accompanied by harsh, rhythmic scratching sounds, as if two bricks were being grated together repeatedly. The reverend entered the room first, her cross held high, the others close behind.

They saw Donna with her back to them, standing at the far wall by the wide rectangular hole of an unfinished window which had most definitely not been there before. It opened onto the site, but a cage of scaffolding on the outside of the unfinished house would have stopped her from climbing out and escaping, if that had been her intention. It obviously wasn't. Instead, she was scratching at the mortar around one of the breeze blocks on the bottom edge of the opening, using a fragment of broken brick but also picking at it with her left hand, digging and plucking sharp fragments loose with her bare fingertips and throwing them aside. Her flesh was shredded, and the masonry wet with her blood. And all the while she sang in a high, childlike voice, something that sounded like a nursery rhyme except that the language was either nonsense or else so old that they couldn't understand it.

'Donna?' ventured the reverend.

Donna stopped both digging and singing, but didn't turn around. When she spoke, the voice that came from her was still that of a child but there was something deeper underneath it, something hoarser and immeasurably older. 'You sanctimonious cunt,' it snarled. 'I knew a priest once. He was a good man. He took a dying stranger into his home and nursed him even though he knew it meant his own death. What have you ever done but hide behind a barrier made of your own precious piety and self-righteousness? You dare preach *hospitality* and *protection* here, of all places?' She resumed digging and scratching, having succeeded in loosening the brick that she was working on a good way already, so that it rattled in its hole like a rotten tooth as she worried at it.

'Heavenly Father,' the reverend prayed, 'in the name of Jesus Christ, we bind this child to the will and purpose of God and we loose her from every attempt of the evil one to influence any part of her life. We ask, Lord, that you cover this child with the blood of Christ—'

'You refused us what pittance of charity it was in your power to bestow,' the voice continued as she chipped, scratched, dug. 'You turned us away when we were most in need. You killed us. And now you, who should know better than most about succouring the needy, you come here to my home. *MY HOME!*' she shrieked, so loudly and suddenly that some quirk of the echoes in the building's shell magnified it and hammered it into their skulls so that they clapped their hands to their ears and cried out. '*And you talk to me of blood!?*'

With a grunt she succeeded in pulling the block free in two great chunks. Peter wasn't surprised to see that it was hollow; true to Nash's cost-cutting priorities the houses in this development were constructed with cheaper hollow blocks reinforced by metal bars running up through them. She'd pulled the block apart, using her bare hands in a way which hurt just to look at, and in the gap had exposed the rusted rebar from inside.

That done, Donna stood and turned to them, but she wasn't Donna Russell, Director of Financial Services for Haleswell Village Trust, anymore. Her face was ravaged with black lesions that leaked a foul-smelling pus, her throat bulged with grotesque swellings, and the glittering scorn in her eyes was something that he had only ever seen on one other face.

'You think it is your piety that protects you from me?' Hester laughed. 'You cannot keep me out forever. In time the Lord will deliver me unto you, "for He shall bring down their pride together with the spoils of their hands. And the fortress of the high fort of thy walls shall He bring down, lay low, and bring to the ground, even to the dust".' She crossed the room in a heartbeat, and before Rev. Dobson could flinch away clasped the reverend by the face with Her ruined hand, its fingers black with gangrene, painting her crimson from brow to chin. Dobson gagged at the smell. Hester pressed Her mouth to the back of her hand so that without it between them the two women might have been kissing, closed Her eyes and sighed, 'Oh, there will be so much blood.'

For one of the very few times in his life, Nash found himself frozen with indecision. It wasn't fear – fear was a child's reaction to the threat of getting caught, more like the adrenalin high of an extreme-sports junkie. This paralysis was a total systems crash as his brain struggled to find an appropriate response to a completely alien set of circumstances. He couldn't understand what he was seeing, as he watched the impossibly diseased Donna attack Joyce, and in the end he decided that he didn't need to. It was actually very simple: the woman who kept him safe from the thing that wanted him dead was under threat.

'Donna, get off her!' he shouted, hefting the heavy Bible in both hands and raising it at her like a club. 'Snap out of it, woman!'

She rounded on him, snarling, her dead black fingers hooked into claws, and he brought down the Bible to protect his eyes, but the blow never came.

When he looked, she was reeling away from him in baffled fury. 'Where did you get that?' she demanded. 'How dare you have that!'

In the chaos of the moment he was only aware that everybody seemed to be shouting at once; it was only afterwards that he thought there was anything odd about it.

'Give it back!' she raged. 'That belonged to a man who should have been a saint! You're not fit to lie with his dogs!'

Sensing an advantage, he pressed it, raising the Bible and advancing towards her. She backed away another step, and he grinned. He didn't know why it was causing her such consternation, and he didn't much care. 'You're welcome to take it off me, if you can.'

Her scream of frustration split the air, and she spun to face the window opening again, with its waist-high gap in the brickwork filled only with the upthrust spike of the rusted rebar. Too late, he realised what she was going to do, and he screamed, 'For God's sake, Donna, NO!'

But she planted her hands either side of the gap, raised her head high and slammed it down face-first onto the spike. There was a crunch which sounded like someone driving a knife into a cabbage, her legs spasmed for a moment, and then she was still, bent over as if praying, and fixed in place by the rebar through her skull.

'Oh my God, Toby?' Maya's eyes were wide with fear. 'What's going on?'

From their hiding place behind a stack of pallets, they could clearly hear the shouting coming from inside the half-built house.

'I don't know,' he replied. 'But I think I need to go and see.'

Maya put a hand on his arm and dragged him back down. 'You can't!' she said. 'We're not supposed to be here, remember?'

He remembered. This had turned out to be a bad idea, pretty much right from the start when he'd had to come up with a story about why his parents were involved. He obviously couldn't tell her the truth, and what had started out in his head as a harmless bit of spying on a bunch of dumb adults had quickly mutated into a nightmare of awkward questions.

He shook off her hand. 'Something's gone wrong!' he said. 'I need to help them.'

'Then call the police,' she told him. 'Actually, I will.' She dug out her phone but he grabbed it from her. 'Hey! What the fuck? Give that back!'

'You can't call the police.'

'Give me my phone back, you asshole!' Her eyes were blazing with fury. She tried to seize her phone but he kept it out of reach behind his body.

'*You can't call them,*' he insisted. 'They won't be able to do anything. Besides, you were the one who said we're not supposed to be here, remember? We'll both be in the shit.'

'Fine! Let them…' she waved in the general direction of the building. 'Whatever this is. Now give me my phone or I'll tell Rajko that you brought me out here to have your wicked way with me.'

Toby handed the phone over, and she started backing away. 'I'm sorry,' she said. 'I don't know what this is all about but I have to go.'

'I understand. I'm the one that should be sorry. I thought this was going to be just a bit of a laugh, you know? I'll talk to you about it later, yeah?'

She nodded, turned and ran. In the end he never did get the chance to talk to her about it, and the last he ever saw of her was as she disappeared amongst the towers of scaffolding. When he turned his attention back to the situation, someone was reeling out of the front door – it looked like Al Pankowicz, and he was weeping. Then his dad appeared, supporting his mum, and they fell at the threshold.

'Mum! Dad!' he screamed, and ran to help.

His dad looked at him dazedly. 'Toby? You shouldn't be here.'

His mum was trying to get up again, so he got his hands under her arms and pulled. She swatted at him. 'Get away!' she gasped. 'Don't go inside…'

'What happened? Mum, what happened in there?'

Then Mr Nash appeared, supporting Reverend Dobson, whose face was streaked with blood, and Mr Singh who looked like he was sobbing.

That was the point at which he pulled out his phone and dialled 999.

29

THE PILGRIM BADGE

'TELL ME AGAIN WHAT THIS THING ON THE BOTTOM is,' said Nash, sliding the embroidered bookmark across the desk to Simms. It wasn't so much the bookmark itself that he was interested in, as the gleaming metal badge-like object which had been sewn onto it at the end. The archaeologist had told him once, when he'd first found it and passed it on to Nash just as an historical curio. Once he'd realised that it wasn't especially valuable, Nash had given it to the reverend because it seemed like a church thing, but that had been a year ago and he wanted to hear Simms again in case he'd missed something important the first time around. Nash was fidgety and out of sorts. Partially it was the shock of seeing Hester make Donna do that to herself yesterday. The rest of Sunday had been written off by interviews with the police, who thankfully seemed to be going with a theory of suicide brought on by some kind of religious fervour. But

.f a bottle of whisky hadn't made sleep come any easier or him.

Markes and Singh hadn't come into the office that morning, and he couldn't blame them. Pankowicz was probably holed up at the White Hart, letting his bar staff run the pub – wherever he was, he wasn't returning Nash's calls. The Feenans – actually, he didn't give a fuck what the Feenans were doing, just as long as their wankstain of a kid didn't come near him. The reverend was at the rectory with the doors locked and the curtains tightly drawn. Nash didn't think she'd noticed that he'd taken the bookmark, but if she had she wasn't making a fuss about it. It would have seemed utterly trivial. Nash was hoping that it was the exact opposite.

'It's a pilgrim badge,' said Simms. 'Fourteenth century. Pewter. Not that rare or valuable, I'm afraid.'

'Spare me the *Antiques Roadshow* bullshit and just tell me what it means.'

Simms crossed his arms and sat back. 'If you want a professional consultation you can make an appointment tomorrow and I'll invoice you. If you're here in my home on a Monday evening asking for a favour you're going the wrong way about it.'

Nash closed his eyes and breathed deeply, pinching the bridge of his nose as if suffering a headache. 'Lewis, I'm sorry,' he said. 'It's been a…' He uttered a short, high laugh. 'Well it's been a bit of an awkward few days, to be honest with you. I'm sorry. Please…' He gestured for the other man to continue.

Simms sighed and picked up the badge again. 'Lots of

people went on pilgrimages in the Middle Ages,' he said. 'From all walks of life, not just the clergy. They'd go to the shrines or burial places of saintly figures, like Thomas Becket at Canterbury, for worship and miraculous healing. A pilgrimage over long distances on foot was a dangerous undertaking and when they got to their destination they found people selling these decorative badges as souvenirs of the journey. They were cheaply made, cast in pewter, and depicted the shrines, a bit like postcards, or faces of the saints themselves, or stories from their lives.'

'So this is just a piece of medieval tourist tat?'

'In a sense. Some of them were quite sexually graphic, too – flying phalluses and vulvas with arms and legs. There's evidence that pilgrims enjoyed the opportunity for casual sex along the way, so some historians think that these badges could have been a way of letting other pilgrims know you were available and what you were into.'

'Seriously?' Nash shook his head, amazed. 'So it was basically a medieval Club 18–30 booze cruise?'

'For some, yes. But that didn't stop it from having deep religious significance for them at the same time. It's only our modern culture which separates sexuality and spirituality. A pilgrim badge was also a status symbol to the people when you got home that you'd fulfilled one of your obligations as a Christian of good standing in the community.'

'So it could have been owned by literally anybody.'

'Yes. This one, of a ship with figures, is from Becket's shrine, illustrating his exile to France following a confrontation with Henry II.'

Nash took the badge back and examined it more closely. It was exquisitely detailed, showing every board of the steeply curved clinker-built keel, the rudder and the anchor, figures in chain mail at bow and stern and the saint standing by the central mast at the centre, and not just ropes running from deck to topmast but even the twists in each rope. Many hours of devotion had gone into crafting its original – for thousands of copies to be cast and sold a penny a piece to make a quick profit. Nothing new there, he supposed. 'Is it something that people might think would protect them from the Devil?'

'I wouldn't have thought so. A good old-fashioned cross would do the job better, wouldn't it?'

Nash pocketed the badge and stood. 'Well, thanks for that,' he said.

'Does that help?'

'I don't know,' Nash replied. He couldn't think of a reason why a piece of mass-produced junk would have had such an effect on Hester. It was like discovering that a vampire could be repelled with a piece of Lego. 'I honestly don't know.'

Nash was sitting on one of the park benches by the village pond, staring blankly at the squabbling ducks when the man from the Diocesan Deliverance Ministry found him. The dwindling twilight of a summer evening streaked the world with long shadows.

'Richard,' he said, sitting down beside him.

Nash nodded, but didn't look up. 'Malcolm.'

If it hadn't been for his dog collar Father Malcolm

Powell might have been mistaken for someone doing an impersonation of a seventies geography teacher, with his unruly mass of curly brown hair, glasses and a scruff of beard. 'I would ask after your health,' said Father Powell, 'but in the light of recent circumstances…' He shrugged and tailed off awkwardly. 'Please accept our deepest condolences.'

Nash wasn't so easily disarmed. 'You're doing the rounds, I take it, now that the police are finished? Who have you spoken to so far?'

'Just Joyce. She blames herself, obviously.'

'I don't think there was anything she could have done differently.' He waited, but the priest just shuffled his feet and scratched his nose. 'That was your cue to tell me that we should have waited for your lot before taking matters into our own hands.'

'I'm not here to apportion blame, Richard,' Powell said gently. 'I'm just here to find out what happened.'

'You're recording this, I take it?'

Father Powell took his phone out of his jacket pocket. 'Do you mind?'

Nash uttered a short laugh. 'Why would I mind? You can add it to all the other records that have been collected over the last few hundred years and have done fuck-all good. You can put it next to Donna's bloodstained clothes in a nice little plastic bag.' It didn't make any sense but he didn't care. He was pissed, and scared, and he hated feeling the latter most of all. 'I mean what good does your ministry actually *do*, beyond replacing those of us that She manages to bump off?'

Father Powell ignored Nash's little rant. 'Joyce told me that the entity actually retreated from you when you confronted it with the pulpit Bible from St Sebastian's. Is this true?'

Nash sighed. Might as well play the game, then. 'Yes, it is.'

'You understand how unprecedented that is. Short of the parish stones we have never found anything that the entity has been repelled by. What do you think was different this time?'

With the pilgrim badge resting against the skin of his chest, hidden underneath his shirt and hanging on a slim silver chain about his neck, Nash looked at Father Powell squarely and said, 'No idea. You lot are the experts.'

Father Powell looked at him for a long time without answering. Nash thought it was likely that the priest knew he was lying, but what could he do about it? There was no way Nash was going to give up the one thing that could save his village from that dead little bitch.

'I did examine the Bible, obviously,' Powell said eventually. 'It's quite a nice one. I was particularly taken by the number of ornately embroidered and decorated bookmarks it has, although one of them, I did notice, appeared to be missing something. There were a number of loose threads as if something which had once been sewn onto it had been subsequently cut or ripped off. Do you know what that might have been?'

'You'd have to ask Joyce that.'

'I did. She said it was just an old pilgrim badge that must have fallen off either some time earlier or in the commotion. I checked with the investigating officers, who said that they'd found nothing like it at the scene. I mean it's probably got nothing to do with the entity, although interestingly, Joyce told me that it was you who had originally given the badge to her, nearly a year ago.'

Nash waved his hand airily. 'I have this archaeologist fellow I know who looks out for interesting things for me. I thought she'd like it.' That much at least was the truth. 'As you say, probably nothing to do with "the entity" at all. But if I see it I'll be sure to let you know.'

'I'd be very grateful.' Father Powell stopped the recording on his phone, put it away, and stood. 'You know,' he said after a moment, 'we really do want nothing more than to help protect Haleswell.'

Nash rose and shook his hand. 'So do I,' he said, maintaining his grip. 'More than literally anything else in the world.'

He nearly added *or anyone*.

The priest left, his shadow trailing after him along the grass.

Hester had not thought of Father Cuthbert's pilgrim badge for longer than it would have taken several generations of men to die, and it disturbed her.

He had arrived in Clegeham as a fourteen-year-old servant to the old village priest, Father Euan; lanky and awkward, in robes that were too big for him, wrestling to carry Father Euan's books and belongings. She had been ten, but remembered his arrival clearly. She decided from the moment she saw him that, priest's servant or not, she was going to marry him.

She found or manufactured occasions to help Cuthbert with his work around the church, taking him gifts and quizzing him on what their life would be like together. She stole ale and food for him and endured her father's beatings for this gladly, and Cuthbert tried to teach her what little learning he had.

And then, when Cuthbert was sixteen and she was twelve, Father Euan was kicked in the stomach by a cow and died, and the parish priest at Haleswell decided that Cuthbert would take his place. The Church would be his only bride. Moreover, he would undertake a pilgrimage to Canterbury to pray for the Lord's guidance in his new vocation.

Hester was distraught. She had been as far as Warwick, and that had been adventure enough; the notion of travelling for weeks on the road to somewhere as far as Canterbury seemed dangerous and foolhardy. She clung to him and wept and offered to run away with him and threatened unspecific but dire retribution if he abandoned her, but he gently disentangled her hands from his and said that he had been called and so must answer, and that there was no greater love he could offer her than to shepherd her soul into the Lord's care where they could be together for eternity.

In the end she had no choice but to let him go.

He returned three weeks later – leaner and with his clothes much stained from long travel, but there was a brightness to his gaze and in the way he greeted his old neighbours that told her his pilgrimage had indeed changed him. He seemed to have been filled up with something, as if there had been an empty space in his soul that even he had not known was there. She saw that and loved him even more, but she put aside her childish infatuation and tried to turn her love into something more befitting an unmarried woman for her priest, and accustomed herself to calling him Father. In token, perhaps, of this, he gifted her the pilgrimage badge that he had bought as a memento.

It was a pretty thing. She liked the way the light flashed on the pewter. It was fashioned after the image of a boat with a steeply curved keel, knights on the high fore and aft castles, and the saint himself standing by the mast, and Father Cuthbert told her the tale of how Saint Thomas had fled to exile in France for defying the king's orders. Hester liked that story, secretly relishing the fantasy of saying *No, I will not* to a king. She never wore it openly, as it would have invited the envy of the other girls and opened Father Cuthbert to accusations of impropriety, but hid it within the straw of her bedding to take out at night and admire and dream impossible fantasies of escaping far away over the ocean with her beloved.

Then the pestilence came and took him from her.

She was the last to tend him, the other women having more than enough to contend with in caring for their own sick menfolk and children. The pestilence had ravaged his smooth skin with black lesions and open sores, but she endured the stench of it and helped him to sip as much water with his cracked lips as he could take. And when he died, she made sure that he was buried with the pilgrimage badge to guide him on his last and furthest journey.

No, she had not thought of this in a long, long time. It disturbed her.

It disturbed the black thing inside her which gave her the strength to punish her enemies.

The *gwrach clefyd*.

30

CATASTROPHIC CIRCUMSTANCES

RAJKO KNEW SOMETHING WAS WRONG WHEN HE SAW the light from the living-room window – it was two in the morning and everybody should have been in bed. Maya and the Ant had school in the morning, Papa was on an early shift at the sorting office, and Mama simply didn't stay up that late. He killed the engine and got out of the car, staring up at the house. Had his parents argued? Was someone hurt?

He let himself in, and was halfway upstairs when he surprised himself by succumbing to a massive yawn that felt like it threatened to split his head in half at the jaw. He hadn't realised he was so tired; it certainly wasn't the latest he'd come home from a night out with the lads from college. *Must be getting old*, he thought with a quiet laugh. *Old man, nineteen soon, responsible man of the family.* Or maybe it was just the comedown from the coke. As he climbed he idly wondered whether he could use the Feenan kid as a way into the Trust's cosy little middle-class bubble; had to be some friends there he could supply.

There was someone up on the landing ahead of him.

Wait – no, no there wasn't. The landing was empty. But just for a moment it had seemed like there was the silhouette of a girl standing by his front door.

'Maya?' he called. 'Maya, have you locked yourself out?'

There was no reply, because nobody was there.

'Losing it,' he muttered to himself.

Another yawn hit him on the landing as he was opening the front door, this one so hard that it left him a little dizzy. No, this was more like being stoned. He didn't like it.

Down on the right-hand side of the hallway was the living room, with a line of bright light streaming underneath the door. And now he could hear the television; some kind of heavy rock music accompanied by metallic clanging sounds and a voice-over that he couldn't quite make out.

This definitely wasn't right – if he could hear it from the hallway, Mama would definitely be able to hear it from the adjoining room, and there was no way she would put up with that kind of noise at this time of night.

Another wave of dizziness washed over him, and he steadied himself with one hand on the wall. What the fuck? Had someone spiked him? And if they had, why was it kicking in only just now?

He pushed open the living-room door, and heaved a sigh of relief. Papa was asleep in his armchair with a can of lager next to him and the television on – some reality show about blokes trying to forge ancient weapons out of car parts. One of the presenters was testing the sharpness of a contestant's blade by slicing at a pig's carcass. Rajko switched the TV off and shook his father by the shoulder.

'Come on, Papa, time for bed,' he said.

This time when he yawned, the dizziness persisted until spots appeared before his vision and only went away when he shook his head fiercely. Something was wrong. And his father wasn't stirring. His head didn't even loll properly like it should have done if he was asleep – in fact, it moved with his torso, stiffly, as if the man were tied to a rigid framework.

'Papa? What's wrong?'

If his own head hadn't been feeling like it was stuffed full of cotton wool Rajko would have seen right from the start what he only noticed now: his father's skin was too pale, and his lips were blue. And he wasn't breathing.

'*Papa!*' he screamed, shaking him with both hands.

His father's corpse toppled forwards like a broken deckchair collapsing over itself, all hinges. His head struck the floor with a dull thud, like a block of wood in a sack. There was absolutely no chance that he might have been alive.

'*Mama! Come quick!*' In that moment Rajko wasn't a young man on the brink of responsible adulthood but a little boy again. He backed away from the horror lying on the floor and ran to get his mother. She would know what to do.

He flung open the door of his parents' bedroom and lurched across to the bed, shaking the figure that was lying there. She was lying on her side, facing away from him. 'Mama!' he sobbed. 'Come quick! Papa's hurt!'

It felt like trying to shift the trunk of a felled tree. Other than rolling slightly beneath his hand, she didn't move, but the covers fell away from her shoulder to reveal the strap of a nightdress over pale, waxy flesh.

Oh Jesus no.

Then: *Maya. Antony.*

Despite his panic, he hesitated a little before opening the door to Maya's bedroom, because in the last year she had started to get ferocious about her privacy, and heaven help him if he barged in on her while she was practising one of the Feminine Mysteries. The head and foot of her bed frame were strung with fairy lights, so that he could see her, sitting propped up against her pillows, with her phone in one hand as if she'd fallen asleep in the middle of chatting with her friends about whatever it was that girls chatted about. She was wearing a fluffy pullover with the words 'Cool Vibes' spelt out in letters shaped like doughnuts and ice lollies. It had been a favourite when she was younger and even though she never wore it in public anymore she still liked it for slobbing around at bedtime. The fairy lights were dim, but they couldn't hide the blueness of her lips, or the thin line of drool which hung from them and made a damp spot in the front of her pullover.

'No...' he moaned. '*Noooo...*'

Black blotches rushed in from every side then, and almost overwhelmed him, but he smacked his head against the door frame until the pain chased them away. Whatever it was, it was getting worse. The only time he'd ever felt anything like it had been the only time he'd tried laughing gas – it hadn't made him laugh at all, just feel sick and panicky because he knew that he wasn't breathing proper air.

He wasn't breathing proper air.

Dear God, the boiler the boiler THE FUCKING BOILER!

He staggered across Maya's bedroom to the window and wrenched it open, and the flood of fresh air was like a bucket of cold water to the face. He took a couple of deep lungfuls and then doubled up as his stomach cramped, and he vomited an evening's worth of booze and the remains of a kebab between his feet.

'Sorry... sorry...' he whimpered, not sure if he was apologising for the sick, or the fact that he had to abandon Maya to look for his baby brother, or for the broken boiler which had probably been filling their flat with carbon monoxide for hours, or maybe all of it. Shivering, weeping, hanging on to the walls for support, he left her room.

He found Antony curled up in bed as if fast asleep, thumb in his mouth, Simba clutched in the crook of one elbow. There were ten other people in the building who he knew he should have checked on too, but at the sight of his dead baby brother all rational thought for their survival, or even his own, disappeared. Rajko must have called the emergency services at some point, although he didn't remember it, because when the paramedics arrived they found him on the floor beside the bed, rocking Antony's body in his arms and howling like a soul newly damned.

The shrilling of Nash's phone woke him and he fumbled it from the bedside table. It buzzed in his grip like an angry wasp while he tried to blink away the fog in his head. He frowned at the screen; without his glasses it was blurry even this close. Christ, his eyes were getting bad. It looked suspiciously like two something in the morning, but that couldn't be right. Even his ex-wife wasn't stupid enough to call at this hour.

Incoming call: Ingram, Daniel

He sat up straighter. Sergeant Dan Ingram was the officer in charge of Haleswell Neighbourhood Policing Team and a cog in the workings of the Trust machinery that Nash had worked very hard to keep turning smoothly for their benefit. Ingram's children went to the grammar school, his wife's law firm handled a lot of the Clegg Farm contracts, a sizeable chunk of their savings had been invested in the development – in return for which they were getting a sweet deal on one of the premium units – and all of this kept it in Ingram's interests to alert Nash to anything which might throw a spanner in its delicately balanced workings.

So if he was calling the Trust's chief executive at stupid-o-clock in the morning it wasn't going to be for anything good.

'What?' he grunted.

Then, as he listened: 'Oh *shit*.'

By the time Sergeant Ingram had finished, Nash was halfway towards being dressed and out the door.

Even though Rajko was breathing the clean night air again, sitting safely in a police car with the back door open, it felt like the carbon monoxide had worked its way into every last atom of his soul: he was totally numb. The freezing cold of the early hours didn't touch him. The strobing lights of ambulances, fire engines and police cars washed over him in waves of red and blue without making him blink. The chatter of radios as fire crews and paramedics tried to make sense of the situation remained meaningless and distant; even his skin felt as tight and lifeless as the oxygen mask that they'd given him. He wasn't real, and here and alive – how could he be, given what had happened to the world? With so much dead, how could he not be too? The paramedics would have taken him to the hospital first, a lot earlier, if there'd been enough ambulances, and until they'd realised the scale of the disaster. He was able to pick at least that much information out of the insect buzz of their voices. Disconnected words and phrases slipped through:

...must have been building up for hours...

...detectors?...

...shitty ventilation...

...probably didn't feel a thing...

Everyone on the first three floors of the house was dead. Of course nobody was saying that officially – there'd have to be a proper investigation first – but it was obvious from the futile resuscitation efforts going on around him and conversations between people in uniforms who had forgotten he was there (because he wasn't; he was numb, dead, gone). Nine of his neighbours. Tamanna the teacher and her husband Stuart and his brother and the entire Ashok family. A nice baker's dozen if you included his own family. Only old Mr Griffiths from the topmost floor, where the carbon monoxide hadn't yet reached a lethal concentration, had been wheeled out alive.

And Rajko himself, of course.

Since he was conscious and talking lucidly the paramedics had been content to let him sit out front while they worked on those more urgently in need of help, which was just as well because even if they had tried to take him to hospital in one of the first ambulances to arrive he'd have fought them. He was not leaving while his family were still inside, it was as simple as that. So he sat, numb, waiting for the horror of it all to break through and shatter him into a million pieces all over again.

Then standing at the edge of everything, watching, he saw Maya.

Or at least, it wasn't exactly Maya. It was a girl who looked a bit like his sister, an illusion strengthened by the fact that she was wearing Maya's 'Cool Vibes' sweater. Then he remembered that girl he had thought he'd seen on the staircase landing.

'Hey,' he murmured. This wasn't right. Had she sneaked back in and stolen Maya's clothing off her dead body? Was she somehow responsible for all of this? She was looking right at him across the crowd of paramedics, fire crew and onlookers like she was taunting him.

'Hey!' he got out of the police car, but nobody was paying any attention to him.

She turned and started to walk away, into an alleyway between two houses.

'Hey! Someone stop her!'

Faces turned his way but by that time he was runnir.
weaving his way between stretchers, emergency vehicles
and the people in uniforms, until he collided with two men
standing on the periphery.

'Fucksake, watch where you're...' started the larger of
the two, and Rajko saw who he'd hit.

'You!'

Richard Nash stumbled away as much from the shock of
recognition as the physical contact.

'Oh so *now* you turn up? *Now?* Come to see the results of
all your hard work, have you?' He threw himself on Nash,
locking hands about his throat and bearing him backwards
against a wall, snarling, 'You want to see it? You want to
fucking *see* it?'

In moments other hands were pulling him away, pinning
his arms to his sides, and a female police officer was in front
of him. 'Easy, mate,' she said. 'There's no need for this.' She
turned to Nash. 'Sorry about that, sir. Are you all right?'

'Of course I'm not all right!' snapped Nash. 'This little
bastard assaulted me! You saw him!'

Rajko tore uselessly against the hands. 'You murdered
my family, you motherfucker!' he screamed. 'I'll kill you! I'll
fucking kill you!'

'Are you going to stand there and let him threaten me like
that?' Nash demanded.

The second man, who Rajko only now noticed was
wearing the kind of police uniform which meant that he
was someone in charge, stepped between them. 'The boy
is in shock, Richard, look at him. He's just witnessed

mething nobody should, and he needs to be looked after. Karen, please take him straight to the station and find an Appropriate Adult for him. An uncle, social worker, teacher – I don't care who.'

'Yes, Sergeant.' The PC turned back to Rajko. 'Are you going to let me look after you?'

But Rajko wasn't ready to let it go yet. 'He killed them, don't you understand? His negligence! It's his responsibility!'

'Well you can tell me all about that in the warm with a cup of tea. Come on.'

Rajko felt the numbness slide back into his bones, and let himself be led away. It wasn't until the patrol car was moving that he remembered the girl in his sister's sweater, but by then it was too late to look for her.

Ingram was right, there was nothing Nash could do right at that moment. In time there would be a coroner's investigation at which the Trust would be called on to give evidence, but that was weeks away. He should go home, try to get some sleep, and Ingram would update him first thing in the morning.

Nash thanked his old friend and agreed, having absolutely no intention of going home. He was supposed to sit patiently on his arse and wait for the unholy shitstorm that was certain to come rolling out of that house full of dead immigrants, was he? Fuck that straight to hell with brass knobs on. The Trust needed to be insulated from this as soon as possible.

He drove across town, just a little apprehensive about leaving the parish boundary after dark and in such circumstances. He didn't think She would have had anything to do with the accident – what did She stand to gain by it? – but Hester and death were like sharks and blood, and there was no telling how She might react. On balance it was a risk worth taking. He certainly wasn't going to trust a phone, hackable as it was, for the conversation he needed to have right now.

The house he pulled up at was large, detached, and expensive – the kind of property owned by a man who made the kind of money that a close association with the Trust brought. The man in this case was another of Nash's cogs: Hugh Watkins, owner of ProTherm Heating and Electrical, the company which maintained the Trust's properties at a price which was very favourable to their annual budget. Although 'maintained' in this particular case now clearly seemed something of an overstatement. It was tempting to let Watkins swing in the wind for the accident, but Nash hadn't been lying when he'd told Peter Feenan that things with the Clegg Farm development were at a delicate stage financially, and this was precisely the wrong time to have his investors spooked by accusations of multiple deaths by criminal negligence.

He rang the front doorbell several times and stamped his feet impatiently in the cold. In the driveway next to him was a freshly minted Subaru SUV with personalised plates: W4TK1N5.

'You're doing altogether too well out of me,' he murmured.

Lights went on behind curtains and footsteps thumped towards the door which Watkins opened on the security chain as he peered out. He had a face which was all chin and no forehead, like the top and bottom halves of his head were made from different skulls, the smaller on top.

'Morning, Hugh,' he said amiably.

'Morning?' Watkins whispered, incredulous. 'What the fuck do you mean by "morning"? As in fucking four o'clock in it? Richard, what the fuck are you doing here?'

'I've come the bearer of bad news, I'm afraid. Can I come in?'

'No you can't fucking well come in! I—'

'Who is it, darling?' asked a female voice from deeper inside, probably at the top of the stairs, clutching her hair curlers.

Watkins turned and called, 'Nothing, dear. Just a work thing.'

'At this time of—'

But he'd shut the door and was standing out on the front step with Nash in a bright tartan dressing gown. 'What,' he hissed. 'Do. You. Want?'

As Nash told him about the carbon monoxide poisonings on Pestle Road, Watkins seemed to deflate, growing paler and smaller until he was leaning against his front door for support and muttering, 'Oh shit oh shit oh shit,' on a loop.

'By my reckoning,' Nash continued, 'it's going to take the coroner a week minimum to arrange for an examination of the boiler and the heating system, which gives you plenty of time to get in there and make sure that what they find doesn't point back at us. And by us I mean you, obviously.'

'You know what that's called? "Perverting the course of justice", that's what.'

'How does "manslaughter through gross negligence" sound instead? Any better?'

Watkins ran both hands over his face as if trying to scrub it off the front of his head, and groaned. 'But I don't understand. We put detectors in all the flats. Didn't any of them go off?'

'You mean those cheap-arse Chinese ones? What do you think?' Nash could see Peter Feenan in his office right now, waving one of them around and lecturing him about safety standards. What made the whole thing worse was that he'd been right. If he got so much as a whiff of an I-told-you-so from Mr Peter Holier-than-fucking-thou Feenan after this he'd gleefully tear the skinny little mick's throat out with his teeth.

'Everything I put in that building was legal,' Watkins insisted. 'Everything you told me to use was legal. They can't do us for negligence.'

'Maybe not,' Nash conceded. 'But the scandal will ruin the Trust, and it will take you, me, and everybody else down with it. Good luck making the payments on this place when nobody will trust you to fix a dripping tap. You'll be lucky to get a job rodding the bloody drains.' He paused to let this mental image sink in with Watkins. 'Obviously you can't make it look like there's nothing wrong with the boiler at all,' Nash continued. 'Bang it about a bit, make it look like the residents were fiddling with it, use your imagination.'

'But the cops will be all over the place. I'll never get in!'

'That's the bit you leave to my imagination.'

He watched Watkins pace up and down the length of

his driveway, back and forth past his expensive car parked in front of his expensive house inhabited by his no-doubt expensive wife, all the while muttering to himself as he built up the guts to agree, as if he had a choice. Finally he stopped.

'All right then,' he said. 'But if I get caught—'

'Yes, yes, yes,' Nash waved it away. 'Let's skip the fine print, shall we?'

31

REMEMBRANCE

TOBY HAD ONLY EVER TRIED WEED ONCE, AT HIS OLD school. There'd been an old shipping container at the bottom of the playground which was used to store sports kit, but all the kids called it the Smokehouse since that was what happened in the bushes behind it. A kid had got hold of some stuff from his older sister, allegedly, and word had got around and Toby had gone along that one lunchtime to see what it was like – partially out of peer pressure, partially out of sheer curiosity. It hadn't made him feel blissed out or mellow or whatever it was they said he was supposed to experience; it had just made him feel dislocated from reality, as if he was observing his actions in the world as part of an out-of-body experience, but hollow and detached. He hadn't enjoyed it, and he'd never tried it again, but going to school the day after the gas accident felt exactly like that all over again. Judging from the way a lot of the other kids in his year were behaving, they were experiencing much the same thing. There were visits from grief counsellors and the police, special assemblies, opportunities to talk it through with the few teachers capable of having a human conversation. But still, every so often a girl or a boy would suddenly leave the classroom in tears, or pick a fight for no reason, or be found just staring into space.

They congregated at the Rec, that passing-through place which wasn't a park and wasn't a field but was uniquely their space because its nature was indeterminate and nobody knew what to do with it, just like them – at least for a few more years, until they'd finished passing through from childhood in the supermarket playground to the adult space of the village green. Mostly they chatted about what they always chatted about, taking comfort in each other's company, huddling close in their circles under the trees because any gap big enough for a person to fill only reminded them of the one person who never would again. They sat and played through Maya's favourite YouTube streams or the Spotify playlists she'd shared, laughing at or singing along with whatever she'd laughed at or sang to, or else they got high or drunk or just cried and held each other. In the absence of a funeral or a body to say goodbye to yet, they held their own digital wake and celebrated what lived of her online.

Toby avoided the Rec to begin with, knowing what was buried under there, but had no choice when people started to comment on his absence.

krishdog181:
u avoiding us or sthing toeB?

astrobwoy:
toeB or not toeB lol

cheekynando7:
Leave off. He'll come if he wants.
Some of us need more alone time than others.

damo666:
unless hes hiding

krishdog181:
from? got no reason 2 hide among friends

damo666:
think we all no why. Trust issues lol

cheekynando7:
STFU!!!

Everyone knew what had happened, and none of them did. There was a gas leak, that much was certain. It was a faulty boiler, or else it was Rajko's fault for fiddling with it; he was on a mechanics course, wasn't he? And where was he, anyway? He was dead too, or arrested, or run away, or living with an uncle in Sheffield. Or else it was a murder-suicide which had escalated catastrophically. It quickly became common knowledge that Maya's building was managed by Haleswell Village Trust, and that was when the trolling started – anonymous accounts accusing the Trustees of murder, hoping that they died of cancer/poison/suffocation, or any menu item from the trolls' drop-down list of abuse. They posted sick images and jokes about gas chambers, calling Toby's mum a fucking Nazi, threatening to set fire to their home. He switched off all his social media and went dark. Then he switched it all on again half an hour later because hearing nothing at all was somehow worse.

Because of course he accepted that it was all his fault. If he'd given Maya the secret priority emergency contacts then Rajko might have had them and help might have arrived soon enough to save her life. If he'd done what Rajko had asked him in the first place and got his mum to push for their boiler to be fixed, none of this would have happened, but instead he'd been too fixated on finding out everything he could about Hester – and this was the sickest ironic twist of all: killing a building full of innocent people by his obsession with one who was already dead. Even if She had somehow arranged it, it must surely have been only to get at him, and through him his parents.

That first night after he'd heard about the accident he'd gone out to the garden stone, looking for Her.

'Did you do it?' he called to the empty darkness. 'Did you kill those people because of me? Because you can't get to me or my parents? Is that how this works?' There had been no reply. She would not be granting an audience, it seemed. Neither his questions nor his pain would be answered, and it suddenly enraged him. '*I know where you're buried!*' he screamed, snot-faced and weeping like a spoilt child. '*I'll dig you up and piss on your fucking bones!*'

He knew how this must have looked to his parents – losing it and shouting at thin air, but who knew? Maybe they thought it was good and cathartic, finally getting something out of his system. It was certainly more of a reaction than he'd shown in the aftermath of the break-in. He didn't want to hear what they were saying about him – he didn't even want to hear the murmur of their voices downstairs and have to imagine what they were saying. He plugged his ears into his phone and sketched, or pored over Mrs Drummond's books, and then eventually bowed to the inevitable and went down the Rec to be with his friends. At least if someone wanted to have a go at him they'd have to do it face to face.

The press got hold of it, obviously – first the local papers, then the nationals. The Trust did a good job of circling the wagons, putting out a press statement and coaching his mum what to say if reporters came knocking, but since she wasn't on the Executive Committee nobody did. Richard Nash got his face on the TV news, looking full of concern and empathy as he said that of course the Trust would cooperate fully with any investigations to determine the cause of this appalling tragedy.

A scumbag tabloid newspaper hack even came to the Rec to get dirt from the victim's schoolfriends, trying to bribe them with cash and iTunes vouchers (as if anybody actually used iTunes anymore) to say that the flats in Maya's building were crammed with illegal immigrants ten to a room. The reporter's smarmy insinuations were met with a wall of sullen adolescent silence, and that moment of solidarity to the memory of their friend was one of the few bright spots for Toby in an otherwise dark week. The hack wrote his story anyway, making it up completely, with the headline IMMIGRANT GAS CHAMBER OF HORRORS, so they bought up as many copies of the paper as they could find and had a nice bonfire in one of the dumpsters behind the supermarket.

Someone who knew someone who knew someone else found out that since the post-mortems had definitively established the cause of death as carbon monoxide poisoning, the coroner had issued a Certificate of the Fact of Death for each of the victims, even though her investigation would probably take many weeks to establish the exact cause of the poisoning, which meant that grieving relatives could finally lay their loved ones to rest.

The funerals were staggered over several days, at various churches and mosques, while the burials would be at a large municipal cemetery rather than St Sebastian's, which was too old and small and had been closed to new interments for decades. On the day that Maya and her family were buried Toby stayed at home, drinking mint tea and reading 'The Secret Life of Walter Mitty'.

After the words, the tears, the prayers and the earth swallowing his family, Rajko stood by the row of graves alone. He had told his Uncle Andrii that he'd be along soon, as people would be gathering at the *daca* to pay their respects; although his family hadn't been practising, Orthodox tradition was still strong, and he was going to need some time to get himself together if he was going to be able to cope with a massive meal and the condolences of distant relatives whom he barely knew.

The two largest graves were in the centre, the smallest on the right, the middle-sized one on the left. Almost like in a fairy tale about bowls of porridge and chairs and beds. Not too hot, not too cold. There should have been a fifth one for him in the middle – *just right* – but there wasn't, and that was wrong, because he was dead. He had to be. It wasn't possible to have had so much life ripped away and still be living – it was just that his body hadn't caught up to the fact yet.

The only part of him which felt remotely alive was the rage burning low down in his guts. It had always been there, flaring up now and then and getting him into trouble; the last time had been when he held Richard Nash's throat in his hands. Over the years he'd tried to keep it under control to stop it from burning his loved ones, except now his loved ones were all dead so that didn't matter anymore.

It was a bright morning in early June but the summer sun didn't touch him because he was dead. Flowers covered the graves and blossom was on the trees along the cemetery's paths but he couldn't smell it because he was dead.

This was not a season for the dead.

And yet there She was, standing behind Maya's headstone, wearing his sister's Cool Vibes jumper over a ragged smock. The dead girl showed Her wounds to him openly, and he probably should have been scared, but then fear was for the living. It was entirely possible that he had simply lost his mind. She didn't threaten, however. If anything, Her deeply shadowed eyes seemed to be regarding him with sadness.

'You're dead, aren't you?' he asked, just to be sure. His voice was rusty, and it barely worked above a rasp.

She nodded. *Yes.*

'Is my sister with you?'

She shook her head. *No.*

'Do you know where she is?'

Yes. She pointed at the grave between them.

He swallowed thickly. The words, when they came, were like grit spat from between his teeth. 'Did you do it?'

No.

'Then *why?*'

She shrugged, gesturing around – up at the trees, down at the ground, everything and nothing.

'What – you're trying to tell me that it *just happened*? There was no reason? They're dead and there was *no reason at all*? Fuck that! And fuck you too if that's all you came for! Why are you here? What the fuck do you want from me?'

Her mouth moved but he couldn't hear what She was saying. Thinking that She was whispering, he drew a little closer, but found that She wasn't making any sound at all, or what sound She was making couldn't reach him. She wasn't entirely *there* – he couldn't see through Her like a storybook ghost, but he noticed that She didn't cast any shadow.

'I can't hear you! You're not, I don't know – not close enough!'

The dead girl considered him closely, narrowing Her eyes, assessing. Then She reached under the sweater and brought out a knife – a small and crude thing, just a scrap of black metal with a wooden handle.

Rajko laughed. 'No,' he said. 'You're going to have to do better than that if you want to scare me.'

But scaring him wasn't Her intention. She held out Her other palm and slashed the blade across it. Instead of the bright splash of red blood, what oozed out of the new wound was sludgy and dark, more like mud. She reached over the top of Maya's headstone and held Her hand out to him, as if inviting him to shake it.

It was obvious what She wanted him to do.

He stepped back a pace, shaking his head. 'That's not going to happen.'

She looked him up and down in withering contempt, then very deliberately wiped Her wounded palm across Maya's sweater, or the illusion of it, obliterating the writing with a thick black smear. She turned to go.

'No, wait!'

He looked around; on a nearby grave was a glass vase, murky with age and full of dead flowers. He tipped out the dry stems, smashed it over Maya's headstone and took up a jagged shard. Before he could second-guess himself, he sliced it across his left palm. The blood came an instant before the pain, deep and burning. He stuck out his wounded hand.

'Here. Do it.'

She raised her eyebrows. *Really? Are you sure about this?*

'Here!'

She leaned across the headstone and grasped his living hand with Her dead one. The shock of Her dead blood entering his was like being injected with frozen battery acid. He gasped, fighting for breath as it crept up his arm like a tide and the blue veins under his skin turned black. Her grip was iron; he couldn't have pulled away even if he'd wanted to. The world dimmed and a great rushing filled his ears as if he was surfacing from deep underwater, but through it he was aware that She was experiencing something equally traumatic, screaming silently as his living blood burned into Her. The black ice spread up his arm and past his shoulder, and now he could hear Her talking to him through gritted teeth, faintly at first but growing louder as it neared his heart.

There were promises of blood and fire and vengeance.

He listened and agreed.

There were instructions.

Then Her dead blood touched the core of him and his heart gave a great staggering leap of protest, almost stopping completely. He reeled away from Her grip, light-headed and retching, and fell on the grass.

When his eyesight returned he saw that She was gone. What an idiot he'd been, to imagine himself dead earlier. What stupid, childish self-delusion. He knew what death felt like now – its merest fingertip had brushed his soul and that had almost finished him. But he had a taste for it now, and he knew exactly who to take it to. Hester had shown him how.

Her will be done.

32

DESECRATION

FOR SOMETHING DESIGNED TO KEEP DEATH ITSELF AT bay, thought Rajko, the parish boundary stones were pitifully easy to destroy.

He started with the Epistle Stone by the postbox, since it was on the corner of two relatively quiet streets where he was least likely to be disturbed. Hester had said that he probably wouldn't be able to get to all of them before being caught, but the more he could desecrate the weaker the blessing would be against Her. The stone here was at the base of a waist-high wall made up of odd-shaped natural rocks, mortared and whitewashed, but with plenty of gaps and crevices between them. It was some kind of granite, with carvings that had been eroded over time. He set down the heavy sports holdall and looked around for any witnesses. It was after one in the morning, but he wanted to make sure. He wanted to do this right. For Her.

Satisfied that he remained unobserved, he took from the holdall a foot-long cold chisel of the kind used on construction sites for breaking up lumps of concrete, and a short-handled sledgehammer. He wedged the tip of the chisel into a gap next to the boundary stone and gave it an experimental tap with the hammer. It bit into the mortar and held. He drew the hammer back and whacked the chisel as hard as he could. The shock of the blow jarred his arm and put a spike of pain through his wounded hand but the chisel drove deeper, so he whacked it again, driving it deeper still until it became stuck and he had to knock it from side to side to loosen it so that he could pull it out and drive it in on the other side of the stone.

It shifted, like a loose tooth in its socket.

He looked around again; nobody seemed to have been disturbed by the noise. At least, nobody who was coming out to do anything about it.

He worked around the stone methodically, knocking it looser and looser with each blow until there was a big-enough gap above it that he could get his fingers over the top and pull it free from the wall, toppling it onto the pavement where it lay in a litter of mortar fragments.

He paused, hands on his knees, to catch his breath. His arms ached and he had a thumping headache – worse than yesterday's, despite dosing up on paracetamol and a line of ketamine. The aches and chills had started after his communion with Hester, and he knew that She had passed something on to him through Her blood, so he'd got together what he needed as quickly as he could without alerting his

Uncle Andrii or any of the other members of the extended Gorić clan who had stayed after the *daca*. He suffered an evening of being the focus of their awful pity, their drunken, tearful hugs, their sympathy that he was so young to have to become a man when all he wanted to do was scream at them *How am I supposed to be a man when there is no family left to be a man for?!*

He grabbed the hammer with both hands and brought it down on the stone from overhead, and with a crack like a gunshot it split in two.

And She was there, standing on the other side of the wall, smiling Her blessing at him. He felt the aches and fatigue melt from his bones in Her presence.

'One,' he said to Her.

She nodded. *Continue.*

He packed his tools back in the holdall and went off to find the stone above the Oxfam shop.

He managed to take out the Horse Stone, the Red Stone on the village cenotaph, and the Bumping Stone – which only had to be levered out of the pavement with a crowbar – and She followed him each time, waiting just on the other side of the intangible barrier which he was taking apart piece by piece, and with each one She seemed to come closer, clearer.

Things began to unravel at the Sunrise Stone by the Rec.

He'd cut the lock off its protective railing with a pair of bolt cutters and was pissing on the stone while he worked out how to destroy it, because it was easily the largest of the parish stones and his exertions had taken their toll, when he heard voices, low in murmured conversation, coming towards him. Hurriedly he tucked his dick away and crouched down by the stone which, large as it was, couldn't hide him completely. He could only hope that the semi-darkness would take care of that; it was nearly three in the morning but streetlights still didn't help.

The murmurers came closer – one male, one female, walking with heads close together over the glow of a phone screen, and he thought great, he was going to get away with it; the brightness of the phone would bugger their night vision and he'd just be one shadow amongst many. They were passing him, and he saw with surprise that they were two students he vaguely recognised from the year above him in college, when a fit of coughing struck.

It didn't just strike him – it grabbed him, clenched his ribcage in giant fists and squeezed a volley of harsh barks from his lungs so violent that it felt like he was hacking himself inside out, and when it finally released him he was light-headed and gasping for breath. There was wetness on his hands and the stone in front of his face. It gleamed black in the streetlight, and he knew that it was his own blood.

'Is somebody there?' The boyfriend.

A phone camera-torch lit up and found him.

'Oh my God...' The girlfriend.

'Wait – is that Rajko?' said the guy. 'Raj, is that you? It's me, Ben – Ben Hannan, remember? Jesus, man, are you okay?'

Rajko used the stone to drag himself to his feet. 'Hi Ben,' he said. 'Hi, uh...'

'Izzie. Porter.'

'Sure. Izzie.'

He remembered now. Ben was round and ginger and studying something to do with business, and Izzie was into eighties retro and doing something with electronics. It was exam season so they'd obviously been doing a bit of late-night revision of human anatomy and reproduction in the Rec. Out of the corner of his eye he saw Hester and Her followers, almost close enough to touch the railings. Could Ben and Izzie see them too? Were they that close?

Ben was still babbling on. 'We heard you'd left. Sorry to hear about what happened to your family. Jesus, that's awful. What are you doing here, man?'

'Oh just desecrating some stuff. You know.' He wasn't going to get the chance to physically damage the stone now; his piss and blood would have to do.

'Ben,' murmured Izzie, 'we should go.' She was wide-eyed and nervous, and had a right to be. Rajko's reputation went before him, never mind that right at this moment he must have looked terrible. He wiped the blood from his mouth with one sleeve and picked up the nearest thing to hand, which was the bolt cutters. He was feeling better already, though he knew it was only temporary.

'No, sorry,' he said. 'I don't want to hurt you but I will fuck you up if you try to run away.'

Ben tried to laugh it off, a high-pitched, quavering bray of a laugh. 'That's not funny, man—'

Rajko didn't bother answering, just took a couple of quick strides out of the railed enclosure, bunched a fist in the front of Ben's hoodie before the other lad could do much more than back away a step, pivoted, and flung him inside. He bounced off the stone with an *oof!*

Izzie screamed.

He grabbed her too and held up the heavy jaws of the bolt cutters in front of her face. 'Shut up,' he suggested, 'or I'll hurt you. A lot.'

Her screams subsided into snivelling, and he bundled her inside the cage with her boyfriend.

'Give me your phones,' he ordered.

They obeyed, and he smashed their phones on the pavement.

He made them take their arms out of their hoodies' sleeves and then used the empty sleeves to tie them to the railings like straitjackets on opposite sides of the stone so that they couldn't help each other get free. He couldn't do anything to stop them shouting for help, but then this wasn't a residential area and it would take time for someone to respond, and he only needed a breathing space to get the last two done.

There was no way he was going to be able to break into the White Hart without setting off the burglar alarm and getting grabbed by the pigs long before he had a chance to do damage to the Ale Stone. Fortunately, the stone was part of the hearth at the base of the main chimney – all he had to do was get up onto the roof.

A table in the beer garden gave access to the sloping roof

above the delivery yard, from which it was easy to boost himself up onto the tiles of the single-storey restaurant. He went along that to the main building, and then used the old iron guttering to get up onto the steep roof, finally following the corner of two adjacent slopes for purchase along old and cracked tiles up to the spine of the roof where he found the main chimney stack.

Sick as he was, it was physically draining, and all the climbing was doing terrible things to his bad hand. He rested to catch his breath, stifling another coughing fit in the crook of his elbow. Gingerly he unwrapped his wound and examined it, though it was impossible to see much in the glistening mess.

Still, it was a decent view from up here, he thought, looking over the immediate environs of Haleswell, north across the neighbouring suburbs to the bright glow of the city centre and south to the dark countryside of Warwickshire. From a vantage point like this a man could watch a whole empire burn.

He'd left the holdall below, but carried up the few things he needed in a smaller drawstring bag around his neck, which he set out carefully along the roof ridge: a plastic funnel, a packet of children's party balloons, a cigarette lighter, a packet of Rizla rolling papers, and an aluminium camping thermos full of petrol.

As a kid he'd always loved making water bombs.

The chimney pot was covered by a wire mesh anti-bird guard, but he kicked that free, unconcerned about the clatter it made falling down the roof. Filling the balloons in the dark was actually easier than he'd feared; a little trickier fitting a Rizla into the knot of each balloon's neck as he tied it closed, but not impossible. He lit and dropped each one in quick succession down the chimney. Some would go out, but only one had to take.

And take they did.

He was rewarded by a bright yellow bloom and a gush of heat from the chimney pot, followed by the almost immediate shrilling of a fire alarm inside. Abandoning his gear, he slithered as quickly as he could without breaking his neck back to the ground, grabbed the holdall and ran as flames rose in the pub windows. He wished he could stay to watch it burn. He really should have left this until last, but he'd wanted to save a treat for himself: there was only the Feenans' stone to go.

The fire alarm ripped Alan Pankowicz from sleep and he thrashed out of bed, tangling himself in the bedclothes and falling to the floor. The manager's flat was on the inn's second floor at the back, above the kitchens and the office where the alarm control box was situated. Gritting his teeth against the braying noise, he opened his bedroom door and headed for the staircase without stopping to put on either his dressing gown or his slippers. It was his bare feet which felt something small and furry brush past them as he reached the first riser, and then the exquisite, bone-deep sting of small teeth which bit into the Achilles tendon of his left ankle. His scream was lost in the noise of the alarm. Howling, he bent, twisted, swatting at his foot as he pulled it up, horrified at the tugging weight of something which had its jaws locked into the back of his ankle *and wasn't letting go*. His fingers closed on the plump body of a rat – one of Hers, obviously – and squeezed with vicious glee, but by then he was already losing his balance and toppling towards the drop. He flailed with his other arm, and his fingertips briefly slipped over the smooth wood of the banister before losing contact with it and he was falling, tumbling headfirst, a series of concussive jolts as he hit the stairs with pelvis, rib, shoulder, and then there was a tremendous *crack!* as his neck snapped and then there was nothing else at all.

33

INTRUSION

WHEN THE LIGHT WOKE TRISH SHE THOUGHT THAT Peter had got up to use the loo, so she pulled the covers over her head and turned away, already drifting back to sleep, until her knee grazed his thigh and he rolled away from her with a snort, which couldn't be right because how could he be in bed if he was in the bathroom too? Plus, the light was coming from the other direction – from the bedroom window.

And now she could hear grunting and metallic ringing noises like a blacksmith's anvil coming from outside.

She jack-knifed into a sitting position, wide awake and terrified. Bright, cold halogen light was streaming through a gap in their bedroom curtains from the security floodlight bolted to the rear of the house.

They were being burgled.

'Peter!' She kicked him awake.

'Whudizzit?' he mumbled.

She was already reaching for her phone. 'There's somebody in the back garden. I'm calling the police.'

'*What?*' He struggled up, knuckling his eyes.

'Don't do anything!' she hissed, dialling 999. 'Let the police look after this!'

'What, you mean like last time?' he growled. 'Fuck that.' He started climbing out of bed.

'999, what service please?' asked a female operator.

'Peter!'

'Miss?' said the operator. 'Do you need the police?'

'What? Yes!'

'Transferring you now.' She rushed after Peter and got a hand on his shoulder as he opened the bedroom door but he shook her off and carried on downstairs, dressed only in his t-shirt and boxers. Then there was a male police emergency operator asking for her address and whether she was in any danger, and by the time she caught up with Peter he was gripping a poker from the fireplace and heading towards the back door.

'Mum?' Toby was on the upper landing in his pyjamas and Aston Villa hoodie.

'A patrol is on the way,' said the operator. 'Can you stay on the line please, Miss?'

'Toby, go back to your room and don't come out until I say so.'

'Miss?'

'Mum, I think Maya's brother Rajko is trying to wreck the stone.'

'*What?*' She hung up and flew after her husband in only her nightshirt.

In the glare of the security floodlight she saw everything. She saw Peter running at the Gorić boy with the poker upraised in his fist like a sword, yelling, 'Get the fuck away from my family!' She saw Gorić's triumphant grin as he stood above the parish stone that he'd managed to halfway unseat – it was sitting aslant in a yawning hole with the pry bar that he'd used, and she saw that in a gesture of infantile vindictiveness he'd spray-painted on the stone a cock and balls in poisonous green. She saw his crudely bandaged hand, dripping red, come up to meet Peter's attack. They grappled. Gorić fell and Peter went with him, the pair of them rolling on the grass, punching and kicking, Gorić finishing on top, kneeling on Peter's forearm so that he dropped the poker with a grunt of pain, planting his bloodied hand in Peter's face as he pushed himself back up. Peter grabbed at his ankle as he tried to lurch away, the lurch turning into an uncontrolled fall, arms outstretched, hitting the stone with one hand and his forehead which made a dull *crack!* and the stone was finally shoved past its tipping point, toppling onto its side. Gorić fell beside it, groaning. Peter climbed to his feet, wiping his face and spitting out whatever had got into his mouth.

'Mum? Is Dad okay?' Toby had been watching all of this from the back doorway.

She wheeled on him. 'What did I tell you?' she snapped. 'Get back upstairs! The police will be here soon!'

Peter advanced on Gorić. 'They're going to lock you up

and throw away the fucking key,' he said. 'Should have happened a long time ago.'

Gorić's groans had turned into a strange kind of laughter; giggling mixed with phlegmy coughing. Blood streamed from a gash in his forehead.

'What's so funny?' Peter demanded, standing over him.

'Peter, please, leave him alone,' Trish pleaded. 'Let the police take care of him.'

Gorić giggled again. 'Police aren't going to be shit all use to you.'

'What are you on about?'

'She's here... She's here... and all of you... all of you are fucked!'

'*Mum...*' Toby's voice was the low mewl of a terrified animal, and he was pointing to the end of the garden, where Hester and Her followers were emerging from the shadows into the brilliant glare of the security light. There was nothing to hide their wounds or their weapons, or the naked hatred on their faces. Peter scrambled away from Gorić, grabbed up the poker and rejoined his family.

The dead girl walked up to the fallen stone which had for so long marked the limits of Her reach. She prodded it with Her bare big toe, and smiled.

And stepped over it.

'Get in the house, now!' Trish ordered.

They darted into the utility room and slammed the back door. Trish locked it, then twisted the small knobs at top and bottom which engaged the deadbolts.

'Deadbolts,' she said, and uttered a high little laugh.

'What?' Peter was staring at her.

'Bolts to keep out dead people.'

'That's not fucking funny!'

'I know.' She felt herself on the edge of bursting into tears or hysterical laughter. The door was solid oak with a steel core and its panes were of toughened and laminated glass, but she wasn't sure if that made any difference to something like Hester. The dead girl came right up to it, Her nose almost touching the glass, shading it with Her hands against the glare coming from behind Her and peering in. Trish towed her husband and son deeper into the shadows, in the doorway to the kitchen.

'Mum,' whispered Toby. 'When will the police get here?'

'Soon, darling, soon.'

'Did you use that priority contact Mr Nash gave us?'

Her hand flew to her mouth. She hadn't. She'd done just what Richard had said when Toby's hand was being treated: panicked and dialled 999 out of habit. And he'd been right – she didn't care if any other people's emergencies might have been more important right at that very moment. But she didn't have her phone and she couldn't remember where she'd left or dropped it – in the bedroom? Outside?

There was a polite knock at the door.

'*Go away!*' she screamed. 'Just why can't you leave us alone?'

When Hester spoke, Her voice was as clear as if She were in the room with them. It was that of an ordinary girl, but there was a deeper note to it, a coarse undertone as if two people of vastly differing sizes were fighting for the same vocal cords. Trish thought that must be what seven hundred years of undying rage must sound like.

'Come out, Custodian,' Hester said. 'I promise to make it quick. I may even spare your family.'

'Why are you doing this?' Trish sobbed. 'I don't understand! I've never done anything to you!'

'You think your deeds matter in the slightest? You think your ignorance excuses you? It does not matter what you have or have not done. The moment you joined the Trust you took share in the guilt of their forebears, the ones who murdered my people.'

'But I didn't know! How could I know? It's not fair!'

'*It's not fair,*' Hester whined in mockery. 'Do you know how much the *gwrach clefyd* cares for your notions of what is *fair*?' She drew the silhouette of Her head back and spat on the back door's window. Black phlegm slid down the glass. 'That much. Now let me in. It is the only chance you have to save those you love.'

From the kitchen came a sudden thud at the window above the sink, followed quickly by a second, and on the third accompanied by a deep cracking sound as the laminated safety glass began to give. At the same time the front door was rammed hard enough to make the safety chain and the brass letter flap rattle. Rationally she knew that there was little to no chance that even a gang of intruders could break through its steel core, but that took a back seat to the sudden terrified realisation that her home was surrounded. 'Peter, what do we do?'

'Upstairs to my room!' said Toby. 'It's at the top of the

house, and it's got the narrowest doorway right at the top of the stairs. We chuck all the furniture down the stairs and make a barricade.'

'Did you think of that before?' she asked.

'It's why I chose that room,' he said.

'Don't tell me you knew this was going to happen.'

'Of course not!'

'No,' said Peter, looking across the kitchen at the connecting door to the garage. 'I'm not having us trapped. We don't know how long the police will take, or what they'll even be able to do if they get here. We go for my van and we get the fuck out.'

There was a tremendous crunch and the window blind above the kitchen sink tented inwards as whatever implement was being wielded forced its way through. Sounds of thudding and hammering echoed from all parts of the house; it sounded like Hester's people weren't just focussing on obvious things like windows and doors but were trying to smash through the very walls themselves in some places.

'NOW!' Peter yelled, grabbed Trish and Toby each by a wrist and ran for the garage door.

The kitchen blind was ripped from its fittings and fell onto the sink unit, carrying the drainer to the ceramic-tiled floor, where cutlery bounced away in a cacophony of spinning steel and drinking glasses exploded into glittering shrapnel. The crazed window glass looked like a huge spiderweb with human silhouettes crowding close on the other side.

Something like a rusted boat hook withdrew from the black hole at its centre and dead hands replaced it, curling around the broken edge and ripping at the laminated glass, peeling it back as if it were a pane of toffee.

Peter yanked at the garage doorknob. It didn't move. He stared at it stupidly. 'It's locked!'

'Of course it's locked!' Trish yelled.

'Keys…' Peter ran for the hall. Next to the main burglar alarm console in the cupboard under the stairs he'd installed a board with hooks for all the household keys – doors, windows, even the ones for bleeding the radiator and opening the electricity meter cupboard. He hauled the cupboard open. A small amber light on the alarm console was flashing helpfully to let him know that someone had tripped the motion sensor in the back garden. The keys – all labelled, neat and sane – jittered, dancing away from his panicky fingers, enjoying the fun. A battery of fists and weapons thundered against the front door, and he heard something in the study off to his left fall with a crash.

Behind him, Toby moaned, 'They're inside…' and Trish screamed.

He grabbed the tag for the garage key and ran back to the kitchen, scooping up his van keys from the bowl on the hall table and slamming the door shut behind him.

A head and shoulders were pushing through the hole in the window. Beyond the fact that he had a beard, and his mouth was open in a wordless snarl, the man's ruined face made it impossible to tell what he might have looked like in life. He had one arm through ahead of him and was gripping the sink tap with gangrenous fingers, pulling himself deeper into the house.

'Trish!' Peter tossed the key to her. 'Open it!' He threw his back against the kitchen door just as footsteps thumped down the hall and whoever had got in through the study window barrelled into it from the other side. Toby ran over to help, bracing himself next to his father. The door shoved open an inch, but they slammed it back again. For the moment the pair of them had the advantage of numbers, but that wasn't going to last long.

Trish fumbled with the key, inserting it into the lock, turning it, and opening the door to the garage. It was dark inside, no telling if anything had already broken in, and Peter wondered for a moment whether or not Toby's idea of barricading themselves in upstairs might have been the better idea. Still, they had no option now; the dead intruder was up to his waist in the window, both arms through, grunting as he flailed for anything to get a purchase on.

'Come on!' she yelled.

Peter glanced at Toby. 'Ready?'

Toby's terrified eyes were stark in his pale face, but he nodded. 'Ready.' Peter felt a rush of mingled love for his son and murderous rage for the bastards who were terrorising him like this.

'Go!'

They leapt from the kitchen door, which sprang open under the assault, and ran for the garage door as the man in the window fell through completely, going headfirst into the floor with a crunch. Trish slammed the door and locked it behind them. A moment later it shuddered as something which sounded like it was very heavy and sharp tore a chunk out.

The garage was dark and smelled thickly of motor oil. The wide bulk of Peter's van was a deeper shadow in the gloom, with just a red LED on his dashboard glowing through the windscreen. He thumbed the unlock button on the key fob, and Trish and Toby climbed into the cab. He tossed the keys in after her. 'Get it going. I have to open the garage door.' The pull-up mechanism wasn't motorised; he was going to have to do it manually and hope that if there was anything outside waiting for him he could leap back into the van before it got him.

'Be careful!' she whispered.

He got his hands on the twist-handle in the middle of the wide metal garage door and listened, trying to hear above the thudding of his own heartbeat whether anything was waiting on the outside. Certainly nobody was hammering to get in. Come to that, the chopping at the internal door from the kitchen had stopped, as had the noises of intrusion from deeper in the house. He didn't dare hope that Hester had just given up and left. More likely Her people were simply waiting.

Then Trish got the engine going and he was enveloped in a cloud of exhaust fumes and couldn't hear anything over its roar.

Peter drew a deep breath, and in one swift movement twisted the handle open and heaved as hard as he could. The metal door rolled upwards and backwards in a smooth arc on oiled rollers, but with a lot more force than normal so that it crashed into its fully open position with a noise like a scrap-metal gong.

The interior of the garage was bathed in the flashing blue of police lights, and a voice called, 'Is everything all right in there?'

They abandoned the van and fled to the sanctuary of the police car, Toby's parents both yelling at once.

'Now hold up, hold up, one at a time!' shouted the first uniformed officer. He had a craggy shaven head and his bulky stab vest made him look even larger than he already was, and his arms were outstretched as if trying to herd the chaos, patting the air with his palms, calming them down. His partner, the driver of the patrol car, was still in his seat, on the radio to dispatch. Behind and above everything was the snarling burr of a police helicopter hovering close overhead, unseen in the dark. 'You,' the cop said, singling out his dad. 'Sir, you have blood on you. Is anybody hurt?'

Peter wiped his face and looked at his hand in surprise, as if he'd forgotten his tussle with Rajko. 'No, thank God, but you have to call for backup or something because there's a load of them and I think they're still here and they've got fucking *scythes*... oh, Christ...' He retched, hawked and spat. 'Have you got any water?'

'Yes sir, we can sort you out with that just as soon as you're all safe. I'm PC Owen, that's PC Karim in the car just letting the station know that we're here. I'm going to ask you all to get in the back of the car while we have a quick look around.'

'I really wouldn't recommend that, officer,' said Toby.

'Why's that?'

'Like my dad says, two of you aren't going to be enough.'

'Just get in the car, son, and don't worry about us; this is what we do.' PC Owen turned back to Peter. 'When you say *a load*, how many do you mean?'

His mum jerked as if stung and slapped her hand to her cheek, eyes wide with sudden realisation. 'Oh shit!'

'What?' Peter took her shoulders, alarmed. 'Honey, what is it?'

'The others! The other Trustees! We have to warn them! She'll be after them too and there's nothing to stop Her! She's going to kill all of them!'

'Who is going to kill who?' asked PC Owen.

'Toby,' she said. 'Have you got your phone?'

He shook his head. 'Sorry. It all happened so quickly.'

'*Who is going to kill who?*' the cop demanded.

'A girl… look, it's not going to make any sense. I have to get my phone and warn them…' She started back towards the house, but PC Owen headed her off.

'Mrs Feenan, I'm sorry but no. Intruders might still be inside. There's absolutely no way I'm letting you back in there until I'm sure it's safe, and if your husband is telling me that there's a group of them and that they're armed, we're all going to have to wait for more units.'

'But…'

'The helicopter,' he said, overriding her, 'is keeping an eye on things, and right now they're telling me that they can't see anybody outside or in the immediate area, so as far as I'm concerned right here is the safest place you can be. You're not the only one having a bit of a busy night – we're dealing with several other reports of vandalism and assault and one major fire. If you think there is someone you know who might also be in danger, give us their names and addresses, and we'll send someone to check on them as soon as we can, okay?'

His mum muttered, 'Okay,' and slumped suddenly, shivering as the adrenalin crash began to take hold. His dad helped her into the back seat and between them they started to give the cop in the driver's seat the contact details of the other Trustees. Toby, who at least had something warm to wear, remained standing next to the patrol car. Its lights strobe-painted the front of the house in blue and black shadows, picking out the rips and gouges in the front door, and the sparkling of broken glass on the lawn. The helicopter clattered overhead in widening circles, presumably using its thermal imaging camera to look for anyone fleeing the scene. They wouldn't see anything. The danger, at least for the moment, seemed to have passed.

Inside the car, he heard his dad start to cough.

34

THE NIGHT BEFORE

THE SOFT WHISPER OF TRICKLING WATER FILLED THE silence of St Sebastian's church. The holy spring bubbled up into its granite basin and flowed away through the culvert in the west wall as it had done for centuries, its echoes rippling back upon themselves from ancient walls and dark oak, magnifying them into the music of a woodland stream, but in the dim hours of the early morning its sound gave Reverend Joyce Dobson no solace. The stream was ice-cold from its birthplace underground, and the columns that it ran between were petrified trunks of dead stone.

She sat in the rearmost pew, listening, hearing nothing. Ever since she had been a girl she had loved the sound of water. Throughout her childhood in the Lakes it had been part of the background heartbeat to her life, whether she and her sister had been crossing it on arched bridges on the way to school or chasing it in tumbling white streamers down the sloping sides of the fells. Whenever she'd been troubled she had always sought out quiet places where the sound of water could get into her head and rinse it clean, allowing her to think clearly and find her answers. In time she had come to recognise in it the voice of the Lord, and when she learned that the church in Haleswell had a holy spring inside its walls it had seemed nothing less than a sign. Unlike Nash, who had been born to the role of Trustee, or Patricia, who had been manipulated into it, Joyce had embraced the position voluntarily, eager for the opportunity to shepherd a flock so spiritually threatened, in the full knowledge of what she was letting herself in for.

Full knowledge. She uttered a short, hard laugh, and its echoes ricocheted. What arrogance. She could still taste the palm of Hester's hand – the dead cold salt of it, like drowned leather. Hester might have been wearing Donna's flesh and blood, but in that intimate physical contact couldn't disguise what She truly was.

Joyce's mistake had been to assume that in attempting to bless the house she was confronting something malicious but essentially human – the unquiet spirit of a girl, far removed from her own experience in time, perhaps, but knowable for all that. She acknowledged now that whatever had once been human in Hester Attlowe had long since soured into something wholly evil, and she blamed herself for not following her instincts in the first place to contact the Deliverance Ministry, rather than letting herself be swayed by Nash's arguments. Unable to sleep, and at a loss for how to respond in the face of all this, she had returned to St

Sebastian's Well for guidance, but the sound of water was just mindless babbling, as heedless of her as it had been of the countless other vicars of this church who had served and died over the centuries.

There came a tentative knocking on the church's heavy wooden door, and a male voice: 'Is there anybody in there? Please, can you help me?'

Joyce looked at her watch: it was after three in the morning. Too late for conmen to come calling, and thieves looking for lead off the roof would simply climb up there and have at it. She approached the door, and laid her hand on its dark timbers as if she could feel her way through them to whoever was on the other side. 'Who is it?' she called.

'My name is Rajko Gorić,' he said, and coughed heavily. 'Please, I've been beaten up.'

The poor boy who had lost his family in that dreadful business on Pestle Road. Despite Nash's protestations to the contrary she couldn't help feeling that the Trust could have done more to prevent it, and she wished she could have provided more than just a memorial service, but they were Eastern Orthodox and in any case he'd moved away after the funerals. What was he doing back in Haleswell? Joyce heard his hand on the other side of the door, mirroring her own, and a soft thump which must have been his forehead leaning to rest on the wood. 'Please,' he implored, and coughed again. 'Can't you do anything to help me? I don't know where else to go.'

She should have left the door shut and called an ambulance for him. She should have helped him sooner after his loss.

She should have gotten to know his family way before any of it. Too many opportunities lost.

She slid back the heavy cast-iron bolts top and bottom and opened the door, gasping when she saw the state of him. His hair was matted with blood, which also caked one side of his face, seeping from a nasty-looking gash above his right eyebrow. His other eye was bruised purple and his lower lip was split and swollen. He was rail thin and hugging himself, dressed only in a t-shirt and jeans against the night's chill.

'Oh you poor boy!' she said, reaching out to draw him inside. 'Come in and let's have a look at you.'

'Thanks,' he grinned, and looked back over his shoulder. 'I hope you don't mind, but I've brought a few friends.'

From the darkness behind him, something growled – something obviously much larger and heavier than a person – the sound rising and unknotting itself into a single intelligible syllable: '*Priest*.' A girl appeared, framed in the doorway with a crowd of people massing behind Her, and for a moment She looked terrifyingly familiar.

'Dear Lord,' Joyce breathed. '*Claire?*'

Hester laughed.

Joyce backed away and down the aisle towards the altar, shaking her head in meaningless denial. No. This wasn't possible. No. The blessing of the plague stones still held. No. If the boundary had been broken she would have been warned. Surely she would have been told.

'Sorry, Reverend,' said Rajko, stepping aside to make way for his *friends*. 'But we can't have you blessing the stones again after all the trouble it took to bring them down.' He was seized with another coughing fit, bent double with his hands propped on his knees, and blood spattered the floor between his feet.

'Priest,' repeated Hester. 'Come out and I will make it quick for you.' When Joyce didn't move She added, 'Get a move on, slowcoach!' and giggled.

'The God of my rock; in him will I trust,' Joyce babbled, the words falling over themselves in her panic. 'He is my shield, and the horn of my salvation, my high tower, and my refuge, my saviour; thou savest me from violence...' Still backing away, her heels bumped against the step up to the chancel and she fought to keep her balance. A tiny and utterly superstitious part of her was convinced that if she could stay upright they wouldn't be able to get her.

But they came for her anyway. The dead villagers of Clegeham poured into the church, hacking apart the pews with mattocks and billhooks and smashing the stained-glass windows into rainbow shards with rakes and pitchforks, gouging the memorial boards and ripping down from the walls the pictures drawn by Sunday school children. They seized her with cold, black hands and dragged her back down the aisle to where Hester was waiting by the well and forced her to her knees at Hester's feet so that she could see her own face reflected in the water.

'Please...' she whispered. 'We're sorry...'

'And if thou draw out thy soul to the hungry,' declared Hester, preaching to the chaos, 'and satisfy the afflicted soul; then shall thy light rise in obscurity, and thy darkness be as the noon day. And the Lord shall guide thee continually, and satisfy thy soul in drought, and make fat thy bones.'

'I'm sorry that I wasn't able to help you find peace.'

Hester paused in Her preaching. 'Save your pity for yourself,' She sneered. 'Though doubtless you have faith that the Lord will save your soul. He won't. There is no God, nor is there a devil. There is only the *gwrach clefyd*. Only the rake or the broom.'

The reflection of the dead girl rose up high behind Joyce, and she saw now that in Her hand was a sickle of the kind used for reaping crops. Joyce struggled then, but the dead hands held her fast, bending her lower, one fist bunched in her hair and stretching her throat out taut over the brimming water of Saint Sebastian's holy well. It wasn't just terror for her own life, though that was sharp enough – it was a soul-deep horror at the desecration Hester Attlowe was about to commit.

'And thou shalt be like a watered garden,' Hester said, finishing the verse from Isaiah, 'and like a spring of water, whose waters fail not.'

The sickle swept across Reverend Dobson's throat so swiftly and deeply that at first she felt nothing except a numb surprise at how the water seemed to have darkened. The realisation that it was her own life blood jetting into the water hit her at the same time as the pain, but then both flooded away into oblivion.

They bled her body into the well and left it amongst the rest of the carnage. The flow of water wasn't especially fast, so it took some time for all of the blood to rinse clear through the culvert and out into the world where it joined the network of streams and rivers which eventually fed into the ocean, but before long the spring ran as clean as if nothing had ever happened, and the church was silent again except for the soft whisper of trickling water.

Rajko found himself standing in a dark side street behind a different expensive-looking house with no clear recollection of how he'd got there beyond the fact that Hester and Her people had brought him. There was a dim sense of cold hands all around him, pulling, pushing, urging, and carrying him rapidly through some non-place that was all shadows, but that might have been caused by the fire in his head. He might simply have just taken to his heels and run, and somehow managed to escape the helicopter. He heard it throbbing in the distance, but again that could have been just coming from inside his burning head. The gash in his forehead was swollen and sticky with blood and he was running with sweat, but at the same time shivering as if he was naked in the snow.

'Where are we?' he asked through chattering teeth.

'At the house of the bailiff,' She replied. 'The man responsible for your pain.'

'You mean Nash?'

'His name is not important.'

'His name might not be but his security fucking is. How are we going to get in there? His place is going to be even harder than the Feenans'.' They hadn't meant to be first –

they were just a target of opportunity – but it had nearly finished him all the same. The priest and the bailiff were the main threats. With them out of the way, Hester could pick off the rest of the Trustees at leisure.

'He will come when I call. He possesses an object that he believes protects him, and in his arrogance he will not be able to resist the chance to flaunt it in my face.'

'Is he right?'

Her answer came slowly, as if extracted with pain. 'It is an object which I find... disagreeable. But he will not be expecting you; you will take it from him and destroy it, and then I will take vengeance for all of us.'

'What does this thing look like?'

She described the pilgrim badge. He didn't understand why such a thing would make a difference to Her, but She'd been as good as Her word so far, and besides, it hurt so much to think that it was easier to simply agree.

Nash's back garden was a lot larger than the Feenans' and more expansively landscaped. Rajko crossed a wide koi pond by a replica Japanese bridge and worked his way around the side through the shadows of sculpted topiary while Hester and Her people marched right up to an elaborate conservatory which took up most of the back of the house. If there was a security light, it didn't trip, which meant either that their cold, dead bodies were invisible against the background, or that they weren't really there at all and he was simply insane.

'Bailiff!' cried Hester. 'Come out and I promise to make it quick!'

Rajko waited. Sirens wailed in the distance, along with the helicopter's grumble.

'Bailiff!' She called again. 'You will—'

A light went on in the conservatory, and Nash was standing there by its wide double sliding doors. Despite the early hour he was fully dressed in suit and tie, with his hands in his trouser pockets as if out for nothing more adventurous than a stroll in the moonlight. His official Haleswell Village Trust lanyard hung around his neck, and attached to that was something small that glinted silver which must have been the pilgrim badge that She'd described.

'I heard you,' said Nash, and he opened the conservatory doors to walk outside and parley with the dead.

There was nothing very original in seeing his suit as a form of armour, Nash knew, but that didn't stop it being true. As a schoolboy, the neatness of his uniform was a source of pride in the face of the older boys' bullying. At the age of eleven he was ironing his own shirts. At college and university through the seventies and eighties, when white kids wore their hair like Africans and everybody seemed to want to look like they lived in a van despite coming from cosy, affluent middle-class families, Nash turned up to lectures in jacket and tie because that was exactly where he did come from, and that was what he was. He scorned their counter-cultural affectations as a form of childish self-delusion. *Look how individual and free I am*, their Doc Martens and badge-covered army surplus jackets said. If his suits said anything, it was *Stop fucking around and just get on with it.*

There was a very good chance that Hester was going to tear him to pieces, but if so he wouldn't be naked when it happened. He'd thought he would be more frightened, but he felt strangely calm, as if there were something familiar about all of this.

'I heard you,' he said. 'I would ask what you want, but that's pretty obvious.' He nodded at the farm tools carried by Her people. 'The answer is what it has always been: no. Fuck off back to hell or wherever it is you come from.' It was just noise to provoke a reaction, but none of the dead mob had made a move towards him yet. He removed his left hand from its pocket and grasped the lanyard just above the badge, took a deep breath and a step forward.

He saw Hester's glare flicker down to the pilgrim badge, and what might have been a twitch of something like pain snag the corner of Her mouth.

She retreated a step, and his soul blazed with triumph.

'Oh you stupid dead bitch!' he crowed. 'I'm going to—'

Then a shadow with grasping hands launched itself at him from the left.

He jumped back into the doorway of the conservatory, withdrawing his right hand from where it had been holding a personal self-defence Taser the size of a Dictaphone, pivoted into the attack and unloaded the device's ten thousand volts full in his attacker's throat. There was a sound of dry twigs cracking, and the man fell to his knees over the threshold, clutching his neck with both hands and making agonised gargling noises. Nash watched with distaste as he writhed.

'Did you actually think that I wouldn't see you climbing over my wall?' he asked, and turned to Hester. 'Or that I wouldn't be alerted the moment you started desecrating the stones? I let you get this far to see if this…' and he waved the pilgrim badge at Her, '…works, and it looks like it does. This is what we call in the trade a game-changer, my dear.'

Abruptly, without appearing to move, Hester was gone, and Her mob with Her.

Nash let out a great shuddering sigh of relief and sat down heavily on one of the conservatory chairs, propping his elbows on his knees and leaning forward as if he were about to pass out or vomit, and right now he felt like doing both. His attacker was still choking, but also trying to squirm to his feet, so Nash leaned forward and Tasered him again in the neck. He screamed and flopped, and for the first time Nash got a proper look at him.

'Oh, it's you,' he muttered to Rajko. 'Well I suppose it's not that surprising.' There was probably only one charge left but hopefully the police would be here soon. They were going to be having a busy night. Not all of his fellow Trustees would survive until dawn, which was a shame, and he wished he could have warned them that Hester had broken the Beating, but it would have made luring Her much more difficult if they'd all been running around like headless chickens. Assessing the effectiveness of the pilgrim badge was much more important than any single one of their lives, even his own. It was the first time anything approaching a weapon had been found that could be used against Her.

The very future of the village was at stake – a future in which they might not need the Beating, or even the Trust at all. Why put a whole committee of other people's lives needlessly at risk when one man, properly protected, could take charge of the whole thing?

'I'm doing this for you, you know,' he said to the semi-conscious young man at his feet. 'All of you.'

35

THE MORNING AFTER

'HE'S NOT ANSWERING,' MUTTERED NATALIE, PACING the living-room floor of her apartment with her phone. 'It just keeps diverting me to voicemail.'

'He's probably giving a statement to the cops,' said Peter. He was sitting at one end of the sofa with Trish at the other and Toby lying with his head in her lap, looking pale and haggard despite having finally been able to shower off the mess of Rajko's attack. The extra police units had eventually arrived to confirm that their attackers weren't hiding in the house, but there was no guarantee that they wouldn't return and with so many windows broken PC Owen wouldn't let her and Peter and Toby go back in for anything more than to pick up some belongings. When he'd asked if there was anybody that they could stay with – friends or relatives – Trish had laughed bitterly, remembering her conversation with Peter in which they'd joked about running away to draw Hester down on someone they didn't like. The only people that they could turn to for refuge were the other Trustees, who were in just as much danger, and the only one of them left that Trish felt comfortable enough with was Natalie.

The White Hart would have been the more sensible choice, if it hadn't been gutted by fire – besides which, nobody had been able to contact Al either, and the thought that Hester might have already killed him made her feel sick. Joyce Dobson had been her next best choice. PCs Owen and Karim had driven them into the village to the rectory, but pulled up short at the sight of the church door wide open and all its windows smashed, light pouring out into the night. Telling the Feenans to stay in the car, the two police officers had radioed it in and checked out St Sebastian's with great caution. But PC Owen had come back to the car looking ashen and shaking his head in disbelief; he wouldn't tell them what was inside but Trish knew that Joyce was dead when he asked her if there was anybody *else* that they could stay with.

So they'd gone to Natalie's to answer the police's questions. Full statements weren't needed right at that moment, besides which Trish gathered from the half-conversations she heard through their personal radios that the emergency services were a bit stretched tonight. The one piece of good news that they could offer was that the Gorić boy had been arrested at Nash's house, but, other than calling them to say that he'd been attacked, the chief executive himself was nowhere to be found. By the time the police left it was well after dawn.

'Nash would only be making a statement if something

had happened to him,' Trish replied.

Peter flapped a hand distractedly. 'Oh, I don't know,' he protested. 'I'm sure he's fine.' He'd complained of a growing headache and taken a couple of paracetamol, but they didn't seem to be having much effect. Trish put it down to exhaustion and the after-effects of the attack; she felt like she was ready to drop herself. 'If anybody can take care of themselves it's your chief executive.'

'But what if Hester's got him?' said Anik Singh. His hair was in wild tufts and he was chewing and picking at the corners of his fingernails.

'Well then there's not a huge amount we can do about it, is there?' Sean Trevorrow called in from the balcony where he was having a vape. Rather than the large detached houses of the other Trustees, Natalie Markes had opted for a penthouse apartment in a discreet but luxuriously appointed complex on the edge of the village but still within the boundary of the plague stones, for whatever good that was worth now. An intruder would have to go through a concierge and seven lower floors, though whether that would deter Hester was anybody's guess. 'Seriously though,' Trevorrow added, blowing a billowing cloud. 'What does She want?'

'I think it's pretty fucking obvious what She wants, don't you?' Anik retorted. 'She wants us dead!'

'So why has She stopped, then? Why are we still alive?'

'Maybe because it's daylight?' suggested Natalie.

'Why would that make a difference?' said Trish.

Anik stared at them, his brown eyes very wide. 'Because She's one of the walking dead – all right, yes, I said it, shut up – so maybe it's like vampires.'

Trish wasn't so sure. 'Daylight doesn't seem to have been a problem before, when all She could do was trick us. I don't see why it would be now, when She can actually do physical harm. And anyway, vampires aren't real.'

Anik uttered a short bark of laughter. 'Will you listen to yourself? Go outside and ask anybody if a dead medieval peasant girl walking around killing people with a fucking scythe is real!'

'I'm trying to keep a level head about this,' replied Trish. 'Someone has to.'

Esme Barlow, who had been quiet for most of the morning, said, 'Maybe it's just because it's easier to get away with it in the dark, like any other criminal.' She was nursing a large mug of coffee but Trish could see from the way she kept glancing at the bottles of wine in Natalie's kitchen that the sun might be going over the yardarm a lot earlier for her today.

'She's not just—' protested Anik.

'Okay, okay, we get it,' interrupted Natalie. 'Anik, do us a favour – Peter's looking pretty grim there and I don't have anything much stronger than paracetamol. Can you go out to the pharmacy and get something for colds and flu? We're also almost out of milk and I don't know about you, but I need another brew.'

Anik looked like he was about to argue the toss but looked at Peter, who was pale and clammy, with red-rimmed eyes and a damp cloth on his forehead. Peter gave him a tired thumbs-up. 'Okay, fine. But I'm not going out there on my own.'

'I'll go with you,' Esme sighed, and got to her feet.

After they'd left, Trevorrow came back in from the balcony and shut the sliding door.

'Let's track this back,' said Natalie. 'Rajko wrecks the stones between two and three in the morning. Hester attacks Trish's house because it's the last stone, but is chased off by the police and goes straight for Joyce just after three. Why Joyce first? Because of the attempt to bless Hester's resting place? The rectory is right in the centre of the village; some of us live a lot closer to you,' she gestured at the Feenan family, 'so why ignore us and go straight for Joyce?'

'It's raiding tactics,' said Toby, and everybody looked at him. It was the first thing he'd said since they'd arrived, and he'd been curled up on the sofa between his parents with his head in his mother's lap and his eyes closed, so the others had assumed he was asleep. He pulled himself into a sitting position. 'If you're pillaging a town repeatedly from a remote stronghold you need to stop the inhabitants from rebuilding their defences so you kill off the stonemasons and the builders, or you wreck their quarries. The reverend could have blessed all the stones again first thing and kept Hester out, so she was a priority target.'

The four adults stared.

'I play a lot of computer games.'

'Okay,' Natalie continued, 'so She attacks Joyce to stop her from reconsecrating the stones but it's still not much more than half past three in the morning and sunrise won't be until a quarter to five, so if dawn is a limiting factor She's still got over an hour in which She could easily take out a few more of us but She doesn't. Why not? It can't be just the daylight. Let's assume that She went for Richard next because he's the chief executive – except he's not at home and not answering his phone. So something must have happened to stop Ser.'

Trevorrow shook his head. 'Are you saying that he, what? *Talked Her down?*'

'I'm saying that I don't know, but that we need to find out, and quickly. We need to find *him*. He's lied to us about some fairly important things, but you have to admit that he has a knack of being able to tell people what they want to hear.'

Trevorrow threw his hands up in frustration. 'And so we're back to square one: what does She want? Beyond killing us, obviously.'

'Bread and salt,' said Toby.

'What's that supposed to mean? Is that another gaming thing?'

'It's a Bible thing, sort of. Hospitality, but an older and more powerful kind, older even than the Bible, not just the "can I borrow a cup of sugar" kind. The ancient Greeks called it *xenia* – the duty which you owe to guests, that got you cursed by the gods if you withheld it. The medieval church of Hester's time called it *hospitium*. Maya's mum…' he stopped and swallowed thickly. 'Maya's mother gave me bread and salt as a guest to her home. I think that Hester wants what She never got in life, which was to be given refuge by Her neighbours, but the people of Haleswell denied Her God-given right as a traveller in need, and She's cursed this village in punishment.'

'Christ, he sounds just like Stephanie!' said Trevorrow. 'That's exactly the same kind of mystical bollocks she kept spouting!'

Toby turned to his mum. 'I've been reading Mrs Drummond's books,' he explained.

'Yes, well she'd been losing her marbles for years, and I'll tell you now what I told her then: the notion of actually welcoming Hester into our home is simply fucking insane! It's suicide!'

Toby shrugged. 'She seems happy enough to break the door down and come for you instead. Maybe there's nothing to lose by trying.'

Trevorrow opened his mouth to retort, but Natalie got in before him. 'I think we've got a way to go before we try anything quite that drastic. Let's focus in the meantime on trying to find out where Richard has taken himself off to and whether he knows anything helpful.'

Before anything else could happen, Peter doubled over in a fit of violent coughing. When he pulled his hands away from his mouth he stared at them, horrified, and turned his palms to show Trish: they were slimy with green mucus, streaked with the vivid red of blood. 'Honey?' he said.

She texted Esme: *I think we're going to need something stronger than a decongestant.*

It was a few hours before the duty doctor could see the Gorić boy, by which time the state of him was such that she marched straight back to the custody sergeant and insisted that he be taken to Accident and Emergency immediately.

'Just as soon as his uncle gets down here from Sheffield and we can get someone from CAMHS,' said the sergeant. 'I don't know if you've noticed, but it's only just gone seven.' It was the last hour of a long shift and he was due on a plane at six the next morning to visit his sister in Sydney. This was the last thing he needed.

'Mental health isn't that boy's priority,' the doctor objected. 'Even the head laceration – which needs stitches, by the way, never mind that he's likely got concussion – isn't the worst of it. It's his hand. It's already badly infected. He's got a raging fever, vomiting, abdominal pain, and his lymph nodes are up like golf balls. I don't know what particular bug this boy has but he needs some serious antibiotics, right now.'

The duty sergeant sighed and reached for his phone.

Banahan:
hey Iz u there?

IzPorter:
just about. Knackered. 2hrs sleep if that. U?

Banahan:
Same. Cops asking me all sorts of questions about Raj.
Parents went absolutely skitz on me. I heard he got arrested?

IzPorter:
I heard he killed someone.

Banahan:
WTAF?!?!

IzPorter:
don't believe it tho.

Banahan:
That's it. Not coming into college today. Can't face it.

IzPorter:
dont blame u. Me neither.

Banahan:
also feel like shit. think I'm coming down
with flu or something.

36

RECKONINGS

THERE WAS A BORED-LOOKING POLICEMAN SITTING on a plastic chair outside the door to Ward 28, the Infectious Diseases Unit of Heartlands Hospital, when Toby's dad was taken in for observation. It seemed an odd coincidence, given the events of the previous night, but he didn't give it any more thought. The cop could have been there for any one of a dozen reasons, and Toby was too exhausted to pay attention to much beyond what was happening with his dad.

Esme and Anik had returned to Natalie's apartment with a load of prescription antibiotics, but they hadn't done any good. They moved his dad into one of the bedrooms, where he kept hacking up great gobs of phlegm and blood. He couldn't stomach food and struggled to keep down a glass of rehydration salts. Every half hour during the rest of the day Esme had checked his vital signs, and his pulse had become faster while his temperature had steadily climbed to the point where she declared that she couldn't see any signs of him improving overnight and it might be best to get him to a hospital sooner rather than later.

Ward 28 was primarily for HIV sufferers but it also treated everything ranging from tonsillitis to malaria. It consisted of two bays of five beds apiece and another twenty-one separate rooms, with two high-security isolation suites at the far end with their own dedicated entrance, so that those suffering from the worst of conditions didn't have to be wheeled past other patients on the ward. The nurses welcomed his dad with warmth and calm professionalism, and firmly but gently threw Toby and his mum out to get some rest while they made him as comfortable as possible. It would be at least twenty-four hours until the samples that the doctors had taken came back from the lab to tell them what Peter was suffering from, and in that time all they could do was wait.

Seeing his strong father totter from wheelchair to bed on unsteady legs, wheezing like an old man, was easily more terrifying than anything Toby had seen yet, and he was happy to leave.

The last person he'd expected to see in the corridor outside was Rajko.

He'd been to a vending machine around the corner from the ward entrance while his mum dealt with the paperwork, and noticed the cop was up and moving, escorting a nurse and a porter who were wheeling a bed-bound patient towards Radiography. Clustering about the patient were drips and monitoring equipment, and he had a large dressing above his left eye and a surgical mask covering the lower half of his face, so that Toby didn't recognise him until he lashed out and grasped Toby by the wrist as they passed each other.

'Hey there, little landlord,' he croaked, his voice muffled by the mask.

'Rajko?' Alarmed, Toby pulled away; Rajko's grip was so weak it was easy to shake off.

'Oi!' warned the cop. 'We'll have none of that!'

'It's okay, officer,' said Toby. 'We, well, we sort of know each other.' He didn't know why he felt the need to defend Rajko – maybe because he looked so catastrophically ill.

The surgical mask shifted as Rajko's mouth curved into a ghastly smile beneath. 'Best buds.'

The nurse escorting the bed tutted. 'I'm sorry, but we do need to move on,' she said, so Toby followed alongside.

'What have you got?' he asked. 'Whatever it is, you've given it to my dad.'

'They don't know,' said Rajko. His voice sounded like someone sawing raw meat. 'They're doing tests. But we both know better, don't we, landlord? We know what She gave us.'

Toby couldn't even say it; its name stuck in his throat, choking. *The Black Death.* 'Jesus,' he whispered. 'It's not going to stop with the Trust this time, is it?'

'Not Nash. He's going to get away with it. I fucked up again. I'm sorry.'

'What do you mean? Get away with what? How?'

'He's got something. Something She doesn't like. Or can't touch. Or…' Rajko shook his head and coughed in wet, ripping sounds.

'That's enough now,' warned the nurse. 'You're distressing him. You need to go.'

Toby ignored her. 'What's he got, Raj? Where is he? How do I find him?'

'Son,' said the cop, who was now in front of him, stopping him from following. 'That's it. You're done.'

'*How do I find him, Rajko?*' he called over the cop's shoulder.

He thought Raj wasn't going to reply, but as he was being hustled away by the policeman he heard a croaking laugh come back to him along the corridor with the words: 'Ask Her!'

But She was busy.

She had Her father's tally sticks, and the ancient rage of the *gwrach clefyd* brimming within Her. There was a reckoning to be had.

Anik Singh got as far as Birmingham Airport. The Trust's director of human resources had a large family scattered all over the globe, and he had no intention of sitting in one place waiting for death to come to him. He didn't know how far She was prepared to pursue him, how quickly She could catch up with him, or how long he could keep moving until the money ran out, but he literally had nothing left to lose by trying. He bought a last-minute flight to Sweden, hoping there would be room at his cousin's place in Malmö, threw some clothes in a bag and endured a nail-biting train journey from Birmingham New Street, jumping at sudden noises and keeping a wary distance from any young women who looked even remotely like Her. Paradoxically, he had chosen public transport over driving because he felt safer amongst other people; anything which might make Her think twice about attacking him. He began to relax only once he had passed through check-in and security; there were so many airport guards with guns about the terminal that She couldn't possibly go for him. His reasoning was that if She was capable of direct physical assault then She must surely be vulnerable to a physical defence, and who was better defended than the passengers at an airport?

All the same, as the minutes ticked away until his gate opened for boarding he felt his anxiety rising. He watched from the gate lounge as the ground crew busied about the Lufthansa 727, making it safe. Then there were the final checks, and he heaved a sigh of relief as he set off down the slope of the boarding tunnel, with a family of four ahead of him and his cabin luggage trundling along behind him on its little wheels, and behind that the footsteps of the other passengers. The boarding tunnel dog-legged, and for a moment the family were out of sight around the corner, and when he followed them around it they weren't there anymore.

There was only Hester, in the ticking flicker of a faulty strip light, tally sticks in one hand, bloodstained sickle in the other. There had only ever been Hester, and he had been a fool to think otherwise.

The footsteps behind him were still there, but he knew that it wasn't the other passengers who were following him. He felt himself shoved violently from behind, and looked down in surprise at something that had appeared in his peripheral vision. The twin steel tines of a hay fork protruded from his chest just below each nipple, and he tried to gasp in surprise except that he couldn't breathe. He would have fallen, if whoever was holding the handle hadn't been helpfully holding him up. Then Hester stepped towards him with a swift, sideways swipe of Her hand, and he was watching the purple and grey loops of his intestines spilling out over his waist and onto his feet, emptying him, hollowing him utterly.

Natalie hadn't meant to fall asleep. She hadn't thought that she'd be able to so much as catnap, what with everything that was happening. She'd decided to just have a little lie-down because she'd been up since the early hours and she could feel the tell-tale signs of one of her migraines coming on. The darkness of her bedroom and a damp washcloth over the face usually did the trick, but her body had obviously decided that it needed something a bit more substantial because her bedside clock told her that it was nine o'clock in the evening. She'd been asleep for four hours. Her stomach growled, reminding her that she was also starving.

'Why didn't either of you wake me?' she muttered, stretching out the stiffness in her shoulders and shuffling towards the hall in her socks. Anik had disappeared earlier that afternoon, despite everything that they could do to persuade him that whatever safety there was lay in numbers, leaving

Trevorrow and Esme in her apartment. She didn't even know if they were still here. There was no sound of either television or conversation coming from the living room.

'Guys? Are you there?'

The smell stopped her in her tracks like a physical wall. Once when she'd been seventeen and her grandmother had gone into hospital because of a fall, she'd had to look after Gran's aged cat Hector who, because of Gran's conviction that tinned food was bad for cats, was fed on meat scraps and liver from a nearby butcher's. It was stored in little plastic bags in Gran's freezer, and Nattie would have to thaw out each bag before feeding Hector, and she quickly discovered that the smell of liver was sickening. It was thick and heavy, like a nosebleed clot of jellied blood trapped in your skull.

That smell hit her again, only it was a thousandfold strong and coming from the doorway to her living room.

Sean Trevorrow and Esme Barlow had been laid out side by side on her dining table, naked and holding hands, in a lake of their mingled blood which covered its entire surface and spread over much of the surrounding floor. At first glance it looked like they'd simply been hacked to death; their bodies were slashed and gouged in hundreds of small wounds. That would have been bad enough, but as she edged closer she saw that their limbs had been tied off at each joint – shoulders, elbows, wrists, hips, knees, ankles, and each individual finger and toe – with tourniquets that in some places were so tight they sank deeply into flesh and couldn't be seen, and each part of Sean's and Esme's divided bodies had been systematically cut open and bled. Death from a single wound would have been too quick, presumably. This way they could watch themselves and each other being emptied bit by bit. How long must they have suffered while she was asleep in the next room, and why hadn't she heard anything? More importantly, why hadn't Hester come for her too?

'Because you need us to see it, don't you?' she said to the empty air. 'You need us to know what's going to happen to us. Well I get it!' she screamed suddenly. 'Okay? I fucking get it! Somebody hurt you a long time ago and you can't get at them so you're taking it out on us. Well boo fucking hoo! This isn't justice – it's murder, and you're not some avenging angel, you're just a petty little vindictive bitch! So come on then! What are you waiting for? *Come on!*' She screamed this last so loudly that her voice broke on the last syllable and ended as a hoarse rasp.

The shadows in the corners of the room shifted and took on substance, stepping forward into the ragged shapes of men and women armed with bloodstained tools, and Hester at their head.

Nattie took a step backwards, towards the sliding glass doors which led out onto her seventh-floor balcony. Outside, the sky was still lambent with the long slow dusk of a summer's evening. 'Fuck you,' she spat at them. 'I'm not your meat to butcher.' And she turned, ran, and vaulted the railing into the twilight.

When Hester came for Trish, she was praying at Peter's bedside – although not literally so, since, having worsened throughout the day, he'd been moved into Ward 28's other negative-pressure isolation room and was behind several layers of sterile glass and Perspex. She was in the anteroom where the nurses changed into and out of their protective clothing; it had a large window looking into the room where Peter lay surrounded and dwarfed by monitors, lights, cables, and respirator units. He was sedated, having been drifting in and out of lucidity and distressing both himself and her with his violent reactions to the hallucinations that his fevered brain kept spawning. She knew that in the room next to this, Rajko Gorić was in an even worse way. The doctors' laboratory tests had yet to confirm Toby's claim that both men were suffering from bubonic plague, but they were acting on the assumption that it was since everything about their symptoms matched up – except for the extreme speed and virulence with which the bacterium was spreading, and the inability of all but the strongest antibiotics to put even a dent in it. She and Toby had both been advised that, since they had been in such close proximity to him, it was best that they stay in one of the smaller side suites, where they were being given prophylactic antibiotics and having their vitals monitored regularly. On the few occasions when she'd left Peter's bedside to pay any attention to what was happening in the outside world, she heard stories in the hospital corridor about increasing numbers of the general public reporting severe flu-like symptoms, but that held no significance for her. The only world that she had any concern for was lying in that hospital bed.

Trish was sitting on a plastic chair with her forehead leaning against the isolation-room window, hands clasped under her chin, pleading with the Lord to spare her husband and the father of her child, when she felt the cold whisper of a blade stroke the hairs on the nape of her neck.

She froze, glancing at her reflection in the window. It showed nobody behind her, but the blade continued to stroke, almost lovingly. Slowly, she let out her breath, and without moving from her position said, 'I don't have time for you right now. I'm busy.'

Hester laughed softly, Her mouth right behind Trish's right ear. 'Take time,' She whispered. 'Take time to watch him die. Watch him die like my mother watched her own husband die, and then you will join him.'

Then she heard the door to the anteroom open and Toby's voice: 'I was wondering when you'd get here.'

Trish whirled away from the window. 'Toby!' she shrieked. 'Get out!' She would have rushed to shove him out of the room except that Hester was between them, and the dead girl's presence was an impassable barrier.

'It's okay, Mum, I've got this,' he replied. It was plain that he was terrified, but he kept his eyes locked on Hester. *Got this?* By what measure of suicidal insanity could he be said to have *got this?* While she stood with her mouth hanging open, her son was addressing their enemy.

'I want to offer you a deal,' he said.

'No deals,' Hester whispered. 'No bargains. No pacts. You have nothing I want, save for your deaths.'

'You want what Nash has,' Toby countered. 'Or you want

it gone, at least, and I know you can't or won't take it from him. Raj told me everything.'

Hester's face contorted with disgust.

'I'll take his place,' Toby continued. 'I'll find whatever this thing is and get rid of it.'

Hester cocked Her head. *If?*

'You leave my mother alone.'

'No!' Trish screamed. 'Toby, you will not agree to do anything for Her! I need you here! I can't lose you too!'

'*Mum,*' he said, in a tone she'd never heard before – the voice of the man he might become one day, if he survived this. 'Please, shut up. I know what I'm doing.' He turned back to Hester. 'What do you say?'

She frowned, considering. Then gave a curt, reluctant nod.

When the duty nurse came to see what all the shouting was about, she found Trish curled up in a sobbing ball against the wall below the observation window, in an otherwise empty room.

37

BADASS MOTHERFUCKER

STRIPS OF POLICE TAPE FLUTTERED FROM THE doorway of Lot 9 like the discarded streamers from an autumn village fete, and dim yellow light glowed from the empty sockets of its windows. Toby knew he shouldn't have been surprised that this was where Nash had gone to ground, but he thought that the man would have chosen somewhere with a few more creature comforts to wait out the end of his world.

Hester remained unseen, but he felt Her presence around him all the same, like a shiver that wouldn't stop. He couldn't recall exactly how they'd got here, and he didn't want to.

While it had been easy enough to sneak out of the busy hospital ward, he had no idea how he was going to steal the pilgrim badge off Nash. He thought about waiting until the man was asleep and trying to steal it off him. He thought about luring him out and smacking him over the head with something, and even went so far as to find a piece of scaffolding pipe – two feet of heavy steel which fit nicely in his palm. He thought about calling the police and making up some story about being abducted so that the cops would take the badge from him along with the rest of his belongings when they threw him in a cell. He thought of a lot of different things, each as implausible as the other.

'Fuck it,' he said finally, and walked in through the front door.

The light came from a battery-powered lantern, which had been set up on a small tower of bricks in one of the empty rooms. Nash was wearing a woollen beanie and a thick down jacket against the chill, and he was in the process of jumping up from a folding camp chair in front of a kettle on a gas stove. Over the top of the jacket hung a small metal pendant, gleaming and flashing in the light of the lantern as he moved.

'Jesus Christ, Toby Feenan!' Nash barked. 'You scared the shit out of me!'

'I'm sorry!' said Toby, hoping that he sounded surprised to see Nash here. 'I saw the light and I didn't know who it was. I thought it might have been Her.'

'What? Making a cup of tea? Don't be obtuse. What are you doing here?'

He didn't have to feign his distress and anger in answering this one. 'She's killing everyone, and my mother's next. I thought, I don't know, I have nothing to lose by coming here and begging Her to stop.'

'Where are they – your parents?'

'Dad's really sick in hospital. Mum's looking after him.'

'Oh. What about the others?'

'The last I saw they were holed up in Ms Markes' flat, but I haven't heard anything since we took Dad to A&E. We think Reverend Joyce is dead.'

'Ah.' Nash lowered himself into the camping chair again, hands in the pockets of his jacket. Although the June evening wasn't especially cold, there was a chill in this half-built house that came from something more than just being surrounded by bare concrete. Nash glanced down at the length of scaffolding pipe that was still in his hand. 'You plan on doing something with that?' he asked carefully.

'What? Oh, no, sorry.' Toby laid the pipe on the floor, close to his foot. 'So what are *you* doing here? This isn't exactly the kind of place I expected to find you.'

'How the mighty have fallen, eh? Don't worry, this is just temporary. Just until things die down.'

'Things. People, you mean.'

Nash shrugged. 'If you like. Fancy a brew?' He set out two tin mugs and produced a packet of biscuits from a rucksack against the wall. The kettle was starting to hiss as the water in it approached boiling.

'But you could hide out anywhere,' Toby pointed out. 'You're here for a reason. It's to do with Her, isn't it?'

'Huh,' Nash snorted. 'Everything's to do with Her. But you're right, sharp little soul that you are. She needs to learn Her place. Specifically She needs to learn that Her place is now *my* place.' He took one hand out of a pocket to stroke the shining pendant.

'What's that?'

'Oh cut the bullshit,' Nash sneered. 'You know exactly what it is, and I know exactly why you're here.'

Toby picked up the pipe again. 'I'm only here for my mum. I don't want to hurt you.'

'Yeah you do.'

Toby thought about this. 'Actually yes, I do. Maya and her family died because of you. The Trustees are dying and you've found something that could help but you're sitting here nice and safe until "things die down". Yes. I want to fucking hurt you. Even if you get away with it, what do you think will happen? You can't keep this a secret. The Deliverance Ministry are going to be very interested in what you've found. They're not going to let you keep it.'

Nash snorted contemptuously. 'Deliverance Ministry my left bollock. Do you know why the Deliverance Ministry always reconsecrated the stones after each time that She managed to break through and kill everyone? Why they put another group of Trustees' lives at risk? We're bait, boy, nothing but fucking bait. If you've got a wild tiger prowling around your town and you can't get rid of it, the next best thing is you give it a nice distraction to play with. The Trust is nothing but a goat tied to a stake in the woods to keep the tiger away from town, and that's all we've ever been, for six hundred years. Except now, because of this,' he stroked the pendant again, 'everything's changed. She had Her lair and Her prey, but now Her prey are all dead, or as good as, and She can't come back to Her lair. So what does She do now?'

'I don't know.'

'Neither do I!' Nash laughed, his eyes bright with glee.

'Maybe She'll just give up and disappear. My best guess is that She'll still try to come for me, but won't be able to because of this.' He waved the badge. 'If the village is run by just one person from now on, and that one person wears this, nobody ever needs to get hurt again. But who knows? Maybe She'll go absolutely batshit and kill everyone. It's going to be interesting either way.'

Toby shook his head, more awestruck than angry. 'You really are a complete psycho, aren't you?'

Nash's laughter vanished as quickly as it had appeared. 'And you really are an arrogant little shit, aren't you? Look at you, swinging that pipe around like you think you're going to do something with it. Think you're a badass now?' He laughed, his mockery scorching. 'I hope you've got your inhaler with you this time...'

Toby didn't hear whatever it was that Nash said after that because his head was suddenly ringing and the world was tipping in lazy circles around him like a drunk carousel. *I will fuck you up in ways you can't imagine.*

He tottered backwards, eyes wide. 'You...!'

Nash stopped in mid-flow and frowned at Toby as if he genuinely had no idea what had just happened. 'What?'

Toby could barely speak. It felt like someone had punched him hard in the guts. The ringing was getting louder. 'You were Green Skull!' he gasped.

Nash's laugh was genuine this time, huge and rolling. 'Oh and there you go,' he said, wiping his eyes. 'Just when I think you're too clever for your own good you go and say something asinine like that, just like your father. Of course

I wasn't your dreaded Green Skull!' He shrugged. 'That was just some thug I paid, but he did bring me back a very accurate report.'

'But... why...'

Nash sighed, as if having to explain something idiotically obvious. 'Because your wonderful mummy and daddy were fucking cowards, that's why, and they needed a push. They were given every incentive, every possible reason for leaving that shitty little rat-hole of a flat and their shitty little zero-hours jobs, and taking up a life with some actual meaning. But no. It was all, "we're not sure if it's the right move for our son", so I made it the right move for them. You were never in any actual danger. If you think about it I've actually done you a favour. Look at you now, every inch the badass—'

'*Stop saying that—!*' Toby threw himself at Nash. All through his speech the ringing in Toby's ears had been getting louder, just like when he'd punched Rajko, and shoved George Cox's head through the classroom window, and every one of the other times he'd been unable to stop himself flying into a rage since the break-in. Correction: since Nash's thug had broken in. 'You put this in me!' he screamed, swinging wildly with the scaffolding pipe.

Nash was older and outweighed him considerably, but had obviously been prepared for intruders of some kind because he stepped smartly away, knocking over the folding chair, and pulled from the pocket of his down jacket a small, black, torch-like object. He thrust it at Toby just as Toby brought the pipe down and the two connected. There was a loud crack and a bright blue flash, and Toby felt the pipe smashed out of his hands as if he'd struck solid concrete, the blow numbing his arms to the shoulder and making him fall backwards onto his arse with a thump that jarred his coccyx and made his teeth snap shut.

Nash advanced on him. He was shaking his hand as if it had been stung. 'No,' he said. 'No, I didn't put anything in you. It was already there, thanks to Daddy dearest. What you have to understand, boy, is that at the end of the day we're all just puppets, dancing to the same tunes that our daddies did, and their daddies before them. Someone else is always pulling the strings.' He reached for Toby with the Taser again.

The only thing that was within reach was the kettle on the gas hob by his feet. He hooked out with his left foot, kicking the kettle towards Nash so that its lid fell off and near-boiling water splashed over Nash's ankles. A hissing cloud of steam flew up and Nash danced away, screaming. Toby levered himself to his knees with arms that were no more than jelly filled with pins and needles, but managed to exert enough control over his hands to pick up the camping stove. It was one of those low, blocky square stoves which had a single hob and a compartment down the side to slot a butane canister – low and solid enough that it hadn't toppled over when he'd kicked the kettle, and still burning with a fierce blue flame. Nash was coming for him again, bellowing, so he raised the stove with the flame burning out in front and slammed it into Nash's stomach.

The polyester covering of his jacket melted instantaneously and caught fire. It was obviously too well designed to go up in flames completely, but Nash screamed and batted in panic at the patch of localised burning, smearing molten plastic all over his hands, which made him scream even more shrilly. Toby dropped the stove and reached in close, choking on the stench of burnt plastic and human flesh, grabbed the cord which held the pilgrim badge, and yanked it free with a snap.

He stumbled to the other side of the room. Nash fell to his knees, moaning, scrubbing his hands on the concrete floor to scrape off the plastic. The battery lantern was knocked from its pile of bricks and rolled across the ground, casting shadows that swooped and pitched like the wings of some vast beast flying low overhead, and out of the rolling billows of darkness stepped Hester Attlowe and the murdered villagers of Clegeham. They stood close about Nash, with their scythes and pitchforks and billhooks.

'Please,' Nash sobbed. 'Toby, help me! You can't let them do this!'

Hester turned and looked quizzically at Toby, inviting him to stay and watch.

Clutching the pilgrim badge, Toby ran from the house.

38

WHAT WE INVITE IN

HE RAN HOME TO STONE COTTAGE THROUGH A
neighbourhood which didn't seem to know that it was
dying. He saw ordinary people going about their lives –
heading out to the pub for a drink with friends or coming
back from meals with loved ones, dressed up or dressed
down, going to corner stores, walking dogs, riding bikes,
jogging. There were kids still sitting under trees at the Rec
as he ran past, aching to stop and warn them of the plague
that was brewing but knowing exactly how he would
have looked. How many of them had Rajko passed it on
to? Where had She infected him and how long ago? This
was how it began, he realised, right at the start. Not with
ambulances in the streets and soldiers in hazmat suits and
machine guns. It began with people feeling a bit under the
weather, certain that it was just a summer cold, or at worst a
touch of the flu. They would take over-the-counter remedies

which would mask the worst of the symptoms so they could get an early night, and sleep through the hours while the *Yersinia pestis* bacteria raged through their lymphatic systems so that by the time they woke up they were already in need of hospitalisation. And even then they would make the best of it, put on a stiff upper lip, call in sick to work but not want to visit the doctor because it was just a case of flu after all, wasn't it, and all the advice they were given was to stay at home to avoid infecting their neighbours in the waiting room. Nobody wanted to trouble the Accident and Emergency departments because there were so few of them nowadays and they were so understaffed and there were bound to be people worse off than themselves and the doctors would just send them home anyway. And by the time that they started vomiting blood, and the buboes were huge and hard in their throats, armpits, and groins, and patches of their skin were starting to blacken with gangrene and somebody finally called for an ambulance, the emergency system would be so overwhelmed that they'd begin to die in their homes.

He didn't sprint, as an asthma attack now would delay him catastrophically; he took it easy, or as easy as he dared, and texted his mum as he ran: *Am at home. Plz can u come get me?* His phone started buzzing immediately but he ignored her attempts to call him because then he'd have to explain what had happened, and he wasn't up to that yet. He didn't know how long he had. If Hester's bloodlust blinded Her to the fact that Toby still had the pilgrim badge, and if She took Her time over Nash, and if She decided to chase him rather than go straight for his mother...

He couldn't do anything about ifs. All he could do was try to ignore the growing tightness in his chest, and run.

He stumbled through the gate of Stone Cottage, clutching a runner's stitch in his side and wheezing. The house was still locked but there hadn't been time to arrange for the broken windows to be boarded up yet, so he climbed in through the study window and headed for the upstairs bathroom. His spare inhaler was in the medicine cabinet and he jammed a couple of puffs with trembling hands. When his breathing had steadied he went back down to the kitchen. The floor was littered with cutlery and smashed crockery and glass, but there were still plenty of the things he needed, and he hurriedly set them out on the table.

Waiting was torture. He paced the house, went up to his room and looked at his books, his posters, his games. It was like a different world now.

A few minutes later he heard tyres crunching on the gravel of the drive and saw headlights washing the side of the house. He ran downstairs as the front door opened with a jingling of keys and his mother calling out, 'Toby? Toby, are you here?'

'I'm here!' he called. 'I'm okay!'

'Oh thank God!'

They met in the hall and she gathered him up in a rib-crushing hug, sobbing with relief into his shoulder. 'Don't you ever...' she said. 'Don't you ever...' Then she pulled away, taking him by the hand. 'There's a taxi waiting outside. Come on, let's get you back.'

'No,' he said, and took his hand back. 'It's not finished.'

'What do you mean it's not finished? Toby, we are going back to the hospital now, to be by your father's bedside. You can tell me all about everything that happened on the way.'

Toby retreated down the hallway. 'I'm sorry, but I don't have time to explain,' he said. 'We have to do this now. I can't risk Her getting here before.'

'What are you talking about? Before what?'

'Before I've invited Her. Don't worry, She can't hurt us if She accepts an invitation. If She lets Herself in it won't work.' He went into the kitchen.

'*Toby!*' She hurried after him, but by the time she caught up he'd already started.

'Hester Attlowe!' he called. 'I invite you into my home, to be honoured as my guest, to eat at my table and to rest beneath my roof!'

'Toby, what in God's name are you doing?!'

He ignored her and called again. 'Hester Attlowe! I invite you into my home, to be honoured as my guest, to eat at my table and to rest beneath my roof!'

His mother seized him by the shoulders and shook him. 'Stop it!' she yelled.

He shouted over the top of her: '*Hester Attlowe, I invite you into my home as my guest, to eat at my table and to rest beneath my roof!*'

And She was there, but She was obviously not happy about it. Her face twisted and winced as if being in the room was causing Her physical pain, and She darted sharp glances to and fro. 'What is this?' She snarled.

'Leave us alone!' screamed his mother, putting herself in front of him, but he gently pushed her to one side.

'It's okay, Mum,' he murmured. 'I told you, I've got this. She's bound by the law of *hospitium*.' She looked at him, stunned and confused. He turned to Hester. 'This is what you've always really wanted. It's the welcome you were always denied. It's your right, as a traveller on the road, to expect refuge and hospitality.' He sat down at the table and gestured at what he had set out there. 'Bread and salt. Please, will you sit and eat with me?'

It was half of one of his mother's loaves, a small bowl of cooking salt, a jug of water and two glasses.

'No!' Hester snapped. 'I will not!' Her black fingers opened and closed like claws, obviously itching to kill, and yet She didn't move from the spot. Her face wore the expression of a hunted animal at bay.

'But you must,' said Toby gently. 'It's the law of *hospitium*. It's what has kept you here all this time. You must obey it. You can't break it and still be you.'

'Where is the token?' She demanded.

'I destroyed it, and don't change the subject.'

'Liar!' Black spittle flew from Her teeth. She flew at him, and his mother wailed, but Hester stopped inches from him as if She'd slammed into a wall. Her contorted, centuries-old rage filled his field of view and Her pestilential breath swamped him. 'You lie!'

Somehow he managed to maintain an even tone. 'If I had

it, and it really is something you can't bear to be near, then surely I'd have given it to my mother to protect her, wouldn't I? Mum, did I give you the pilgrim badge?'

'No,' replied his mum in a tiny voice.

Toby spread his hands. 'See? Now, please, as my guest, will you break bread with me? The bread is togetherness for my family, and the salt is prosperity and happiness for our guest.'

Slowly and painfully, as if dragged by hooks, Hester retreated to the other side of the table and took a seat. Toby poured each of them a glass of water from the jug. Then he tore off a chunk of the bread, sprinkled it with a pinch of salt and ate it, washing it down with a mouthful of water. 'My mother baked this bread,' he said, and pushed the plate towards Hester. 'The water is from Saint Sebastian's Well. Some of it, at least. We had a small bottle from the church, so I tipped it in there. It's what you wanted, isn't it? You believed it would have healed your people, didn't you?'

'They kept it from us,' She whispered. 'They had no right.'

'I'm keeping it from you no longer,' he said. 'I want you to have what you were always owed, so that you'll be at peace and stop all the killing.'

Hester's voice was so small, so afraid. 'I never wanted any of this.'

Her dead fingers tore off a large hunk of bread, and afterwards he thought She must have known, because why take such a large piece? She raised it to her mouth and bit off a portion, and when She took Her hand away there was a gleam of pewter in the piece that She was left holding, just like a lucky sixpence. It had been the easiest thing in the world for him to cut a slit in the base of the loaf and push the pilgrim badge deep inside. 'Cuthbert,' She whispered, with the faintest of smiles, and She began to cry.

'I could have given it to you,' he said to his mum. 'But that would have just pushed the problem further down the line. They always said that the Trust looks after its own, and that's been the problem all along. It has to stop somewhere. The reverend said that Hester was empty of everything except rage, but I don't think that's true.'

The tears came out of Her like black oil, far too much of it to be normal, pouring down Her face and quickly soaking Her ragged tunic, and then pooling on the floor underneath Her chair. As She wept, the pool grew and spread towards the walls of the kitchen, and Hester seemed to shrink, the marks of Her disease diminishing until She was little more than an ordinary-looking girl, somebody that Maya might have been friends with in another world and time. Then the angle of the light must have changed somehow because the blackness seemed to be rising up behind Hester like a vast shadow of a much larger figure whose head brushed the ceiling, clothed in shifting veils of darkness. Whatever the pilgrim badge meant to Hester, its effect had been to fill Her with something that left no room for whatever had ridden Her for six hundred years. Toby knew that it was aware of him, and with that recognition came the knowledge that it was ancient, immeasurably older than the spectre of the dead girl. Six centuries of purgatory was probably no more than a blink of the eye for it. He also realised how massively he had underestimated what he was facing – how arrogant and naïve he was to think that he could do anything to stop a power like this.

'I don't know who you are,' he said. He couldn't stop his voice from shaking this time, and he knew it lacked conviction. All he wanted to do was crawl under the table, find some deep hole in which to escape its pitiless regard. He was vaguely aware that his mother was praying, her eyes closed, murmuring fervently. 'But you weren't invited. Get out of my home.'

If anything, the shadow loomed larger.

'She is the *gwrach clefyd*,' said Hester. She looked utterly spent, like the last flame of a dying candle, ready to blow away at the slightest breath. 'From the land of my mother's people. She is winter, and plague, and the promise of death whispering to you from the moment you are born. She is the rake; She is the broom. She is everywhere. She needs no invitation.'

With a banshee wail, the *gwrach clefyd* boiled towards him through the air like a thunderhead, and straight through the shape of Hester who unravelled completely at its touch. He cowered, waiting for the blow that would kill him, but the *gwrach clefyd* veered away from him at the last moment and plunged at his mother as she prayed to her Lord for deliverance. Tornado clouds of shadow tore around her, enveloping her from head to foot, battering at her, ripping at her clothes, hair and flesh, seeking for a way in. But his mother was no hollow vessel to be possessed, and the *gwrach clefyd*, repulsed, turned its violence outward into the house. It screamed through the halls and bedrooms like an arctic gale, ripping doors from the hinges, slamming furniture against the ceilings, tearing pictures and shelves and light fittings from their fixings and flinging them into a maelstrom of destruction that eventually narrowed and concentrated itself into a seething funnel of rage which finally poured itself into the shape of a huge grey rat in the middle of the dining table. It glared at them both for a moment, and then leapt out through the broken kitchen window and was gone.

Toby and his mother helped each other out to the Uber which was still waiting in the road. It seemed impossible that the events in the house had taken only a matter of minutes, and that the driver had been sitting out here with his headphones on, humming away, oblivious to the noise and destruction. The world had tilted on its axis; surely an age must have passed at least. They sat in shocked silence with their hands tightly entwined all the way back to the hospital. It was only when they were standing in the anteroom, watching Toby's father fighting for his life, that either of them said anything about what had happened in the kitchen.

'It didn't come for me,' he said. 'Right at the end. It was going to, but it veered off and went for you instead. Why?'

'I don't know,' she replied. 'But I felt Her and what She wanted when She was trying to get inside me. She was – *is* – too much for a male to contain.'

Toby said, 'She's still out there, along with the disease. Did we stop it?'

'I don't know. You stopped Hester. Isn't that enough?'

It should have been, he told himself. Saving one soul should be enough for anyone. They watched the slow wheeze of the respirator, the blinking LEDs that tracked his dad's blood pressure, heartbeat, temperature. The pallor of his face, and the fevered flickering of his eyelids as he dreamed. He stood close to his mother and held her hand, watching his father, waiting to see if the world would tip on its axis again, and if so, which way.

Some unguessable amount of time later a doctor came in and confirmed what they already suspected: that Peter Feenan had been infected by a mutated and highly virulent form of the *Yersinia pestis* bacterium. For the moment the antibiotics were just about holding it at bay, but the hospital wasn't prepared to give him better than a 50/50 chance. Trish resumed her earlier position, seated in the plastic chair with her head against the glass and her hands clasped under her chin, praying.

After a while she asked Toby if he wanted to join her. He thought it over and pulled up a chair beside her.

He figured it couldn't hurt.

39

SAFELY DOWN

'EXCUSE ME, SIR, YOU'RE GOING TO HAVE TO WAKE UP – we've landed. Sir? Sir?'

Poh Min Yuan shook the passenger in 32A gently by the shoulder, but he only muttered something and his head lolled in a way which set every one of her alarm bells ringing. She tried again in Russian and French for form's sake, but by then she was already convinced that the man was seriously ill.

She looked up and towards the front of the aircraft's economy cabin where Omar was going along the aisle with a plastic bag, taking in the blankets. The rest of the seats were empty, the other passengers having deplaned only moments earlier.

'Omar!' she called.

He smiled, but his smile dropped as he saw the expression on her face.

'Get Celine,' she ordered. He was young, only in his

second year as a flight attendant, but to his credit he didn't ask why, he just dropped the bag and hurried forward to get Celine Lim, the in-flight manager.

In Min Yuan's six years as cabin crew for Singapore Airlines she had seen a few passengers become ill during long-haul flights, but nothing worse than mild food poisoning – and never where the passenger had deteriorated as rapidly as this. He'd been fine when he'd come on board at Heathrow – a little snuffly, perhaps, but had satisfied them that it was nothing more than a head cold. In her experience, Britain was a cold, damp, and generally miserable country where colds were to be expected. She'd given him a complimentary boiled sweet to suck at take-off for his ears, and that had seemed that. He'd been up and down to the toilet quite a few times but had otherwise remained undemonstrative and undemanding throughout the journey to Changi International, and given the other demands on her time that had been a blessing. She saw now the small drift of crumpled tissues and blister packs of medication between his feet that his blanket had hidden, and kicked herself for not having been more vigilant.

'What is it?' Celine was approaching with clipped strides, an avatar of efficiency – her hair and make-up immaculate, her flight manager's purple kebaya as neat and uncreased after twelve hours as if she'd only just put it on.

'He's ill. I can't get him to wake up.' His colour was very pale and she gasped when she felt his forehead. 'He's got a terrible fever.' There was a smell rising from him too – pungent and hot. The stink of illness. Her grandfather had reeked of it in the months before his cancer took him. 'Who is he?'

Celine leaned over her and tried to rouse the man, but with as little effect. She checked his wrists and throat for any medical jewellery, but found nothing. 'Get away from him,' she said, straightening up. Cursing quietly, she took out her tablet and called up the passenger manifest. 'David Liam Corr, UK national, no medical alerts. One security flag: he's a policeman, apparently. Checked through to Sydney.' She tucked away her tablet. 'Somehow I don't think he's going to make it that far.'

The man with no medical alerts began to cough violently, and his eyes snapped open, though it was obvious that what he was seeing existed only in his feverish imagination. 'She's here!' he screamed, and coughed again. A fine spray of red droplets hit the screen in the seat-back in front of him. Both Min Yuan and her manager jumped back in alarm. 'She's here! She's come for us all!' Bloody mucus streaked his mouth and chin.

Min Yuan's alarm turned to disgust as she saw the front of the man's trousers darken and then the stench hit her as he soiled himself. His coughing worsened and he doubled over in his seat as it turned to a deep, spasmodic retching, and he vomited in a sudden bright-crimson gush. She clapped a hand to her mouth and backed away, horrified. Celine was barking something into her Bluetooth. Min Yuan cast a terrified glance up the plane in case any of the other passengers had also lingered and seen this. But other than Omar, staring wide-eyed and terrified, there was nobody. All four hundred men, women and children were on their way through the airport's customs and immigration systems to catch connecting flights and continue their journeys all over the world, finally to be safely home and in the arms of their loved ones.

Then she looked at how many seats there were between here and the toilets. How many other people he would have had to pass. How many he would have brushed against, or coughed over. How many would have used the same cubicle.

Through the window, she saw blue flashing lights screaming across the tarmac towards the plane.

AFTERWORD & ACKNOWLEDGEMENTS

IN LATE SUMMER OF 1349 A SHIP CARRYING WOOL
from Norfolk landed in Bergen, Norway – the story goes
that its entire crew was already dead from the plague which
was carried by the rats on board, and whether or not that's
just a bit of gruesome dramatic licence, the fact remains that
the Black Death wiped out somewhere between a half and
two thirds of the Norwegian population in the following two
years. How does a culture with no knowledge of bacteria,
let alone epidemiology, handle a catastrophe like that?

They invent a new myth, that's how.

Along with the disease, tales began to spread of a
terrifying hag called Pesta who travelled from town to town
and village to village, killing all she met. She was described
as old and bent-backed, wearing a black hood and a red
skirt, and she carried either a broom or a rake to sweep
away the lives before her. If she was carrying a rake when

she arrived at your village you might be one of the lucky ones who escaped through its teeth, but if she was carrying her broom you'd best set your affairs in order, because nobody would survive.

It's interesting to note that the plague wasn't being blamed on the displeasure of God or the wickedness of Satan – almost as if the Black Death was so completely unnatural and aberrant that it couldn't be accounted for by anything as normal as the actions of heaven or hell. You could pray your way out of trouble with the Lord, or failing that you could try dickering with the Devil, but none of that worked with this disease. It was utterly implacable and relentless. Pesta wasn't anything as mundane as a witch, casting spells on her neighbours. She was a force of nature given form: a plague hag, a goddess of death. Similar figures in British folklore include the *cailleach*, a female creator deity from Scotland and Ireland also known as the Queen of Winter or the Veiled One; as well as the *cyhyraeth* from Wales, a wailing banshee-like spectre. I know this is Norwegian folklore and not English, but can you blame me? I couldn't write a tale about the Black Death and not have her in there somewhere.

It helps that by a linguistic coincidence the name Pesta (presumably deriving from the same Latin root as the word 'pestilence') rhymes nicely with Hester, which is as close as I can get in English to Hestia, the Greek goddess of the hearth, home, and state – all of which are central themes to this story. I just like patterns and rhymes.

So that's the one place where I deliberately mashed up a set of folkloric references because it seemed like a fun thing at the time. The *gwrach clefyd* is my own fictional version of the same thing, so blame me for the dodgy Welsh name. That and any other accidental historical mistakes are on me, though I am indebted to the following people for helping me to keep them to a minimum:

Cat, Jo and Hayley for their keen editorial eyes and for making me learn a load more about medieval history than I ever wanted to – not to mention everybody else at Titan, especially Sarah and Lydia for general unflagging promotional loveliness, and Miranda just because.

Iain Grant, for his copy of *The Time Traveller's Guide to Medieval England* by Ian Mortimer, who got it back significantly more dog-eared than when he loaned it to me, and patiently answered all my questions about What Fourteenth-Century Peasants Thought About God. And while we're on the Ians, my agent Ian Drury for just letting me get on with it.

Tamara for help with the Serbian material. Sorry for all the swearing.

Caz, who marked my spelling, punctuation and grammar and demanded dragons. Maybe next time.

Dan for the mind-clearing rambles around the Worcestershire countryside.

Jamie-Lee, bookseller extraordinaire. You rock.

...and the triumvirate goddesses of my own hearth: TC, Hopey and Eden.

ABOUT THE AUTHOR

JAMES BROGDEN IS A PART-TIME AUSTRALIAN WHO grew up in Tasmania and now lives with his wife and two daughters in Bromsgrove, Worcestershire, where he teaches English. He spends as much time in the mountains as he is able, and more time playing with Lego than he should. He is the author of *The Hollow Tree*, *Hekla's Children*, *The Narrows*, *Tourmaline*, *The Realt* and *Evocations*, and his horror and fantasy stories have appeared in various periodicals and anthologies ranging from *The Big Issue* to the British Fantasy Society Award-winning Alchemy Press. Blogging occurs infrequently at jamesbrogden.blogspot.co.uk, and tweeting at @skippybe.

THE HOLLOW TREE

JAMES BROGDEN

WHO DANCED WITH MARY BEFORE SHE DIED?

After her hand is amputated following a tragic accident, Rachel Cooper suffers vivid nightmares of a woman imprisoned in the trunk of a hollow tree, screaming for help. When she begins to experience phantom sensations of leaves and earth with her lost hand, Rachel is terrified she is going mad… but then another hand takes hers, and the trapped woman is pulled into our world. She has no idea who she is, but Rachel can't help but think of the mystery of Oak Mary, a female corpse found in a hollow tree, and who was never identified. Three urban legends have grown up around the case; was Mary a Nazi spy, a prostitute or a gypsy witch? Rachel is desperate to learn the truth, but darker forces are at work. For a rule has been broken, and Mary is in a world where she doesn't belong…

Praise for James Brogden:
"NICELY DONE"
Daily Mail

"CAREFULLY CRAFTED"
Publishers Weekly

"YOU SIMPLY CAN'T AFFORD TO MISS THIS"
Rising Shadow

TITANBOOKS.COM

HEKLA'S CHILDREN
JAMES BROGDEN

A decade ago, teacher Nathan Brookes saw four of his students walk up a hill and vanish. Only one returned – Olivia – starved, terrified, and with no memory of where she'd been. After a body is found in the same woodland where they disappeared it is first believed to be one of the missing children, but is soon identified as a Bronze Age warrior, nothing more than an archaeological curiosity. Yet Nathan starts to have terrifying visions of the students. Then Olivia reappears, half-mad and willing to go to any lengths to return the corpse to the earth. For he is the only thing keeping a terrible evil at bay...

"A VISCERAL, SEAT-OF-THE-PANTS THRILLER"
The Guardian

"AMBITIOUS, SKILFULLY PLOTTED AND EVOCATIVELY REALISED"
SFX

"A SMART BLEND OF SCIENCE FICTION AND HORROR"
Barnes & Noble

TITANBOOKS.COM

THE SILENCE

TIM LEBBON

In the darkness of an underground cave system, blind
creatures hunt by sound. Then there is light, there are voices,
and they feed... Swarming from their prison, the creatures
thrive and destroy. To scream, even to whisper, is to summon
death. As the hordes lay waste to Europe, a girl watches to
see if they will cross the sea. Deaf for many years, she knows
how to live in silence; now, it is her family's only chance
of survival. To leave their home, to shun others, to find a
remote haven where they can sit out the plague. But will it
ever end? And what kind of world will be left?

"A TRULY GREAT NOVEL WITH A FRESH AND
ORIGINAL STORY"
Starburst

"A CHILLING AND HEART-WRENCHING STORY"
Publishers Weekly

"THE SILENCE IS A CHILLING STORY THAT
GRIPS YOU FIRMLY BY THE THROAT"
SciFi Now

ANNO DRACULA

KIM NEWMAN

It is 1888 and Queen Victoria has remarried, taking as her new consort the Wallachian Prince infamously known as Count Dracula. His polluted bloodline spreads through London as its citizens increasingly choose to become vampires.

In the grim backstreets of Whitechapel, a killer known as 'Silver Knife' is cutting down vampire girls. The eternally young vampire Genevieve Dieudonné and Charles Beauregard of the Diogenes Club are drawn together as they both hunt the sadistic killer, bringing them ever closer to England's most bloodthirsty ruler yet.

"COMPULSORY READING... GLORIOUS"
Neil Gaiman

"ESSENTIAL FOR ANY FAN OF GOTHIC LITERATURE"
The Guardian

"UP THERE WITH BRAM STOKER'S CHILLING ORIGINAL"
Daily Mail

TITANBOOKS.COM

AN ENGLISH GHOST STORY

KIM NEWMAN

The Naremores, a dysfunctional British nuclear family, seek
a new life away from the big city in the sleepy Somerset
countryside. At first their new home, The Hollow, seems to
embrace them, creating a rare peace and harmony within the
family. But when the house turns on them, it seems to know
just how to hurt them the most – threatening to destroy
them from the inside out.

"IMMERSIVE, CLAUSTROPHOBIC AND UTTERLY
WONDERFUL"
M.R. Carey, *New York Times* bestselling author of
The Girl With All the Gifts

"THOROUGHLY ENJOYABLE, MASTER
STORYTELLING"
Lauren Beukes

"DESERVES TO STAND BESIDE THE GREAT
NOVELS OF THE GHOSTLY"
Ramsey Campbell

TITANBOOKS.COM

For more fantastic fiction, author events, competitions,
limited editions and more

VISIT OUR WEBSITE
titanbooks.com

LIKE US ON FACEBOOK
facebook.com/titanbooks

FOLLOW US ON TWITTER
@TitanBooks

EMAIL US
readerfeedback@titanemail.com